Debbie Macomber

The Manning Brides

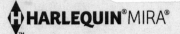

HARLEQUIN®MIRA®

Published in Great Britain 2012. This edition 2013.
Harlequin MIRA, an imprint of Harlequin (UK) Limited,
Eton House, 18-24 Paradise Road,
Richmond, Surrey, TW9 1SR

THE MANNING BRIDES © Harlequin Books S.A. 2012

The publisher acknowledges the copyright holder of the individual works as follows:

Marriage of Inconvenience © Debbie Macomber 1992
Stand-In Wife © Debbie Macomber 1992

ISBN 978 1 848 45080 6

58-0312

Debbie Macomber is a number one *New York Times* bestselling author. Her recent books include *44 Cranberry Point, 50 Harbor Way, 6 Rainier Drive*, and *Hannah's List*. She has become a leading voice in women's fiction worldwide and her work has appeared on every major bestseller list. There are more than one hundred million copies of her books in print. For more information on Debbie and her books, visit www.Debbie Macomber.com.

Rich's Story

in

Marriage of Inconvenience

To Yakima's Iron Maidens:
Cheryl Nixon, Ellen Bartelli, Joyce Falcon,
Jill Seshiki, Faye and Victoria Ives

One

"I'm so stupid," Jamie Warren wailed, tossing the crumpled tissue over her shoulder. Rich Manning, who was sitting across the kitchen table from her, held out a fresh one. "I trusted Tony, and he's nothing more than a...jerk."

She yanked the tissue from Rich's hand and ingloriously blew her nose. That tissue took the same path as the previous one. "I feel like the biggest fool who ever lived."

"It's Tony who's the fool."

"Oh, right. Then why am I the one sitting here crying my eyes out?" Jamie really didn't expect him to answer. Calling Rich at an ungodly hour, sobbing out her tale of woe, wasn't the most considerate thing she'd ever done, but she had to talk to *someone* and he was the first person who'd come to mind.

He was the kind of friend she felt comfortable calling in the middle of the night. The kind of friend who'd immediately drive over if she needed sympathy or consolation. They'd been close ever since they'd worked together on their yearbook in high school. Although they didn't see each other often, Jamie had always felt their relationship was special.

"At least crying's better than getting drunk, which is what I did when I found out Pamela was cheating on me," Rich admitted with a wry twist of his mouth. He got up and poured them each another cup of coffee.

"You haven't seen her since, have you?"

"Sure, I have. I wouldn't want her to think I was jealous."

Despite everything, Jamie laughed. "You're still dating her? Even *after* you learned she was seeing another guy behind your back?"

Rich shrugged carelessly, as though the entire situation was of little consequence, something Jamie knew not to be the case. Although he'd been devastated, he'd worn a nonchalant facade. He might've fooled everyone else, but not Jamie. His flippant attitude couldn't camouflage the pain.

"I took her to a movie a couple of times," Rich continued. "I played it cool. But as far as I'm concerned, it was over the minute I heard about that other guy."

"It's over with me and Tony, too," Jamie murmured. Just saying the words produced a painful tightening in her chest. She was truly in love with Tony and had been for nearly a year. They'd often talked about getting married and raising a family together. Jamie wanted children so badly. The weekend before, they'd gone shopping for engagement rings. Her mother, who was crazy about him, had been thrilled. Since Jamie was over thirty her mom tended to worry about her marriage prospects, but even she said that waiting for a man like Tony Sanchez had been time well spent. Sharing the bad news with her widowed mother had been almost as upsetting as learning about the betrayal itself.

"You're *sure* the other woman's baby is his?" Rich asked, reaching for her hand. "She could be stirring up trouble."

"He didn't bother to deny it." In the beginning, Jamie had hoped the woman was lying. She'd searched Tony's face, praying it was all some malicious joke. His beautiful dark eyes had turned defensive, but gradually the regret, the doubt, had shown, and he'd slid his gaze away from hers. It had been a mistake, he'd told her, a momentary slip in judgment. A one-night fling that meant nothing. He felt terrible about it and promised nothing like this would ever happen again.

Tony was cheating on her before they were even married, and Jamie didn't need a crystal ball to know that pattern would almost certainly continue.

"This isn't the first time," she admitted, biting her lower lip to control the trembling. "Margie, in New Accounts, mentioned seeing Tony with a blonde a month or so ago. He'd told me he was out of town and I…I was sure it was just a case of mistaken identity. I should've known then."

"Don't be so hard on yourself," Rich said, bending to brush a wisp of dark brown hair from her temple. "There were plenty of signs that Pamela was playing me for a fool, too, but I was so taken with her—"

"Bust line. Which was always your primary interest."

"That's probably why I never dated *you,*" he countered, grinning.

Jamie smiled. The joke was an old one between them. When they'd first been assigned to work together on the yearbook, Rich had been a popular football player and she'd been a nondescript bookworm. They'd clashed constantly. One day, after a particularly nasty confrontation, she'd shouted that if she had a bigger bust, he might actually listen to her. Rich had gone speechless, then he'd started to laugh. The laughter had broken the ice between them and they'd been friends ever since. The best of friends.

"I hear there's help in the form of surgery," he teased, leveling his gaze at her chest.

"Oh, honestly." Her breasts weren't that small, but it was comfortable and easy to fall into their old banter. Focusing on something other than what a mistake Tony had turned out to be provided her with a good—if momentary—distraction. She'd wasted an entire year of her life on him. An entire year!

Rich reached for his coffee, then leaned back in the chair and sighed. "I'm beginning to wonder if anyone's faithful anymore."

"I'm the last person you should be asking that," she said, taking a sip of her coffee. She didn't blame Rich for having doubts. Relationships all around her seemed to be failing. Friends, whose marriages had appeared strong and secure, were divorcing. At work affairs were rampant. Casual sex. Jamie was sick of it all.

"When Mark Brooks cheated on my sister Taylor, she took that teaching position in another state," Rich went on to say. "You know, I never much liked Mark. From the first I felt there was something off about him. I wish I'd spoken to Taylor about it."

"I felt so bad for her."

"The whole family was worried. Then she moved to the backwoods of Montana and a few months later, she married Russ Palmer. Everyone was sure she'd made a terrible mistake, marrying a cowpoke on the rebound, but I've never seen her happier. And now Christy's married to Cody Franklin."

"Christy's married to whom?"

"The Custer County sheriff. She's living in Montana, too."

"But I thought she was engaged to James Wilkens! Good grief, I was at her engagement party just a few months ago."

"It's a long story, but James is out of the picture."

"Christy dumped James?" It was hard to believe. Jamie had assumed they were perfect for each other. They'd acted like the ideal couple at the engagement party, sipping champagne and discussing wedding dates with their families.

Rich chuckled. "If you're surprised by that, wait until you hear this. While Christy was still engaged to James, she was *married* to Cody."

Jamie was shocked. She didn't know Rich's youngest sister well, but she would never have imagined Christy doing anything so underhanded. "I *am* surprised."

"There were mitigating circumstances and it's not as

bad as it sounds, but Christy is yet another example of how fickle women can be."

"Women?" Jamie protested. "Men are notoriously untrustworthy—they always have been."

It looked as though Rich wanted to argue. He straightened and opened his mouth, then shook his head. Sighing, he drank the last of his coffee. "I've begun to think commitment means nothing these days."

"I hate to be so cynical, but I agree."

Standing, Rich carried his mug to the kitchen sink. "Are you going to be able to sleep now?"

Jamie nodded, although she wasn't convinced. However, she'd taken enough of Rich's time for one night and didn't want to keep him any longer.

"Liar," he whispered softly.

Jamie smiled and got up, too. He slipped his arms around her and she laid her cheek against his shoulder. It felt good to be held. Rich's comfort was that of a loving friend, someone who truly cared about her without the complications of romance or male-female dynamics.

"You're going to get through this."

"I know," she whispered. But she hadn't been confident of that until she'd talked to Rich. How fortunate she was to have him as her friend. "We both will," she added.

A sigh rumbled through Rich's chest. "Don't you wish life could be as simple now as it was in high school?"

That remark gave Jamie pause. "No," she finally said, then laughed. "I was so shy back then."

"Shy?" Rich argued, releasing her enough to cast her a challenging look. "You were a lot of things, Jamie Warren, but *shy* wasn't one of them."

"Maybe not with you."

"I wish you had been, then you might've done things my way without so much arguing."

"You're still upset that I didn't use your picture on the sports page, aren't you? We've been out of high school for thirteen years and you haven't forgiven me for using that shot of Josh McGinnes instead."

Rich chuckled. "I could be upset, but I'm willing to let bygones be bygones."

"I'm glad to hear it." She led him to the door of her condo. "Seriously, though, I really am grateful you came."

"Call if you need me?"

She nodded. The worst of it was over. She would pick up the pieces of her life and start again, a little less trusting and a whole lot more wary.

Two months later, Rich was sitting in his office at Boeing when the image of Jamie Warren's tear-streaked face drifted into his mind. It was as if their conversation had taken place just the night before—even though he'd talked to her two or three times over the holidays, and she'd sounded good. Cheerful, in fact. Certainly in better spirits than he'd been himself.

She hadn't made any attempt to fool him. Tony had hurt her badly. From what she'd said, he'd made several attempts to resume their engagement, but she'd rejected the idea in no uncertain terms. It was plain to Rich that

Tony Sanchez didn't really know Jamie Warren. The woman was stubborn enough to impress a mule. Once she made up her mind, that was it. Oh, she appeared docile and easygoing, but Rich had collided with that stubborn streak of hers a time or two and come away battered and bruised.

It bothered Rich that Jamie had never married. She'd always loved children, and he'd fully expected her to have a passel of kids by now.

Most men, he realized, passed Jamie over without a second glance. That bothered him even more.

The problem, not that *he'd* call it a problem, was that she didn't possess the looks of a beauty queen. She wasn't plain, nor was she unappealing. She was just— he hated to admit it—ordinary. Generally, there was one thing or other that stood out in a woman. A flawless face. Cascades of shining hair, blond or gold or black… Jamie's wasn't blond and it wasn't brunette but somewhere in between. And it wasn't long, but it wasn't short either. Some women had eyes that could pierce a man's soul. Jamie had brown eyes. Regular brown eyes. Not dark or seductive or anything else, just brown eyes. Nice, but average.

She was about five-five, and a little on the thin side. Giving the matter some consideration, Rich noted that there didn't seem to be any distinguishing curves on her. Not her hips, and certainly not her breasts. He could be mistaken of course, since he hadn't really looked at her that way…. To be honest, he'd never looked at her in any way other than as a friend.

She didn't have a body that would stop traffic. The thing was, a woman could have an ordinary face, but if she had curves, men fell all over themselves. Rich hated to admit something so derogatory about his fellow men, but he felt it was true.

What few took the time to see was Jamie's warm heart and generous spirit. He'd never known a more giving woman. What she'd said about being shy was true, even though he'd denied it. Yet she had spunk and she had spirit. Enough to stand up to him, which was no easy thing.

Pushing against the edge of his desk, Rich rolled back his chair and stood up. He headed down the hallway with determination.

"Bill," he said, striding purposefully into his friend's office. "Got a minute?"

"What's up?"

Rich had never played the role of matchmaker before, and he wasn't sure where to start. "There's someone I want you to meet."

"Oh." Bill didn't look too enthusiastic.

"A friend of mine."

"Widowed or divorced?"

"Single."

Bill's brows arched toward his receding hairline. "You mean a leftover girl."

Rich wasn't comfortable thinking of Jamie as leftover, but this wasn't the time to argue. "We went to high school together."

"High school? Exactly how old is she?"

"Thirty-one." Her birthday wasn't until April. Their

birthdays were both in April, and Jamie loved to point out that she was a whole week older.

"She's never been married?" Bill asked, his voice rising suspiciously. "What's the matter with her?"

"Nothing. She's one of the nicest people you'll ever meet."

Bill reached for his In basket and took out a file, flipping it open. "I can't tell you how many times friends—" he paused and glanced up "—*good* friends, have set me up. They always claim the girl's one of the nicest people I'll ever meet. No thanks, Rich."

"No thanks? You haven't heard anything about her."

"I've heard enough."

"What's the matter with you?" It was hard to keep the irritation out of his voice. Bill was thirty-five and twenty pounds overweight, not to mention the receding hairline. Frankly, Rich didn't think his friend had any right to be so damn choosy.

"Nothing's wrong with me."

"I thought you wanted to remarry."

"I do. Someday, when I find the right woman."

"You might well be passing her over this minute," Rich said. "I'm not going to lie to you—she's no Miss America, but she's not ugly, if that's what concerns you."

"Why don't you ask her out yourself, then?"

The question took Rich by surprise. "Well, be-cause…because it would be like dating one of my sisters."

Bill released an impatient sigh. "Why haven't you said anything about her before?"

"She was involved with someone else."

Bill shook his head emphatically. "Forget it. You're a good friend and all that, but I've been set up too many times in the past few years. Frankly, your friend's everything I want to avoid in a woman. She's over thirty and never been married. It doesn't help that she's just out of a relationship, either. I'm sorry, Rich, I really am, but I'm not interested."

Rich found Bill's attitude downright insulting. Before he could stop himself, before he could analyze his actions, he reached for his wallet.

"What are you doing?" Bill wanted to know when Rich pulled out two tickets.

"These are for the Seahawks play-off game against Green Bay. The scalpers are getting three hundred bucks each for these. If you agree to call Jamie for a date, they're yours." His older brother would have his hide for this, but Rich would deal with Jason later.

Bill's eyes rounded incredulously. "You mean you're willing to give me two tickets to the Seahawks play-off game if I go out with your friend?"

"Yup."

Even then Bill hesitated. "One date?"

"One date." But once his fellow engineer got to know Jamie, he'd realize how special she was. In a few weeks, Bill would be looking for ways to repay him for this. Rich would keep that thought in mind when he told Jason he'd *given* away their play-off tickets.

"Someplace nice, too. No pizza in a bowling alley, understand?"

Bill's hand closed over the tickets. "Dinner at the Space Needle followed by an evening at the ballet."

"Good. Just don't *ever* let Jamie know about this."

Bill laughed. "Do I look that stupid?"

Rich didn't reply, but in his opinion, any man who'd turn down the opportunity to meet Jamie Warren wasn't exactly a candidate for Mensa.

"Here's her phone number," he said, writing it on a slip of paper. "I'll give her a call, clear the way, but the rest is up to you."

"No problem," Bill said, pocketing the tickets.

Rich felt downright noble as he returned to his own office. Jamie was one hell of a woman and it was about time someone figured that out. Bill Hastings wasn't nearly good enough for her, but he was an amiable guy. Without too much trouble Rich could picture Bill and Jamie a few years down the road, raising two or three kids.

He felt good about that, better than he'd felt about anything in quite a while.

That evening, Rich went to Jason's apartment on his way home and was relieved to find his brother was out. That meant he could delay telling him what had become of the play-off tickets. It was definitely something he had to do in person, he told himself.

After killing an hour or two at his own apartment, Rich decided to drive over to Jamie's. He rang her bell and waited. It hadn't occurred to him that she might not be home. He was ready to turn away when he heard activity on the other side.

"Who is it?" she called.

"The big bad wolf."

The sound of her laugh was followed by the click

of the lock. She opened the door and Rich saw that he must have gotten her out of the tub. She'd hastily donned a white terrycloth robe that clung to her damp skin.

"Rich," she said, surprise elevating her voice, "what are you doing here?" As she spoke, she finished knotting the belt around her waist.

The robe fell open below that, revealing a glimpse of thigh. Rich was having trouble taking his eyes off it and didn't answer right away. His gaze followed a natural progression downward, and he was momentarily astounded to see what long shapely legs she had. Funny, he'd never noticed them before. He grinned, thinking Bill was in for a very pleasant shock.

"Go ahead and finish your bath," he said casually, walking into her kitchen. "I'll make myself at home while I wait."

"I'm almost done."

"Take your time," he called out. He stuck his head inside the refrigerator and helped himself to an apple. He'd just taken his last bite when Jamie returned. As best he could tell, she'd run a brush through her hair and put on slippers. But that was it. The robe rode over her slender hips like a second skin.

"Do you have any plans tonight?" Generally he went out on Fridays, but there wasn't anything he particularly felt like doing that evening.

"Got anything in mind?"

"A movie. I'll even let you choose."

"I suppose you're going to make me pay my own way?"

"I might." He grinned, pleased with himself for coming up with the idea. The suggestion that they attend a movie had been as much of a surprise to him as it obviously was to Jamie. As much of a surprise as offering Bill the play-off tickets...

Actually, it was a damn good idea. This way he could lead naturally, casually, into the subject of Bill. The last thing he wanted Jamie to think was that he'd arranged anything.

The movie was indeed a stroke of genius, Rich decided as they drove to the theater. He'd always enjoyed Jamie's company and never more so than now. An evening with her was an escape from the games and pretenses involved in taking out someone new—and it was exactly what he needed to settle his nerves. He didn't like to say much, particularly to his family, but Pamela had hurt him badly. He no longer trusted his judgment when it came to women. Oh, he dated. Often. But he was tired of all the games. Pamela hadn't just broken his heart; the damage she'd inflicted went deeper than that. She'd caused him to doubt himself.

Rich pulled into a movie complex in the Seattle suburbs, close to Jamie's condominium. He bought their tickets, but she insisted on buying the popcorn and the chocolate-covered raisins.

He was just thinking how nice it was to be with a woman who wasn't constantly worrying about her weight when she leaned over and whispered, "You ate more than your share of the raisins."

"Do you want me to buy more?"

"No. Just remember you owe me."

It took him several minutes to realize he had no

reason to be grinning the way he was, especially since the film was actually quite serious.

"We don't do this often enough," Rich said as they left the cinema two hours later. He meant it, too. He'd been at loose ends for a couple of months but hadn't thought about contacting Jamie. Now he wondered why.

"No, we don't," she agreed, buttoning her coat. She wore jeans and a pale pink sweater. The color looked good on her. He was about to say as much when he remembered the reason for his impromptu visit.

"How about a cup of coffee?" he suggested, linking his arm with hers. There was a coffee shop in the same complex as the theater, and he steered them in that direction.

He waited until they were seated and looking over their menus before he brought up the subject of Bill. "There's someone at work I'd like you to meet."

Jamie didn't raise her eyes from the menu. "Who?"

"Bill Hastings. You'll like him."

"Is he tall, dark and handsome?"

"Yes. No and no."

"Sounds like my kind of man," she joked, setting aside the menu. The waitress filled their mugs with coffee and Jamie stirred in a liberal measure of cream. "From everything I've heard, it's best to avoid the handsome ones."

"Oh?" He could guess what was coming. He wasn't conceited, but Rich knew he was easy on the eyes—a fact that hadn't gone unnoticed from the time he was in his early teens. Rich had never lacked for female attention, some he'd sought and some he hadn't.

"Yes," she said. "The handsome ones can't be trusted."

"Who says?" Rich demanded, feigning outrage.

"Everyone," Jamie returned without a pause. "They're too impressed with themselves. Or so I hear."

Rich chuckled and, motioning for the waitress, ordered a chef's salad. He felt like having a decent meal for the first time in weeks. He didn't even complain when Jamie stole his olives, claiming it was the least he could do for hogging the chocolate-covered raisins.

Tuesday morning, Bill marched into Rich's office, pulled out a chair and plunked himself down. His face was creased with a heavy frown. "It didn't work."

Rich tried to figure out which project Bill was referring to and came up blank. They were both part of an engineering team working on a Boeing defense contract. Rich had volunteered for this job, knowing it would entail plenty of overtime hours. The challenge was something he needed at this point in his career—and his life.

"What do you mean?" he asked Bill.

"She turned me down flat."

Bill couldn't possibly be talking about Jamie. He'd paved the way for him! He'd managed to casually drop his name into the conversation at least three times. Enough to pique her curiosity, but not so often that she'd suspect he was setting them up.

"She turned you down?" Rich echoed, still unable to believe it. "Obviously you didn't try all *that* hard."

"If I'd tried any harder, I would've been arrested," Bill muttered.

"What the hell did you say to her?"

"Nothing. I called her Saturday afternoon, just like you suggested. I mentioned your name right off and told her we worked together and have for several years. I wanted her to feel comfortable talking to me." He hesitated as though he was still trying to understand what had gone wrong.

"Then what happened?" Rich could feel himself losing patience. He'd risked his brother's wrath by giving up those tickets and he wasn't about to let Bill off so easily.

"That's just it. *Nothing* happened. We must've talked for ten or fifteen minutes and you're right—she sounds nice. The more we talked, the more I realized I wouldn't mind getting to know her. She said you two were on the yearbook staff together.... She even told me a few insider secrets about your glorious football days."

"What the hell were you doing talking about me?" Rich demanded.

"I was establishing common ground."

Rich brought one hand to his mouth in an effort to hide his irritation. "Go on."

"There's not much more to tell. After several minutes of chitchat, I asked her out to dinner. Honest, Rich, I was beginning to look forward to meeting her. I couldn't have been more shocked when she turned me down."

"What did she say?"

"Not much," Bill admitted, his frown deepening. "Just that she'd given up dating and although she was sure I was a perfectly fine guy, she wasn't interested."

"You didn't take that sitting down, did you?"

"Hell, no. I sent her a dozen roses Monday morning, hoping that would convince her. Red roses, expensive ones. I didn't get them in any grocery store, either. These were flower shop roses, top quality."

"And?"

"That didn't do it, either. She phoned and thanked me, but said she still wasn't interested. Said she felt bad that I'd gone to the expense of sending her flowers, though."

Rich muttered under his breath. Bill had just encountered that stubborn pride of hers. Rich knew from experience that once she'd made up her mind, nothing was going to change it. Not flowers, not arguments, nothing.

Bill sighed unhappily. "You aren't going to make me return the Seahawks tickets, are you?" he asked.

Two

Jamie was sitting at her kitchen table, reading the application from the adoption agency, when the doorbell rang. A long blast was immediately followed by three short, impatient ones. By the time she'd stood and walked to the door, whoever was on the other side was knocking loudly.

She checked the peephole. Rich. And from the look of him, he was furious. Unbolting the lock, she opened the door.

Without a word, he marched into the center of her living room, hands deep in the pockets of his full-length winter coat. Damn, but the man was attractive, Jamie noted, not for the first time. Much too handsome for his own good. His blue eyes were flashing, which only added to his appeal—even if they were flashing with annoyance, not laughter or warmth.

"You turned down Bill Hastings's dinner invitation and I want to know why," he said without preamble.

Jamie sighed. She should've realized Rich would be upset about that. He'd obviously gone to a lot of trouble to arrange the date and even more trying to conceal it from her. The seemingly impromptu visit Friday night, the movie and coffee afterward, had all led up to his singing Bill Hastings's praises. He'd listed Bill's apparently limitless virtues at length and actually seemed to think he was being subtle about setting her up.

To be fair, she'd enjoyed talking to Bill. He'd seemed cordial enough, and he had sent her the roses, which really were lovely. But he hadn't said or done anything to change her mind. It did seem rather harsh to turn him down sight unseen, but she was saving them both future heartbreak and disappointment. Bill accepted her decision with good grace, but that clearly wasn't the case with Rich.

"Well?" Rich demanded. He walked around her couch, as though standing still was impossible, but if he didn't stop circling it soon, he was going to make her dizzy.

"He sounds very nice."

"The guy's perfect for you," Rich argued, gesturing toward her. "I match the two of you up and then you turn him down. I can't believe you refused to even meet him!"

"I'm sorry, but I'm not interested."

"One date," he cried, waving his index finger at her. "What possible harm could there be in one lousy dinner date?"

"None, I'm sure," she said calmly. "Listen, do you intend to stay long enough to take off your coat, or are you just dropping in to argue with me on your way to someplace else?"

"Are you going to let Tony do this to you?" he challenged, disregarding her question. He plowed his fingers through his hair, something he'd done often today if the grooves along the side of his head were any indication.

"Tony has very little to do with this." Rather than discuss the man who'd wounded her so deeply, Jamie moved into the kitchen and poured them glasses of iced tea, which gave her a few minutes to compose her thoughts.

"Obviously Tony has everything to do with this, otherwise you wouldn't have told Bill you'd given up dating. Which, by the way, is the most ridiculous thing I've ever heard." He shrugged off his coat and draped it over the back of a kitchen chair.

"Really?" Leaning against the kitchen counter, she added sugar and ice to her glass, stirred, then sipped from her tea. Rich ignored the glass she'd poured him.

"It's not true, is it?"

He glared at Jamie as though he expected her to deny everything. But she couldn't see any reason to lie. "As a matter of fact it is."

Rich's jaw sagged open. "Why?"

"You really need to ask?" Jamie said with a light laugh.

"How can you deny that Tony's responsible for this?"

She lifted her shoulders in a shrug. "In part he is, but this decision isn't solely due to what happened with him. It's just one more disappointment. If anything,

I'm grateful I found out what kind of man Tony is *before* we were married."

The timer on her oven dinged. Setting aside her tea, Jamie reached for a pot holder and took out a bubbling chicken potpie. The recipe was one she'd come across in a women's magazine and it had looked delicious. True, the meal was large enough to feed a family of four, but she intended to freeze half of it.

"Have you had dinner? Would you like to join me?" She extended the invitation casually as she set the steaming pie on top of the stove to cool.

"No," Rich answered starkly. "I'm not hungry."

"It seems to me you've lost weight. Have you?"

"I'm not here to discuss my weight," he barked, "which hasn't changed since high school, I might add."

His attitude was slightly defensive, but Jamie decided to ignore it. He *had* lost weight; she'd noticed it soon after he'd broken off the relationship with Pamela. Jamie had never met the other woman and it was all she could do to think civilly of her. If anyone was ever a fool, it was Rich's former girlfriend.

"You didn't answer my question," Rich said. His voice had lowered and he seemed less persistent now. Jamie suspected he'd spent the day seething over her decision not to date his friend.

"Which question didn't I answer?" she asked, putting the pot holder back in the top drawer.

"What made you decide to give up dating?"

"Oh." She pulled out a chair and sat down. Rich did, too. "Well, it wasn't something I did lightly, trust me. It was a gradual decision made over the past few months.

I honestly feel it's the right one for me. I feel better than I have in years." She tried to reassure him with a warm smile. He was frowning at her as though he wanted to argue. Rich had always been passionate when it came to people he cared about. "I'm nearly thirty-two years old," she added.

"So?"

"So," she said with a laugh, "there aren't many eligible men left for me."

"What about Bill Hastings? He's eligible."

"Divorced, right?"

"Right. But what's that got to do with anything?"

He wasn't going to like her answer, but Jamie wouldn't be less than honest. "I've dated plenty of divorced men over the years. My experience may not be like anyone else's, but I've discovered that if their wives left them, there's generally a damn good reason. And if there isn't, they're so traumatized by the divorce they've become emotional cripples."

"That's ridiculous! And furthermore, it's not fair."

"I'm sure there are exceptions. I just haven't found any."

"In other words, you wouldn't date Bill because he's divorced."

"Not…exactly. It's more than that. I don't want to date *anyone* right now, divorced or not."

"What about single men? You're only thirty-one, for heaven's sake. There are lots of single men out there who'd give anything to meet a woman like you."

Jamie had to swallow a sarcastic reply. If there were as many eligible single men as Rich seemed to think, she certainly hadn't met them. "Obviously I haven't had much luck with that group, either," she said. "I hate to burst your bubble here, but single men aren't all they're cracked up to be. If a man's in his thirties and not married, there's usually a reason for it. Besides, single men over thirty are so set in their ways, they have problems adjusting to the natural give-and-take of a healthy relationship."

"That's downright insulting."

"I don't mean it to be." She stood up to get two plates. "You're having dinner with me, right?"

He nodded.

"I'm not going to lie to you and claim Tony had nothing to do with this," she went on. "He hurt me, and it took me weeks to work through the pain. As strange as it may seem, I'm actually grateful for what Tony taught me. He helped me reach some sound, honest decisions about my life."

"If this no-dating stand of yours is one of them, then I'd do some rethinking if I were you." Rich opened the silverware drawer and took out two knives and forks. Without glancing at the adoption papers, he placed them to one side and had the table set by the time she brought over their plates. Jamie couldn't help being pleased that he'd agreed to join her for dinner.

"My biggest, and probably most significant realization," she said while smoothing the napkin across her lap, "was that I like my life the way it is. I don't need a man to feel complete."

Several minutes passed before Rich spoke. "That *sounds* healthy, but to lock the door on any chance of a relationship—"

"I'm not locking the door," she interrupted, eager to correct that impression. "I'm just not looking for one. I've wasted years trying to fulfill my dream of being married and raising children."

Rich took a bite of the chicken potpie and raised his eyebrows. "Hey, this is great."

"Thank you." She tried it herself and was satisfied with her culinary efforts. Taking the time to cook real meals instead of throwing together a sandwich or resorting to frozen entrées had been another decision she'd reached. It might seem silly, but cooking gave her a feeling of permanence and purpose. She was doing something healthy for herself, and she felt good about it.

"Everything you've said makes sense," Rich admitted reluctantly.

"Don't sound so shocked."

"It's just that I've always pictured you with kids...."

"I've got that covered," she said enthusiastically, removing the top sheet of the papers Rich had stacked on the other side of the table. "I intend to adopt."

"I know they let single people adopt children now," he said, "but two-parent families are better for kids."

"Ideally, yes," Jamie agreed. "But sometimes there's no alternative. Anyway, from what I've read, I don't think it's going to be easy or anytime soon, especially if I want a newborn."

"Which you do?"

Jamie nodded. If she was only going to be a mother once, then she wanted as much of the experience as she could have, including midnight feedings, teething and changing diapers. "I have an appointment with a coun-

selor at an adoption agency tomorrow afternoon. I
haven't been this excited about anything in years."

"I'll bet you haven't told your mother."

Jamie rolled her eyes at the thought. "It's better if I
don't say anything, at least for now. Mom's wonderful,
but she'd never understand this."

Rich chuckled, but as the laughter drained from his
features, his eyes took on a faraway look. "You know
what?"

"What?" she asked softly.

"I've basically come to the same conclusion about
dating. I'm sick to death of the games and women
whose only interest is getting me in the sack. I never
knew women could be so aggressive."

Intrigued, Jamie could only nod. She would never
have believed Rich was experiencing the same difficul-
ties she had. For years she'd been expecting him to
marry, but she'd never felt comfortable enough to ask
why he hadn't.

"I've spent ten years looking for a woman who
believes love lasts longer than an hour," he added
grimly. "As for commitment and honesty, I don't think
they exist anymore. Or if they do, then I can't seem to
find anyone who believes in them. After Pamela cheated
on me I realized I'm a self-reliant adult—and if I never
married, it wouldn't make my life any less worthwhile."

"That's how I feel," Jamie said. "I just never
thought that—"

"I did, too," he finished for her.

"Exactly."

They exchanged a look—a look wrought with understanding and empathy. They'd been friends for years and Jamie had never known how much they actually had in common.

"I had no idea it was happening to you, too," she whispered. She felt as though she was deprived of oxygen. Everything in the kitchen seemed to fade from view. Everything except Rich. If anything, his dark good looks came into sharper focus. As she had a thousand times before, Jamie acknowledged how very handsome Rich Manning was. But there was much more there, more than she'd ever noticed. This was a man of character and strength. A man of substance. He looked older; the years had marked their passage. There were wrinkles on his forehead and shadows beneath his eyes. The well-defined angles of his cheeks as well as the lines bracketing his mouth only made his face more masculine, more appealing.

The silence between them stretched to embarrassing lengths. It was Jamie who pulled her eyes away first. With a weak smile, she picked up her fork and managed to swallow a bite of her dinner.

"This turned out well, didn't it?" she said in a casual voice.

"Excellent." He seemed equally intent on putting their conversation back on an even keel. He attacked his dinner as though he'd entered a speed-eating competition.

They chatted for several more minutes, teased each other, exchanged the banter that was so familiar to them. Rich insisted on helping her clean up, but as soon as the last dish was put away, he made his excuses and left.

Jamie felt weak afterward. As weak and trembly as

the first time she'd stood on the high dive. The feeling wasn't any more comfortable now than it had been all those years ago.

Hard though he tried over the next few days, Rich couldn't forget the look he'd shared with Jamie at her kitchen table on Tuesday evening. He'd tried to define it, decipher its meaning. It was the kind of look longtime lovers exchanged. The kind he'd witnessed between Taylor and Russ, as though they didn't need words to say what was in their hearts.

But he and Jamie had never been lovers. To the best of his knowledge, they'd never even kissed. *Really* kissed. A peck on the cheek now and then. A friendly hug, perhaps. That was it. Their relationship had always been strictly platonic. It was the way they'd both wanted it. Anything else would have destroyed the special closeness they shared.

Rich shook his head in an effort to banish the disturbing thoughts that had taken up residence there. Until Tuesday, he'd seen Jamie as ordinary. Not anymore.

Still, nothing had changed, not really. At least nothing he could put his finger on. Jamie Warren was the same person she'd always been.

Not so, he corrected. Her eyes had been different.

To think he'd once believed her eyes were an average shade of brown. He'd never seen eyes the precise color of Jamie's. They were a blend of green and brown; some would call it hazel, he supposed. That night they'd been more green, reminiscent of the mist rising off a moss-covered forest floor....

But it wasn't her eyes that had intrigued him. It was

something more profound than that. Something more baffling, too.

His musing was interrupted by the phone. Rich grabbed the television remote and muted the volume. He didn't know why he'd bothered to turn it on—from habit, he guessed. For the past hour he hadn't heard a single word of the local or national news. He'd been too busy analyzing what had happened between him and Jamie.

"Hello," he answered briskly. Pamela sometimes phoned him, and he braced himself in case it was her.

"Hi," came the soft feminine voice he recognized immediately as Jamie's.

"Hi, yourself." He felt a bit ill at ease, which he'd never experienced with her. It was as though they hadn't found their stride with each other yet, which made no sense. Perhaps he was taking his cue from Jamie. She didn't sound quite like herself; she sounded tense, as if it had taken some courage to call him.

"I was just thinking about you." He probably shouldn't have admitted that, but it had slipped out.

"Oh?"

"Yeah, I was going to give you a call later and find out how the appointment with the adoption agency went."

She paused, and he heard her take a deep breath. "Actually, that's the reason I'm calling you. Are you busy?"

"Not really. What do you have in mind?"

"Would it be all right if I came by for a few minutes? There's something I need to talk over with you."

"Sure, you're welcome anytime." He glanced

around the apartment to see what kind of shape it was in. Not bad. Not especially good, either, but he'd have time to pick up the newspapers and straighten the cushions.

As it turned out, he had time to wipe down the kitchen counter, as well, and stick his dirty dishes in the dishwasher. The best meal he'd had in weeks had been the chicken potpie at Jamie's place. He didn't remember her being such an accomplished cook. She certainly seemed full of surprises lately.

Jamie arrived about ten minutes after her phone call. She wore jeans and the same pink sweater she'd had on the night they went to the movies. He was about to tell her how nice she looked, but stopped himself. Curiously, his heart stopped, too. Just a little.

"That didn't take long," he said instead.

"No… But we only live four or five miles from each other."

"Yeah." He led the way to the sofa and sat down, resting one ankle on the opposite knee and draping his arm along the back. "So, what's up?"

Jamie sat down, too, but he noticed that she sat on the very edge of the cushion and rubbed her hands nervously down her arms. He wondered if she was cold.

That prompted him to say, "Would you like a cup of coffee?"

"Please," she said eagerly.

Rich couldn't shake the impression that she was interested in the coffee more as a delaying tactic than out of any real desire for something to warm her.

He made a pot of coffee, and a few minutes later,

brought two steaming mugs into the living room. He had to look around for coasters, but once he found them, he sat down on the recliner across from her and resumed his relaxed pose.

"How'd the appointment with the adoption agency go?" he asked, when she didn't immediately launch into her reason for the visit. She hadn't really answered his question earlier.

Her hands cradled the mug and she stared into its depths. "Not very well, I'm afraid. Naturally, the agency prefers to place newborns with established families. Besides, the waiting list is years long, and I don't feel I have all that time to wait."

"I'm sorry to hear it." Rich could feel her disappointment.

"If I'm going to have a child, I want to be young enough to enjoy her."

"Her?"

"Or him," she amended quickly, briefly glancing his way.

"So what's next?"

For a long time she didn't say anything. Rich might have grown impatient with anyone else, but he found himself more tolerant with Jamie. He watched the emotions move across her face and tried to read her thoughts. It was impossible to know what she had on her mind, but whatever it was seemed to burden her.

"You're going to think I'm a candidate for intensive counseling when I tell you this."

"Try me."

"I…I've made an appointment with my gynecologist.

I want to discuss the possibility of being artificially inseminated."

Rich was relieved that his mouth wasn't full of coffee, otherwise he would've choked to death. "You're going to do *what?*"

Jamie stood abruptly and walked around the back of his recliner. She braced her hands against the sides as she stood behind him. "I know it sounds crazy, but I plan to have a child, and if I can't adopt, this was the best idea I could come up with."

"What about checking with another adoption agency?"

"I did. Five others, and the story's the same. If I want an infant, it'll mean years on a waiting list. Two of the agencies wouldn't even talk to me. The others tried to persuade me to become a foster parent with the hope of adopting at some point in the distant future. I want a baby. Is that so wrong?"

"No," he assured her gently.

"I'm nearly thirty-two years old, and my biological clock is ticking. Not so loud it keeps me awake nights, but loud enough. If I'm going to do this, it's got to be soon." Jamie's eyes filled with tears, but she was too proud and too stubborn to let them fall. Her gaze met his without wavering. Did she regret being honest because it forced her to reveal her deepest secrets?

"What about the father?" he mumured.

"I...I'm not sure. I've read everything I could find on the subject, which isn't all that much. I understand there's a sperm bank in our area. I don't know what else to tell you, since I haven't been to the doctor yet. I'll have more answers once I've had a chance to talk it over with him."

"I see." Rich could hardly believe they were even having this discussion. "You're positive you want to go through with this?" The minute he asked, he knew he'd made a mistake.

Steely determination shone from Jamie's eyes. "I'm going to do this, Rich, so don't try to talk me out of it."

Her warning wasn't necessary; he was well aware that any attempt to dissuade her would be pointless. "Are you worried about what people might say?" he asked. "Is that what's bothering you?"

She shrugged. "A little. The biggest hurdle will be my mother, but I'm not too worried. It's my life. Besides, she's been after me to have children for years. Of course, she'd prefer it if I were married, but I've decided against that." Her eyes met his again. She seemed nervous, edgy. Rich couldn't remember Jamie being either. Until tonight.

"Something's troubling you."

She closed her eyes and nodded. "You're just about the best friend I have."

"I'm honored."

"I have several close girlfriends. I've been a maid of honor twice and a bridesmaid three times. But when I found out about Tony, it was you I turned to. You're the one I felt I could wake up in the middle of the night."

"I feel the same way about you."

Her smile was genuine, if a little shaky. "That pleases me more than you know. We're good friends."

"Good friends," Rich echoed. Good enough for him

to hand over two fifty-yard-line play-off tickets on the off-chance she might find happiness with Bill Hastings. He'd done it without pause, too.

"I'd do just about anything for you," she said, eyeing him closely.

Rich didn't know why he felt that was a leading statement, but he did. The door was wide open for him to echo the sentiment. "You're special to me, too. Do you mind telling me exactly where this conversation is heading?"

Jamie came around the chair and sat on the sofa again. She leaned forward and rubbed her palms together, as though she was outside in below-freezing temperatures. She seemed more sure of herself now.

"You're such a handsome guy."

Rich frowned. "What's that got to do with anything?"

"You come from a wonderful family."

That was true enough. "So?"

"You're tall. What I wouldn't give for an extra two inches."

"Jamie, what the hell are you talking about?"

She stood up, still rubbing her palms. Once more she positioned herself behind his recliner. "I…I was having dinner when it dawned on me exactly what I'd decided to undertake. I want a child and because I do, I'm willing to be subjected to heaven knows what kinds of medical procedures. I don't care. It's a small sacrifice, and I'm amenable to whatever it takes. The only aspect of this entire scenario that disturbs me is giving birth to a stranger's child. A man I've never met, never even seen. Then it came to me. There's one person, a man I admire and trust above all others. It didn't make sense to go through all this and have a stranger's baby when…when there's already someone in my life who's tall, dark and handsome. Someone with excellent chromosomes who might be willing to contribute to this project."

"What are you saying?" Maybe she didn't mean what he thought she meant. Maybe this was all a dream and he'd wake in the morning and have a good laugh. Maybe Jamie wasn't wrong about the counseling. There seemed to be a hundred *maybes* in this. Rich didn't like the answer to a single one of them.

Jamie looked into his eyes and smiled, the softest, sweetest smile he'd ever seen. "I'm asking you to be the sperm donor for my baby."

Three

"Naturally, I don't expect you to make a decision tonight," Jamie added, walking around the recliner and sitting down again. She leaned back and crossed her legs, striking a relaxed pose.

Rich frowned. She sounded so casual, so comfortable with the idea. Mentioning it had obviously demanded courage, but now that her baby plan was out in the open, she seemed completely at ease.

But Rich wasn't. His thoughts were in chaos.

"I...don't know...what to say," he stammered.

"I'm sure the whole thing comes as a shock," she said. "I wish there was some way I could've led up to it with a little more tact, but I couldn't think how to say it other than flat out. I didn't want there to be any room for misunderstanding between us."

Rich was standing now, although he couldn't remember getting to his feet. "No...this is the best way." He paced back and forth in front of the coffee table. "A baby," he muttered, needing to hear himself say it aloud. He was trying to assimilate exactly what it was Jamie had suggested. He paused, waiting to be overwhelmed by objections, but apparently he was too numb to think clearly. Not a single protest occurred to him. Not one.

Questions. There were plenty of those. A few doubts and a whole lot of shock, but no real opposition. Although he'd thought there would be. *Should* be.

"Our baby," she said, her smile serene—as if she was already pregnant and counting the days before their child's birth.

Her attitude, the calm way she was watching him, unnerved Rich more than anything. He stalked into the kitchen, emptied his coffee mug and then refilled it. When he returned, he saw that Jamie was studying him closely.

"Say something." Her confidence seemed to be shaken, and for his own peace of mind, Rich was relieved to see it. She'd been taking this in stride a little too easily.

"I don't know what to say," he admitted bluntly.

"It sounds preposterous to you, doesn't it?"

"Yes," he nearly shouted. *Preposterous* was putting it mildly. She was talking about creating a new life, one that would link them forever.

"Why?"

"Why?" He couldn't believe she'd even ask such a thing. "You want me to father your child. A baby—any baby—is a huge responsibility and—"

"But that responsibility would be mine," she said quickly, interrupting him. "Don't worry, I wouldn't ask for any support, financially or emotionally."

That didn't sit well with Rich, either. He put down his coffee, sank into the chair again and leaned forward, pressing his elbows to his knees. He needed to think but couldn't seem to form a single coherent thought. "Let me see if I understand this correctly," he said after a moment. "You don't want anything from me other than a...biological contribution. I'd father your child, and that's all."

"For this to work, you'd—we'd both need to separate ourselves emotionally from the procedure. The baby would technically be yours, but only because of his or her genetic makeup. For all intents and purposes, the pregnancy and the child shouldn't be any different than if I'd gone to a sperm bank."

"In other words all you really want from me is my genes."

"Yes," she said, nodding emphatically. Her eyes briefly met his, and she appeared to have immediate second thoughts. "I know I'm making it all seem so callous, but that's not my intention. There's no one I trust more than you, no one else I feel comfortable approaching with this idea. If the doctor were to line up ten guys—ten strangers—and ask me to choose one of them to father my baby, I'd pick you instead. Knowing you and trusting you means so much to me. We've been friends since high school and that adds a whole other dimension to this."

"I don't know...."

"I...I considered seducing you."

This time, Rich was unfortunate enough to be in the process of swallowing a mouthful of coffee. It stuck halfway down his windpipe and completed its course only after a bout of violent coughing.

"Are you all right?" Jamie asked.

"You honestly considered seducing me?" That idea was even more ludicrous than the first one she'd had.

"Briefly," she admitted. "But sex between us would upset everything, don't you think? Your friendship's far too valuable to me to ruin it over something physical."

"I'm glad to hear it." So she'd considered luring him into her bed. Jamie Warren was certainly full of surprises this evening.

"I'm...not sure I could've done it," she said as she lowered her gaze to her hands, which were tightly clenched in her lap. "I mean...well, you know what I mean."

Rich wasn't convinced he did, but he pretended otherwise and simply nodded.

Jamie reached for her coffee and took one tentative sip. "Do you have any questions? I mean, I'm sure you do, and I want to reassure you in any way I can."

"Not yet." He couldn't seem to think clearly, let alone form sensible questions. "You say you're not looking for emotional or financial support?"

"Correct."

"So I'm not supposed to feel anything toward this child?"

Her eyes widened. "I...don't know. I hadn't thought about it in those terms. If it would make things easier for you, I could move out of the area after the baby's born, or...before. Whichever you prefer."

He didn't like that strategy at all. "What about our parents?"

"What about them?" She seemed puzzled.

Rich couldn't speak for Jamie's mother, but he knew his own, and she'd give him an earful the minute she heard about this craziness. "You don't expect our parents to accept this sitting down, do you?"

"I don't plan to tell them."

He gaped at her. "What do you intend to do? Run off and have the baby and then go home and present our parents with a surprise grandchild?"

"My mother, yes, but not yours. I don't intend to tell anyone you're the baby's father. That'll be between you and me. No one else needs to know. As far as my mother's concerned, all I'm going to say is that I was artificially inseminated, but not by whom. That would only complicate matters, don't you think?"

This didn't work any better for Rich than Jamie's other ideas, especially the one about moving away. He rubbed his face, hoping that would help him sort out his thoughts. It didn't.

"I suppose you'll want a few days to think this over?" She eyed him speculatively. It was apparent she'd like her answer as quickly as possible, but that was just too bad. This was too important a decision to be made quickly. He needed to weigh all the concerns carefully, think through the pros and cons.

He found the whole situation unsettling. Sure he'd like to be a father, but he'd prefer that it happened in the traditional way. His first instinct was to reject her suggestion outright, but Jamie was staring at him with those big, round eyes of hers, obviously doing her best not to sway him. To his regret, Rich discovered that he couldn't turn down her request without at least considering it. Their friendship was worth that much.

"Give me a week," he said after a strained minute or two.

"A week," she repeated slowly. "Should I call you or will you call me?"

"I'll call you."

She nodded and stood up to leave, pausing at the front door. "Before I go, there's one more thing I'd like to say."

"Yes?"

"I...I truly believe we'd have a beautiful child, but if it isn't meant to be, then I can accept your decision. I'm going to have a baby. I'd just rather it was yours than some stranger's." With that, she was out the door.

After she'd left, Rich resumed pacing, unable to stand still. His thoughts were a tangle of confused reactions, and part of him was laughing at the absurdity of Jamie's proposition.

Their baby! Their baby?

They'd never even kissed, and she was proposing they create a child together.

She'd told him she expected nothing from him, other than the pregnancy. Although he was sure she hadn't meant to sound so cold and calculating, that was exactly what Rich felt. She'd made it seem so...impersonal. Even that parting shot about having a beautiful child got to him. With those hazel-green eyes of hers and his height... He forcefully pushed the idea from his head.

Although he'd asked for time to make his decision, Rich already knew what his answer would be.

He wanted no part of this craziness.

Jamie made a genuine effort not to think about Rich for the next few days. She'd stated her case, explained what needed to be explained without resorting to emotions.

A hundred times since their talk, she'd thought of all the things she might've said to get him to agree....

Her mind was muddled with regrets. Rich was a good friend. Too good to risk ruining their relationship because she was determined to have a child.

She'd insulted him. She'd known, from his stunned look, that his immediate instinct had been to say no. Good grief, who wouldn't? It was only because of their friendship that he'd been courteous enough to consider her proposal.

Not for the first time, Jamie repressed the urge to call him and withdraw the suggestion. With everything in her, she wished she hadn't said a word. And in the same instant she prayed with all her heart, with all her being, that he'd say yes.

If only she'd approached him differently.

If only she'd told him how much his child would mean to her, how she'd love that child her whole life.

If only she'd assured him what a good mother she was going to be.

If only...

Rich had made plans to go to his brother Jason's apartment on Sunday afternoon to watch the Seahawks football game. Since Rich had given Bill Hastings their fifty-yard-line tickets, the least Rich thought he could do was bring the beer.

Close to one, nearly an hour late, Rich arrived at his brother's with a six-pack of Jason's favorite beer in one hand and a sack full of junk food in the other.

"About time you got here," Jason muttered when he opened the front door. "The kick-off's in less than five minutes."

"I brought a peace offering," Rich announced, holding up the six-pack. It wasn't like him to be late, and he half expected an interrogation from his brother. He was grateful when it looked as though he was going to escape that. If Jason did grill him, Rich didn't know what he'd say. Certainly not the truth. That he'd been so consumed with indecision over Jamie's proposal, he'd lost track of the time.

"It's going to take a whole lot more than a few beers to make up for the loss of those tickets, little brother," Jason complained as he led Rich to the sofa. "Last I heard, scalpers were getting three hundred bucks for this game, and my brother *gave* ours away." There was more than a touch of sarcasm in Jason's voice. "I still don't understand how Bill Hastings ended up getting *our* tickets."

Rich had been purposely vague about the exchange. "He did me a favor."

"You couldn't have bought him dinner?"

"No." It wouldn't help to tell Jason that the big favor Bill was supposed to have done him had fallen through.

Damn, Jamie was stubborn. Stubborn enough to go ahead and have her baby without him.

That stopped him in his tracks. It was her decision. What bothered Rich, what caught him so completely by surprise, was the rush of resentment he felt at the thought of her having another man's child.

"Hey, you all right?" Jason asked, claiming the seat next to him on the overstuffed sofa.

"Of course I'm all right. Why shouldn't I be?"

"I don't know, but you got this funny look all of a sudden."

Rich dropped his gaze to the can of beer he clutched in his hand. He offered his brother a weak smile and then relaxed on the sofa. It was a few minutes before his heart rate returned to normal. But he kept thinking about Jamie. She'd have a stranger's child. Yes, she would. She'd do it in a second. More than once Rich had collided with that pride of hers, and there wasn't a doubt in his mind.

She'd do it!

"You ever thought about being a father?" Rich found himself asking his older brother. He attempted to make the question sound casual but didn't know if he'd succeeded or not.

"Who, me?" Jason teased. "I'm not even married, and frankly I don't ever plan to be."

"Why not?" This was news to Rich. Jason dated as often as Rich did—although, come to think of it, Rich might have implied that his social life was more active than it really was. Jason never seemed to lack for gorgeous women. The only time he'd gotten serious, the relationship had turned out badly, but that was years ago.

"I'm not the marrying kind," Jason said, tearing open a bag of potato chips with his teeth. "All women think about is reforming me. Hell, if I want to kick off my shoes and watch a football game on a Sunday afternoon, I don't want to feel guilty about it. Most married men are henpecked. I prefer my freedom."

"So do I," Rich agreed. Marriage wasn't for him, either. Or for Jamie. He valued his independence. So did she. Jason apparently felt the same way—marriage was too much trouble.

"If I want to dry my socks in the microwave, there's no one around to yell at me," Jason added, then took a deep swallow of his beer.

"You dried your socks in the microwave?"

Jason shrugged. "I forgot to put the load from the washer into the dryer the night before. I needed a pair for work. So it was either that or pop them in the toaster."

Rich chuckled. That sounded exactly like something his brother would do. Jason was right: A woman would've been horrified had she known about his method of drying socks.

For the next ten minutes they were both engrossed in the game. At the commercial break, Jason propped his ankle on his knee and turned to Rich.

"Why'd you bring up this marriage thing?"

"No reason. I was just wondering."

"What about you?" Jason asked. "Isn't it time *you* thought about settling down and fathering a houseful of kids?"

"Me?" Rich asked.

"Yes, you. Mom knows any future Mannings will have to come from you and Paul. She's thrown up her hands in disgust at me."

"I don't think I'll get married, either."

Jason's eyes widened with disbelief. "Why not?"

"Don't look so surprised."

"I am. You, Richard Manning, are definitely the marrying kind. Women flock to you."

Plainly his older brother had an inflated view of Rich's sexual prowess, and Rich couldn't see any reason to disillusion him. "True, but not one of them, in all these years, has appealed to me enough to want to marry her."

"What about Pamela?"

"That woman's a—" Rich decided not to say it. "Put it this way. We don't have much in common."

"I thought you were still seeing her."

"I do occasionally." He took a swig of his beer and set it down, then reached for a bowl of popcorn. Leaning back, he rested his feet on the coffee table, crossing his ankles. "This is the life." He made a point of changing the subject, growing uncomfortable with the topic of marriage, although he'd been the one foolish enough to introduce it.

"It doesn't get much better than this," Jason said enthusiastically.

Once again their attention reverted to the television. The Seattle football team, the Seahawks, was playing the Green Bay Packers in a heated contest for the National Football Conference title. The winner would go on to play in the Super Bowl. All of Seattle was excited about the game.

"What about kids?" Rich wanted to kick himself the instant the question left his lips. What the hell was the matter with him? He'd had no intention of talking to Jason about any of this.

"Children?" Jason's attention didn't stray from the game. "What about them?"

"If you don't plan to marry, how do you feel about not having a child of your own?" This bothered Rich the most. He really would like a son or a daughter. Or both.

Jason took a long time answering, as though the question had caught him unprepared. "I don't know… I hadn't given children much thought. I guess I'd like a couple of kids someday, but on the other hand, I don't want to get married in order to have them. But then—" he hesitated "—there's no need to marry…not these days. We live in an enlightened age, remember?"

"Not marry the woman pregnant with my child?" Rich gave his brother a sour look. "I don't care what age we live in. We both know better than that. A word of advice—don't let Mom or Dad ever hear you say such a thing."

Jason exhaled. "You're right, that was a stupid idea." He reached over to the bowl of popcorn Rich was holding and grabbed a handful. "Is there something you're not telling me?"

"Not telling you?"

"Yeah. There's something on your mind."

"I'll tell you what's on my mind," Rich said, picking

up his beer. "Football. In case you haven't noticed, we're down by seven points and Green Bay's got the ball on the fifteen-yard line." He laughed, but his brother didn't.

"You're sure?" Jason asked a few minutes later. "The score's the only thing bothering you?"

"Positive," Rich assured him, feigning a smile. A man didn't tell his older brother, especially one who assumed women flocked to him, that he was thinking about becoming a sperm donor.

Six days had passed, and if Rich didn't call her soon, Jamie was convinced she'd have a nervous breakdown. Every time the phone rang, her heart shot to her throat and she started to tremble like an October leaf.

Rich had made a point of saying he'd be the one to call her, and he'd promised to do so within a week's time. Nevertheless, the wait was killing her, and each day that passed seemed to increase her anxiety.

She'd just put a casserole in the oven when the doorbell chimed. Jamie's gaze flew apprehensively toward the door. Even before she answered it, she knew it was Rich.

Inhaling a deep breath, she walked unsteadily across the carpet and opened the door.

"Hello, Jamie."

"Hi, Rich."

His eyes refused to meet hers, and her stomach twisted into a tight knot as he entered her home. He removed his coat and hung it in the closet as though he intended to stay for a while. Jamie didn't know whether she should take encouragement from that or not.

"Dinner's in the oven. Will you join me?"

He nodded, although she suspected he hadn't heard what she'd said.

"It's a new recipe…. I seem to be in a cooking mode lately. Tamale pie—I found the recipe on the back of a cornmeal box. I've always liked Mexican food."

"Me, too."

"Would you care for some coffee?"

"Sure."

He followed her into the kitchen and sat down at the table. "I suppose you're wondering what I've decided," he said when she brought him his coffee.

It was all she could do not to demand he tell her right then and there. Waiting even one more minute seemed too long. She pulled out the chair across from him and sat down. She was so anxious, her hands were trembling and she clasped them in her lap, not wanting to give herself away.

"I've done a lot of thinking since the last time we spoke," he began.

If the lines around his eyes and mouth were any indication, his thoughts had been serious indeed. It didn't look as though he'd slept much in the past week. For that matter, neither had she.

"I'm sure it hasn't been an easy decision."

"No, it hasn't," he said pointedly. "Before I say anything else, there are a few things I'd like to get straight. Once I do, you may change your mind."

"I'm not going to do that," Jamie said confidently.

His eyes held hers. "Don't be so sure. First and foremost, I want full parental privileges. This child will be as much a part of me as he or she is of you." He spoke forcefully, as though he anticipated an argument.

"What…what exactly do you mean by parental privileges?"

"I want a say in how the child will be raised, as much of a say as you. That means when it comes time to choose a preschool, I'll expect you to confer with me. I don't want you moving out of the area, either. At least not without me being informed and in full agreement, but I can tell you right now, I won't agree."

"Okay," she said hesitantly. The only reason she'd even brought up the subject of moving was to simplify the situation for him. It wasn't what she wanted at all. "Anything else?"

"I'm just getting started. If we go ahead with this, I want visitation rights."

"Of course. I have no intention of hiding the child from you."

"That's not what I understood earlier," he said, frowning.

"I…know. I should have thought this through more carefully before I approached you. I'd come up with the idea of you being the baby's father the same night I talked to you. When I showed up at your place, the idea was only half formed."

Rich seemed cold and distant. It was almost as if they were negotiating something highly controversial and there was no room for friendliness. No room for personal feelings.

"Does that mean you've changed your mind?" he asked.

"No…no, just that I hadn't worked everything out as extensively as I should have before I came to you. It hadn't dawned on me that you'd care one way or the other about the child. I realize now how insensitive that was of me. I apologize for that, Rich, I really do."

"Of course I'd care about the child!"

"I know. If you want full visitation rights, and a say in how the child's brought up, then that's only fair. I have no objections. None whatsoever."

"I'm also going to insist you accept child support."

"But, Rich, that really isn't necessary. I make a decent wage and—" She stopped abruptly at the way his eyes hardened.

"Then the deal's off."

She took a moment to compose herself. "Since that's clearly an important issue to you," she said carefully. "I'll be willing to accept whatever monetary support you deem necessary."

"Emotional support, as well. I don't want you walking the floors at night with a colicky baby."

"What do you expect me to do?"

"Phone me."

He was making everything so much more complicated than it needed to be. "You don't expect me to call you over every little thing, do you?"

"Yes," he said emphatically. "I want all the arrangements between us clear as glass *before* the blessed event. We'll share the responsibilities."

When she didn't respond, he asked, "Having second thoughts yet?"

"Not…really. Is this everything?"

"It isn't." He stood and opened the oven, checking the casserole that was baking inside. He let the door close slowly.

"You mean there's more?"

"One small item."

"One small item," Jamie repeated, assuming she wouldn't have any more trouble with this than his other demands.

"If we do decide to go ahead and have a child together…"

"And I think we should," she said, smiling over at him.

"Fine. Great. Wonderful. If you're sure."

"I'm sure."

"Good. In that case, I insist we get married."

Four

Jamie was too confused to think clearly. Surely Rich didn't mean what he'd just said. It made no sense. "Married...but...you can't be serious."

"I've rarely been more serious in my life," Rich answered, stalking to the far side of her kitchen. He removed two dinner plates from her cupboard and set them on the table. "Naturally, this wouldn't be a conventional marriage."

"Naturally," Jamie echoed, still too bewildered to understand his reasoning. "Then...why are you insisting on a wedding?"

"I want the child to have my name. I don't care if that no longer matters to most people. It matters to me."

"Oh."

"We'll continue to maintain our separate residences. For all intents and purposes, nothing will change, at least not outwardly. Except that we'll be sharing the care and custody of a child."

Jamie stood in front of the silverware drawer and closed her eyes, trying to force her heart to stop pounding so hard. Rich had made it plain this wasn't any love match—not that she'd ever suspected it would be. Nevertheless, her heart had reacted fiercely to his insistence on a wedding. Because she couldn't help associating marriage with love, despite a great deal of evidence to the contrary.

"What about the pregnancy? I mean…how do you think I should get pregnant?" By the time the question was complete, her voice had dwindled to a whisper.

"You could always seduce me."

Furious, Jamie whirled around and glared at Rich. She could feel the hot blush warming her cheeks, "I should never have admitted that. You're going to throw it in my face at every opportunity, aren't you?"

"No," he denied, but his eyes were sparkling with the blue light of laughter. "I agree with you. Sex between us would ruin everything. I don't want to risk our friendship any more than you do."

The tension eased from between Jamie's shoulder blades.

"We'll need to keep the marriage a secret."

"For how long?" If their child was to have his name, they'd eventually have to tell their families. Jamie wasn't keen on facing her mother with a surprise marriage to go along with a pregnancy. Doris Warren wouldn't take kindly to being cheated out of a wedding any more than Rich's mother would.

"We'd only stay married until the baby's born," Rich explained, revealing no hint of indecision, and certainly no doubts. He apparently had the whole situation worked out to his own satisfaction.

Unfortunately, he'd completely unsettled Jamie. She'd had everything organized and none of her plans included marriage, even a marriage of convenience. The questions were popping up faster than she could ask them.

"What are we going to say after the baby's born?" she demanded.

"That we're getting a divorce."

Jamie felt the sudden need to sit down again. "That we're getting a divorce?" she repeated. Already she could imagine her mother's shock and dismay. Not only would Jamie have married without telling her, but she'd be obtaining a divorce.

"It makes sense once you think about it," Rich continued with matchless confidence.

Maybe it did to him, but Jamie felt as though she were wandering through the dark, lost and confused, bumping into walls she didn't know were there. It had all seemed so simple the night she'd approached Rich.

He pulled out a chair and placed his foot on the seat, resting his right elbow on his knee. "We'll get married at the courthouse as quietly as possible. There's no reason for anyone to know."

"That much I understand…. I'm just not convinced it's necessary."

"I am," he said adamantly.

"All right, all right," she muttered, swiping one hand through her hair. What had seemed such an uncomplicated idea had suddenly taken on more twists and turns than a country road.

"You'll agree to the wedding?"

"I don't know yet."

"Don't sound so enthusiastic."

"I'm not." She sighed loudly.

"As soon as the ink's dry on the marriage certificate, we can make an appointment with the gynecologist…."

"Good grief, what are we going to tell him?" Jamie didn't relish that task. If Rich wanted to explain why two healthy, normal, *married* adults who wanted a baby would choose such an unconventional method, then more power to him.

"We won't tell him anything. He's a professional— he isn't going to ask a lot of questions. It's none of his business, anyway."

"Rich…I don't know about this."

"If you have doubts, then I suggest you spill them now."

"I'm not sure getting married is the right thing. We don't have to go through a wedding ceremony for the baby to have your name. Couldn't you legally adopt him or her after the birth?"

"Why complicate everything?"

"And marriage *isn't* going to do that?" Jamie cried.

"Marriage will accomplish the same thing now without the legal hassles of adoption later. As I said, it'll be in name only."

"Yes, I know, but…" She hesitated, trying to shape her objections in the form of a reasonable argument. When she spoke, her eyes met his. "You're going to think I'm terribly old-fashioned."

"The woman who asked me to be a sperm donor? Hardly!"

Jamie had the feeling it would take a long time to live that down. "Yes," she said vehemently, "I suppose it has to do with my upbringing, but I've always considered marriage sacred. Somehow, it just doesn't feel right to sneak off and get married and…and then arrange for a divorce nine months later."

Rich was quiet for a moment. "I agree," he finally said, "but this isn't a normal marriage."

"What marriage is?" Jamie asked, thinking of all the friends she'd known over the years who'd married. Each relationship was different from the others. She'd stood by and observed how some couples had grown closer in their love and commitment. Others had drifted further and further apart until it was too late.

"Nothing's going to change, at least not outwardly," Rich tried to reassure her once again. "We're doing this for the child's sake. And for yours."

"For *mine?*"

Rich's eyes narrowed slightly, and when he spoke his voice was cold. "I won't allow your reputation to be damaged by an out-of-wedlock pregnancy."

That was all well and good, but it was *her* reputation and if she had no objections, then he needn't be concerned. "But Rich—"

"Furthermore," he said, interrupting her. "I refuse to allow my son or daughter to be born a bastard." He raised his hand. "Before you argue with me, I feel the same way about this as I do about the baby having my name. I don't care if it's important to anyone else. It is to me. Besides, why make a kid's life any harder than it has to be?"

"You've got a point," she whispered.

"Still, I can understand your hesitation."

Jamie lowered her eyes. "It's just that I expect you'll want to marry someday. Sooner or later a woman's going to come into your life and this marriage is going to complicate everything for you. What are you going to tell her about me—and the child?"

"The truth."

"But Rich—"

"It's not going to happen. If I believed I was eventually going to marry, I wouldn't have agreed to this."

Any doubts Jamie entertained were wiped out with the certainty of his smile.

"So you'll marry me?" he asked.

Jamie nodded. She still wasn't convinced it was the right thing to do, but he'd insisted on it so she felt she had no choice.

"One last thing," Rich said, placing his foot back on the floor.

There was *more?* Jamie's head was still reeling from his last announcement. "Now what?"

"You're important to me. Our friendship's important. For the sake of that friendship, I think we should have everything drawn up legally. I don't want any misunderstandings later on."

This seemed logical to Jamie. "Okay, but most of the lawyers I know through work handle real estate and wills and business mergers. This isn't their kind of contract."

"I know an attorney who'll do it. One I trust."

"Who?"

"James Wilkens, Christy's ex-fiancé."

* * *

James Wilkens's office reminded Rich of his youngest sister, Christy. She used to work here, and he'd stopped by a couple of times over the past year to take his sister to lunch. He half expected her to come around the corner at any moment.

Christy was married to Cody, however, not James. Sheriff Cody Franklin. Rich wasn't likely to forget how he'd interrupted their wedding night, nor was Cody going to *let* him forget it. Rich had arrived at her apartment soon after he'd found out about Pamela's little fling. He'd been disgusted and disheartened, convinced women didn't know the meaning of the word *faithful.* He hadn't included Christy in that, though. Not his little sister; she'd always been so sweet and virtuous. Then, not knowing they were married, he'd stumbled upon her in bed with Cody, and his opinion of women had fallen to an all-time low.

Sitting in the plushly decorated waiting room next to a five-foot potted philodendron brought back an abundance of memories. The plant was on one side of him, with a fidgeting Jamie on the other.

He glanced at her. She was flipping through the pages of a magazine so fast she'd created a draft. She was on her third issue of *Good Housekeeping* and they hadn't been seated for more than five minutes.

She remained ambivalent about the idea of marriage, but she wanted the child enough to agree to his terms.

Unlike Jamie, Rich felt comfortable with the plan, for all the reasons he'd given her. He wasn't sure what anyone else would think, especially his family—if they ever found out—but frankly that was their problem. He was doing his best friend a favor.

Rich had the almost overwhelming urge to laugh. Never had he thought he'd agree to anything like this. According to Jason, women gravitated naturally toward him. In some ways that was true, but they were usually the wrong women. What he wouldn't give to have fallen in love with a woman as genuine and compassionate as Jamie.

The need to touch her, to reassure her, even in the smallest of ways, was as strong as the urge to laugh had been a few minutes earlier. He reached for her hand, entwining her fingers with his own.

She looked up at him. "I'm sorry."

"For what?"

"I…I can't seem to sit still."

"We aren't at the courthouse, you know. This is a meeting with James. He's a decent guy, and a darn good attorney. He isn't going to laugh or make snide remarks."

"I know…. It's just that…" She let the rest of the sentence fade.

"You're nervous."

"I'm nervous," she said. "I don't understand why, exactly, but my stomach's in knots and I can't seem to read, and I keep thinking of everything that could go wrong."

"Like what?"

Jamie turned from him and stared down at the open magazine in her lap. "I… You wouldn't understand."

"Try me."

"Marriage shouldn't be taken lightly. I know I've said that before, but I can't seem to explain it in a way that you'll understand. Something happens to a couple when they marry—even when it's only a marriage of convenience. Something…spiritual. I know you don't agree with me, but we're both going to be affected by this. I can't shake the feeling that deep down we'll regret it."

"We aren't going to have a physical relationship."

"I know all that," she said, "but it doesn't change what I feel."

Her hand was trembling in his, and he could tell from the way her voice quavered that she was close to tears. "Do you want to call it off?" Rich would accede to Jamie's wishes, but he hoped she wouldn't back out now.

"That's the crazy part," she said, her expression even more anguished than before. "I want this marriage and our child more than I've ever wanted anything in my life."

"So do I," Rich admitted, realizing how true it was. "So do I."

"Rich," James greeted him as he came into the waiting room. Rich stood and they exchanged handshakes. "It was a pleasant surprise to find your name on my appointment calendar this morning." The attorney looked from Rich to Jamie, and he smiled warmly.

"This is Jamie Warren," Rich said.

"Hello."

"We met briefly…a while back," she said, suddenly

biting off her words. She cast an embarrassed glance at Rich, as though she'd made a dreadful blunder. Fortunately James didn't react at all. It wasn't until they were inside James's office that Rich remembered the two of them had been introduced at James and Christy's engagement party.

"Come on in and sit down," James said, motioning toward the two upholstered chairs positioned on the other side of his desk. James, who was of medium height with broad shoulders and a hairline just beginning to recede, had a rather formal manner and a natural reserve.

Rich knew from mutual acquaintances that he'd taken the broken engagement hard. He'd loved Christy and been deeply wounded when she'd married Cody instead. Rich had heard that James rarely dated. If so, that was a shame. James had a lot to offer a woman. He was a junior partner with the firm these days and his talents were in high demand. It would take one hell of a woman to replace Christy, and Rich could only hope that James would find someone just as special.

"So," James said, reaching for his pen and a yellow pad, "what can I do for you?"

Rich leaned back in his chair. "Jamie and I would like you to draft a prenuptial agreement."

The attorney's gaze flew to Rich's. "Congratulations! I'm delighted to hear it. I didn't know you were engaged."

"We aren't...exactly," Jamie said hurriedly. When James focused his attention on her, she shifted in her chair and gestured at Rich. "You'd better explain...everything."

"This will be a marriage of convenience," he announced.

"A marriage of convenience," James echoed, as though he wasn't sure he'd heard correctly.

"There are...extenuating circumstances."

"We're going to have a baby," Jamie inserted, then as she realized what she'd implied, her eyes grew wide. "I'm not pregnant, at least not yet, but if everything goes according to schedule, I will be in the next couple of months."

James lowered his pen. "This doesn't sound like a marriage of convenience to me."

"We aren't going to destroy a perfectly wonderful friendship by having sex," Jamie declared vehemently, slicing the air with her hands. "We agreed on that first thing."

The pen was carefully placed on the polished mahogany desk. James frowned at Rich, then cleared his throat. "Let me see if I understand this. You plan for Jamie to become pregnant, but there isn't going to be any sex?"

"Before we go any further, I want the details of the divorce clearly spelled out," Jamie added, sliding to the edge of her cushioned seat. She slipped her hands under her thighs, but continued to fidget, crossing and uncrossing her ankles. "They should be as explicitly drawn up as the particulars of the marriage. And by the way, we won't be living together. But that shouldn't matter, should it?"

"You're planning the divorce now?" This time, James made a few notations on the pad, frowning again.

"You don't expect us to stay married after the baby's born, do you?"

"Rich?" James gave him a stern look. "Would you kindly explain what's going on here?"

"We're getting married, having a baby and getting a divorce. A, B, C. Points one, two, three. It's not nearly as complicated as it sounds." Rich found he was enjoying this. James, however, obviously wasn't.

"A prenuptial agreement—okay, fine. We have several forms already drawn up that you can read over. The two of you can decide which one suits you best and amend it as you see fit. But—"

"But what about the baby and the divorce?" Jamie asked nervously. Turning to Rich, she added, "I don't think James understands what we're planning."

"You're right about that. The marriage I understand—at least I think I do. Unfortunately it's everything else that's got me confused."

"There's a logical explanation for all this," Rich assured him.

"No, there isn't," Jamie said sharply. "Rich insists we marry and I don't feel it's necessary, but nothing I say will convince him. If I didn't want a baby so much, I'd never agree to this."

"Rich?" Once again, James looked at him, clearly more baffled than ever.

"It's not as confusing as it seems," Rich told him a second time. "A bit unconventional, perhaps, but not confusing." He spent the next ten minutes explaining their plans and answering a long series of questions from the attorney.

"It sounds crazy, doesn't it?" Jamie said when Rich had finished. "You probably think we both need appointments at a mental-health clinic. I don't blame you, I really don't."

James took his time answering. He continued making notes, then raised his head to look pointedly at Rich. "Are you *sure* this is what you want?"

"I'm sure." Rich shared few of Jamie's concerns regarding the marriage. It was merely a formality. She kept talking about it as though it were a deep spiritual experience. For some couples, marriage might well be that. But not for Jamie and him.

"What about you, Jamie?"

Her head came up sharply.

"Are you sure this is what *you* want?"

She hesitated, then nodded emphatically. "I'm sure."

James paused, rolling the pen between his open palms as he collected his thoughts. "Does your family know about your plans?" The question was directed at Rich.

He gave a short, scoffing laugh. "You've got to be joking. I don't intend to let them find out, either. At least not right away. They'll learn about the marriage and the baby eventually—that much is inevitable. But the longer I can keep this from my parents, the better."

"On that, I can agree."

"So you'll write up an agreement for us?" Rich asked. He hadn't missed the subtle note of concern in James's voice.

"I'll have one drawn up within a week."

"Good." Rich took Jamie's hand. They both stood,

and she tucked the long strap of her purse over her shoulder. "Then we'll go off to the courthouse now and apply for the wedding license."

"Might I offer you two a bit of advice?" James asked, standing himself. He rubbed the side of his jaw as if he hadn't decided exactly what he wanted to say.

"Please." Jamie's tone suggested that she hoped someone would talk her out of this scheme. If that was the case, Rich would be the first to remind her that she was the one who'd started the whole thing.

"I'll write up whatever you want me to," James said thoughtfully, "but I don't believe there's any reason to rush into anything. You've both waited this long to have a family—a few more months isn't going to make any difference."

Rich looked to Jamie for confirmation, but he couldn't read her thoughts. "We'll talk about it," he promised.

James nodded. "I'll give you a call later in the week and you can stop by and read over the agreement."

"Great." Rich steered Jamie toward the door, although she didn't need any encouragement. She seemed downright eager to escape. "I'll be talking to you soon then," Rich said over his shoulder.

"Soon," James promised.

Jamie was quiet on the way to the parking lot. For that matter, so was he. Although James Wilkens hadn't explicitly stated his misgivings, they were all too apparent—from the questions he'd asked and the hesitation Rich had heard in his voice.

Rich unlocked the passenger door and held it open for

Jamie. He waited until she was inside, his hand on the frame. "Do you want to take some time to think this over?"

"No," she said instantly. "Do you?"

He shook his head. "No."

Their eyes met and held until they were both smiling broadly.

Rich woke early Tuesday morning, before the alarm went off. He turned on the shower and stepped under the plummeting spray, enjoying the feel of it against his skin. He was whistling cheerfully when the tune slowly faded, one note at a time.

He quickly finished showering, reached for a towel and headed directly from the bathroom to the phone at his bedside. He punched out the number from memory and waited impatiently for Jamie to answer.

"Good morning," he said enthusiastically.

"Good morning," came her groggy reply.

"You know what today is, don't you?"

"Of course I do. It isn't every day a woman gets married."

"Second thoughts?"

"Third and fourth if you want the truth, but now that I've had a chance to think it over, I'm more certain than ever."

"Good." He'd grown anxious in the shower, convinced Jamie would change her mind at the last minute. He had to be assured one final time, although they'd talked of little else in the past week.

James had contacted him Friday afternoon, and Rich

had stopped at the attorney's office on his way home from work. The agreement was several pages long, but when he asked for the bill, James had insisted it was a wedding present. The gesture took Rich by surprise. James was the only person who knew what they intended, and he was acting as though this was a conventional marriage. Of all people, James was well aware exactly how unconventional it was going to be.

"You think we're nuts, don't you?"

"No," James had responded with a wry grin. "I think you're both in love and just don't know it yet."

James's comment had caught Rich off guard. He would never have taken the attorney for a romantic.

I think you're both in love and just don't know it yet. On this, the morning of his wedding, Rich tested James Wilken's theory once again. Sure, he loved Jamie, but not in the sense James implied. They were friends. Pals. Not lovers. Not soulmates. Just friends.

"Have you arranged for a witness?" Jamie asked, pulling Rich out of his reverie.

"A witness?"

"Rich—" she groaned "—don't you remember? When we applied for the license, we were told we'd each need to bring a witness. What do you plan to do, drag in someone from outside the judge's chambers?"

Rich thought about it for a moment. "I suppose so."

"Don't forget the ring," she said, beginning to sound nervous.

"I won't."

"As soon as the ceremony's over, I'll return it." Rich intended to use a small diamond that had once belonged to his grandmother. Jamie had objected, until she'd hit upon the idea of returning it after the ceremony. Wearing a diamond would raise too many questions, she'd decided. The only reason they even needed one was for the exchange of vows.

"Who's going to be your witness?"

Jamie paused. She couldn't very well ask any of her friends. "I…I'm not sure yet. I was thinking of Margie from New Accounts. Margie can keep a secret. But then I thought it might not be a good idea if anyone from the bank knew I was getting married."

"What do you plan to do?" he asked, mimicking her words. "Drag in someone from outside the judge's chambers?"

"I suppose so," she returned, and laughed. It had been at least a week since Rich had heard her laugh. It encouraged him, and he chuckled, too.

"You haven't heard from anyone?"

"No. You?"

Their biggest concern was that one or more of their family members would somehow find out that they'd applied for a marriage license.

In his worst nightmare Rich could envision his mother sobbing hysterically, interrupting the ceremony. She'd be furious that he was marrying Jamie without the large church wedding she'd looked forward to having for Taylor and Christy. Both of Rich's sisters had chosen small private weddings without any family present. For that matter, so had Paul. And he was doing the same thing.

The family honor now rested in Jason's hands.

Jason.

"Rich." Jamie's voice cut into his thoughts. "Don't worry, I'll have a witness."

Rich got dressed in a hurry, his movements filled with purpose.

He grabbed his raincoat on his way out the door and found himself whistling once more as he unlocked his car. He checked his watch and realized he had plenty of time. More time than he knew what to do with.

He drove to his brother's veterinary hospital in the south end of Seattle. There he saw three people in the waiting room. Two in the section marked Dogs and one little old lady clinging tightly to her cat on the other side of the room.

"Is Jason in?" he asked the receptionist.

"He's with a Saint Bernard, but he'll be out soon."

Sure enough, Jason appeared five minutes later. He wore a white lab coat, but underneath, Rich knew he had on jeans and a T-shirt.

"Rich, what are you doing here?"

"Can you take an hour off later today?"

"You buying me lunch?" Jason asked.

"No. I need you to be the best man at my wedding."

Five

Jamie was at the courthouse at the agreed-upon time, pacing the corridor outside Judge Webster's chambers. Ten to two.

She was there, but Rich wasn't.

If he left her standing at the altar—so to speak—she'd personally see to his tar and feathering.

She called his cell phone. No answer.

For the tenth time, she checked her watch.

Seven minutes late. The man would pay for this.

A woman Jamie assumed was the judge's secretary stepped into the hallway. "It's almost two. The judge can see you now."

"Ah...hello," Jamie said, giving the middle-aged woman her brightest smile. "My... The man I'm going to marry seems to have been detained. I'm sure he'll be here any second."

"I see." She glanced at her watch as though to say the judge was a busy man.

"I'm sure he'll be here," she repeated. A slow death would be too good for Rich Manning if he wasn't. "I was wondering…when Rich does arrive, would it be possible for you to be my witness?" She shouldn't have left it to the last minute like this, but she hadn't known who to ask.

"Of course." The gray-haired woman returned Jamie's smile. "Let me know as soon as your young man shows up."

"I will, thank you."

Jamie tried his cell again, and again he didn't answer. She resumed her pacing. She'd made the mistake of asking for the whole day off. If she'd only taken half a day, she wouldn't have all this time to contemplate what she was doing. In the last five minutes she'd vacillated between thinking marriage was the best solution and feeling convinced that it was the most foolish decision she'd ever made.

"Jamie." Breathless, Rich came around the corner at a half run.

"Where have you been?" she cried, her voice cracking under the strain. She was caught halfway between abject relief and total fury. Halfway between hope and despair, trapped in a world of nagging questions and second thoughts.

Rich pulled her into his arms and hugged her close. His breathing was labored, as though he'd raced up several flights of stairs. "I got stuck in traffic."

Jamie was about to chastise him for not allowing enough time, but she swallowed her irritation. What did it matter? He was there now. Suddenly she felt a relief so great all she wanted to do was wrap her arms around him and weep.

"Judge Webster's secretary said we should go into his office as soon as you arrived," she said, composing herself.

"Just a minute. We have to wait for my witness," Rich said, smiling down at her. His beautiful blue gaze was filled with a teasing light.

"You actually brought someone with you? Who?"

"Me," Jason Manning said, hurrying around the same corner Rich had a moment earlier. He, too, was out of breath. "Rich left me to park the car," he said, pressing his hand over his heart. "Said if he was late for his wedding, you'd skin him alive."

"He was right, too."

Jamie's gaze flew to Rich, whose expression was both tender and amused. He'd brought family! They'd discussed the subject at length and had agreed not to let any of their immediate relatives in on their plans. Not until it was necessary, which they'd calculated would be when Jamie entered the fifth or sixth month of her pregnancy.

"Bringing Jason seemed like a good idea at the time," Rich said with a chagrined look. "He spent half the morning arguing with me. According to Jason, we're both candidates for the loony bin."

"We weren't going to tell anyone, remember?" They'd decided that the fewer people who were in on this, the better. But at the rate Rich was telling people, Jamie wouldn't be surprised to see her picture splashed across the front of a grocery-store tabloid.

"Don't worry," Jason inserted smoothly, "I've been sworn to secrecy."

"I'll explain everything later," Rich promised in a low voice. He draped his arm over her shoulder and inhaled noisily, as though he still needed to catch his breath. "But right now, we've got a wedding to attend."

Jamie knew the ceremony itself wouldn't last more than a few minutes; she'd taken comfort in that. They'd be in and out of the judge's chambers in five minutes, ten at the most.

They stood before Judge Webster, their backs stiff and straight. The judge attempted to reassure them with a smile.

Jamie needed to be reassured. Her knees were shaking, her hands trembled and she wasn't sure she'd be able to go through with this.

When it came time to repeat her vows, she hesitated and raised her eyes to Rich. How could she promise to love him and honor him for the rest of their lives, knowing full well their marriage wouldn't last the year?

Rich must have read her confusion and her fears. Some unfathomable emotion flickered in his eyes, and she wondered if he was experiencing the same doubts. When his hold on her hand tightened, Jamie was grateful. She felt the need to be close to him. She didn't know why, any more than she understood the reason she'd agreed to go through with this wedding ceremony.

When she spoke, her voice shook, then steadied and grew strong. Her heart was pounding, then gradually returned to a normal, even beat. She realized that the calmness she felt, the serenity, had come from Rich. His eyes didn't leave her, and his own voice was confident and sure.

They exchanged rings, his hand holding hers as he slipped the delicate diamond that had belonged to his grandmother onto Jamie's finger. He revealed no hesitation. Once the ring was secure, her gaze slowly traveled up to his face. She stopped at his eyes, so blue and clear. They were just as steady as his hand.

The judge pronounced them husband and wife, and with a naturalness Jamie didn't question, Rich drew her into his embrace. Her hands gripped his shoulders as he lowered his mouth to hers. To the best of Jamie's memory, this was the first time they'd kissed, *really* kissed.

Rich made it worth the wait.

His mouth slid possessively over hers, coaxing open her lips. His own were warm and moist, gentle and teasing, giving and demanding.

Jamie was overwhelmed by the variety of sensations he evoked. She felt light-headed and giddy. Appreciated and adored. It seemed that her entire world had been inadvertently turned upside down and she was groping to find her balance.

She shouldn't feel this way, she told herself. She shouldn't be feeling *any* of these sensations. Rich didn't love her—not like this. Nothing like this. One kiss, and he made her feel as though she'd never been kissed before, as though she'd never experienced love before.

Maybe she hadn't. Maybe this was all in her imagination, her mind creating a warm romantic fantasy in order to appease her conscience. Maybe this was a subconscious effort to wipe out the ambivalence she'd felt during the ceremony.

The sound of Rich's older brother clearing his throat brought Jamie back to reality. Rich—her husband— reluctantly let her go and just as reluctantly turned his attention to Judge Webster. The two men exchanged handshakes.

"Thank you so much for being my witness," Jamie said to Judge Webster's secretary. She never did catch the woman's name.

"I was pleased to do it," the secretary told her. She stepped forward and gave Jamie an impulsive hug. "The judge marries a number of couples every year, but I have a good feeling about you and your young man. I think you two are going to be just fine."

Jamie didn't know what to say. She felt like the biggest phony who'd ever lived. It was happening already—the very thing she'd tried to warn Rich about. The feeling of connection. She'd sensed it during the ceremony and even more so with his kiss. But their marriage wasn't supposed to be about any kind of spiritual or emotional connection. It was supposed to be a convenience, a legal shortcut to giving Jamie what she wanted—a child.

They were making a mockery of everything marriage was meant to be. Jamie had never felt more like crying in her life.

She'd tried to convince herself they were doing the right thing. Rich was so confident, so certain, and she believed him because…because she'd always believed him.

But if they were doing what was right, why was her stomach in knots? Why did she feel as though she was going to burst into tears? And why, oh why, had Rich kissed her the way a husband kisses his wife—the most cherished wife in the world?

"Congratulations," Jason said, moving toward her.

She tried to smile, but her mouth started quivering and tears fell from the corners of her eyes, running down the sides of her face.

"Jamie?" Jason asked, giving her a hug. "Are you okay?"

"No."

Jamie didn't know how Jason managed it, but within minutes they were out of Judge Webster's chambers and Rich was at her side, his arm around her middle.

"All right," he said gently, guiding her down the hall, "why the tears?"

Jamie rubbed her hand across her cheeks, suspecting she'd smeared mascara over her face in the process. She'd dressed so carefully in her new pale pink suit. Like a romantic fool, she'd had her hair styled and nails manicured—and for what? So she could stand before God and man and say vows they'd never be able to keep.

"You honestly want to know what's wrong?" she wailed, snapping open her purse and rummaging around for a tissue. She found one, tucked her handbag under her arm and noisily blew her nose. "You mean you haven't guessed?"

"No."

"I…I feel dreadful."

"Why?" Rich looked completely bewildered.

"Because I just lied."

"Lied?"

"So did you!"

"Me?" He sounded even more confused.

"How can you justify what we did? We stood before Judge Webster and said vows. Vows! Vows are serious. We made promises to each other, promises neither one of us intends to keep."

"I can't speak for you, but I certainly intend to honor my vows."

"Oh, right," Jamie muttered sarcastically, rubbing her hand beneath her nose. "You're going to love me in…in sickness and health and everything else you said."

"Yes." Rich didn't so much as blink.

"How…can you?"

"True, this might not be a traditional marriage. Nevertheless, it is a marriage. And like I said, I fully intend to honor every promise I made for the full duration of the marriage."

"You do?" she asked on the tail end of a sniffle.

"You mean you don't?"

"I…I suppose so. It's just that I hadn't thought about it like that. I do love you, you know…as a friend."

As Rich walked her toward the elevator, his hands were clasped behind his back and his head was bent. Ever diplomatic, Jason remained a few steps behind them. "The problem," Rich said, "is that we've each put years of effort into finding the perfect mate. We've spent years looking for that special person—someone we'd be willing to commit the rest of our lives to—but neither of us found what we were looking for. So when we stood before Judge Webster…" He hesitated as though he'd lost his train of thought.

"What we were pledging…the seriousness of our decision hit us hard," Jamie finished for him.

"Exactly," Rich agreed, nodding.

"Then you felt it, too?" She stopped walking and turned to face him, her heart in her throat. Rich had experienced the same reaction she had while they were repeating their vows. He, too, had felt the solemnness of it all.

"I did…very much," he whispered. "A wedding ceremony is a sobering affair. If you didn't understand it before, I want to make it clear now. I'm committed to you, Jamie. That commitment will be the same for the baby once he's born."

"Or she," Jamie murmured, gnawing on her lower lip. Rich *had* said as much before, only she hadn't understood it. He planned to provide financial support for their child and emotional support for her. He'd also insisted they marry so the child would bear his name. But she hadn't thought of that as a commitment until he'd put it in those terms. A sense of contentment stole through her.

They continued walking side by side, toward the elevator, which was at the far end of the corridor. Rich matched his stride to hers. He was several inches taller than Jamie, and every once in a while, his shoulder would brush against her. His touch felt intimate and special. Jamie was sure he didn't intend or expect her to feel anything at his touch, but she did. She couldn't help herself.

"It's going to be all right, isn't it?" she asked when they stopped to wait for the elevator.

"Not if our parents find out, it won't be," Jason answered for Rich.

"They won't anytime soon unless you tell them." There was a clear warning in Rich's words.

"Hey," Jason said, raising his right hand. "I've already promised not to say a word—to anyone. Mom and Dad would have to torture it out of me."

Rich chuckled and slowly shook his head. "All Mom would need to do is offer you homemade bread fresh from the oven."

"Maybe so. But be aware that the fur's gonna fly once she learns she missed out on another one of her kids' weddings."

"She'll adjust," Rich said, looping his arm over Jamie's shoulder.

"Are you as full as I am?" Rich asked, leaning back against the upholstered circular booth. His hands rested on his flat stomach and he breathed in deeply.

"I couldn't eat another bite if I tried."

Rich had made reservations for their wedding dinner at the restaurant on top of the world-famous Space Needle. He'd planned every aspect of their wedding-day celebration, from the matinee tickets he'd purchased for a musical at the Fifth Avenue Theater, to a special dinner.

"What did Jason mean when he said you kidnapped him?" she asked. Not that it really mattered, she thought, basking in the pleasures of the most memorable day of her life.

Rich reached for the wine bottle and replenished both their glasses. "To be honest, I did kidnap him. Why…is another story. I'm not sure myself, especially when I knew he'd try to talk me out of this."

"He did try, didn't he?" That went without saying.

"Not at first." Rich arched a brow as though he was still a bit surprised by that. "He actually seemed excited—until he heard the full details."

Jamie groaned. "You told him…everything?"

"He's my brother." Rich picked up his wineglass and sipped. "When I first told him about you and me, he was thrilled. He said he's always admired you and felt I couldn't have made a better choice."

"He said that?" Jamie couldn't help feeling a little incredulous. She barely knew Rich's older brother. Oh, they'd met on several occasions, but the longest conversation they'd ever had was at Christy's engagement party, and that couldn't have lasted more than five minutes. Jason had been miserable in a suit and tie, and kept edging his finger along the inside of his collar. Actually, Jamie had spent more time that night talking to Jason than she had to Rich. Her now-husband had escorted some blonde to the elegant affair, and the woman had stayed glued to his side all evening.

A surge of irritation flashed through her. She'd never been keen on Rich's choice of girlfriends. She swore he could spot a bimbo a mile away.

He attracted them—and he attracted *her.*

That was a brand-new perception, a brand-new awareness.

Until he'd kissed her in the judge's office, Jamie had never thought of Rich in a physical way. He'd always been attractive, too handsome for his own good. But what she'd experienced earlier that afternoon had nothing to do with his looks. Instead, it had a whole lot to do with sensuality.

Rich made her feel vulnerable. Exposed. Powerless. And yet…powerful, too. Everything, all the emotion, all the sensations, had come rushing toward her at once.

Afterward, he'd been so concerned. So understanding. Allaying her fears, answering her doubts. He'd dried her tears and made her laugh. He'd turned this into the most special day of her life.

What he'd said about how they'd each searched for someone to love was true. Jamie had wanted to be married for so many years. She'd hungered for that special relationship and all that went with it, only to be disappointed time after time.

Their dinner check arrived, and while Rich dealt with that, Jamie finished her wine. As she raised the glass to her lips, her gaze fell on the diamond ring on her left hand. It was a simple design, a small diamond set in the center of an antique gold rose. When Rich had first mentioned it, she hadn't felt right about wearing it, but the fit was perfect, and now that it was on her finger she wished she didn't have to take it off.

"I suppose I should drive you home."

Jamie's heart soared at the reluctance she heard in his voice. She wasn't any more eager for this day to end than he was.

"I suppose," she said with an equal lack of enthusiasm.

"You have to work tomorrow?"

Jamie nodded. "You?"

He nodded, too.

They stood, and Rich helped her on with her coat.
His hands lingered on her shoulders, and he drew her
back against him and breathed in deeply. "Thank you."

"For what?" Jamie twisted around, and the restaurant
noises that surrounded them—the laughter and conversation, the clinking of silverware on china—seemed to
fade away.

"For marrying me," he whispered. "For agreeing to
bear my child."

Jamie pulled the straight skirt over her hips and
clipped it to the hanger. She hung it in her closet along
with the jacket, then wandered into the kitchen as the
teakettle whistled.

Sitting at the table in her full-length slip, she propped
her nylon-covered feet on the opposite chair and cradled
the mug of hot tea in both hands.

"I'm married," she said aloud, testing the words.

They came back sounding hollow, as hollow as she
felt. She hadn't wanted Rich to leave—not so soon. It
was barely ten. But when she'd offered him an excuse
to stay, he'd turned her down.

So this was her wedding night. In her dreams she'd
created a magical fantasy of champagne and romance.
See-through nighties and wild, abandoned passion. If
this was a traditional marriage, she'd have all that.
Instead, she'd chosen something else. Something far less.

She should be happy. Excited. In love.

She *was* all those things—in a manner of speaking. Then why, she asked herself, did the aching loneliness weigh so heavily on her heart?

Rich bent the thick goose-down pillow in half and bunched it beneath his head. Rolling over, he glanced at the clock radio and sighed. Nearly one. The alarm was set for five-thirty and he had yet to fall asleep.

It wasn't every day a man got married, he reminded himself. It wasn't every man who spent his wedding night alone, either.

Rich had dropped Jamie off at her condo, and although she'd suggested he come in for coffee, he'd refused. He didn't even know why he'd turned her down. Coffee had sounded good.

"Be honest," Rich said aloud. It wasn't the coffee that had enticed him, it was Jamie. She wasn't the most beautiful woman he'd ever met. But she was lovely. It seemed impossible to him that he'd missed it all these years. Was he blind?

He'd had beautiful. Pamela was beauty-queen gorgeous—and so empty inside, so lacking in values and morals, that he had to wonder what had attracted him in the first place. She'd appealed to his vanity, no doubt.

Rich rolled onto his back, tucked his hands beneath his head and stared up at the dark ceiling. It hadn't felt right to leave Jamie. With real disappointment, he'd turned around and walked to his parked car. He'd paused halfway down the steps, resisting the urge to rush back and tell her he'd changed his mind, he'd take that coffee, after all.

Instead he'd returned to an apartment that had never seemed emptier and a bed that had never felt so cold.

The phone on Rich's desk rang, and he automatically reached for it. "Engineering." He didn't take his eyes from the drawings he was reviewing.

"Hi," came the soft feminine reply.

Rich straightened. "Jamie? You're back from the doctor's already?" He checked his watch and was surprised to discover it was nearly four.

"I just got back."

"And?" He couldn't keep the eagerness out of his voice. They'd already had one appointment to see Dr. Fullerton. Rich had gone in with Jamie for the initial visit. They'd sat next to each other in Dr. Fullerton's private office and held hands while the gynecologist explained the procedure in detail.

"And," Jamie said quietly, confidently, "we're going to try for this month."

"This month," Rich repeated. "In case you didn't know, I've always been fond of March. March is one of my favorite months."

"Don't get too excited. It…it might not take, it generally doesn't with the first try."

"April, then. April's a good month. Another one of my all-time favorites."

"It could easily be three or four months," Jamie said with a laugh.

"June, July, August. Who can argue with summer?" Rich found himself smiling, too. He was calculating what month the baby would be due if Jamie got pregnant in March.

"December," she said, apparently interpreting his silence. "How would you feel about a December baby?"

"Jubilant. How about you?"

"It could be January or February." She sounded hesitant, as though she was afraid to put too much stock in everything going so smoothly.

"It'll happen when it happens."

"That was profound!" she said. "The doctor gave me a chart. Every morning, I'm supposed to take my temperature. It'll be slightly elevated when I ovulate. As soon as that happens, I'm to contact his office."

"I'm going with you."

"Rich, that really isn't necessary. It's very sweet of you, but—"

"I thought you knew better than to argue with me."

"I should," she said with mock exasperation. "We've been married nearly a month and I don't think I've won a single argument."

"No wonder married life agrees with me." He kept his voice low, wanting to be sure no one in the vicinity could overhear him. Only Jason knew he was married and he wanted to keep it that way as long as possible. "Call me in the morning," he said.

"Why?"

"Because," he said, leaning back in his chair, "I want to keep my own chart."

The following morning, Rich was in the shower when his phone rang. He turned off the faucet, grabbed a towel and raced across the bedroom.

"Hello!" he yelled into the receiver.

"Ninety-eight point six."

He pulled open the drawer on his nightstand and searched blindly for a pen. Water was raining down from his hair, dripping onto the bed. "Got it."

"Talk to you later."

"Great."

Wednesday morning, Rich waited in bed until he heard from her.

"Ninety-eight point six." She sounded discouraged.

"Hey, nothing says it has to happen right away."

"I keep trying to visualize it."

"What is this? Think yourself pregnant?"

She laughed. "Something like that."

"Call me tomorrow." He reached for his chart and made the notation.

"I will."

Thursday showed no difference, but Friday, Rich knew from the tone of her voice that something was up, and he hoped it was her temperature.

"Ninety-eight point seven...I think. Darn, these thermometers are hard to read. But it's definitely higher."

Rich could envision her sitting on the edge of her bed, squinting, trying to read the tiny lines that marked the thermometer. He made a mental note to buy her a digital one.

"Call Dr. Fullerton."

"Rich, I'm not even sure it's elevated. It could be wishful thinking on my part."

"Call him anyway."

"If you insist."

"I do." He hung up the phone and headed toward the shower, whistling.

* * *

It wasn't until later that afternoon that the idea of taking her out to dinner occurred to him. Although they'd been married a month, they didn't see each other often. It had been a conscious decision on Rich's part following their wedding day. In light of how he'd felt when he kissed her, it seemed the safest thing to do. He'd taken her to a movie the weekend after their wedding, and they'd both been ill at ease. Foolish as it seemed, it was almost as if they were afraid of each other. Not once during the entire movie had they touched. Jamie didn't invite him in for coffee afterward. Even now he wasn't sure what he would've done had she offered.

Still, they talked every day. Only last weekend he'd changed the oil in her car while she sewed a couple of loose buttons on his shirts. It was a fair exchange and afterward they'd gone out for hamburgers. Nothing fancy. The tension between them didn't seem to be as great as when they'd gone to the movie.

It was time to try again. There could well be a reason to celebrate, and a night on the town appealed to him. Someplace special. It wasn't every day his wife's temperature was elevated by one tenth of one percent.

Jamie was on her lunch break, and Rich didn't leave a message. He'd call her later.

When he did, she was tied up with a customer. The next time he tried, the bank was closed, so he left a message for her at home.

"This is Prince Charming requesting your presence

for dinner. Don't eat until you talk to me. I'm on my way home now. Call me there."

Rich expected a message from Jamie to be waiting for him when he arrived at his apartment. There wasn't.

He tried her again at six, six-fifteen, six-thirty and six-forty-five, leaving a message all four times.

By seven o'clock, he was worried. A thousand possibilities crowded his mind, none of them pleasant. He paced the living room in an effort to convince himself he was overreacting, then dialed her number one last time. He listened to her recording yet again, and seethed anxiously during the long beep.

"Jamie, where the hell are you?" he demanded.

Six

Jamie checked her watch, keeping her wrist below the table, hoping she wasn't being obvious. Eight-thirty! She'd been trapped listening to the endless details of Floyd Bacon's divorce for three solid hours.

"Don't you agree?" he asked, looking over at her.

She nodded, although she had no idea what she was agreeing to. A yawn came and she attempted to swallow it, didn't succeed and tactfully pressed her fingers to her lips. Floyd was such a nice man and she was trying hard to disguise her boredom.

"My goodness, look at the time," Floyd said.

It had all started so innocently.

Jamie had dated Floyd about five years ago. He was a regular customer at the bank and they'd seen each other off and on for a six-month period. Nothing serious, nothing even close to serious. Then he'd met Carolyn and the two of them had fallen in love and married. Jamie had attended their wedding. She remembered what she bought them for a wedding gift—a set of stain-less steel flatware with rosebuds on the handles. He and Carolyn had bought a house a few months later. Jamie had handled the loan application for them, but when they'd moved, they'd switched their account to a branch closer to where they lived. In the past three years, Carolyn had quit work to stay home with their two young children.

"I can't tell you how sorry I am the marriage didn't work out," Jamie said, wondering what could possibly have gone wrong between two people who so obvi-ously loved each other. She would never have suspected this would happen to Floyd and Carolyn, of all people. Of all *couples*.

"I'm sorry, too," Floyd said. His dark eyes touched her with their sadness. He'd moved into an apartment and had stopped at the bank to open a checking account. But a new account was only a pretext, Jamie soon learned; for airing his frustration with Carolyn, his mar-riage, his two preschool children and life in general.

Floyd had arrived just before closing time, lingered until he was the last customer in the bank and then asked Jamie to join him for a drink. She'd hesitated, but he'd looked so downtrodden and miserable that she'd gone against her better judgment. A drink soon turned into two and then Floyd suggested they have something to eat. At the time, it had seemed reasonable, but that was an hour and a half ago.

"I really should be going home," she said, reaching for her purse. It was Friday night and the work week had seemed extra-long and she was tired. Keeping track of her temperature and charting it was draining her emotional energy.

No, she decided, talking to Rich every morning was responsible for that. Speaking to him first thing, discussing the intimate details of her reproductive system, hearing his enthusiasm…talking about their child. Nothing had prepared her for the effect all this was having. She lived for those brief two-minute calls. It was almost as if he were in bed beside her…almost as if he were holding her in his arms. This closeness she felt toward him frightened her. The magnitude of what they'd done, of what they were planning, the child they'd conceive together, had brought subtle and not-so-subtle changes to their relationship.

Earlier in the day she'd hoped and planned to have a relaxing Friday night—to soak in a hot bath and cuddle up in bed with a good book. She might have given Rich a call and invited him over for dinner. There was a new recipe she wanted to try and he seemed to enjoy her home-cooked meals. She'd only seen him twice in the past month, and it didn't seem enough.

"I'll follow you home," Floyd said, breaking into her thoughts. He tossed some money on the table for the waitress.

It would be too late to call Rich now. Tomorrow was her Saturday morning to work, but she could call him then and ask him over for dinner on either Saturday or Sunday. Friday nights were probably busy for him, so it wasn't likely he would've been home anyway.

"Jamie?"

"I'm sorry. My mind was a million miles away. There's no need for you to see me home, Floyd."

"I know, but I'd feel better if I knew you got there safely."

She nodded. Floyd really was a nice man, and she did feel sorry for him. If lending an ear had helped him, she shouldn't complain. The time would come soon enough when she'd need a shoulder to cry on herself. Once the baby was born, she'd be filing for divorce. The thought was a cheerless one.

Jamie lived less than fifteen minutes from the bank and it was on Floyd's way to his new apartment, so she didn't object strongly when he insisted on following her.

When she pulled into her assigned parking space, he waited until she was out of her car. She waved to let him know she was safe and sound.

Floyd lowered his car window and said, "I appreciate being able to talk to you, Jamie. You're a good friend to both Carolyn and me."

"I'm happy if I was any help."

The sadness returned to Floyd's eyes. "I really love her, you know."

Jamie nodded. She believed him. Divorce was usually so ugly and there was so much pain involved. Jamie had seen several of her friends traumatized by the breakup of their marriages.

"Are you sure you really want this divorce?" she asked impulsively. Surely if two people deeply loved each other, they could work something out, couldn't they?

He shook his head. "I never did want a divorce.

Carolyn's the one who…well, you know." His shoulders rose in a deep sigh.

"You're sure about that?"

Floyd hesitated. "I'm pretty sure. When I told her I was moving out, she didn't say a word to stop me. The way I figure it, if she really loved me, she would've asked me to stay."

"What if she assumed that if you really loved her, you'd never *want* to move?"

Floyd stared at her. "You think that's what she might've thought?"

"I don't know, but it's worth asking, don't you think?"

"Yeah…I do," Floyd said, his voice revealing the first enthusiasm she'd heard all evening. He raised his car window, then quickly lowered it again. "Jamie?"

"Yes?" She was halfway toward the outside stairs that led to her second-floor condominium.

"Would you mind if I used your phone? My cell's dead, and I'd like to give Carolyn a call to see if she wants to talk."

"Sure." Smiling, she opened her purse and took out her key. If she'd mentioned this earlier she thought wryly, she might've been home two hours ago.

Floyd parked his car, then hurried up the stairs with her. He resembled a young boy, he was so eager. She unlocked the door and flipped on the light switch. Floyd immediately headed for her phone.

Jamie made herself scarce for a couple of minutes, going into her bedroom to remove her shoes. She hung up her jacket and eased her gray blouse from her waistband. Before leaving her bedroom, she slipped her feet into her fuzzy open-toed slippers. Then she went into the kitchen and put the kettle on the burner. As soon as Floyd was gone, she planned to relax with a cup of herbal tea.

"Carolyn agrees we should talk," Floyd announced triumphantly as he replaced the telephone receiver. "She sounded pleased to hear from me. Do you think she's lonely? I doubt it," he answered his own question before Jamie had a chance. "Carolyn always did have lots of friends, and she isn't one to sit home and cry in her soup, if you know what I mean."

Jamie nodded. "I hope this works out for you."

"Me, too. I'll be heading out now," Floyd said. "She's getting a sitter for the kids and she's going to meet me for a cup of coffee."

The doorbell chimed then, in long impatient bursts. Floyd's gaze swung to Jamie. She couldn't imagine who'd be arriving this late.

She walked past Floyd and opened her door. No sooner had she turned the lock than Rich raced in as though he was there to put out a fire.

"Where the hell have you been?" he demanded. "I've been half out of my—" He stopped midstep and midsentence when he caught sight of Floyd and the color drained from his face. His eyes widened with shock, disbelief and…could it be pain? Slowly he turned toward Jamie.

"Floyd, this is Rich Manning," she said, gesturing from one to the other. "Rich, Floyd Bacon."

Floyd held out his hand, and for a moment, Jamie

feared Rich wasn't going to take it. He did so, but with ill grace. "I take it Jamie didn't mention me," he said sarcastically.

"Ah…no," Floyd said, rubbing his palms together. He eyed the front door. "Listen, I was just leaving."

"No need to rush," Rich said, sitting down on the sofa and crossing his long legs. He stretched his arm against the back of the cushions, giving the impression that he had plenty of time to sit and chat. "I'm interested in hearing how the two of you spent the evening." His smile lacked warmth or welcome.

"Rich," Jamie said, stepping forward. She'd never seen him like this, so sarcastic and ill-mannered.

One look from him cut her to the quick. Rarely had anyone looked at her with such…disdain. He studied her, from her slippers to the blouse she'd pulled free from her skirt, and his eyes narrowed, damning her.

"Jamie's an old friend," Floyd explained. "I was in the bank this afternoon and…well, you see, my wife and I have separated, and Jamie—"

"So you're married, *too*."

"Too?" Frowning, Floyd turned to Jamie for an explanation.

"Yes," Rich said in a deceptively calm voice. "Jamie and I've been married…what is it now, darling, a month?"

"Rich," she warned him under her breath. He might be her legal husband, a man she'd known and respected for more than a decade, but seeing him behave like this, talk like this, he seemed like a total stranger.

"Jamie. My goodness," Floyd said, sounding astonished. "You didn't say a word about being married. Congratulations! I wish you'd said something earlier."

"So do I," Rich added caustically.

Once again Floyd glanced at the door. "I'd like to stay and chat, but I really should leave. My wife and I are going to meet and talk… Jamie was the one who suggested it. Well, actually, I came up with the idea of calling Carolyn, but Jamie helped me see that it was the right thing to do." He spoke rapidly, the words coming out so fast they tumbled over one another. "I'll see you later."

Jamie held the door for him. "Thanks for dinner," she said as graciously as the circumstances allowed.

"Thanks for dinner," Rich mimicked derisively as Floyd went out the door.

Jamie felt a storm threatening. One of anger and frustration. The thundercloud was sitting directly behind her, and she did her best to restrain her indignation. After taking a moment to compose herself, she turned around. "Is something bothering you, Rich?" she asked in a level voice.

He leapt off the sofa as though he'd been sitting on a giant spring. "Is something *bothering* me?" he repeated coldly. "What do you think you're doing, dating that joker?"

"It wasn't a date."

"I heard you thank him for dinner." He spat out the words as though to have to say them was a detestable task. "At least you could've returned my phone calls."

"I…haven't checked my messages. Good grief, I didn't get home until five minutes ago." Moving across the room, she went to her phone to listen. Six messages, all from Rich, played back, each sounding progressively less patient and increasingly anxious. The last one had been to demand to know "where the hell" she was.

"When I couldn't stand waiting for you to call, I drove over here to wait for you. Lo and behold, your car was in your parking space and you were here—with *Floyd.*"

"I can understand your concern," Jamie said calmly, willing to grant him that much.

"You're my wife, dammit! How am I supposed to feel when you turn up missing?" He raked his fingers through his hair and stalked to the opposite side of the room.

Jamie drew in a long, soothing breath, determined not to let this escalate into a full-fledged argument. "I was never missing. I'm sorry I worried you, Rich, but you're overreacting, and frankly, it's beginning to annoy me."

"Annoy *you?* I've been pacing the floor for the past three hours…."

"I would have phoned."

"You brought a man home with you!" He made it sound as though that was grounds for divorce.

"Floyd's an old friend."

The kettle whistled, and Jamie hurried into the kitchen and turned off the burner, all thought of tea forgotten. The boiling water bubbled from the spout, nearly scalding her. Rich had followed, stalking into the room behind her.

"Apparently you don't have a problem letting *old friends* take you out to dinner," he accused her, his words inflamed with impatience.

Jamie gritted her teeth, biting back an angry retort. "He needed someone to talk to, someone who'd listen to his problems. You're making it sound as though I did something underhanded. I was just being a friend."

"You're a married woman," Rich bellowed. He slammed his fist on the counter. "*My* wife. How do you think it makes me feel, knowing you chose to go out to dinner with another man instead of your own husband?"

"I didn't choose Floyd over you! Good heavens, how was I supposed to know you wanted to take me to dinner? I'm not a mind reader."

"If you'd come home after work the way you're supposed to, you would have heard the first of my six messages."

"That's ridiculous! I can't run my life according to your whims." She'd managed to keep her temper intact, but she didn't know how much longer her precarious hold would last.

"I thought you were different." A spark of pain flashed in his eyes.

"What do you mean by *that?*"

"I would've trusted you with my life, but you're like every other woman I've ever known. The minute my back's turned, you think nothing of seeing someone else."

The emptiness in his voice cut at Jamie's heart. "That's so unfair."

"We're married, and even that didn't make a difference." His eyes accused her of—what? Being unfaithful? That was completely irrational!

"This isn't a real marriage and you know it," she said heatedly. Her voice was shaking with the effort to keep from shouting. "You're the one who insisted on the ceremony, but it was for convenience."

"We're married!"

"Maybe, but you have no right to storm into my home and insult my guests."

"And *you* have no right to bring a man home with you."

"That's ridiculous." Jamie couldn't believe they were having this conversation. "Our marriage is in name only for…for obvious reasons."

"We said our vows."

"Don't remind me." The promises they'd made to each other continued to haunt her.

"Clearly someone has to."

"Oh-h-h," Jamie seethed. Tightening her fists at her sides, she exhaled sharply and resisted the urge to bang her cupboard doors to vent her frustration.

"Temper, temper."

"I think you'd better leave before we say something we'll regret." Instinct had told her that getting married wouldn't work, and she'd ignored it. Now she was suffering the consequences.

"Not on your life."

"This is my home," Jamie cried, quickly losing her grip on her rage. She'd never known Rich could be so unreasonable, so rude, so…impossible.

"You're just like every other woman I've ever known," Rich repeated in unflattering tones.

"And you're just like every other man, so wrapped up in your own ego that it'd take a whack on the head with a two-by-four to see what's right in front of your nose."

"It wasn't *me* who went out behind *your* back," he shouted. He leaned against the kitchen counter and crossed his arms.

"Why do you care if I had dinner with a dozen men?" she demanded. "It never bothered you before!"

"We weren't married before."

"I'm not your possession," she said. "You have no right, husband or not, to tell me who I can see and who I can't."

"The hell I don't."

Jamie squeezed her eyes shut. "I *knew* this wasn't going to work... I told you it wouldn't, but would you listen? Oh, no, you knew so much better."

"I still do."

Jamie couldn't help it, she stamped her foot. She hadn't done anything so childish since junior high. "Look at us," she cried, her voice shaking with anger. "I'm...I'm not even pregnant yet and already we're fighting. We're going to ruin everything fighting over something so...stupid."

"It isn't stupid to me."

"Floyd is just a friend. For heaven's sake, he's married!"

"So are you."

"Why are you doing this?" she cried.

"All I'm asking is that you keep your part of the bargain and I'll keep mine. That shouldn't be so difficult."

"Oh, right," she said, walking around the table and leaning on the back of a chair. "There's a lot more involved in this arrangement than I ever knew about or agreed to and—"

"Like what?"

"Like…like your caveman attitude toward me."

"Caveman? Because I don't want my wife dating another man—another *married* man?" He glared across the room at her. "Forgive me if I'm wrong, but I seem to remember a phrase or two in the wedding vows that state—"

"Don't you dare." Jamie pointed an accusing finger at his chest. "Don't you *dare,*" she repeated. "I never wanted to go through with the wedding, and you knew it. Using it against me now is the height of unfairness."

"We're married, Jamie, whether you like it or not."

"I don't like it, I hate it. I hate everything about it— this is the biggest mistake of my life." Unable to bear any more arguing, she whirled around and covered her face with her hands. If there was any decency left in him, Rich Manning would go. He'd leave her alone.

Jamie's nerves were raw, and the hair at the nape of her neck bristled as she heard Rich walk toward her. The clipped pace of his steps did nothing to reassure her.

"Did he kiss you?"

"No!" she shouted, furious that he'd ask such an outrageous question.

"Good, because I'm going to." His hands moved over her shoulders, clasping them, holding her in place.

"No." She made one weak protest, but she didn't know who she was talking to, Rich or herself. He'd kissed her once, the day of their wedding, and it had obsessed her ever since. She couldn't allow him to destroy her equilibrium again, destroy her peace of mind.

Although she resisted, Rich turned her around to face him. Jamie was on fire, and he'd barely touched her.

Rich took hold of her chin, his fingers firm, yet oddly gentle. Without another word, he bent down and covered her mouth with his own. Jamie knew she shouldn't let him do this. Not in the heat of anger. Not when they were fighting. Not when his kiss would only create a need for more.

He tasted so good, so wonderful. It wasn't *fair.* Nothing about this so-called marriage was fair.

He moved his mouth over hers, shaping her lips with his own until she moaned. It seemed to be what he was waiting for. The instant her lips parted, his tongue swept inside.

Shock waves vibrated through her at the small, ruthless movements of his tongue. Jamie could feel herself melting against him. The need continued to build within her, licking at her senses, growing hotter and stronger and fiercer....

Not satisfied with her lips alone, he kissed her eyes, her throat, until Jamie felt as if she was about to ignite.

A frightening excitement exploded inside her, going beyond mere pleasure and quickly advancing to a demand so intense there would be no turning back for either of them.

"Rich…no." She braced her hands against his chest, wanting to use that leverage to break away.

"Yes," he countered with a groan. His arms circled her waist, and he lifted her effortlessly from the floor, adjusting her hips against his own so she was aware of what she was doing to him—of the need she'd created in him.

Jamie slipped her arms around his neck, inclined her head and kissed him back. She felt sensual, wanton… and a little scared.

A low, rough sound rumbled from deep within his throat.

"Rich…please, oh, please, we've got to stop." Her heart was reeling with excitement but she was terrified of where this might lead. Terrified that, after tonight, she'd never be able to live with a marriage that wasn't a marriage.

"Not yet." He pressed his lips to her neck, running the tip of his tongue across the smooth skin of her throat and up the underside of her jaw. Jamie threw back her head. A ribbon of warm pleasure braided its way down her spine.

She buried her fingers in his hair and sighed, feeling breathless and hot. So breathless she could barely gulp in enough air. So hot. Hotter than she'd ever been.

He lifted her higher, leaning her against the kitchen counter. His hands worked the buttons of her blouse, sliding it from her shoulders. Her bra closed in the back, and he reached for and found the clasp.

"Tell me what you want," he whispered, caressing her thighs, stroking them as he spread delicate, moist kisses across her neck.

"I...don't know."

"Funny, I do," he countered with a lazy, sexy laugh. "You want me."

Jamie couldn't disagree. She could barely speak as a powerful coil of need tightened within her.

"Deny it." His tongue moistened a trail from the hollow at the base of her throat to her trembling chin.

"I can't."

"Me, neither." He swept her from the counter, shifting her weight until she was completely in his arms. He carried her as if she weighed nothing at all and headed out of the kitchen. He paused to turn off the light.

"Rich." She had to say something before it was too late. "We'll regret this in the morning." Even as she spoke, she wound her arms around his neck.

"Maybe." He didn't bother to deny it, but it didn't stop him, either.

Her bedroom was dark. Moonlight splashed through the open drapes, and Rich slowly lowered her onto the bed.

There was no turning back now.

Seven

They were silent afterward, their breathing labored, their chests heaving. Rich wished Jamie would say something. Anything. She didn't, and slowly reality returned, inexplicably linked with the glory of what they'd shared.

Rich kissed her softly, gently, with none of the urgency he'd felt earlier. He slid his fingers into the silky length of her hair and sighed with satisfaction. He kissed her again, reveling in her warm, sweet taste. He longed for her to tell him she experienced no remorse over their lovemaking. He'd been so angry, such a jealous idiot, and one thing had led to another. Before he could stop it, they were making love. She'd warned him, claimed they'd be left with regrets, but he felt none. Only a powerful sense of honesty.

Rich realized his weight was too much for her, but when he tried to move, she resisted, tightening her hold on him, hooking her ankles over his.

"Don't leave me," she whispered.

"No." He had no intention of doing so. "But I'm too heavy for you."

"Stay with me like this. Please." She stroked his back, her touch featherlight.

He would stay like this because she asked, but only for a little while. They both needed sleep and the thought of waking up beside her thrilled him almost as much as the memory of everything they'd done together in the last hour.

The silvery moonlight illuminated her face. He noticed that her eyes were languorous, her face flushed with pleasure. Her lips were turned up slightly in a secret smile. A serene, womanly smile. Just watching her, *loving* her, brought him peace. Because he did love her, and he was astonished that he hadn't recognized it earlier. Astonished at his own lack of perception. The love he felt for her burned within his chest, literally burned. The depth of emotion he felt had everything to do with this woman, and the profound pleasure he'd experienced was only part of that.

Her skin felt like silk beneath his hands as he brushed his fingertips down the side of her face. She sighed, and her breath caught in her throat.

Rarely had Rich experienced such contentment. The magnitude of it left him feeling weak and humble. Tucking his arms securely around Jamie's waist, he rolled onto his back, taking her with him. She made a small sound of surprise, then smiled peacefully, nestled her head on his chest and closed her eyes. Within minutes, she was asleep.

Slumber didn't claim him as quickly. He remained in awe of the emotions crowding his heart. For years he'd been blind and deaf when it came to his feelings for Jamie. Others had seen it. James had immediately recognized the love Rich felt for her and said as much. Rich had been quick to laugh and deny what was obvious to everyone but himself.

It had taken an argument to push him over the edge, push them both past the point of no return. If he had any regrets, it was that this discovery had come so late—and on the heels of a heated exchange.

He sighed and watched Jamie in the moonlight. She slept, utterly tranquil, and his heart swelled with a love so strong it was all he could do not to wake her and tell her what he was feeling. He wanted to, but it would be selfish not to let her sleep. He kissed her temple and closed his eyes, content to keep his wife secure in his arms.

Sometime toward dawn, Rich woke. Jamie was sleeping on her side and he was cuddling her, their bodies pressed intimately together. He smiled, a smile that came from his heart. They were like a long-married couple, completely comfortable with each other, as though they'd been sleeping together for years.

This was exactly what Rich intended, to continue sleeping with Jamie night after night for the rest of their lives. They'd grow old that way, gracefully, together. God willing, they'd raise several children, who'd be sheltered by the love their parents shared.

Rich stirred once more a little after six. Yawning, he stretched his arms above his head. He'd been working a lot of extra hours on a contract Boeing had with the government and he needed to get to work soon, despite the weekend.

He slipped out of bed and gazed down on Jamie, then leaned over and gently kissed her forehead. Hurrying to the shower, he whistled a cheerful tune.

In a joyous mood, Rich sang at the top of his lungs. He expected Jamie to be awake when he returned to the bedroom, but was disappointed to discover she was still asleep. He dressed and went out the door. He'd phone her later, as soon as he had a chance. He tended to get involved in his work and forget about the time, but he'd try not to let that happen. They had to talk.

Jamie woke at eight. Although she was sleeping on her side, facing the wall, she sensed almost immediately that Rich had gone.

He'd left without a word. Abandoned her to deal with the emptiness of the morning. Alone.

Closing her eyes, she bit her lower lip. The feeling of betrayal, of total isolation, was unlike anything she'd ever experienced.

Their argument played back in her mind, over and over. Every ugly word they'd said, the accusations, the hurt, echoed in her mind, taunting her again and again.

His reaction the night before made perfect sense in the bright light of morning. It must've been more than his pride could take to find her with Floyd. Something inside Rich had cracked.

Her evening with Floyd, no matter how innocent, must've been like a slap in Rich's face. He'd reacted in anger and pain, not because he cared. The reason for his outburst was directly related to his male ego. What had started out as an argument had eventually progressed to a physical exchange.

Rich had kissed her. First in anger. Then in need. A need fed by frustration and jealousy. He might not want a real marriage, but his pride demanded at least the pretense.

The image of her husband standing in her kitchen was unforgettable. He'd been furious with her. Although she'd had her back to him at the time, she knew she'd outraged him when she'd said that their marriage was the biggest mistake of her life.

A terrible tension had followed, so impenetrable that Jamie doubted she could've said or done anything to relieve it. Sitting up in bed, she pushed her tangled hair away from her face.

Rich hadn't kissed her for any of the right reasons. He'd done it because he hadn't believed her. He assumed Floyd had kissed her, and he couldn't tolerate another woman cheating on him—even if it was only in his imagination.

During all the years of their friendship, Jamie had seen Rich as distinct from the other men she'd known. That had been the first of several mistakes. Rich was exactly like them, competitive and territorial.

A few weeks earlier, he'd attempted to set her up with his engineering friend, Bill whatever-his-name-was. Now Rich couldn't stand her speaking to another man, even someone as blameless as Floyd Bacon. Good grief, Floyd was married! Did Rich honestly think she'd stoop to that level? Apparently he did, which didn't say much for his opinion of her.

She'd never seen Rich act more irrational. He'd refused to listen to her explanation, had been rude and arrogant in the extreme. And for what reason? None! At least none she could understand.

What he'd said about their being married was true enough—on paper. But their relationship wasn't any different now than it had been before the ceremony.

Except that it was. Everything she'd feared was coming to pass.

They'd been married a month, and look what had happened. It wouldn't depress her quite as much if Rich hadn't left her to face the morning alone. The questions tormented her, eroding her pride and self-confidence.

If only he'd said something afterward.

If only she'd said something.

It had all been so beautiful. Their lovemaking had captured her heart, her soul.

Jamie had longed to tell him everything she was feeling, but she'd been afraid. Afraid he hadn't experienced the same wonder. Afraid he'd be embarrassed. Afraid he had regrets. She couldn't have borne knowing that, not when everything had been so perfect for her.

Evidently he'd had second thoughts, otherwise he wouldn't have abandoned her, slipping away like a thief in the night.

Reluctantly, Jamie climbed out of bed and into the shower. The pulsating spray struck her skin like dull needles. The need to release her anguish in the form of tears left her throat aching and raw, but she refused to cry. She didn't have the time. It was her turn to work the Saturday morning shift at the bank. She was already behind schedule.

Wrapping a towel around herself, she went back into her bedroom—and came to a sudden stop. She covered her cheeks with her hands, mortified to find her carelessly discarded clothes from one end of the room to the other. The memory of how eager they'd been for each other added to her shame and humiliation.

Jamie dressed quickly, then hung last night's clothes in the farthest reaches of her closet and hurried out the door, not bothering with more than a cup of instant coffee.

Rich tried phoning Jamie at quarter to ten. Surely she'd be up and about by then. The phone rang three times before he was invited to "leave a message." He hung up. Later, he promised himself. He'd try later.

It was noon before he had a chance to call again. When she still didn't answer, he became irritated and set the receiver down harder than he'd intended.

"Problems?" Bill Hastings asked, walking into Rich's office.

"Not really." He did his best to appear nonchalant.

"Don't try to kid me," Bill said, sitting on the corner of Rich's desk, his left foot dangling. "I know the look when I see it—I've worn it often enough myself. You've got woman problems."

It wouldn't do any good to deny it, so he said nothing.

"Pamela?"

"Not this time."

Bill's eyebrows shot upward. "Someone else? You've been lying low lately. I didn't know you were seeing anyone."

"I'm not…exactly." It was a half-truth, which also made it a half lie. He *wasn't* seeing anyone. He was a married man, only Bill didn't know that and Rich wasn't in any mood to announce it now. Not when he didn't know what was going on between him and Jamie.

Last night had been good for them. Every time he remembered their lovemaking, his head spun and he felt warm inside. It wasn't a sensation he was familiar with, since he'd never experienced anything like it in other relationships.

He'd thought, at least he'd hoped, that Jamie had shared in the magic they'd created, but apparently that wasn't the case.

At two, Rich decided to try Jamie one last time. He might be reading more into her not answering the phone than she intended. Maybe she simply wasn't there to answer it. After all, Saturdays were often busy with errands.

He'd phone again and if there still wasn't any answer, the hell with it. A man had his pride.

He'd wait until she called him.

The phone was ringing when Jamie, struggling with a bag of groceries, tried to remove the key from her purse and unlock her front door. Once she'd thrown open the door she raced across the room, praying with everything in her that it was Rich.

"Hello," she cried breathlessly after making a leap for the phone. Whoever it was had apparently just hung up, and a buzz droned in her ear.

She knew the caller couldn't have been Rich. He'd left six messages the night before. He wouldn't be shy about leaving another.

On the off chance he had, she listened impatiently through all the messages she hadn't yet erased.

Nothing new from Rich. Nothing.

The emptiness around her seemed to swell. Her heart felt like a lead weight in her chest as she walked across her living room and closed the door. She'd dropped her bag of groceries on the sofa as she dashed for the phone. The apples had tumbled out, along with a box of cold cereal and a bottle of imported wine.

Like a romantic fool, she'd gone and purchased an expensive bottle of wine. Her morning had been hectic—Saturdays at the bank generally were. But no matter how many customers she served, or how many loan applications she reviewed, Jamie hadn't been able to stop thinking about Rich.

She'd been wrong—he *wasn't* like other men she'd known. She'd loved him too long to condemn him on such flimsy evidence. There were any number of reasons he might've had to leave. She was a sound sleeper, and for all she knew, he could've tried to wake her. By the time she'd left the bank at a little after one, Jamie was confident she'd hear from Rich. Confident enough to rush out and buy a bottle of wine and a small sirloin tip roast just so she could invite him over to dinner—so they could talk.

There was a lot to say.

* * *

Rich stared at the phone accusingly, willing it to ring. He'd arrived home late Saturday afternoon. He was in such a rush to listen to his messages that he didn't even stop to check his mail. He bounded up the stairs to his apartment, taking two and three steps at a time, sure there'd be some word from Jamie.

The blinking red message light made him feel almost cocky with relief. Until he discovered it was Jason who'd phoned. Jason, not Jamie. His brother, not his wife.

So this was what it meant to be married, to wear his heart on his sleeve and mope around like a besotted fool. So this was how it felt to truly love another person. To care so much that his whole life hinged on a single phone call.

Rich was through with waiting. He'd already ruined one night pacing the floors like a madman, yearning to hear from Jamie. He'd be damned before he'd do it again anytime soon.

Furthermore, he mused darkly, he was through with allowing a woman to rule his heart. Apparently he hadn't learned his lesson, after all.

Pamela had strung him along for weeks. He'd been duped by one woman and he wasn't going through *that* again.

If Jamie was foolish enough to throw away the best thing that had ever happened to either of them, then so be it. The choice rested entirely with her and he wasn't going to say a word to persuade her. Not a single word.

Clearly she felt none of the beauty of their night

together. None of the wonder and the magic. It stung his pride that he could have misread her so completely.

Rather than dwell on his marriage, Rich reached for the phone and viciously punched out his older brother's number. Jason answered on the second ring, and they made plans for the evening. Nothing fancy. Paul, their oldest brother, had invited them over for a round-robin of pinochle. A card game sounded a lot more inviting than sitting home all night waiting for a silent phone to ring.

Call him. Jamie had never spent a more restless Saturday afternoon and evening in her life. Pride, she soon discovered, made poor company.

For all she knew, he could be just as eagerly waiting for her to call him. But that didn't make sense, especially since he'd been the one to slip away in the early morning hours. Even so, she was willing to give him the benefit of the doubt. *More* than willing.

Although her stomach was in knots, she'd gone about cooking an elaborate dinner, just in case Rich did phone. The roast and small red potatoes gave her a perfect excuse to invite him over. Now the meal sat on her stove untouched. Unappreciated. Forsaken. Just like her.

When she could bear the silence no longer, Jamie walked over to the phone. Her hand was trembling and she paused to clear her throat twice while she was dialing. She forced herself to smile, determined to sound as cheerful as a robin in springtime when Rich answered the phone.

Only he didn't.

After four rings, his machine came on.

Jamie was so stunned, she listened for a couple of seconds, then reluctantly hung up. For several moments, her hand remained on the receiver as the futility and the discouragement overwhelmed her.

She was being silly. Naive. But it had never occurred to her, not once, that Rich wouldn't be home.

Apparently he'd gone out for the evening. No doubt he was having fun, laughing it up with his friends, enjoying himself while she sat home alone.

There were places she could go, people to see, fun she could have, too. She contacted three friends and suggested a movie. It was a sad statement on her life that the most exciting entertainment she could think of was a movie.

All three of her friends already had plans for the evening. Which was just as well, since Jamie wasn't all that keen to go out anyway. It was the kind of night for watching reruns on television with a box of crackers in her lap and a six-pack of diet soda at her side.

Rich had a great time Saturday night. They'd played cards into the early hours of the morning and thoroughly enjoyed themselves. There'd been whole stretches of time when he didn't think of Jamie at all. Five- and ten-minute blocks of time.

Things would've gone well if it hadn't been for Jason. His brother seemed to like walking close to the edge, Rich thought with annoyance.

"So how's the marriage of *in*convenience working

out?" Jason had asked on the drive home. He made it sound like a joke, but Rich wasn't in a laughing mood.

Rather than go into any of the details, Rich gave an unintelligible reply.

"What's that?" Jason pressed.

"I didn't say anything."

"I know."

"Just drop it, Jason." Rich was serious and he made sure his brother knew it. He didn't want to discuss his relationship with Jamie. What she'd said the night before about their marriage being the worst mistake of her life was beginning to have the ring of truth to it.

"So," Jason added after a few minutes, "marriage isn't exactly a bed of roses, is it?"

"I never claimed it would be."

"Is she pregnant yet?"

"Pregnant?" Rich repeated the word as though he'd never heard it before. "Pregnant," he said again, his voice dropping. Vividly he recalled their conversation Friday morning and how excited he'd been when he learned her temperature had been slightly elevated. They'd spoken every morning for several days running, discussing the chances of pregnancy. It was the reason they were married! Only, they'd planned to conceive the child by nontraditional means....

Twenty-four hours following his conversation with his brother, Rich continued to mull over the possibility of a pregnancy.

He hadn't heard from Jamie all day Sunday, either. He'd decided he probably wouldn't. That woman was so stubborn. Fine, he'd wait her out. If she didn't contact him, it was her loss.

He changed his mind Monday afternoon. It was either call her or resign from his engineering job. He'd made one mistake after another all day. Every time the phone rang, he felt as though an electrical shock had gone through him and nearly leaped off his chair. Although he strove to sound cool and collected, he couldn't keep his heart from speeding like a race-car engine.

Obviously Rich would have to be the one to call. It felt like blackmail, which did little to improve his mood. He stood and closed the door to his office.

He walked all the way around his desk twice, then sat heavily in his chair and picked up the phone.

The bank's receptionist answered almost immediately.

"Is Jamie…Warren available?" He stopped himself from asking for Jamie Manning just in time.

"I'll transfer your call," the woman said, cutting him off. The phone rang three times, frustrating Rich even more.

"This is Jamie Warren's office. How may I help you?"

"Ah…" Rich had expected Jamie would answer. "Is Jamie available?"

"No, I'm sorry, she's home sick today. May I help you?"

"Ah…" Jamie was home sick? She'd seemed in perfect health Friday night. Perhaps she was ill. Too ill to call him.

"Sir? May I help you?" the woman repeated

"No…no, thanks. I'll phone later."

But first he was going to find out exactly what was wrong with Jamie.

Eight

Jamie felt wretched. Not only had she spent the most miserable weekend of her life, but late Sunday afternoon she'd come down with a ferocious case of the flu.

Monday morning she'd phoned in sick. For most of the day she'd stayed in bed, trying to convince herself that it was a twenty-four-hour virus and she'd be fine by Tuesday morning.

Her head throbbed, her muscles ached and she was sure she had a fever. If she wasn't so sick, she'd get out of bed to take her temperature. The only times she'd risked leaving the comfort of her warm cocoon had been to make trips to the bathroom.

The phone at her bedside rang and she reached for it blindly, nearly toppling a glass of liquid flu medication left from the night before.

"Hello," she croaked. It was probably some salesman hoping to sell her a cemetery plot. The timing couldn't be better.

"Jamie?"

"Rich?" Naturally he'd phone her *now,* when her defenses were down and she was too weak to react. She'd waited three painful days to hear from him. Nightmare days.

Now that he'd called, Jamie experienced absolutely no emotion. Certainly not relief. Or anger, although she'd spent most of Sunday furious with him, and so hurt it was all she could do not to simply give in to self-pity.

"I phoned the bank and they told me you were home sick," he explained, as though he needed a reason to call her.

"I've got the flu."

A slight hesitation followed. "You're sure? Have you been to the doctor?"

"I'm too sick for that." She found his concern laughable. He'd walked out on her. Ignored her. Hurt her. And now he was upset because she hadn't seen a doctor over a twenty-four-hour flu bug?

Once again Rich hesitated. "I think you should make an appointment with Dr. Fullerton."

"Dr. Fullerton?" she echoed. Rich wasn't making sense. "Why would I see a gynecologist?"

"Because what you have might not be the flu," he returned, his words sounding as though they were spoken from between clenched teeth.

Maybe she was being obtuse, but she didn't understand what he was saying. "Trust me, it's the flu. I've got all the symptoms."

"Didn't it dawn on you that it might be something else?" His voice rose with impatience.

"No. Should it?"

"Yes!"

It hit Jamie like a bolt of lightning. Rich thought she might be pregnant! If it wasn't so ludicrous she'd cry. He actually seemed worried.

"It's too soon to tell," she said in her most formal voice, as if she were relaying the bank's decision regarding a loan application. "But it's unlikely."

"Your temperature was elevated, remember?"

"Not that much. Don't worry, you're safe."

His angry sigh told her that either he was exasperated or furious—Jamie didn't know which.

When would she learn? Time after time she'd foolishly handed her heart to a man, and the outcome was always the same. Within a few months her heart would be broken, shattered, and she'd be limping away. Some women were meant to find love, but apparently she wasn't one of them. Some women were destined to have forty or fifty years of contented marital bliss. She'd be lucky if *her* marriage lasted two months.

"Do you need anything?" Rich asked.

"No." She made her reply as clipped as she could. If he really cared, he wouldn't have left her on Saturday morning. "I'm perfectly fine."

"Then why weren't you at work?"

"Because I've got the flu," she said again.

"Then you aren't *perfectly fine,* are you?"

How like a man to argue about semantics. "Other than the flu, I'm feeling wonderful." She tried to sound as if she'd practically be running the bank single-handed if it weren't for this virus. There certainly wasn't any problem in her life—other than an almost-husband who had no regard for her feelings.

"We need to talk," Rich suggested after an awkward moment. The silence between them was strained—as strained as their marriage.

"I…think that might be a good idea."

"When?"

"Uh…" Jamie stalled for a few seconds. She didn't want to see him anytime soon, considering the pitiful way she was feeling. If she looked remotely as dreadful as she felt, Rich would drag her bodily into Dr. Fullerton's office.

"Wednesday night?" Rich said impatiently.

"Wednesday…sure." By then she should be well on the road to recovery.

"The Cookie Jar?"

The restaurant was one they'd frequented in high school. A little hole-in-the-wall diner with a polished linoleum floor and an old-time jukebox in the corner. Jamie hadn't thought about the place in years. "I didn't know they were still in business."

"I happened to be driving down Forty-third recently and I saw it. It brought back a lot of old memories. If you'd rather meet somewhere else…"

"No, The Cookie Jar sounds like fun. I'll meet you there at…how about seven? Right after dinner."

"Fine. Seven. I'll buy you a chocolate sundae for dessert."

Despite everything she'd been through in the last three days—the anxiety, the disappointment and the pain—Jamie found herself smiling. A few words from Rich had wiped it all away. "I'd like that."

He chuckled. "Somehow I knew you would."

A moment later, Jamie replaced the receiver and nestled back on her pillows. She'd been thoroughly chilled earlier and had piled on every blanket in the house. Suddenly she was feeling much better. Good enough to climb out of bed and make herself something to eat.

Wednesday, Rich arrived at The Cookie Jar an hour early, figuring he might as well have dinner there. He slipped into the booth with its tattered red vinyl upholstery and reached for the menu, tucked between the napkin holder and the sugar container. The menu offered four or five varieties of hamburger, in addition to sandwiches and a wide range of ice-cream desserts. He noted the picture of the chocolate sundae, the ice cream swimming in a pool of chocolate, smothered in whipped cream and crowned with a bright red cherry. Jamie's favorite.

He'd made light of discovering The Cookie Jar, claiming he *happened* to be driving down Forty-third when he caught sight of it. That was a lie.

He'd almost gone crazy when he hadn't heard from her by Sunday evening and he'd gone out for a drive in an effort to collect his thoughts. Going past their old high school and the nearby restaurant had been no accident. He would've gone inside The Cookie Jar, but the restaurant had been closed. He wasn't entirely sure why he'd suggested they meet there. Nostalgia? A chance to remember simpler times? To relive the beginning of their friendship?

An impossibly young waitress arrived with a glass of water and a small pad, ready to take his order. Rich asked for a cheeseburger, a strawberry milkshake and an order of fries. He glanced around at the other customers, but the high school crowd had gone home and the few people there were older.

He strolled over to check out the jukebox, thinking it might be fun to hear some of the songs he'd loved in his teens. He was surprised to find he didn't recognize a single tune. Not even one. He fingered a few quarters in his pocket, but after a couple of minutes he decided not to bother and returned to the booth.

He was getting old. He hadn't really noticed it before but he did now. When the waitress didn't look any older than twelve and he didn't recognize a single Top 40 hit, he couldn't deny it—he was past his prime.

The cheeseburger was sinfully delicious. The French fries were just the way he liked them—hot and salty. He savored the sweet, thick shake and couldn't remember a meal he'd enjoyed more.

Wrong.

No point in trying to fool himself. Any meal with Jamie would've been better. He missed her. He missed their early-morning conversations and the sound of her laughter. He missed the intimacy they shared as they talked about their child.

Their child.

Paul's three-year-old twin sons had been up and

about for part of Saturday night, racing around the house in their Spider-Man pajamas. For an hour or so, Jason had played cards holding Ryan on his lap, while Rich held a squirming Ronnie. Rich had always enjoyed being with his young nephews, but he hadn't truly appreciated them until that evening. If all went well, within a year's time he'd be holding a son or daughter of his own. That had filled him with an electrified anticipation. He'd managed to contain those feelings, not knowing what was happening between him and Jamie. But he'd know soon. They were going to clear the air.

When he'd first mentioned marriage, Jamie had been afraid, full of dire predictions that sex would ruin their friendship.

He'd agreed with her then, and he did now. They were in danger of ruining everything unless they acknowledged their feelings in a mature, honest manner. Their night together had redefined their relationship, taking them from friends to lovers.

What a discovery they'd made.

What a *mess* they'd made.

He knew he should never have made love to her, but try as he might, Rich couldn't make himself regret it. If he suffered any remorse, it was that it had taken an argument to realize how much he cared for Jamie.

He'd been in love with her for years, only he hadn't known it. They'd had a special friendship all that time, and they now had a chance to have even more. Rich didn't want to say or do anything that would jeopardize their marriage *or* their friendship.

Things hadn't gone well when he'd phoned her Monday afternoon. The tension during that call still made him wince. Rich had said none of what he'd wanted to say, nor had he done anything to assure her of his love. Jamie had sounded stilted and uncertain. The conversation was over almost before it started—although at least it had ended on a lighter note. Thank goodness for ice cream.

He'd been tempted to call her again several times since, but decided it would be best to wait until they could meet face-to-face. There was less likelihood of misunderstandings that way.

Rich had done a lot of thinking about what he needed to tell her. First, they had to put aside any pettiness, let go of any jealousy, vanquish any fears. Then they'd discuss their feelings. If the conversation went the way he hoped it would, he'd go home with her and spend the night.

Why not?

They were married. It didn't make sense for Jamie to get pregnant by artificial means when they were fully capable of doing it naturally.

Capable and eager.

He didn't plan to bring that up right away, of course, but he planned to let her know it was what he wanted.

During the remaining time he spent waiting for her, Rich entertained several ways of handling their discussion. Furthermore, he felt they should seriously consider moving in together. Since Jamie owned her place, it would be sensible for him to make the switch, but they'd eventually buy a house.

He was mulling over which neighborhood would

suit them when Jamie walked into The Cookie Jar, wearing a full-length navy blue coat.

"Hi. I'm not late, am I?" she asked, slipping into the seat opposite him.

She looked so good. Rich had trouble keeping his eyes off her. "No…no." He summoned the waitress and asked Jamie what she'd like.

"Hot tea, please," Jamie said, smiling up at the teenager.

"Coffee for me," he told the waitress.

"You want your chocolate sundae now?" he asked.

Jamie shook her head. "No, thanks. I'm still recuperating from the flu." She folded her hands primly in her lap, her gaze avoiding his.

This wasn't as promising as Rich had hoped. "So you're still battling the bug?" Now that she mentioned it, she did look pale.

She nodded, her gaze following their waitress.

"They sure are young these days, aren't they?" he said, his eyes following hers.

She glanced at him as though she didn't understand what he meant. Rich motioned toward the teenager.

Jamie nodded, her eyebrows raised. "Pretty, too."

Rich hadn't noticed. A sixteen-year-old in braces did nothing for him. Jamie on the other hand sent his senses into orbit. All he had to do, he reminded himself, was be honest with her. Honesty led to intimacy—which led to the bedroom.

The girl brought their coffee and tea, smiling demurely. Jamie returned her smile and picked up the sugar container, shaking some into her tea and stirring it briskly. Rich couldn't remember her using sugar before, but this wasn't the time to mention it.

"I wanted to talk about what happened Friday night," he said, leaning forward, cupping the warm mug in both hands.

"Why?"

"Well, because…" He sipped his coffee before answering. Her question had caught him off guard. "It's brought another dimension into our relationship."

"H-how do you feel about…our relationship having another dimension?" Once again she cast her gaze around the room, looking everywhere but at him.

"I think it has the potential to be good," he said, striving to sound matter-of-fact. If he let on too quickly that he was crazy in love with Jamie, he might scare her off.

"The potential to be good," she repeated, her voice so low he had to strain to hear her.

"Yes. Unfortunately we weren't able to discuss it Saturday morning." Rich watched as Jamie went stiff. He realized she hadn't liked him leaving and wondered if she'd misinterpreted the situation. He'd do his best to make amends now. "I apologize about heading out early. It might have—"

"Stop." She raised her hand.

"Stop?"

"There's no need to apologize. None. The last couple of days at home I've had plenty of time to think."

He nodded in relief. Apparently Jamie had come to the same conclusions as he had. He sipped his coffee and leaned back.

"You were right."

Rich nodded again. A man always likes to hear the truth.

"Having dinner with Floyd was an error in judgment on my part, although it was completely innocent. After your experience with Pamela, I should've understood your feelings. As your friend...I should've been able to hear what you were really saying. If there's any blame to be placed over...over what happened, I want you to know..."

"Blame," Rich repeated. The word fired his anger, and adrenaline shot into his veins.

"Yes, I just wanted you to know I'm willing to accept the blame."

Hearing it a second time didn't improve his disposition. Rich set his mug back on the table with enough force to slosh coffee over the edges. "No one said anything about placing or accepting blame. If that's what you're here to do, I suggest we end this discussion right now."

"I was just trying to—"

"Then don't."

Jamie's gaze fell to her mug of tea, cradled between her hands. From the rise and fall of her shoulders, Rich could see how hard she was trying to avoid another argument.

He was too angry to make the effort. *Blame.* She wanted to allot blame for the most fantastic night of his life. Hers, too, but she was too proud to admit it.

Everything he'd hoped to accomplish—making this marriage real, moving in together, buying a home and creating a child, a son or daughter who'd be born from their love—seemed to disappear before his eyes. He'd longed for this meeting, hoped it would give them a way to move naturally from being friends to being lovers. Married lovers.

"I've done it again," she whispered.

"Done what?"

"Made you mad."

He knew it hadn't been her intention to offend him. Judging by the bewildered look in her eyes, she didn't understand why he felt angry.

"It's happened already, hasn't it?" Her words were so shaky, Rich half expected her to break into tears. "We've killed our friendship."

"Not necessarily." She looked pale, and here he was, furious with her, when all he wanted to do was take her in his arms.

"I *knew* this would happen," she said with sigh. "Marriage just isn't going to work. Our feelings are all muddled up…we hardly know how to act around each other anymore."

Rich sat silent and morose. What she said was true.

"What do you suggest?" he asked after a while.

"I…I don't know. I thought I knew what I wanted. Now I'm not sure."

Rich didn't know, either. He wanted her as his wife, but he needed to be positive that she shared his feelings. What man *didn't* need that type of reassurance? It had all seemed so straightforward earlier. Now he was floundering.

"Do you feel up to walking?" he asked.

His question obviously surprised Jamie, but she nodded.

"Good." Rich reached for their tab, then left some money on the table.

They were in the old neighborhood now. The brick two-story high school they'd once attended was two blocks over. By tacit agreement they headed in that direction. Jamie wrapped a scarf around her neck and buried her hands in her pockets. Rich did the same, but he would rather have held hands with her.

They'd gone a block before either of them spoke.

"I used to think you were the handsomest boy at school."

"Me?" Rich laughed. "You certainly didn't let me know it."

"I couldn't. You were vain enough."

Rich smiled. "I used to wish I had as easy a time with grades as you did."

"Easy?" she repeated with a short, mocking laugh. "I worked my tail off."

"Remember our ten-year reunion?"

Jamie nodded. "You were with some blonde. You always went for blondes, didn't you?"

He ignored her remark. "You were with that guy who looked like David Letterman," he said.

"Ralph was a nice guy."

"Nice and dull." Rich didn't know why he'd bothered to bring Elaine. He'd much rather have spent the evening with Jamie. As it was, they'd danced nearly every dance together.

"At least all of Ralph's brains weren't located below his neckline."

"Speaking of which," Rich said, grinning boyishly.

Jamie whirled around to face him, her eyes spitting fire. "Don't you dare bring up the size of my bust. Don't…you dare."

Rich couldn't hold back his smile. "You're full of surprises, aren't you?"

"Did I ever mention the karate lessons I took? I learned how to disarm a man in three easy moves. Don't tempt me, Manning."

"*You* tempt me." Rich didn't know what made him say it, but now that it was out, he wasn't sorry. Jamie went still at his side, unmoving in the dim light from the street lamp. Rich raised his hand and glided his fingertips over her face. Her eyes drifted shut.

"I…don't think this is a good idea…."

He stopped her, tracing the outline of her lips with his index finger. He circled once, twice, three times….

"Why not?"

Her eyes remained closed, and she swayed toward him. Rich reached for her, pressing her close.

"There…was something I wanted to say," she whispered.

"Oh." He buried his face in her hair, inhaling its sweet scent. Rich didn't know how they could be at odds with each other when the attraction between them was this strong.

"You…you shouldn't distract me."

"Do you want me to stop?" His lips grazed the underside of her jaw. She tilted her head.

"Not yet…."

"Should I kiss you?"

"Please."

It was all the encouragement he needed. He brought his mouth to hers and wrapped his arms around her, nearly lifting her from the sidewalk. Her arms crept up his chest, pausing at his shoulders. The kissing was even better than it had been before, something Rich hadn't thought possible.

His mouth moved hungrily over hers, and when she sighed and parted her lips, he swept her mouth with his tongue. Jamie reacted with a swift intake of breath, winding her arms around his neck.

Rich had never intended to kiss her like this. Not on a public street half a block from where they'd attended school. He wanted her soft and yielding in his arms. And in his bed. Soon.

The salty taste of tears shocked him. She was crying. He pulled his mouth from hers. "Jamie, what's wrong?"

"Everything…nothing." She kissed him back, her open mouth over his. It was as sensuous as anything he'd ever known.

"You're crying."

"I know."

"Why?"

"Because you're making everything so *difficult*."

"How am I doing that?" She remained in his embrace, his hand pressing the small of her back.

"Kissing me… You weren't supposed to do that."

"I'm not?"

"No…but don't stop."

"I don't plan to." Rich didn't need further encouragement. His kiss was urgent, filled with unleashed desire. They'd wasted precious days, hiding behind their fears. All along, they could've been rejoicing in the discovery of their love.

"Rich…"

Reluctantly, he broke off the kiss, his chest heaving. He took her hand, folding it in his own, and started back toward The Cookie Jar. "Let's get out of here."

"I…suppose we should."

"It's either that or make love to you in the middle of the street."

"Make love to me?"

Surely it was what she expected. A man didn't kiss a woman like that without her knowing what he had in mind, especially if that woman was his wife!

"But…we need to talk."

"Later." His steps were brisk. The sooner he got back to his apartment, the sooner he could kiss her again. He didn't want to give her the opportunity to change her mind.

"There's something we should talk over first."

"What? Can't it wait?

She shook her head. "I would've said it earlier…. I planned to, but then you suggested the walk and…we started kissing and now I'm more confused than ever."

He stopped at his car, unlocked the passenger door, then turned to face her. Resting his hands on her shoulders, he met her gaze, relieved to see the hunger in her eyes. "All right, Jamie, tell me whatever it is."

She brushed the tears from her cheeks, and drew in a deep, steadying breath. "Because of Friday night."

That again! "Yes?"

"I was thinking you might want to…you know?"

Rich thought he did. She was about to suggest what he'd been considering for the last few days—that they take this marriage seriously and move in together.

"If it's what you want, it's what I want," he said, brushing the hair from her face, his fingers lingering on the softness of her skin.

Her eyes closed, and she bit her trembling lower lip. "I don't know what I want anymore…and I don't think you do, either."

"Sure I do," he countered. He wanted her.

"I think we should give serious consideration to…"

"To what?"

"A divorce."

Nine

Rich jerked away from her as though he'd received an electric shock.

"A divorce!" he bellowed.

It wasn't what Jamie preferred, but she felt honor-bound to offer Rich the option. They'd broken their agreement, the promises they'd made to each other before the wedding.

The decision to make love had been mutual; nevertheless everything had changed, and they couldn't continue pretending it hadn't. Their lovemaking was so powerful, so moving, Jamie would treasure the memory all her life. Every time she thought about falling asleep, nestled against Rich, she went weak.

"A divorce," Rich repeated.

Jamie shuddered. He'd never know what it had cost her to make the offer. Jamie prayed Rich would give her some indication that Friday night had been as meaningful and as beautiful for him as it had been for her.

"So you want a divorce?" he said, slamming the passenger door of his car.

"I...I didn't say it's what I wanted."

"Then why did you suggest it?"

"Because...well, because things are different now."

"You're right about that," he muttered. "I don't even know you anymore."

Jamie chose to ignore his outburst. "We'd agreed this was to be a marriage of convenience."

"You didn't exactly fight me off, you know."

Jamie's cheeks exploded with scalding color. "No... I didn't, but it doesn't alter the fact that we breached our agreement—and before we go on with our plans, I feel we should reevaluate our options and our commitment."

"You sound just like a banker. Cold and calculating. What's the matter? Are you afraid of a little emotion?" His eyes were seething with anger.

If Jamie thought he was furious when he'd confronted her with Floyd, his anger on Friday night paled in comparison to the fury she saw now.

"We're not teenagers anymore," she said as calmly as her voice would allow. "We're responsible, mature adults who can make decisions based on something other than hormones."

"So Friday night was nothing more than a roll in the hay for you?"

"I didn't say that." Jamie was growing angry herself. "You're purposely misconstruing everything I've said. Friday night happened. Good or bad, it happened. We can't pretend it didn't."

"I had no intention of forgetting it or ignoring it or anything else."

"Then why did it take you until Monday afternoon to call me?" she cried. "Why did you sneak away in the middle of the night without a word? I woke up feeling like...like a one-night stand."

"You aren't the only one who was disappointed," Rich said loudly. "It wouldn't have hurt you to call me."

"You abandoned me."

"I made you feel like a one-night stand?" Rich paced the sidewalk. He rammed his fingers through his hair. "A one-night stand? That's ridiculous. We're *married!*"

"No, we're not," she argued. "Not really. I don't..."

"I've got the papers to prove it. Talk about denial! A wedding is a wedding, so don't try to add a list of qualifiers to it now."

"Those qualifiers were added *before* the ceremony."

"So you want out." He turned toward her, his face contorted with anger, his blue eyes piercing.

"I'm simply giving you the option. Our relationship has changed, and we can't act as if it hasn't."

"And I am?"

"Yes!" she shouted. "If I hadn't said anything we'd be halfway to your place by now. We both know I would've ended up spending the night, and then what?" She didn't let him answer. "Then tomorrow morning," she resumed, answering her own question, "everything would be awkward again and there wouldn't be time to say or do anything because we'd both need to get to work."

Already Jamie could picture the scene. They'd be

rushing around dressing, embarrassed and uncomfortable with each other, the way they'd been when Rich had phoned her Monday afternoon. There wouldn't be time to talk, but they'd exchange polite pleasantries while he drove her back to Forty-third Street so she could pick up her car. Then she'd have to dash home and change clothes again before going to work.

"It wouldn't have to be that way."

"But it would've been." After a few kisses neither one of them would want to talk, not when they were so eager to make love. There wouldn't be any discussion, no clear exchange of views; that was predictable. And their embarrassment the next morning would've been inevitable.

"What I don't understand is why you're throwing a divorce in my face now."

It all made sense to Jamie. "We were planning a divorce anyway, after the baby's born. There were certain stipulations, agreements we made before the wedding. That's all changed. If you're going to have second thoughts, the time is now."

"Is it me or you who's having regrets?" he demanded harshly.

"We weren't talking about me."

"Maybe we should."

"Oh, Rich, please don't."

"Don't what?"

"Try to turn everything I say around. I didn't mean to hurt or offend you. I just want this to be as clear as we can make it. Having a baby is too important a decision. We can't mix it up with egos."

"Easy to say when my ego's the one that's getting battered."

"I told you, I'm not doing it intentionally. All I want is for us to be honest with each other. If you decide you'd rather forget the whole thing, then I'll understand. Look what's happened so far! We've nearly destroyed the marriage, not to mention our friendship, and we haven't been married six weeks. This isn't going to be as simple as we thought."

Rich rubbed his hand down his face, looking confused.

A divorce *wasn't* what Jamie wanted, but she felt she had to give him the opportunity to end their plans now, before the relationship was further complicated by a child.

"I was so confident about what we were doing," he muttered.

"I…was, too." Jamie could barely stand the suspense, but she wouldn't say anything to encourage him one way or the other. They both had to be completely sure that they were doing the right thing. "Would you prefer to take a couple of days to think it over?"

Rich's gaze found hers. "Maybe I should. I thought I knew, but maybe I don't."

Disappointed, Jamie nodded. "I'll wait to hear from you then." She secured her purse strap over her shoulder and smiled. "Good night, Rich."

"'Night."

As she headed toward her car, which was parked four or five spaces from his, she struggled not to reveal any of what she was feeling. Rich surprised her by walking the short distance beside her.

"I've really made a mess of this, haven't I?" he asked. For the first time since she'd mentioned the divorce, he didn't look as though he wanted to bite her head off.

"We both have," she answered in a small voice. She tried to smile at him and failed. When they reached her car, she opened her purse, searching for her keys.

"It may not make any difference," Rich said, and his eyes burned into hers, "but I'd like you to know I had to work Saturday morning. I probably should've woken you. I assumed my singing in the shower would have—" he gave a lopsided grin "—but when it didn't, I decided to let you sleep. It was thoughtless of me not to leave a note."

"You were at work?"

Rich nodded. "When I did phone, you weren't there."

"But there wasn't any message."

He shrugged. "After what I went through on Friday, I was done with leaving messages. Anyway, you might've phoned *me*." The last remark was made as an offhand suggestion, but it didn't disguise his frustration.

"I did! But you weren't home. I didn't leave a message, either." What a fool she'd been. What fools they'd both been. Jamie wanted to groan at their stupidity.

"You phoned?" His sigh of frustration was audible.

"You did, too?" Her sigh joined his.

Jamie resisted the urge to weep. There'd been so much she'd wanted to say, and hadn't. So much she'd longed to tell him. And couldn't.

"You'll phone me…soon?" she asked, trying not to sound as anxious as she felt.

Rich nodded. One corner of his mouth lifted in a half smile. "I'll leave a message if you're not in this time."

"If you don't call me, then I'm calling you." She refused to leave room for any additional misunderstandings. Not again.

Before he realized where he was going, Rich found himself at Jason's apartment complex. He sat in the parking lot for several minutes.

When Jamie brought up the idea of divorce, he thought he'd explode. Rich couldn't remember ever being angrier in his life. Angry and hurt and confused. They were minutes away from making love, and she dropped the word as though she was talking about something casual, something unimportant.

Divorce.

At one point he'd decided there was no reasoning with her, and the best thing to do was walk away from the whole mess. Then the unexpected happened.

She'd started to make sense.

Jamie had always been the logical one. The perfectionist. Everything had to be just so. It had driven him to distraction when they were on the yearbook staff together. He should've realized that although thirteen years had passed since then, Jamie hadn't changed.

She wanted everything as clear as they could make it. Those were her words.

Rich knew what he wanted, too. He wanted her back in his bed so he could make love to her again. Naturally he didn't say as much. How could he? She claimed that they were denying what had happened, that they couldn't pretend nothing had changed when everything was different. Well…yes, that was true—and no, it wasn't.

Hours later, Rich was still sitting in his car, and he still didn't know what to make of their meeting. He needed someone to talk to, so he elected Jason, whether his brother was willing or not.

The lights were out in Jason's ground-floor apartment, but that didn't deter Rich. He leaned on the buzzer until a sliver of light shot out from under the door.

He waited until he heard the lock snap open, then stepped back.

"Rich?" His brother groaned, tying the knot in his bathrobe. "What the hell are you doing here? Do you have any idea what time it is?"

Rich checked his watch, surprised to discover it was after eleven. "I need to talk," he said, marching past Jason and into the kitchen.

A yawning Jason followed. "Is this going to take long?"

"I don't know. Why? Have you got a woman with you?"

"If I did, I wouldn't have answered the door, no matter how long you rang the bell." Jason pulled out a kitchen chair, sat down and slouched forward over his folded arms. "In case you haven't noticed, I'm not in a talking mood."

"Don't worry, all you have to do is listen."

Rich walked over to the refrigerator and opened it. He took out two cold sodas and pushed one at his brother. "When's the last time you bought groceries?"

"I don't know. Why?"

"All you've got in there is a tin can with a fork sticking out of it."

"Dinner," Jason said, covering his yawn. He waited a moment, then gestured. "Go on…talk. I'm listening."

Now that he had the floor, so to speak, Rich couldn't figure out where to start. He wasn't ashamed of having made love to Jamie, but he wasn't sure how she'd feel if she knew he was talking to Jason about their night together.

"You need some help with this, little brother?" Jason asked, straightening and opening his soda.

"No," Rich said vehemently.

"I'll give it to you anyway. You and Jamie have succumbed to the delights of the flesh and now you don't know what to do about it."

Rich was so flabbergasted that all he could do was stare at his brother, his mouth wide open.

Jason ignored him and guzzled half the can of soda.

"How'd you guess?"

"I knew Saturday night," Jason informed him, wiping his mouth with the back of his hand.

"How… What'd I say?"

"Nothing. I asked you if Jamie was pregnant yet, remember?"

Rich nodded. The question had hit him like a sledgehammer. Jason's curiosity was what had led Rich to call her Monday afternoon. Jamie might well be pregnant from their one night together, although she'd been quick to reassure him otherwise.

"So?" Rich asked, feigning ignorance.

"You looked so shocked and you closed up tighter

than a clam. It was obvious, at least to me, that she might be 'with child,' as they say."

"It's not that simple."

"Marriage rarely is. Why do you think I've avoided it all these years? I tried to tell you before the wedding, but would you listen? Ah, no, this was different, you said. You and Jamie were friends entering into a business agreement. Nothing more and nothing less."

"I remember what I said," Rich muttered, taking another swallow. He'd been incredibly naive about this marriage. The whole thing had sounded like a great idea; he had to admit it still did. Although an even better idea was to turn their arrangement into a till-death-do-us-part marriage.

"What's the matter now?"

Rich crushed the empty aluminum can between his hands. "I just met with Jamie for the first time since… since I spent the night."

"It didn't go well?"

Rich shrugged. "Put it this way. She suggested a divorce."

"A divorce? Good grief, Rich, what did you say to the poor girl?"

Rich found it interesting that Jason immediately placed the blame on him. "Hell if I know. She came up with that all on her own. According to her, I…we changed the rules so we need to reevaluate our relationship."

Jason leaned back in his chair, its two front legs lifting from the floor. "Sounds serious. So are you reevaluating?"

"Yeah," Rich said forcefully. "I think we should throw the whole prenuptial agreement out the window and move in together."

"In other words, you want this to be a real marriage?"

"Yes. Hell, yes."

"But you don't think Jamie would go for that?"

"I don't know." He hoped she would, but he'd suffered more than one setback lately. He wasn't nearly as confident as he had been earlier.

"What are you going to do?"

"I wish I knew."

"Do you love her?"

Rich nodded without hesitation. "Like crazy." Standing, he walked over to the sink and leaned back against the counter, crossing his arms. "No one's more surprised about that than I am. I didn't have a clue that I felt anything for Jamie other than friendship. I didn't even notice how beautiful she is until recently."

"What do you plan to do about it?"

"If I knew that, I wouldn't be pounding down your door in the middle of the night." Rich's response was short-tempered, but Jason should've realized that much for himself.

"Good point." Jason rubbed the lower half of his face. "I don't suppose *sleep on it* is the kind of advice you want."

"Hey, if I could sleep, I'd be home in bed." Rich had lived alone for years, but the thought of returning to an empty apartment filled him with dread. He wanted to be with Jamie. It didn't even matter whether or not they made love; he needed her. Needed her reassurance. Needed her warmth, her laughter. Her love.

"I wish I knew what she wanted," he muttered.

"Who?"

"Who do you think?" Rich tossed his brother a scathing look. "Jamie, of course."

"Don't bite my head off."

"Then don't ask idiotic questions."

Jason yawned loudly, but Rich ignored his brother's broad hint. "She didn't give me a single indication of how she felt about it. Absolutely nothing."

"At the risk of appearing stupid," Jason said mournfully, "an indication of what?"

"The divorce." Rich frowned. "She offered it to me as an option, but when I asked what *she* wanted, she wouldn't say."

"She couldn't."

"Why not?"

"Because," Jason responded between yawns, "you'd be influenced by what she said and she wants the decision to be yours. She's a smart gal."

Rich paced the compact kitchen. "I told her I'd think everything over and get back to her."

"Then go home," Jason said, standing. "Now." He ushered Rich toward the front door. "In case you haven't noticed, I'm not exactly at my brightest, and I've got surgeries scheduled all day tomorrow. I need my sleep."

Rich brushed off his coat sleeves and chuckled. "I can take a hint."

Grinning, Jason shook his head. "No, you can't."

* * *

"Dr. Fullerton's office."

"Hello," Jamie said, her hand tightening on the receiver. "I…need to cancel my appointment with Dr. Fullerton." She gave the date and time.

"Would you like to reschedule now?"

Jamie would've liked nothing better, but not knowing what Rich would decide made that futile. "Not now, thank you. I'll call you next week."

Jamie had delayed contacting Dr. Fullerton's office all day. She'd hoped to hear from Rich early that morning. In her optimistic imagination, she'd had him phoning first thing with the assurance that he felt as strongly committed to their marriage and their child as ever.

When she hadn't heard from him by noon, she had no option but to cancel her appointment. It wasn't the end of the world. Yet she was overwhelmed by her emotions for the rest of the afternoon. She had to struggle to keep her feelings from interfering with her ability to make sound business decisions.

She'd thrown a frozen entrée into her microwave for dinner and munched on miniature marshmallows while watching a cable-TV reality dating show. So much for good eating habits or any semblance of healthy emotion. She'd sunk about as low as she could.

Jamie, normally meticulous about her clothes, didn't bother to change after work. Instead, she wandered around the condo in her suit, her blouse pulled out from the waist. Her slippers made scuffing noises as she shuffled from room to room with no real purpose or direction. She would've liked to blame her lethargy on her recent bout with the flu, but she knew otherwise.

What was really bothering her was her husband. Or rather, her lack of one. A real one. In their discussion the night before, she'd tried to be as forthright and honest with Rich as she could. She'd been careful not to hint at her feelings or preferences. She was no longer so sure she'd made the right decision. Maybe she should've mentioned, even casually, how much Rich's willingness to follow through on their agreement meant to her. Perhaps if she'd assured him she'd be a good mother, their evening might have turned out differently.

No. That would've been emotional blackmail.

She couldn't have said any of those things, any more than she could've admitted how much she loved him. Or how eager she was to explore the sensuality they'd so recently discovered.

Jamie was pacing in front of the television, clutching the plastic bag of marshmallows, when the doorbell chimed.

Her heart lurched. It could be Rich, but she was afraid to hope. More likely it was her neighbor coming to complain that the television was too loud.

Her mouth was full of marshmallows, which she attempted to swallow quickly. It didn't work, although she was chewing as fast as she could. She unlocked the door and nearly choked when Rich smiled in her direction.

"Hi."

She raised her right hand, as though she were making a pledge.

"There's something wrong with your cheeks. Have you got the mumps?"

Pointing at the bag of marshmallows, she chewed some more and swallowed a mouthful of marshmallows. "Hi," she said, her heart leaping against her ribs. "I...I wasn't expecting you."

"I know. Rather than risk leaving a message, I decided to stop over. You don't mind, do you?"

"Of course not." If he had the slightest idea how pleased she was to see him, he'd be *really* smiling instead of grinning at her with those blue eyes of his. She knew she was staring, but Jamie couldn't stop looking at Rich.

"Something doesn't smell right," he said, wrinkling his nose and sniffing the air. He walked into her kitchen, and opened the microwave. Cringing, he waved his hand in front of the now-cooked—*over*cooked—entrée.

"My dinner," she explained, stuffing the bag of marshmallows in the silverware drawer.

"I thought you'd given up on this stuff."

"I did...but I wasn't in the mood to cook tonight."

"Why not?"

"Because I had to cancel my appointment with Dr. Fullerton and I was depressed. I know I'm depressed when I crave marshmallows and turn on junk television. Life doesn't get any bleaker than that."

Rich was looking at her as though he'd never seen her before.

"Go ahead and make fun of me."

"I wouldn't dream of it."

"Sure you would." She swiped the back of her hand

under her nose. "I'll have you know I didn't get into the marshmallows when I broke up with Tony."

"In other words I'm responsible for reducing you to this?"

"Not exactly. I can't blame you for *everything*. Let's just say you're responsible for my choice in TV viewing."

Rich grinned and brushed a strand of hair from her temple. "Would it help if I told you I've come to a decision?"

"Probably." She was almost afraid to hope....

Instead of telling her what he'd decided, he removed her unappetizing dinner from the microwave, carried it to the garbage can and dumped it inside.

"If you want junk food, we'll order pizza, all right?"

She nodded eagerly. The *we* part didn't escape her. Apparently he intended to stay a while, which was fine with her. More than fine.

"While we're at it, I think it would be best if you ditched the marshmallows, too."

Wordlessly she jerked open her silverware drawer and handed him her stash.

"One more thing."

"Yes?" She gazed up at him, her heart in her eyes. She tried not to let her feelings show but it was impossible.

"Why did you cancel the appointment with Dr. Fullerton?"

"Because...you know." She rubbed her palms together. "I didn't hear from you this morning—not that I expected I would. I mean, overnight was much too soon for you to make up your mind. It would've been unreasonable for me to expect anything of the sort." Jamie knew she was rambling, but she couldn't make herself stop. "My...our appointment with Dr. Fullerton is...was for tomorrow and I couldn't very well go through with the insemination process, could I?"

"You've already been through one insemination process." He seemed to enjoy reminding her of that.

"Yes, I know, but...this is different."

His mouth slanted upward, his eyes bright with laughter. "I should hope so."

"I didn't *want* to cancel the appointment."

"Any chance you can reschedule?"

"Uh..." Her eyes connected with his, her heart pounding so loudly she thought he could hear it. "Are you saying you want to stay married and have the baby and—"

"That's exactly what I want."

Jamie couldn't help herself. She let out a cry of sheer joy, threw her arms around his neck and brought his mouth down to hers.

Ten

Rich moaned in surprise and welcome as Jamie's mouth sought his. He wrapped his arms around her as she stepped deeper into his embrace. His breath—and her breath, too—was heavy, abrupt, as if they'd both been caught off guard by the power of their attraction. The power of their need.

Rich tried to discipline his response to her, but his arousal was fierce and sudden.

He wanted Jamie as he'd never wanted anyone. He *needed* her. The kiss, which had began as a spontaneous reaction of joy and excitement, quickly became a sensuous feast of desperation and desire.

Rich groaned. He couldn't stop himself. His wife was in his arms, where she belonged, where he intended to keep her.

Patience, patience, his mind chanted. They'd make love soon, very soon and when they did, it would be a celebration of their marriage. There would be no grounds for regret or misgivings. No room for doubts. It would all come in time. *Soon,* Rich promised himself. *Soon.*

By a supreme act of will, Rich drew in a tattered, shaky breath and buried his face in her hair. "You taste of marshmallows."

"I'm sorry."

"Don't be." It demanded more control than he'd ever imagined to ease himself from her arms. "What about ordering that pizza?"

"Sure." She recovered quickly, Rich noted. Far more quickly than he did. She smiled shakily up at him. "There was a coupon in Tuesday's mail...."

"Do you want pepperoni and sausage?"

"Sounds good to me," she said over her shoulder. She moved away from him as if they'd never touched. Rich envied her ability to do so. He had difficulty disguising her effect on him.

Jamie pulled out a kitchen drawer where she maintained a small file for coupons. Once again he was astonished—although he shouldn't have been—at how organized she was. In no time, she'd located the right coupon and placed the order.

The pizza arrived promptly, thirty minutes later, and by then they were back on an even keel with each other. Rich would've liked to discuss their kiss, but didn't want to say or do anything to destroy this fragile peace. There'd be lots of time later to talk about their feelings. For now, he would bask in the warm glow of his love for Jamie and wait patiently for her to love him back.

It shouldn't take long. He didn't mean to be cocky

about his attractiveness or charm, but their love would be built on the firm foundation of friendship. All he had to do was exhibit patience and tenderness. The way he figured, in a week or two he'd be confident enough to approach her with the truth about his love. By the end of the month he'd be moving in with her.

No one would fault his plan. Least of all Jamie. He'd bide his time, give her the love and attention she needed, prove that he'd be a good husband to her and a good father to their child.

If everything went according to his plans, Jamie would be pregnant long before they could see Dr. Fullerton again.

Soon the pizza box lay open on the kitchen table. Jamie had set out plates and napkins and two cold cans of pop.

"This is delicious."

Rich agreed with a nod of his head. The pizza was excellent, but its taste couldn't compare to Jamie's kisses. In fact, he could easily become addicted to the flavor that was hers alone.

"I'll call Dr. Fullerton's office in the morning," she said casually. "I probably won't be able to get in until next month." Her eyes briefly met his, as though she was seeking his approval.

"That sounds fine to me."

Her dark eyes brightened and her hand reached for his. "We're going to make this work. We can, I know it."

"Of course we can," Rich told her. If things went the way he wanted them to, they'd soon be a family—and that was exactly how they'd stay, at least if he had anything to say about it. Jamie didn't know that yet, but she'd discover his intentions soon, and by that time she'd be as eager as he was.

The alarm blared and Jamie rolled onto her back, swung out one arm and flipped off the buzzer. The irritating noise was replaced with the gentle sounds of the soft rock station she listened to each morning.

The bed was warm and cozy and she didn't relish the thought of crawling out into the dark, cold world, especially on a Monday morning. It was far more pleasant to linger beneath layers of blankets, thinking about the good things that were happening between her and Rich.

They hadn't seen much of each other in the past week because Rich was involved in a defense project for Boeing. He'd worked three to four hours overtime every night, plus both days of the weekend. Yet he called her every day without fail, usually late in the evening.

He sounded so frustrated at not seeing her as often as he wanted. As often as *she* wanted. Jamie had done her best to pretend it didn't matter, but it did. She missed him dreadfully, although their nighttime phone conversations went a long way toward making up for that.

They were like a pair of teenagers talking on the phone. There wasn't really a lot to discuss, yet they often spent an hour or more chatting and laughing as if it had been weeks since they'd last spoken. Afterward, Jamie would spend the rest of the night swaddled in happiness.

Rich was exhausted whenever he called her. Although he'd never said as much, she had the impression he hurried out of the office and drove straight home just so he could talk to her.

Although they hadn't actually seen each other since the week before, Jamie felt encouraged by the way their relationship was developing. They were close, closer than they'd been at any time since high school. It seemed natural for her life to be so closely entwined with his. Natural and right.

Everything was going so well for them, she thought again. Rich seemed pleased when she rescheduled her appointment with Dr. Fullerton. Jamie often fantasized about their child—boy or girl, she'd be delighted and she knew he would, too.

Stretching her arms high above her head, she yawned loudly and kicked away the covers. Although she'd prefer to laze the morning away thinking about Rich and their future, she had to shower and get ready for work.

Still yawning, she sat up and turned on the bedside lamp. The room started to sway. Jamie exhaled slowly and closed her eyes. The sensation worsened until she was forced to put her head back on the pillow. The dizziness was followed by a surge of nausea.

Apparently she was suffering from a relapse of the flu. Wasn't she?

Jason called Rich at the office early Tuesday morning. "I haven't heard from you in a while," he said, giving the reason for his call. "I thought I'd check in to see how everything's going with you and Jamie."

"Fine," Rich said, studying a design layout on his desk. He held the phone to his ear with his shoulder as he worked. "I appreciated your words of wisdom the other night." However, as Rich recalled, Jason had been more concerned with getting him out of his apartment than shedding any new light on Rich's muddled marriage.

Rich had been more shaken that night than he'd realized. The mere mention of the word *divorce* had thrown him. It had also forced him to deal with the depth of his love for Jamie and had set his determination to do everything within his power to make their marriage work.

"So things between you and Jamie are better?"

"So far, so good."

"No more talk of a divorce?"

"None." Thank God, Rich mused.

"Then you've agreed to her terms?"

"More or less." It was the terms they'd *both* agreed to—only he wanted to change the rules now. All he needed was a few days to convince Jamie how crazy she was about him. It shouldn't be that difficult, especially when he was already so much in love with her, as long as he could get a few hours free from work. Which was difficult right now, with that defense contract gearing up.

"What does 'more or less' mean?" Jason wanted to know.

"It means," Rich said, his words heavy with impatience, "that I intend to make this marriage real." He glanced around to be sure no one in the office across the hall from him could hear. This wasn't the way he wanted his fellow workers to learn he was a married man.

"How does Jamie feel about this, or—" Jason hesitated "—does she know?"

"She will soon enough." Rich had never felt more frustrated. The defense project was taking all his time; knowing he'd volunteered for it didn't help, either. He'd been single at the time, but his life had changed and he was a married man. Sort of a married man. One who longed to be a real husband to his wife.

"I don't suppose you've considered telling Mom and Dad that you're married, have you?"

Jason should've gone into police work, Rich mused. He certainly possessed interrogation skills.

"It wouldn't hurt, you know," Jason added.

Rich frowned. "Is there any reason I should tell them?"

Jason's chuckle annoyed him. "Not really," his brother said. "Just promise me you'll let me be there when you do."

Rich didn't find any humor in his teasing. "I will when the time's right." That might take longer than he'd originally planned, thanks to all the overtime he'd been putting in lately. Informing his parents that he and Jamie were married, and had been for the past six weeks, wasn't a task he relished. Of course, the longer he waited, the more offended they'd be.

"Talk to you later."

"Okay," Rich said absently, more concerned about the designs he was reviewing than the conversation with his brother. He hung up the phone and glanced at his watch. The defense project was winding down, and if the day progressed as he hoped, he'd be able to take a break this evening and visit Jamie.

Rich was so involved in the designs that he didn't notice someone standing in the doorway until he glanced
up. When he did, his eyes widened with shock.

"Jamie." Her own eyes were red and glazed with
tears. Yet she was smiling. Rich didn't know which
emotion to respond to first. "What's wrong?"

"Oh, Rich, you won't believe what's happened,"
she cried, and ran toward him, arms outstretched. "You
just won't believe it. I…I know I shouldn't have come
here, not when you're so busy, but I had to, I simply
had to."

Worried that there might be something seriously
wrong with her, Rich got out of his chair and had her
sit down. Then he crouched in front of her, holding the
armrests, forming a protective barricade around her.

"Tell me," he said tenderly.

"I woke up sick yesterday," she muttered, opening
her purse and digging through it for a tissue. When she
found one, she dabbed at the corners of her eyes. Once
again she was smiling broadly and weeping at the same
time. Tears slid down her face, and her mouth trembled
with some as-yet-undetermined emotion.

"I assumed it was the flu," she said, sobbing, "but I
felt fine a little bit later. I didn't even *think* to mention
it when you phoned last night—but this morning my
stomach was queasy again and I felt light-headed, as
though I was going to faint. I wasn't sure what to think
until I checked the calendar."

"The calendar?"

She nodded enthusiastically.

"Jamie?" Rich was afraid to place too much significance on what she was saying—what she *seemed* to be saying. She couldn't possibly mean what he hoped she did. It was ludicrous. They'd only made love that one time.

Once again she nodded wildly. "Rich," she said, her hands gripping his. "We're pregnant."

"Pregnant," Rich repeated in a whisper, stunned. If he hadn't been clutching the sides of the chair, he would've toppled onto his backside. "Pregnant," he repeated slowly.

"I never dreamed it would happen so quickly. My temperature was only elevated a little that morning and...I didn't really think I was fertile yet, but obviously I was. Rich, oh, Rich," she sobbed joyfully. "We're going to have a baby."

"A baby." Rich stared at her. "You're sure? You've been to see Dr. Fullerton?"

"No... I bought a pregnancy test in the drugstore this morning and a few minutes later—"

"You're sure?" he asked again.

"The stick turned blue. You can't get any more positive than that."

"Blue...does that mean the baby's a boy?" His head, his heart, were racing, trying to take it all in.

Jamie laughed and hiccuped and laughed some more. "No, silly, it doesn't mean we're having a son, it means we're going to be parents."

"But we *could* be having a son," he challenged.

"Of course. Or a daughter." She threw her arms around his neck and laughed, an outpouring of joy. It was the sweetest, most poignant song he'd ever heard.

"We're pregnant," Rich said, finally—fully—taking it in. "We're really pregnant."

"Really," she said, brushing the tips of her fingers over his face. "That's what I've been trying to tell you."

"Pregnant." Slipping his arms around her waist, he stood, bringing her with him. His mouth found hers, and he kissed her the way he'd longed to do all week.

Jamie moaned. So did Rich. The kiss created a need for much more, and this was neither the time nor the place.

"Say something," she whispered, her eyes holding his. Her hands pressed against the sides of his jaw. "Tell me you're pleased about the baby."

Everything he wanted to tell her—his joy, his excitement, the overwhelming love he felt for her—it all formed a huge lump in his throat. To his dismay, Rich couldn't utter a single word. Finally he threw back his head and released a shout that sounded like a war cry.

"Rich?" A frowning Bill Hastings appeared in his doorway.

Rich grinned and waved. He broke away from Jamie, but took her hand in his. "Hello, Bill. Have you met Jamie Manning, my wife?"

Jamie's smile grew and grew. "Jamie Warren Manning," she corrected.

"Your *wife?*" Bill frowned again, but recovered quickly. "When did this happen? You never said a word. This isn't the same Jamie Warren you…you know, is it?"

"Yup," Jamie answered for him. "I'm the one he wanted you to ask out."

"You two are *married?*"

"We'd better be," Rich said, tucking his arm around Jamie's slim waist. The time would come when that same waist would expand, her belly filled with his child. Thinking about it, he felt shaky inside. Rich hadn't realized men were susceptible to those kinds of emotions. He'd assumed they were reserved for women. His heart was full. Overflowing with a happiness so profound, it was unlike anything he'd ever experienced. His throat thickened as though he might break into tears. Rich couldn't remember the last time he'd wept. It wasn't something men did often. But knowing Jamie was pregnant with his child, his son or daughter, was enough to reduce him to tears.

"I see," Bill said slowly, clearly not seeing a thing.

"I'm pregnant," Jamie announced.

Bill grinned, then turned to Rich. "But you offered me Seahawks play-off tickets to take her to dinner, and that wasn't more than two months ago."

"You *paid* him to take me to dinner?" Jamie muttered under her breath.

"What can I say?" Rich teased. "I was young and foolish."

"This is all rather sudden, isn't it?" Bill continued, choosing to ignore the whispered conversation between Rich and Jamie.

"Not really," Rich answered. "We've had a fourteen-year courtship."

"Fourteen years!" Bill looked astonished. "It seems congratulations are in order. I'm very pleased for you both."

"Thank you," Jamie returned graciously.

Bill left the office then, and Jamie whirled around to face Rich. "You told him we're married!" she cried.

"You mean we're not?"

"Rich, we can't tell your coworkers and not our families."

Rich hadn't given the matter much thought. It had happened spontaneously. But if a husband had just learned he was about to become a father, he should be able to tell someone, and in this case Bill was that someone.

"Since you told Bill," Jamie said, pacing his office, "then I should be able to tell someone, too. Agreed?"

"Agreed." Personally Rich could see no harm in letting the news out. Especially when revealing the truth might actually help him achieve his goal.

Jamie reached for his phone, hesitated momentarily, then sighed deeply and punched out a phone number. Rich had no idea who she was calling. It didn't matter.

While she was waiting for whomever she'd phoned to answer, Rich moved behind her and slipped his arms around her waist. He closed his eyes and reveled in the emotion he experienced as he held her tight. He wondered how long this euphoric feeling would last. All day? A week? A month? Deep down, he began to doubt it would ever entirely leave him.

So this was love. This feeling of warmth and fullness. The sensual alertness. This knowledge that the woman you loved more than life itself was giving birth to your child.

Rich rubbed his cheek against the side of her neck. She smelled of wildflowers and spring.

"Mom, it's Jamie."

Rich tensed. She'd asked to tell one person and she'd decided to tell *her mother*. Rich didn't know Doris Warren well, but what he did remember of her wasn't reassuring. She loved to gossip. Except she didn't call it that, as he recalled. Doris *networked*.

"Jamie," Rich whispered in her ear. "You're sure you want to do this?"

"Mom, I'm calling because I've got some fabulous news."

"Jamie?" Rich was in a panic.

"I'm pregnant."

He couldn't hear Doris's response, but he knew from the loud, squeaking sound that came from the receiver that Jamie's mother was more than a little surprised.

"The father?" Jamie repeated. She twisted around and grinned sheepishly up at Rich. "That's not important. What *is* important is that after all these years, you're finally going to be a grandmother."

"Go ahead and tell her," Rich whispered. Good news, especially news this wonderful, was meant to be shared. Now that Jamie was pregnant—and now that the situation between them had changed—Rich certainly didn't plan to maintain the confidentiality of their marriage. He couldn't see the point. He was too proud to keep Jamie's pregnancy a secret.

"Yes, Mother," Jamie returned, nodding absently. "Of course, I will. No…no, not yet."

Listening to only one half of the conversation put him at a distinct disadvantage, but Rich didn't mind. He was far more interested in spreading kisses along the side of Jamie's neck.

"Of course I'm sure. One of those home pregnancy tests…. Yes, Mother. Listen, I have to go now, I'm already late for work. Yes, I'll call later. Yes, I promise."

Rich's teeth caught hold of Jamie's earlobe. Her response was immediate; she went weak in his arms. Rich had never felt more powerful in his life.

"Rich," she chastised softly.

"Why didn't you tell her we're married?"

"I couldn't… Rich!" She swatted him playfully, but he couldn't make himself stop nibbling her neck.

"Why couldn't you tell her?"

"I…I thought I'd break it to her gently. A little at a time."

"So you started by telling her you're pregnant?" He found her reasoning a bit irrational, which wasn't typical for Jamie.

"If I told my mother we were married, she'd say something to your parents. We both know she would. Mom's like that."

"Yeah." But somehow the prospect wasn't as intimidating as it had been when Jason had broached the subject earlier.

"It'll cause problems."

"No, it won't," Rich said. He reached for her hand and raised it to his lips, kissing her knuckles. "Because I won't let it."

Jamie glanced regretfully at her watch. "Let's discuss it later. I'm late." She seemed as reluctant to leave as Rich was to let her go.

"Meet me for dinner tonight?" Rich intended to make reservations at the best restaurant in town.

"What time?" Jamie asked.

He tried to judge when he'd be finished, but he had no way of telling. "I won't know until later."

"Don't worry about it. Come to my place when you're through here and we can decide then."

Jamie left a few minutes later.

Rich didn't know how her day went, but his was a total waste. More than once he found himself staring into space, dreaming of Jamie and his child, plotting how to convince her to make their marriage real.

His day wouldn't have been so chaotic, though, if he hadn't been at meetings for much of the afternoon. He'd be taking notes, and before he realized it, his mind would wander to Jamie. He wanted to spend the rest of his life with her, not a few stolen moments out of a hectic work schedule. At the end of the day, he longed to hurry home and find her waiting for him. It was easy to envision walking in the front door after a long day at the office and having Jamie there to greet him. Jamie and their son.

That warm feeling returned, and Rich knew he'd been lost in another world again. Luckily, he hadn't embarrassed himself at any of the meetings.

At seven that evening, when he'd finished at the office, he hurried out the door. Bill and a couple of the other engineers invited him for a drink, but Rich declined. He knew they were eager to hear the details of his marriage, but he was in too much of a rush to get home.

Home to Jamie and his new life. His real life. Now all he had to do was convince her how much he loved her....

Jamie opened the door and smiled.

"Hi."

If he didn't know better he'd say she seemed almost shy. "Hi, yourself. How are you feeling?"

"The truth?"

Rich nodded. Of course he wanted the truth. He remembered she'd told him about the dizzy spells and nausea attacks. He'd listened, but in his excitement had forgotten.

"Don't look so worried," she said, laughing gently. "I feel fabulous. Wonderful. I've been walking on air all day."

"Me, too."

"I should never have told my mother, though," she muttered.

If he didn't kiss her soon, Rich decided, he might lose his mind. "Why's that?" he asked, although he agreed with the sentiment.

Not giving her a chance to answer, he took her in his arms. His mouth met hers, and they strained against each other. Eager. Hungry. The kiss moist and hot. Before he could question the wisdom of his actions, he was unfastening her blouse. He'd freed four tiny buttons before he had the presence of mind to hesitate.

"Rich?"

"Do you want me to stop?"

"I…don't know."

His hand cupped her breast, which was sheathed in a pale cream teddy.

"I thought you'd be starved by now," she murmured hoarsely.

"I am," he said, kissing her once more. Slowly. Thoroughly. Until there could be no doubt of what he wanted. "But it's you I'm hungry for."

"What…about dinner?"

"Later," he whispered, easing the silk blouse from her shoulders and reaching for the zipper at the back of her skirt. "I need you, Jamie."

"I need you, too. Oh, Rich, I need you so much." Her voice was a fleeting whisper.

Rich tracked a row of kisses down the side of her neck. "Is this what you want?"

"Yes…"

He dipped his tongue into the hollow of her throat. "How about this?"

"Yes…"

He eased the straps from her teddy over her shoulders, blazing a trail of warm, moist kisses toward her breast.

The sound of the doorbell went through him like an electric shock.

Jamie tensed. "I…I'm not expecting anyone," she said, picking up her blouse and pulling it on.

"Don't answer it," Rich said urgently.

Whoever was at the door must have heard him because the buzzer sounded again in a long, angry blast.

"I'll get rid of whoever it is," she muttered, buttoning her blouse as fast as her fingers would cooperate. She hurried to the door and checked the peephole, then groaned.

"Who is it?" Rich demanded.

Jamie closed her eyes. "My mother."

Eleven

"What are we going to do?" Jamie cried, looking at Rich. She'd been an idiot to announce her pregnancy to her mother, but Jamie had been so excited and happy. Keeping such wonderful news to herself for even a minute longer than necessary was just too hard. Rich had apparently felt the same way, because he'd told a coworker.

They'd both agreed weeks before not to tell anyone about their marriage *or* the pregnancy until Jamie was five or six months along and her condition was obvious. All of that had flown out the proverbial window when Bill Hastings had stepped into Rich's office.

If Rich had found it necessary to announce their marriage, then surely she was entitled to tell someone about the pregnancy. So Jamie had done what came naturally; she'd called her mother.

"I don't think we have much of an option," Rich said calmly. "Open the door."

"But…" Once again the doorbell buzzed, now in

short bursts. There wasn't time to argue, but the prospect of facing her mother filled Jamie with dread.

She opened the door. "Mother," she said, her voice unnaturally high. "This is a pleasant surprise."

Doris Warren's face revealed dismay. Slowly her gaze traveled to Rich, her eyes widening.

"Hello, Mrs. Warren," Rich said.

"Rich." She nodded stiffly in his direction, then turned to Jamie, her mouth tightening. "You didn't return a single one of my calls, Jamie Marie Warren."

Her mother had called the bank a total of seven times. With uncanny luck, Jamie had managed to avoid speaking to her. However, she was pragmatic enough to realize she'd need to soon. But first she had to talk to Rich so they could decide how much to explain. That hadn't been possible with Rich tied up in meetings all afternoon.

She'd arrived home, eager to see her husband. Her phone had rung three separate times and she'd let the caller leave messages. Not surprisingly, all three were from her determined mother. Jamie hated having to avoid her, but it was necessary until she'd had the chance to talk to Rich. Now the matter had been taken out of her hands.

"Perhaps we should all sit down," Rich suggested, gesturing toward the couch.

"I...don't know if I can," Doris Warren muttered. She immediately collapsed onto the sofa. "I can't remember when I've ever spent a more distressing day. How could you do such a thing to me?" she asked, glaring at Jamie. "I'm beside myself. My only daughter's having a baby! My only child…" She paused. "You're *sure* of this?"

"Yes, Mom, I'm pregnant."

"Who's the father?" It was more than obvious that she suspected Rich, as once again, her narrowed gaze traveled to him.

"I am," Rich announced proudly. He smiled over at Jamie and reached for her hand, squeezing it reassuringly.

Jamie was in the recliner, and Rich sat on the arm, his hand continuing to hold hers.

"There's no need for concern, Mrs. Warren," he began.

"No need for concern!" Jamie's mother shot back. "I can tell you right now, I most certainly am concerned. This is my daughter you've been fooling around with, and I insist—no, I *demand* you do the honorable thing."

"Mother!" Jamie had never seen her mother more agitated. "Rich isn't a criminal. In case you've forgotten, it takes two to make a baby."

"I did seduce you," Rich delighted in reminding her.

Jamie frowned back at him. "You did not."

"See," Doris cried, "he admits it!"

"What would you like me to do now, Mrs. Warren?" Rich asked, seeming genuinely contrite.

If Jamie didn't know better, she'd think he was enjoying this.

"I insist you marry Jamie, of course."

"But are you sure you want me for a son-in-law?"

"I— Yes!"

"Rich!" Jamie was growing angry at this silly game of his.

Rich's fingers tightened around hers. Although he did a valiant job of trying to disguise a smile, he failed miserably. His lips quivered and his eyes fairly sparkled. "I believe we should tell her, darling."

Darling! Jamie couldn't remember Rich using that term even once. She looked up at him, astonished by his nerve.

"Tell me what?" Doris asked.

"It's complicated." Jamie decided to lead into her marriage slowly, giving her mother time to adjust to one shock before hitting her with another.

"Life is always complicated," Doris countered, pinching the bridge of her nose.

"Rich and I have been friends for years."

"The very best of friends," Rich added.

"That much is evident." Jamie's mother raised her chin a notch, as though she needed a great deal of restraint to remain civil.

"Not evident yet," Rich said, "but it will be soon."

"What are you doing?" Jamie muttered under her breath.

"Explaining," Rich answered. Then, turning to his mother-in-law, he smiled serenely down at Jamie and said, "There's no need to worry, Mrs. Warren. Jamie and I are already married."

"*What?*" Doris sprang to her feet. "Jamie, is this true?"

"Yes," she admitted reluctantly. "But I'd hoped to break the news to you a little more gently." She frowned at Rich, not bothering to hide her irritation.

Her mother sat back down and pressed her hand over her heart. "The two of you are married.... When?"

"Several weeks ago," Rich said.

"You didn't say *anything*—not even to your own mother." This was directed at Jamie.

"There's a perfectly logical explanation...."

"I can already guess." Doris's hand flew out, her index finger pointed accusingly at Rich. "The two of you *had* to get married."

"That's ridiculous! No one *has* to marry in this day and age." Jamie felt as if she were in a tug-of-war, caught between her mother's shock and her husband's amusement. She wondered if he'd behave the same way when it came to informing his own family.

"You're right about one thing," Rich remarked. "Jamie and I did marry for the sake of the child."

"Will you stop!" Jamie vaulted to her feet.

"Darling..." Rich stared up at her blankly, as though he couldn't understand what had caused her outburst.

"Don't *darling* me!" she snapped at him, her anger getting the best of her. How Rich could find humor in this situation was beyond her. He made her pregnancy sound like...like a joke.

"Jamie, tell me what's going on here." Now it was Doris Warren's turn.

"Rich and I are married," Jamie explained, facing her mother. "I never would've agreed to the wedding if Rich hadn't insisted on it."

"I should hope he insisted."

"You don't understand, and frankly, Mother, I doubt I can explain now. Suffice it to say, I'm married and pregnant, and you needn't worry about me. I couldn't be happier." Telling her poor confused mother everything at once was sure to complicate things even more than they already were. Someday soon, Jamie would answer all her questions, but not now. Not when Rich was acting as though this had all been contrived for his amusement.

"You're happy?" Doris's bewildered gaze locked with Jamie's.

"Blissfully." It was Rich who answered for them. Jamie needed all the fortitude she could muster not to contradict him.

"Then…I'm happy, too." Doris stood, but seemed surprised to find herself on her feet. She glanced around the room as if she wasn't sure where she was. Taking the cue, Rich walked to the door and held it open.

"Shall I call you 'Mother'?"

"Ah…" Doris Warren stared up at him for an awkward moment. "If you wish."

"Goodbye then, Mother Warren. Jamie and I will be in contact with you soon."

As though in a stupor, Jamie's mother walked out the door. Rich closed it after her. The lock had barely slipped into place when Jamie turned on him.

"What do you think you were doing?" she demanded.

"Reassuring your mother." Rich walked past her and sat nonchalantly in the recliner. His actions only fuelled her anger.

"You confused her." And Jamie, as well. Just when she was beginning to believe there was a chance of something wonderful between them, he'd lapsed into these childish antics. The man obviously didn't recognize a crisis when he saw one. "What's wrong with you?" she cried, continuing to pace.

"Wrong?" His eyes went wide with a look of pure innocence.

"You made everything sound like a joke."

"The pregnancy isn't a tragedy. I couldn't be happier about it. Besides, the sooner we explained everything to your mother, the sooner she'd leave and the sooner we could get back to what we were doing and—"

"You were like this in high school, too." Jamie's anger wasn't going to be appeased that easily. Nor would she allow him to lead her into the bedroom and silence her concerns with his kisses. There was too much at stake.

"You're going to drag high school into this?"

"Life isn't one big laugh, you know."

"I never said it was."

"No," she argued, "you just act that way. We're dealing with my mother here and she has—"

"I'm not the one who told her you were pregnant."

"Oh, no," she cried, throwing her hands in the air. "You had to tell Bill Hastings instead."

"That was better than blurting it out to relatives."

"Mom would know soon enough anyway." Jamie noticed the laughter was gone from Rich's eyes and he was beginning to frown.

"If you expect me to apologize for my part in this marriage then you'll have a long wait. You've obviously got regrets, but—"

"I didn't say that."

Rich glared at her. "As I recall, you made a point of saying that *I* insisted we get married."

"You *did!*"

Rich ignored her outburst and continued without pausing. "You also insinuated you didn't want the marriage."

"I didn't." Jamie's original idea hadn't included any of this.

From the first, her instincts had told her that marriage, even a marriage of convenience, wasn't to be taken lightly. Rich had never shared her concerns and, in fact, had carelessly brushed them aside.

"The only reason I went along with this scheme of yours," she reminded him, "was because you insisted."

Anger flashed from his blue eyes. "If you're so overwhelmed with regrets, you might've said something sooner."

"I did!" She didn't want to rehash old arguments, but they'd need to clear up the past before they could deal with the future. "I tried to explain my feelings before we were married, but you refused to listen to me. You never do."

"I *never* listen to you?" he challenged.

"Okay, to be fair, you listen, then you ignore my worries and tell me how foolish they are. The wedding's a prime example of that."

"Then why did you agree to it?"

"Because…I want the baby."

"Then you should be pleased," Rich said as he marched toward the front door. "You've got your baby—it's just *me* you don't want." With that parting shot, he was gone.

He shut the door with enough force to rattle the pictures on the wall. Jamie's first instinct was to run after him and tell him she didn't mean any of it. True, she hadn't been keen on marrying him, but not for the reasons he believed. She loved him, but she couldn't let him know. She needed to remind herself repeatedly that their marriage wasn't a love match. Rich had never intended it to be. She was the one who had problems remembering that this was a marriage of convenience.

She was the one who couldn't keep her heart out of it.

Rich hadn't meant to argue with Jamie. Fighting was the last thing on his mind when he went to her apartment. From the minute she'd left his office that morning, all he could think about was making love to her again. He longed to hold her in his arms and tell her how thrilled he was about the pregnancy. But nothing had worked out the way he'd planned. Instead, they'd gotten into a shouting match during which she'd repeatedly reminded him that she hadn't wanted to marry him in the first place.

She didn't seem particularly concerned about what she was doing to his ego, either.

All right, so maybe his attitude toward Jamie's mother wasn't the best, but no way was he going to sit there wearing a frown and pretending this pregnancy was some unthinkable disaster. So he'd taken a lighter approach. If Jamie wanted to fault him for that, then fine. Guilty as charged.

He had a sense of humour. He liked to tease. Always had. A fact that Jamie delighted in reminding him. Leave it to a woman to reach back thirteen years to their high school days to dig up something they could fight about.

Rich walked across the living room, loosening his tie as he moved. So, Jamie still regretted their marriage. No wonder she'd been so eager to offer him the option of a divorce.

He lowered himself into his favorite chair, raised his feet onto the ottoman and leaned his head against the back, closing his eyes. He needed to clear his thoughts, erase any trace of pride and negative emotion. Deal with the issues facing him.

What *were* the issues?

Jamie was pregnant. Apparently she was as thrilled at the prospect as he was himself, but for different reasons. He was a means to the end, and now that he'd accomplished what she wanted, he was of no use to her.

He felt a painful tightening in his chest. Over the years he'd met a lot of women. Women who used him, wanted him, manipulated him. He would never have believed Jamie was one of them. It was more than obvious that she was trying to push him out of her life. There wasn't much Rich could do.

He couldn't force her to love him.

Rich must have fallen asleep because the next thing he knew the phone was ringing. His eyes shot open, and he stood abruptly, awkwardly, and walked across the room. He prayed with everything in him it would be Jamie, but it wasn't his headstrong wife.

"Rich?"

This questioning, bewildered tone was one he'd rarely heard in his mother's voice. "Hello, Mom."

"I just had the most...surprising phone call from Doris Warren."

Rich groaned inwardly. "Oh?"

"She's Jamie Warren's mother."

"I know who she is."

"She told me about you and Jamie being married?" She made the statement into a question, as if she expected Rich to immediately deny everything.

"She told you that?" Circumstances being what they were, Rich chose to answer his mother's question with one of his own.

"She also said Jamie's pregnant?"

"Really?"

"Is it true?" Like Jamie, his mother had plenty of experience dealing with his stall tactics. When he didn't immediately respond, she raised her voice and asked him again. "Is it?"

Rich wearily rubbed his face, hoping that would help clear his mind. "Part of it."

"Which part?" His mother's voice was quickly advancing toward hysteria. Rich knew his father wasn't there, otherwise Eric Manning would've made the call. His mother had a tendency to get excited over the smallest details. For that matter, so did his father.

When his parents learned Taylor had married Russ

Palmer in Reno, all hell had broken loose. They hadn't been thrilled to learn Christy had married Cody Franklin on the sly, either. Rich could only guess what their reaction would be when they learned he was married to Jamie. Like his two sisters, he'd married without a family wedding.

"Rather than explain everything over the phone, I suggest Jamie and I drop in tomorrow evening," Rich said. "We can discuss everything then."

"Tomorrow?"

"I should be able to get away from the office around six. I'll check with Jamie to make sure that time is convenient for her, as well."

"Just answer one question. Are you and Jamie Warren married or not?"

Rich hesitated. "Yes and no," he finally said.

"That doesn't tell me a thing," Elizabeth cried.

"I know." Rich couldn't argue with his mother about that. But he couldn't tell her what he didn't know himself.

When he'd finished the conversation, Rich stared down at the phone for a moment. He didn't have any choice; he had to call her. Swallowing his pride left a bitter taste in his mouth, but there was no avoiding it. He reached for the receiver and punched out her number.

Jamie answered on the second ring. Rich didn't bother with any greetings. "I just got a call from my mother. She apparently talked to yours."

Jamie released a slow, frustrated sigh. "I was afraid that would happen. What did you tell her?"

"As little as I could. Naturally she didn't understand, so I told her we'd come by after work tomorrow, around six, and explain." Rich tried to keep the inflection in his voice to a minimum, tried not to let any of his emotions rise to the surface.

"Tomorrow," Jamie repeated.

"If it's inconvenient, then I'll let *you* call and tell her that."

"No...I'll be there."

"I'll see you then." He knew he sounded stiff and formal, but Rich couldn't help it. A man's pride could take only so much abuse.

When he'd hung up, Rich sauntered into his kitchen. He hadn't eaten since early afternoon, but he wasn't hungry. Scanning the contents of his refrigerator, he reached for a cold pop.

On his way out of the kitchen, he paused in front of the phone. Before he could question his actions, he dialed Jason's number and waited two long rings before his older brother answered.

"Tomorrow night at six," Rich announced without preamble. He wasn't in the mood to exchange pleasantries.

"What's happening tomorrow?" Jason demanded, clearly confused.

"I'm telling Mom and Dad I'm married."

Jason's hesitation was only slight. "What brought this on?"

"Jamie's pregnant."

"But I thought she canceled the appointment with—"

"She did." Rich realized he sounded abrupt and disagreeable. Hey, he *was* abrupt and disagreeable. But Jason had asked to be present when Rich told their parents about his marriage.

"If Jamie canceled the doctor's appointment, then how…"

"This baby was conceived in the traditional way."

Jason was silent for a moment. "You don't sound happy about it."

"I *am* happy," Rich snapped. "Real happy."

But it didn't seem a fair exchange. He wanted the baby, but nothing was happening the way he would've liked. According Rich's plan, he and Jamie would've been in bed together right this minute. They would've been in each other's arms, her face nestled on his shoulder. When they kissed, it would've been a leisurely exploration of their need and appreciation for each other. His restless hands would be roaming at will over her body, and he'd spread his palm over her flat stomach, communicating his feelings to his unborn child. When they made love, it would've been a celebration of her pregnancy.

But Jamie didn't need him any longer.

Rich had served his purpose.

Rich had trouble keeping his mind on his work the following afternoon. Every ten minutes or so, he found himself looking at his watch. Each time, he mentally calculated how long it would be before he'd be confronting his parents with the truth.

A few minutes after five, he was sitting at his desk,

reviewing some figures, when there was a polite knock at his door. He grumbled a reply, and the door slowly creaked open.

Jamie stood before him, dressed in a pretty pink suit. "Is this a bad time?"

The last person Rich expected to see waltzing through his office door was his pregnant wife.

"No," he said, rolling back his chair, "you're not disturbing a thing." Maybe his equilibrium...and his heart. But precious little else. "Sit down." He gestured toward the chair on the other side of his desk.

Jamie sat down, and he saw that her gaze fell to her clenched hands.

"What brings you here?"

"I—I thought we should discuss what we're going to tell your parents."

"What do you suggest?" He hoped to give the impression that whatever they decided didn't matter one way or the other to him. He leaned against the back of the chair and locked his fingers behind his head.

"Do they know I'm pregnant?"

"Yes. Your mother told mine."

"I thought she must have," Jamie said, with a sigh. "I feel like such a fool."

"Why?"

She shrugged, still avoiding eye contact. "For telling her. I've complicated the whole situation."

Rich didn't agree or disagree. It seemed that every time he opened his mouth, he said the wrong thing.

"How much do you think we have to explain?" Jamie asked, risking a glance in his direction.

Rich hadn't decided. "Everything," he said without giving it any thought.

"A-all of it?"

"I can't see any reason to hold any of it back." Some of the disappointment and lingering animosity from their argument from the day before seeped into his words.

"I thought we might want them to assume the baby—"

"No," Rich said forcefully.

Jamie's startled gaze connected with his. "You didn't even let me finish."

"I already knew what you were going to say. You want my parents to assume this baby was conceived artificially. I won't be a party to that."

"That *isn't* what I meant."

Rich's phone rang just then. He reached for it, although he would've preferred to ignore it.

"Engineering," he responded automatically. "Rich Manning."

"It's Paul," his eldest brother said. "I just got done talking to Mom. What's going on with you and Jamie Warren?"

"Nothing." So Mom was calling in the big guns. Paul was the responsible one in the family, or at least that was his reputation and his role. When it came to family problems, his parents tended to lean on Paul for support.

"That's not what I heard," Paul said. "I got a call from Mom no more than ten minutes ago with some crazy rumor about you being married."

"It's no rumor."

"Jamie Warren?"

"Jamie Warren Manning," Rich answered without thinking. He had to stop saying that. She'd never be a Manning. Rich could feel her stare, but he avoided glancing in her direction, refusing to give her the power to disconcert him.

"Mom says Jamie's pregnant."

"She is." Rich had no intention of hiding it. In a few months, Jamie's condition would become obvious, and while she might want to hide the truth, he had no interest in colluding with her.

"Why didn't you tell anyone?" Paul asked.

"That's a long story."

"Well, I hope you tell it tonight." Paul's disapproval was all too evident.

Rich rubbed his eyes. Thanks to Jamie, he hadn't slept well the night before. His dreams had been troubling, and he'd tossed restlessly until morning.

"Jamie and I'll be there at six. We'll explain everything then."

"Good. I'll be there, too."

Rich closed his eyes to the mounting frustration. This meeting with his parents was becoming a real spectacle, with Paul and Jason sitting on the sidelines. Rich wouldn't be surprised if his parents brought in Taylor and Christy, too.

His whole family was about to discover that Rich was the biggest fool who'd ever walked the earth.

Twelve

Both of Rich's brothers were there waiting for him when he arrived at his parents' home with Jamie at five minutes to six. Paul and Jason were perched on bar stools, holding pop cans, eager to view the latest family performance. The scene reminded Rich of one that had played out months earlier between his parents and his sister Christy when she'd announced her marriage to Cody Franklin. Rich remembered being amused by the circumstances then. Following in his youngest sister's footsteps, however, was proving to be far less entertaining.

His mother was on the phone, and from the way she was shaking her head and muttering under her breath, Rich realized she was probably talking to one of his sisters in Montana.

He walked into the living room with Jamie beside him. He noticed how close she stood to him, which surprised him. At his office, they'd taken several minutes to review exactly what they planned to say.

To him, the entire matter was cut-and-dried. He was in his thirties, certainly old enough to do as he pleased without his parents' approval. Who and why Rich married was his own business, and that was how he intended to keep it. He'd convinced Jamie that, if necessary, he'd reveal the details of their arrangement, but he doubted it would come to that.

After Rich and Jamie were seated, Eric Manning stalked into the living room. His father was tall and in excellent physical condition; his thick hair was nearly gray, and his hairline had barely begun to recede. He was in robust health and looked it.

Rich's two sisters claimed all the men in the Manning family were black-belt chauvinists. Rich hadn't given it much thought, but he had definite ideas about a man's responsibilities—to his wife and his family.

"Rich," his father said, nodding once. Eric's face was grave, and the glance he shot Rich would have quelled Attila the Hun.

"Dad." Rich nodded, too. He chose to sit on the sofa, Jamie still at his side. He didn't know whose hand reached out first, but their fingers entwined automatically, as though they gained strength from each other. Jamie appeared far more nervous than Rich, which, he supposed, was natural.

"Your mother's talking to Taylor," his father said. "She'll be finished in a few minutes."

So Rich had guessed correctly. His mother had managed to involve his oldest sister in this.

"Would you care for something to drink?" Eric asked Jamie. "There's cold pop, coffee or tea."

"Nothing, thanks," she answered with a smile.

Rich noticed that Jamie rested her free hand against her stomach, then drew in a deep, calming breath.

"Are you feeling all right?" She'd mentioned not being well in the mornings, but he'd been so caught up in his own concerns that it had slipped his mind.

"I'm fine."

"You're looking pale."

"It's nerves," she whispered.

"What about mornings?"

Rich wasn't especially thrilled to have his two brothers and his father monitoring his conversation, but he was worried about Jamie's health and their baby's.

"My stomach's still a little queasy, but I heard it'll get better in a few months."

"The book I read says morning sickness should gradually disappear, starting at about the third month." Rich had devoured the paperback on pregnancy and childbirth in one sitting, eager to read everything he could about the changes taking place in Jamie's body. Eager to learn the most minute details about how his child was forming.

Jamie's eyes brightened. "You're reading a book?"

"It might surprise you to learn I read quite a bit," he chided.

"I know," she whispered, and her gaze met his, faltering slightly. "I guess I'm surprised you're reading one about pregnancy and childbirth."

"Why?"

She shrugged. "It just does."

That didn't say much for her view of him. Rich

would have questioned her further, but his mother chose
to enter the room just then. Elizabeth Manning smiled
warmly in Jamie's direction, but her eyes hardened as
they slid toward Rich. He didn't know what he'd done
that was so terrible. His father had looked at him in
much the same way, as though he should be taken out
to the woodpile to have his backside tanned.

"How's Taylor?" Rich inquired conversationally,
ignoring the censorious looks from both his parents. He
kept his voice cool and even. He was actually proud of
his composure.

"Taylor's fine. So are Russ and little Eric."

"That's great." Rich crossed his long legs and leaned
against the couch. This wasn't going to be nearly as bad
as he'd suspected, as long as he kept a cool head.

"Taylor's decided to do some substitute teaching for
the school district. Russ isn't completely in favor of the
idea, but he's coming around."

Rich knew from experience that his oldest sister's
will was powerful enough to launch a rocket. Russ
would do well to recognize that and act accordingly.

"She was shocked to hear about you and Jamie
getting married," his mother continued, after drawing
in a deep breath. "Which, I might add, came as a significant shock to your father and me, as well."

"Not me." Jason spoke for the first time. "I knew about
it from the beginning. In fact, I was Rich's best man."

Everyone's attention swung to Jason.

"You knew?" their mother echoed, accusation in her
voice.

Jason nodded. "Trust me. I tried to talk him out of

it, but you know how stubborn Rich can be. He refused to listen to the advice of his betters."

"You asked Jason to the ceremony and not your own *mother?*" Elizabeth Manning cried. She pulled a tissue from her pocket and dabbed at her eyes.

"It was a civil ceremony at the King County courthouse," Rich started to explain. He didn't get very far. Once again he was interrupted by his mother.

"You didn't even marry Jamie in a *church?*" Elizabeth sounded as if this was the worst misdeed of all.

"Don't be upset, Mrs. Manning, I preferred it that way," Jamie answered quietly.

"But…why get married in a courthouse when you both belong to a church?"

Jamie turned nervously to Rich. Now was the time to announce the reason for their impromptu wedding.

Rich had it all worked out in his mind. The assurances, the brief but concise explanation of what had led to their unusual agreement. Yet when the moment arrived, Rich discovered he couldn't make himself say it.

"We did it that way for our own reasons," was all the explanation he was willing to give. From the corner of his eye, Rich caught sight of Jason arching his brows.

"According to Jamie's mother, Jamie was already pregnant at the time of the wedding," Eric bellowed. His hands clenched at his sides, he paced the length of the living room, then paused in front of the floor-to-ceiling windows, his back to Rich and Jamie. "A couple doesn't need any more reason to marry quickly than that."

"I hate to disillusion you," Rich reported calmly,

"but as a matter of fact, Jamie wasn't pregnant when we got married."

Elizabeth glared at him, her expression implying it was all a lie. Rich had no intention of arguing with either of his parents; they could believe what they wished.

"Then why did Doris make a point of telling us the two of you had married because of the baby?" his mother asked.

Rich groaned inwardly. "Because we'd decided Jamie should get pregnant as soon as possible."

Jamie exchanged a look with Rich, and added, "We're married because we both want to become parents."

"I tried to tell Rich a wedding wasn't necessary," Jason inserted, "but he wouldn't listen to me. He felt that if they were going to have a baby, he should marry her first. Go figure."

His mother gave Jason a horrified look. "I should certainly hope so."

Eric turned around to face them, frowning. "Trust me, parenthood's not all it's cracked up to be."

"Come on, Dad," Paul teased. "It hasn't been so bad, now, has it?"

"When it comes to weddings," Eric argued, "it's been a nightmare. It was bad enough that your sisters had to get married on the sly—but I never suspected one of you boys would pull that stunt. I want to know when there's going to be a *real* wedding in this family."

"Diane and I had a real wedding," Paul reminded his father.

"But no one from the Manning family was there."

Eric's voice boomed. "The boy goes into the army, ships out to Alaska and returns home a married man."

"It was just one of those things," Paul said, grinning.

"Getting back to Rich and Jamie," their mother said pointedly.

"By all means," Jason agreed, gesturing toward the sofa. "Let's get back to Rich and Jamie. Do you realize, Mom and Dad, that they're married and aren't even living together?"

Rich sent his brother a look hot enough to sizzle bacon.

"Rich?" His mother turned to him expectantly.

"Not living together? Why not? You're married, aren't you?" His father fired rapid questions at them. "What about—"

"We're married," Rich broke in.

"But you're not living together?"

"Not…yet." It was the best evasion Rich could come up with on such short notice. This was a subject he'd hoped to avoid, along with several others.

"They plan to move in together soon, isn't that right, Rich?" his mother asked.

"Of course." It was Jamie who responded, and Rich stared at her. He couldn't help wondering if she was sincere or if her sudden reassurances were all part of an act to appease his parents. Not that Rich had any objection to moving in with Jamie.

"Are there problems with your lease?" his mother asked next.

"Uh, I'm working on it," Rich muttered noncommittally.

"I hope you'll move in with her soon," Eric asserted,

burying his hands in his pants pockets. "A pregnant woman needs her husband."

"You're absolutely positive you're pregnant, Jamie, dear?" Elizabeth Manning's voice was filled with gentle concern.

"Absolutely positive," Jamie said with a firm nod. "The kit I bought at the drugstore is very reliable, but I was at the doctor's this afternoon and he confirmed it."

"You went to the doctor?" Rich asked before he could stop himself. They'd spent half an hour at his office discussing this meeting and she hadn't said a word about seeing Dr. Fullerton!

"It was a short visit."

"Did he give you a due date?"

Jamie smiled shyly and nodded.

"When?" Rich was calculating dates. His best guess placed her delivery date sometime close to Christmas. A child would be the best gift of his life.

"The last week of December," Jamie announced.

"I always did love the winter months," Rich said, having difficulty keeping the pride and elation from his voice. Then, damning caution, he brought her knuckles to his mouth and brushed his lips over her hand.

Elizabeth sighed softly. "Are you experiencing morning sickness, my dear?"

"Some."

"A husband should be with his wife," Eric reminded Rich for the second time.

"We've been talking about Rich moving in with me," Jamie said. This was news to Rich, who couldn't recall a single word of such a conversation. After Doris Warren had unexpectedly dropped by Jamie's apartment, they'd barely been able to resume their conversation.

"I've got a truck," Jason said, again motioning toward them with his pop can. "Anytime you need anything hauled, little brother, just say the word."

"I will," Rich muttered. He didn't know what Jamie was up to, but he wasn't complaining. If she wanted his family to assume this was a love match, he'd play along. From his perspective it was, so this was an unexpected turn for the better.

"It's settled, then," Eric said forcefully. "Rich is moving in with Jamie."

"Shouldn't we hold a reception in their honor?" Rich's mother asked his father. Her eyes were sparkling with excitement. Rich remembered how his mother had thrown all her efforts into the engagement party for Christy and what a disaster that had been.

"We should leave that up to these young folks, don't you think?"

Rich wasn't keen on a reception, especially in light of the fact that Jamie planned to divorce him as soon as their baby was born. Thank heaven no one had inquired too closely.

Rich made a point of glancing at his watch. "If you'll both excuse us, Jamie told her mother we'd be stopping by her house, as well." She'd delivered that tidbit of information when she'd arrived at his office earlier.

The prospect of facing Doris Warren twice in as many days didn't thrill Rich. One set of parents at a time was about all he could handle.

* * *

Jamie didn't know why she'd lied to Rich's family. Normally she stuck to the truth, believing with all her being that a lie was always wrong. Yet when Rich's father had started questioning them about their living arrangements, Jamie found herself uttering a falsehood.

Rich had looked flabbergasted when she'd said they were moving in together. Stunned. To his credit, he recovered quickly and went along with her as though they'd actually reached that decision.

Although they hadn't discussed the prospect even once, Jamie had hoped Rich *would* suggest moving in with her once he learned she was pregnant. He hadn't.

She regretted their argument of the day before. Over and over during the long sleepless night, she'd relived their angry exchange and felt worse each time.

She'd overreacted. Rich was only being Rich. She'd lashed out at him because he'd responded to a tense situation with humor.

His parting shot about her not wanting him now that she was pregnant troubled her the most. He couldn't honestly believe that, could he? Jamie was crazy about Rich. She'd been in love with him for years, but she'd been too blind to recognize it.

After her appointment with Dr. Fullerton, she'd gone to Rich's office at the Boeing Renton complex. She'd hoped they'd have a few minutes alone to clear the air. But when she arrived, Rich was stone-cold and about as friendly.

Only when they were at his parents' home did he lower his guard. He'd taken her hand in his and smiled down on her as though they'd never exchanged a cross word. Of course, it could all be for show, but Jamie prayed that wasn't the case.

"Your mother seems to be in better spirits this evening," Rich said conversationally. He drove at a relaxed pace, weaving through the narrow neighborhood streets.

"She's had time to adjust to our news." Their visit had been short and sweet. Just long enough to offer the reassurances Doris seemed to need. Jamie hadn't found that difficult, because she was perfectly comfortable in the role of happy mother-to-be.

"Have *you* adjusted to the news?" Rich asked.

"Yes. What about you?"

Rich nodded. "I suppose I should be surprised, but frankly, I'm not. By the way, are you hungry?"

"A little." Jamie was famished. She'd woken with a queasy stomach that morning and skipped breakfast. Then at noon, she'd eaten a small carton of blueberry yogurt but nothing since.

"Do you want to go to a restaurant and get something to eat?"

"No," she said, thinking quickly. "We could order pizza and have it delivered to my place."

He glanced at her, as if the suggestion had astonished him. "Sounds good to me."

It was nearly eight by the time they got to Jamie's condominium. While Rich ordered the pizza, Jamie went into her bedroom and changed out of her business suit. She chose jeans and a pale blue sweater.

When she returned to the living room, Rich had loosened his tie and was leafing through the evening paper. He looked up when she entered the room and slowly set the newspaper aside.

"I hope you realize both sets of parents expect me to move in with you now." The thought apparently weighed heavy on his mind.

"I know." She sat across from him, leaning forward, and clasped her hands. "Personally I…don't think it's such a bad idea."

"You don't?" He didn't seem to believe her.

"I mean…this will probably be the only pregnancy for either of us, and since you've been reading so much about it, and seem so interested…it's only fair that you share as much of the experience as possible." Jamie hesitated a moment. "Unless, of course, you'd rather not live with me."

He gave a noncommittal shrug. "I don't mind." His gaze moved past her to the hallway that led to the two bedrooms. "Naturally I'll be sleeping in the spare room."

"Naturally," Jamie concurred. But not for long, if everything went as she hoped. She loved Rich. Truly loved him. So far, she'd bungled their relationship and their marriage at every turn. If he were to share these short precious months with her before the birth of their child, there was a chance he might grow to love her.

It was worth the risk.

Worth the potential heartache.

Worth gambling her pride and even her future for this one opportunity.

The pizza arrived soon after, and they sat at the

kitchen table, the cardboard box propped open in front of them. They both drank tall glasses of cold milk.

"So you've been feeling queasy in the mornings?" Rich posed the question after several minutes of comfortable silence. He too seemed to be working to maintain this fragile peace.

"Only a little. Dr. Fullerton said it would pass soon enough. I haven't gotten really sick."

"Good."

"Dr. Fullerton suggested I nibble on a couple of soda crackers when I wake up."

"I can bring them to you, if you like."

Jamie nodded. She *would* like that, but she was afraid to let Rich know how much it would mean to her. Even now, weeks later, she continued to miss their early-morning phone conversations. They'd shared a special closeness then, one that had gone from her life.

"Would you like a cup of coffee?" Jamie asked when they'd finished.

"Yes, please.

"Go ahead and read the paper and I'll get it for you."

"That's a nice, wifely thing to do."

"Yes, it is, isn't it?" Jamie responded with a saucy smile. She took her time making the coffee. While she waited for it to brew, she cleaned the kitchen, wiped the counters and placed their few dishes in the dishwasher.

Carrying a steaming cup of coffee into the living room, she hesitated when she saw that Rich's eyes were closed, although the paper was still clutched in his hands.

Smiling to herself, Jamie sat on the nerby ottoman.

She took a sip of the coffee as she carefully studied the man she'd married. His features were more relaxed now, his head cocked slightly to one side.

How handsome he was. His good looks were even more appealing in slumber. Not sure what dictated her actions, Jamie set the coffee aside and slipped the newspaper from his unsuspecting grasp. Rich stirred briefly, then nestled more securely in the chair.

Jamie reached for the lamp, dimming it. Then, calling herself a romantic idiot, she slipped into Rich's lap and pressed her head against his shoulder.

"Jamie?" He sounded unsure.

"Were you hoping to find someone else in your arms?" she asked in a small whisper.

"No." A smile faintly curved his mouth.

His grin disappeared as his hand framed her face, and his blue eyes held her captive. Jamie could feel her heart pound frantically. Then his thumb caressed the line of her jaw.

"I never realized how beautiful you are," he whispered. "All these years…"

Jamie dropped her gaze, afraid to meet his eyes. She wasn't anywhere close to being beautiful, and it hurt, a good kind of hurt, that he should think otherwise.

His mouth sought out hers. The kiss started slowly, gently, so gently that Jamie could feel herself begin to melt. A feeling of sublime languor filled her. It was completely unfair—downright decadent, in fact—that he could make her feel such things with a simple kiss.

Simple. Rich didn't know the meaning of the word. Certainly not when it came to kissing.

Jamie heard the whimpering sound before she was aware that it came from her.

Rich ended the kiss as leisurely as he'd begun it. Jamie's eyes remained closed, and her breathing came in staggered gasps. For long, contented moments, he held her. His fingers were at the back of her head, stroking her hair. In those moments, Jamie felt the air vibrate with sweet, unspoken promises.

He wanted to make love to her.

Jamie wanted it, too.

"I should be heading home?" Rich's voice rose softly at the end of his statement, turning it into a question.

"No," she whispered, catching his lower lip between her teeth.

"No?"

"You're moving in with me, remember?"

"Starting tonight?"

"Starting right this minute."

"You're sure?

Jamie smiled and pressed her lips to his. "You want to argue with me?" she murmured.

"No…it's just…"

She didn't allow him to finish, kissing him again, cramming her heart, her soul, her *love,* into a single kiss.

She'd surprised him; his gasp confirmed as much. He groaned anew, then deepened the kiss.

They were both trembling when it ended.

Getting off his lap, Jamie stood and held out her hand to Rich. His smoky, passion-hazed eyes met hers, his gaze questioning.

"You're sure?" he asked her again, his words hoarse with need, his eyes hot with passion and some other emotion she couldn't quite read. Restraint? Doubt? Jamie didn't know which.

"I'm sure."

"You're already pregnant."

Why he felt he had to remind her of that was beyond her. "Yes, I know." As she was speaking, her hands were unfastening the buttons on his shirt. Rich helped her by pulling his tie loose and dropping it to the carpet. Jamie slid the shirt from his shoulders, then ran her hands down the full length of his arms.

His chest captured her attention next. His warm, muscular, chest. She ran her flattened hands over it, marveling at the strength she sensed in him. She closed her eyes, wanting him so badly she felt weak with the need.

"You make me crazy," he whispered.

"I do?" It made no sense to Jamie.

"Yes. I want you so much you make me ache."

"I know…. Me, too."

Rich groaned and took her, in his arms, lifting her against him until she became profoundly aware of his arousal.

For one wild second it was as though the world stood still for them. Rich's blue eyes appeared aquamarine in the dim light. Bright, intense, filled with promises.

Jamie felt completely vulnerable to him. Vulnerable and desirable, more desirable than she'd ever felt in her life. She smiled and moved away from him.

Rich looked confused, but he released her.

Jamie turned and had gone two steps before she turned around again. A smile quivered at the edges of her mouth. "You coming with me?"

"Where are you going?"

She laughed softly, sexily, and held out her hand to him. "You mean you don't know?"

Thirteen

Rich woke in the middle of the night. It took him only seconds to realize he was in bed with Jamie. For the next few minutes he did nothing more than watch his wife as she slept. He drank in every delicate nuance of her beauty. He stared at her as if they'd been separated for months, years, when she'd actually spent the night in his arms.

Gradually his gaze lowered to her lips, parted slightly, her breathing slow and even. She had the most delectable mouth….

Desire came at him unexpectedly. Memories of the gentle way Jamie had led him to her bed suffused him like a mist. She'd held her arms out to him, until the ache of wanting her, needing her, dissolved any will he had to refuse her.

She'd freely opened her heart and her body to him. When she'd cried out in pleasure at her completion, the sound of her joy had echoed in his very soul. The sheer, utter beauty of their lovemaking had marked him in ways he was only beginning to understand.

Jamie stirred and rolled her head to one side. Her hair spilled across her face, and after a moment, Rich risked waking her by gently brushing it aside. His breathing was fast, much too fast considering the simplicity of the gesture.

He leaned forward, intending to kiss her. The way he was feeling, with need clawing at his insides, he knew if he followed through with his intention, the kiss would be too intense, too powerful. By an act of will, he stopped himself just in time.

He'd made love to her only hours before and already he was wondering how long it would be before he could do so again.

He had to think. Pull himself together. Make some sense of this nagging physical ache, this overwhelming need, before he woke Jamie and frightened her. Folding back the covers, he sat on the side of the bed, rubbing his face.

"Rich."

The panic he heard in Jamie's voice made him turn around.

"Don't leave me," she pleaded. "Not again."

"I wasn't going to." He slipped back into the bed and gathered her in his arms. She felt so soft against him. Holding her, he wished he could stay like this forever.

"Don't go," she repeated, almost deliriously, clinging to him.

"I can't." Even if he'd wanted to, Rich could never

have walked away from her. He was so much in love with her, so driven by need…and desire.

He kissed her, hoping to reassure her, but the kiss was everything he'd feared. And wanted. His mouth was hard and demanding, as his hands investigated her warm, perfect skin.

"Jamie…" He slid his mouth down the perfume-scented curve of her neck, down her shoulder to the peaked softness of her breast.

Jamie moaned softly and arched her back, encouraging him, plowing her fingers through his hair, thrashing beneath him.

He lifted his head and kissed her mouth. "I need you…again," he whispered.

Their need for each other was as urgent as their kisses. A strangled cry slipped from her throat as she clutched at his back.

Rich jerked his mouth from hers. "I'm scaring you?" He was afraid he had, or worse, that he was hurting her.

"No…no, love me, just love me."

"Yes. Oh, yes."

Rich intended to do a lot more than simply fulfill their bodies' hunger. But for now, his need was too great to take it slow. Or easy. Ruthless desire dictated his actions.

She lay there, eager and trusting, vulnerable to him. Her dark hair fanned about her shoulders. Her sweet face was flushed with excitement, her eyes wide and misty with an emotion too strong to voice. Her lips were parted and moist from his kisses, and her breath came in tiny gasps of encouragement.

"Jamie…love. My love."

Rich couldn't resist her a second longer. Not another second.

The alarm sounded while it was still dark. Jamie rolled onto her side and reached blindly for the clock radio, shutting off the irritating noise.

Rich moved toward her, cradling her, placing his arm around her middle. "Good morning," he whispered. With familiarity, his hand cupped her breast. Although they'd spent much of the night making love, Jamie was astonished by her body's ready response to his touch.

"Morning." Jamie couldn't help feeling a little shy after the tempestuous night they'd spent. Memories of their lovemaking filled her mind—the brazen way she'd led him into her bedroom, stripped for him, stripped him, sent a surge of color into her cheeks.

"How are you feeling this morning?" Rich asked, his mouth close to her ear. He caught her lobe between his teeth and sucked gently, shooting warm shivers down Jamie's spine.

"I'm…fine."

"Do you want me to bring you some crackers?"

Jamie hadn't immediately realized he was asking about the baby, the pregnancy. "Not…yet." She eased back the covers and cautiously righted herself. When she did suffer bouts of nausea, it was generally when she first sat up. With her legs dangling over the bed, she inhaled a deep breath and was relieved to discover she didn't feel queasy at all.

"Do you want to shower first?" Rich asked from behind her, his hands at her waist.

"Please." She had trouble looking at him. It was silly to be so nervous, she told herself. They were married, for heaven's sake. Married. There was no reason to feel uncomfortable or ill at ease. Rich was her husband, and he had a perfect right to spend the night with her.

Jamie moved into her bathroom and turned on the shower, adjusting its temperature. It wasn't until she was under the pulsing spray that she remembered.

The scene replayed itself, its effect as brutal as a slap across the face.

Rich had been about to leave her again, sneaking out in the middle of the night. If she hadn't half wakened when she did, he would've walked out on her a second time. Once again he'd planned to leave her, to let her face the empty morning alone. Except that this time she'd pleaded with him to stay.

Jamie didn't know how long she stood under the spray. Long enough to regulate her breathing and wait for the pain that rippled through her to subside.

When she finished, she forced a smile and walked nonchalantly back into the bedroom, a white towel around her. "Your turn," she told him, not meeting his eyes.

Rich had made coffee and brought her a mug, as well as a small plate with four soda crackers. "Breakfast is served," he said, bowing before her.

Jamie drank some of her coffee, careful to keep the towel securely in place with one hand. It was ludicrous to act modest after what they'd shared. The things they'd said. The things they'd done. Beautiful things...

Nevertheless she was.

Rich frowned, then left her. Although the bathroom door was shut, Jamie heard him singing at the top of his lungs over the sound of the shower. She took advantage of the brief privacy to get dressed, haphazardly choosing her outfit for the day.

She made the bed, folded Rich's scattered clothes and laid them on top, then hurriedly moved into the kitchen. Generally she didn't pack a lunch for work, but she did this morning, just to pass the time. If there was anything to be grateful for, it was that Rich hadn't called her *darling*. He'd only done that in the presence of others, for the sake of the pretense they had to maintain in front of their parents.

She was putting together a sandwich when Rich joined her. He poured himself a second cup of coffee. Jamie concentrated on making her turkey sandwich and managed to avoid eye contact.

She turned around to get an apple from the refrigerator and stopped short of colliding with Rich. "Oh, sorry," she mumbled under her breath, flattening herself against the counter so he could step past her.

"Would you like some breakfast?" she asked matter-of-factly, as though she often made the same inquiry of men who spent the night with her.

"Just coffee, thanks."

Jamie sighed with relief. The intimacy of cooking a meal for him would've been a strain. She made a point of glancing at her watch. "I guess I'd better head out to the salt mines," she said, striving to sound carefree and happy when all the while there was a lump in her throat that made it hard to speak.

"Me, too." Rich's voice was low and hesitant, as if he wasn't quite sure what was happening, but whatever it was, he didn't like it.

Jamie didn't, either, but she didn't know what to do about it.

She was halfway out of the kitchen when Rich stopped her.

"I'll have to leave with you."

"Why?" She was eager to escape, to be by herself, examine her thoughts and reactions, analyze their relationship.

His smile didn't quite reach his eyes. "I don't have a key to lock up with."

"Oh, right." She opened the closet and pulled out her coat.

"If I'm going to move in with you, we should have an extra one made."

"Move in with me..." She'd suggested it when they'd met with Rich's family. It had seemed like a good idea at the time, and she'd been so eager to find a way to make her marriage work.

"I take it you've changed your mind?"

"No," she said hastily. "I...just think we should re-evaluate the situation before we do something we might regret later."

"'Regret later,'" Rich repeated slowly. "In other words, you regret having made the offer."

"I didn't say that."

"You didn't have to." He moved past her and out the front door, slamming it behind him. The sound reverberated like thunder, leaving Jamie alone to withstand the storm.

Rich had never met a more contrary woman in his life. It seemed that one minute she was leading him into her bedroom, and in the next she was behaving as though she couldn't get away from him fast enough.

Rich wasn't the one who'd announced to his family that they were moving in together. Nor had he invited himself into her home for dinner and then seduced her. It was the other way around. All right, she hadn't exactly seduced him, but the lovemaking had been Jamie's idea.

Then, in the light of day, she'd acted as if she'd never seen him before. As if she would've preferred that he disappear in the middle of the night.

Leaving before she woke was what had gotten him into trouble the *first* time they'd made love.

Rich was damned if he did and damned if he didn't.

He didn't understand it. He'd never been this confused by a woman.

Although Rich tried to work, by midafternoon he felt like calling it quits. Leaning back in his chair, he rubbed his tired eyes. Generally, when he had a problem he wanted to talk over with someone, he called Jason. The two of them had been each other's support system for years.

This time, however, Rich decided to phone Paul instead. Paul had been married nearly five years; surely in all that time he'd gleaned *some* wisdom about women and marriage.

Rich stood and closed his office door before sitting back down and reaching for his phone. Paul worked for the largest of the two Seattle papers and was often out chasing down a story. But his brother answered the phone.

"Got a minute?"

"Sure," Paul teased. "The only pressing thing I have is a three o'clock deadline."

Since it was quarter to three, Rich figured he'd better talk fast. "Did Jason tell you about Jamie and me?"

"Not exactly," Paul said, his amusement evident in his voice, "but I put two and two together. Jason confirmed my suspicions, although I have to admit I would never have guessed you'd agree to artificial insemination."

"It didn't work out that way."

"That's what Jason said."

Rich could picture his brother in the middle of the newsroom, leaning back in his chair wearing that cocky know-it-all grin.

"What can I do for you?"

"Explain something to me."

"If I can."

"Women. And how they think."

Paul responded with a low laugh. "You want me to explain a woman's mind. I hope you're kidding. No one, at least no man, will *ever* be able to understand the way a woman thinks. Trust me, I've got five years' experience in this marriage business. If you don't believe me, ask Dad. He'll tell you the same thing. Take Diane. She wants another baby. Apparently she isn't busy enough with Ryan and Ronnie. For weeks on end she's talked about nothing else. She wants a little girl, she says. The twins run her ragged as it is. Besides, there's no guarantee we'd have a girl. We actually had a big fight about it last week."

"And?" Rich didn't mean to pry, but he was curious to know how Paul and his wife settled their disagreements.

"Well, I stood my ground, if that's what you mean. Not that it did much good," he admitted reluctantly. "I absolutely refused to discuss having another child. I tried to appease her though, I don't want to be dictatorial or unreasonable. I said we'd talk about it this time next year. That way the twins will be in kindergarten when the new baby's born. Planning our family makes sense to me."

"What did Diane say?"

"Nothing." This was followed by a significant pause. "But I should mention that she threw out her birth-control pills."

"Is she always this stubborn?"

"It's not just Diane. All women are stubborn. To make matters worse, she wore this sexy little piece of black lace to bed. I tried to ignore her, pretend I didn't see…you don't need me to tell you what I *could* see."

"No, I don't." Rich would rather not hear. He still didn't know what to make of Jamie's actions that morning. Had he frightened her, wanting her the way he did? Hell, it hadn't seemed like it the night before, but what did he know?

Apparently very little.

"The thing is, Diane will probably get her way simply because I don't have the strength to fight her. I could stop making love to her, but then I'd be the one losing out."

Rich rubbed the back of his neck. "Does Diane ever say one thing when she means another?"

Paul's laugh was abrupt. "Oh, yeah. In my experience, women are often indirect. They figure they're being subtle or giving us hints or something like that. But they won't come right out and say what they want. Oh, no, a man's supposed to guess, and heaven forbid if we guess wrong."

Rich exhaled a long, slow sigh. Paul was confirming what he already knew. "Remember, when we met with Mom and Dad, how Jamie casually said I was moving in with her?"

"Yeah."

"It sure surprised me when she brought it up. We'd never said a word about it."

"You mean you don't want to move in with her?"

"Of course I do! For weeks I've been trying to figure out how to suggest it. Then, out of nowhere, she invites me to live with her, in front of my family. I was so excited it was all I could do not to jump up and somersault across the living room floor."

"So what's the problem?"

It was a logical question and one Rich couldn't answer. "If I knew that, I wouldn't be calling you."

"All right," Paul said. "Start at the beginning."

"I drove home with Jamie last night."

"And?" Paul prompted when Rich didn't immediately continue.

"And I ended up staying the night."

"Everything sounds fine to me."

"It was—until this morning."

"What happened then?"

Rich shrugged, although Paul couldn't see him. "I can't say. The alarm went off and we were cuddling like old married folks. Ten minutes later, Jamie's out of the shower, with this towel wrapped around her middle. She wouldn't so much as look at me. I played it cool, gave her some space. Some women are modest—I understand that—so I left her alone.

"Before I know it, she's in the kitchen making herself lunch like it's the most important thing she's ever done. By accident I happened to step too close to her and she practically threw herself against the counter so we wouldn't touch." Rich paused to take a deep breath. "On top of that, when I said I should get a key to her place, she tells me we should reevaluate my moving in with her."

"I see," Paul muttered.

"What'd I do wrong?"

"*Something,* that's for damn sure. Think," Paul advised. "You must've made some remark that set her off."

"Like what?" They'd done more kissing than talking.

"How should I know? I wasn't there. Just think… review everything you said."

"I've tried that, but I can't come up with a single thing I could have done to warrant this reaction."

"Then ask her."

"I can do that?"

"Yeah," Paul said, but he didn't sound convincing. "It's not the best procedure because…well, you'll learn that soon enough. But if you're honestly in the dark about what went wrong, then you might as well ask. But if you do, be prepared."

"For what?"

"To have your ego shredded. When Diane acts like that, I know I'm in trouble. Often, and this is what's so confusing, Diane can't even tell me what I did. All she knows is that she's furious with me."

"She can't explain why she's mad?" Rich could hardly believe it.

"It's true. She glares at me like I should be arrested. Then, when I can't stand it anymore, I finally ask her what I did that was so terrible."

"And?"

"And," Paul added with a sigh, "she says she's still getting in touch with her feelings. According to her, it has to do with her upbringing."

"How?"

"Well, the way she was brought up, according to her, was all about being taught never to make a fuss or create waves. To be a 'good girl,' which means not to make any demands."

"I see."

"So what are you going to do?"

Rich hesitated. "What you suggest. Ask her."

"You're a good man, Rich Manning," Paul said, as if Rich should be awarded a medal for bravery. "Let me know how it goes."

"I will," he promised. After thanking his oldest brother for the advice, Rich hung up, resolved to bring the situation into the open as soon as he had the chance.

The rest of the afternoon passed in a blur. Because they were putting the finishing touches on the defense project, Rich had to stay late that night. He wasn't pleased about it, but he had no choice. Bill Hastings and the others were working overtime, as well. Rich couldn't very well announce that he'd had an argument with his wife and then leave. Especially when half his colleagues didn't even know he *had* a wife.

At quarter past six, there was a polite knock at his door. He glanced up and did a double take when he saw Jamie standing there.

"Can I come in?" she asked shyly.

"Of course." He stood and gestured toward the chair on the opposite side of his desk. Once she sat down, he did, too. This was the chance he'd been hoping for, but since she was the one who'd come to see him, Rich figured he'd let her start the conversation. Trying to appear as nonchalant as possible, he leaned back in his chair and crossed his legs.

"I want to apologize for this morning," she said in a small voice.

"Thank you." Rich was in a generous mood. Apparently she'd seen the error of her ways and had come to make amends. He felt a surge of relief. Maybe this was going to be easier than he'd expected.

"I…I was completely unreasonable."

"Does this mean you want me to move in with you, after all?"

"Yes, of course…that is, if you're still willing."

Was he ever! "It's certainly something to think about," he said solemnly. Then he added, "I read that women are often unreasonable during pregnancy."

"Your book said that?" Jamie asked, frowning.

He nodded. "It's all those hormones."

"I bought a book, too, but I haven't got to that chapter yet. It makes sense, though." She opened her purse and reached for her wallet, snapping open the change compartment. "I had a key made for you during my lunch hour," she said, handing it to him.

"I'm working late this evening." He hoped she'd suggest he drop in at her place—at *their* place—on his way to the apartment.

"I thought you might be. That's why I came here first."

A short uncomfortable silence passed. Rich wondered if he should raise the subject of her bad mood this morning or let it go. Maybe it was simply the hormonal overload. Or maybe she didn't even know herself and regretted her reaction.

"I was thinking I'd bring some of my clothes over this evening," Rich said, experimentally, waiting to see if she'd offer him some encouragement.

"That would be fine."

It wasn't encouragement, exactly, but it wasn't opposition, either.

"I'll contact Jason and ask if he can help me move the furniture and the large items this weekend." He'd put what he didn't need into storage.

"I'll make sure there's plenty of room for your stuff." Jamie stood up. "I guess I'd better leave."

"One last thing."

"Yes?"

When Rich got to her place, he didn't want to play any guessing games about their sleeping arrangements. "Where will I be sleeping?"

Jamie's eyes widened at the directness of his question. "Uh…that's up to you."

"No, it's not," he returned firmly. "It's completely up to you."

"Anyplace you'd like," she said almost flippantly.

"Where would you *like* me to sleep?" he asked, throwing the question back at her.

She hesitated, then lowered her gaze. "With me."

He felt as though he'd scaled the gates of paradise. "There isn't anyplace else I'd rather sleep," he said, unable to keep the pleasure from his voice. He got to his feet and walked toward her, slipping an arm around her shoulders. Rich walked her to the elevator, and while they waited, he leaned forward and gently kissed her.

As so often happened during their kisses, Rich found himself wanting more. Much more. She braced her hands against his chest, her breath ragged, uneven. A warmth filled his heart and seemed to radiate outward.

When they broke off the kiss, Rich was delighted to see that Jamie was trembling. For that matter, so was he.

"You make me forget," she said in a husky whisper.

Rich understood. She made him forget where he was, too.

Bill Hastings strolled by and smiled affectionately at

them. He stood a discreet distance away, apparently hoping to talk to Rich.

The elevator arrived and although Rich was reluctant to let her go, he still had another hour, at least, of work.

"Goodbye, darling," Rich said. "I'll be home in a couple of hours."

Jamie's reaction was instantaneous. She tore away from him, stepped into the elevator and whirled around. Her eyes, her beautiful dark eyes, were brimming with tears.

"That's the most horrible thing you've ever said to me, Rich Manning."

Rich was so mystified by her irrational behavior that it took him a moment to respond. "What I said? What did I say?"

"You know very well." With that, the elevator doors glided shut.

Fourteen

"**W**hat'd I say?" Rich asked, utterly bewildered. He turned to his coworker, at a loss to understand.

Bill Hastings's blank look confirmed that he was equally in the dark.

"Whatever it was must've been awful. Jamie was crying."

"I don't *know* what I said," Rich told him, baffled.

"Maybe she's upset because you told her you wouldn't be home for a couple of hours."

Rich shook his head. "Maybe…" Although his working overtime had never seemed to bother Jamie before. Not that he was aware of, anyway. Sighing with frustration, Rich decided to give up trying to figure out his wife. Jamie had been a whole lot easier to understand before he married her, back when they were just friends.

"Leave now," Bill urged. "Sort this out before it's too late." That meant he was offering to handle the brunt of the remaining paperwork himself, which Rich didn't think was fair.

He shook his head again. "I'll work it out with her later."

"You're sure?"

"Positive."

Bill hesitated. "Maybe you should reconsider." Bill gave him a look that reminded Rich his friend was divorced. He knew that Bill wished his circumstances were different. Over a beer one night, he'd told Rich that if he had it to do over again, he'd work harder to save his marriage.

Rich's heart was racing. "You don't mind?"

"Not at all. Go! Do what you have to before everything gets blown all out of proportion."

"Thanks," Rich said over his shoulder. "I owe you one."

"Don't mention it.... Only, Rich?"

"Yeah?"

"Be happy."

Rich nodded. "I intend to, even if it kills me." Remembering the furious glare Jamie had sent his way, he figured it probably would.

Although he hurried out of the building and toward guest parking, Rich missed her. Jamie's car was nowhere in sight. He released a breath of frustration as he turned and walked to the employee parking area.

Maybe it was better that he hadn't caught up with her. His mood wasn't too positive at the moment, any more than hers was. Would married life always be this difficult? he wondered. Would his life consist of continually making amends for some unexplained wrong? Must he be constantly on his guard, afraid to speak his mind?

If there'd been something handy to punch, Rich would've done it. Plowing his fist into empty air only discouraged him more.

How fitting. Fighting imaginary ghosts. Didn't that describe his entire marriage?

Jamie had always been a sensible woman, or she had until she'd become pregnant. Yes, he'd read pregnant women could be temperamental, but this was ridiculous.

Jamie felt like a fool. Tears had left moist trails down her cheeks. She wasn't a woman given to such blatant emotion, and her actions surprised her even more than they did Rich.

But he deserved it, she thought in quick reversal. Calling her *darling* in front of his friend, putting on a big show, pretending to love her. As if saying it wasn't enough, he had to go and wear a besotted look, as though parting was such sweet sorrow.

It all seemed to be a game with him, and she couldn't bear to play anymore. If this was the first time, she might've been able to overlook it, but this nonsense had become a habit. When they'd gone to visit his parents, Rich had sat beside her, his hand clutching hers. The tender expression on his face, the loving way he'd smiled down on her, was more than she could stand.

It was all so hypocritical. Counterfeit love.

Would she ever learn? Men were fickle, not to be

trusted. And yet she knew Rich, probably better than she did any other man she'd ever dated. His behavior surprised her. More than that, it hurt.

Driving while crying wasn't safe, so Jamie pulled over to the side, got a tissue from her purse and blew her nose. When she could see clearly again, she sniffled and continued driving.

Once she was home, she wandered around her condo, walking from room to room, wondering if she'd ever be able to erase Rich's presence. A part of her longed to chase him out of her life, run after him militantly waving a broom, demanding he leave her alone.

Another part of her hungered to run toward him, greeting him with open arms.

"This is what happens when you fall in love," she chastised herself loudly. She pressed her hand over her smooth, flat stomach and a smile settled on her lips.

Things were different this time because a child was involved. This time she'd walk away from the relationship with a bonus. A very special bonus.

Making herself a cup of tea, Jamie sat in her kitchen, nursing her hot drink and her wounded heart. The damp tissues had piled up, but she'd composed herself enough to realize her display of anger had been out of character. No doubt Rich had viewed it as totally irrational. When she spoke to him again—*if* she did—she intended to set matters straight.

Pretense was unacceptable and she'd make sure Rich understood that.

There was a noise from her door. Since Jamie always kept it locked, she dashed into the living room, surprised to see it swing open. Rich, tall and ominous, entered her condo. He was supposed to be at work! In fact, she'd suspected he wouldn't show up at all tonight, considering the way they'd parted. One brief glance at the dark, brooding anger shining from his eyes, the tightly clenched jaw, told her he was in a furious mood.

Another surprise—the suitcase he held. It was large and bulky, the kind you'd take on an extended vacation. A three-week European tour. A two-week cruise. No one would confuse it with an overnight bag.

He set it down with a thud and headed toward her. Wide-eyed, Jamie moved out of his way.

"What are you doing here?" A challenge might not be the smartest way to start their conversation, but it told him she refused to be intimidated. He could rant and rave all he wanted, but she wouldn't be browbeaten.

"I'm here because I live here." He said it with enough conviction to make the windows vibrate. "Furthermore, I'll be sleeping in the master bedroom—with you. Is that understood?"

Coward that she was, Jamie nodded. She'd never seen Rich like this. Generally, he treated every situation in a joking manner. He could bluff, cajole and tease himself through just about anything. Jamie already knew what he'd be like when she was in labor. He'd be at her side telling jokes, entertaining the nurses, sharing good-ol'-boy remarks with Dr. Fullerton.

"No arguments?" He sounded shocked that she wasn't going to fight him over the issue of living with her, sleeping with her. Despite her contradictory emotions, she wanted him there. She wanted him in her life more than she didn't, if that made any sense.

She shook her head.

"Good." He nodded once as if to say this was going to be easier than he'd expected. "Now please explain what I said that was so despicable, when you left my office."

Jamie found it difficult to speak. "Darling."

"Yes?"

"You called me *darling*," she said, hating that she had to explain it. She clenched her fists, her long nails digging deep into the tender flesh of her palms.

"So?" He frowned, genuinely bewildered.

"So…I'd rather you didn't." A lump was forming in her throat, but Jamie tried to ignore it.

Rich stalked to the far end of her kitchen, his back toward her. He leaned against the sink, hanging his head as if her words demanded deep concentration. After a moment he turned to face her. "You're sure it doesn't have anything to do with me working overtime?"

"Of course not," Jamie said. "That would be unreasonable."

"And objecting to being called *darling* isn't?"

Jamie lowered her gaze to the polished kitchen floor. "I…wouldn't care if you'd meant it. But we both know you didn't and worse than that—"

"Worse? You mean there's something worse than calling one's wife *darling?* Does the FBI know about this?"

"Being funny isn't going to help you this time, Rich

Manning." She'd known it would be impossible to talk to him. He turned everything into a joke.

"All right," he said, lowering his voice. "Tell me what other horrible felony I've committed."

"It was the way you looked." To illustrate her point, she crossed her eyes and let her tongue dangle from the corner of her mouth.

"I looked like *that?*" he challenged in disbelief. "Don't be ridiculous!"

"Not exactly like that, but close." She held herself stiff.

"What was that silly expression supposed to be?"

"You with a besotted look."

"*Besotted?* Who uses a word like *besotted?*" He gave a short, abrupt laugh.

"I do. And I wasn't trying to be cute."

"I never looked like that in my life." Rich walked over to the round oak table, then frowned when he saw the pile of tissues. "You've been crying?"

"I...I have a cold."

He shook his head. "I thought you were never going to cry over another man."

"I...I didn't intend to.... I probably wouldn't, either, but I'm pregnant and, like you said, my hormones are all screwed up, so don't take it personally."

"What's happened to us?" He advanced several steps toward her, stopping just short of taking her in his arms. "Jamie, love…"

"Don't say that!" she cried, her voice rising to near-hysteria. Calling her his love was too painful, like taunting her with the one thing she truly wanted and couldn't have.

"What?" He raised his hands, palms up, in sheer frustration.

"Don't call me your love."

"Why?" he demanded.

"Because I'm not."

"What do you mean?" Rich glared at her.

"You don't love me and I...I can't tolerate it when you pretend you do." The words poured out of her until she was shouting, shaking with the force of her anger.

"I do love you," he said quietly.

"Oh...right." She wouldn't have thought Rich would lie to her about something so serious. It offended her that he'd try to pass off as truth what she knew to be false.

"You mean you honestly didn't realize that?" He came forward, but for every step he took, Jamie retreated two.

"Because it isn't true!"

"How can you say that after the other night?"

"Don't confuse good sex with love." Jamie didn't know what had made her say that, but she couldn't stop. She wore her pride like a protective cloak. She'd been hurt so many times before. Her trust had been violated, her heart bruised. She couldn't go through all of that again, especially with Rich, whom she loved so desperately. It was safer if he believed she didn't care.

"So that's all it was to you—good sex?"

"Yes, of course. *You* don't think it was anything more, do you?"

With each word she threw at him, his anger increased until it flashed like fire from his eyes.

Jamie's back was flattened against the wall, her fingers splayed against it. She longed to tell him their times together had been the most beautiful, the most meaningful, of her life, but she lacked the strength.

She'd never known how exhausting it was to lie.

"I suppose you want me to prove it," he said.

"Yes," Jamie returned flippantly, since that was an impossible task.

Not meeting her eyes, Rich marched past her with purposeful strides. He slammed his suitcase onto the floor, opened it and dug through his clothes until he found what he wanted—apparently a white business envelope with some kind of logo on the upper left side.

Without a word he stepped over to her fireplace, reached for one of the long-stemmed matches she kept on the mantel and struck it against the brick. The flame sprang to life. Cupping his hand over it, Rich knelt and held the match to the white envelope, which he'd set on the grate. Within seconds the paper was nothing more than charred ashes.

At first Jamie didn't understand what he was doing. It came to her gradually, until each breath she drew was more painful than the one before. Rich had burned the marriage agreement they'd had drawn up before the wedding. The one they'd both signed.

The tears that crowded her throat refused to be contained anymore. They leapt to her eyes, burning, smarting. Her throat ached with the need to breathe, her sobs desperate to escape.

She must've made some sound, because Rich, whose

back was to her, turned slowly. His eyes slid to hers, until Jamie thought she'd drown in those blue depths.

Could she believe? She was afraid to hope that what he'd said was true and that he did indeed love her. Hope was so fragile, so easily shattered.

Dare she believe?

Love had always been so disappointing. It had stripped her of her pride, stolen her aspirations. Cheated her.

Did she dare trust her heart again?

"I'm not interested in a marriage of convenience with you any longer, Jamie," he said evenly. "I haven't been, since the night I found you with Floyd what's-his-face. I realized then that I love you and probably have for years, only I hadn't realized it. Condemn me if you will, but it's the truth."

Jamie's heart quickened. Tears streamed down her face and she brought her fingers to her lips, knowing it would be impossible to speak. Instead, she held out her hand to him, her shoulders trembling.

Rich was there a second later, hauling her into his arms. His mouth unerringly found hers, and he lavished warm, moist kisses on her quivering lips.

"I hope all this emotion means what I think it does," he murmured against the curve of her neck.

Jamie's tears fell without restraint. The emotions within her were too primitive, too deeply rooted to allow her the luxury of responding with words. Her hands framed his face as she spread eager kisses wherever she could. Trying to convey everything in her heart, she cherished him with her lips, kissing him again and again until they both shook with passion.

"Jamie…" Rich tore his mouth from hers and stared searchingly into her face.

"I love you," she managed in a breathless whisper.

His smile was more brilliant than a rainbow after the fiercest storm. "I know." He wore a cocky grin as he swung her effortlessly into his arms and walked to the bedroom.

Tenderly he placed her on the bed and moved over her. When he kissed her, their passion flared to life, with no reservations, no holding back.

"Tell me what you said wasn't true," he pleaded. "Tell me our lovemaking touched you the same as it did me."

Jamie tried to answer him, reassure him it had been her pain talking, her disillusionment, but she couldn't speak for the lump in her throat. Smiling, she gazed up at him, letting all the love in her heart spill into her eyes. She wrapped her arms around his neck and kissed him.

They made love gently, slowly, and when they'd finished, they held each other. For a long time neither spoke.

They kissed after a while and Rich rolled onto his back, taking her with him. His hand caressed the small of her back. "I love you," he whispered. "I love our baby, too."

"I know…. I'm sorry I doubted you."

Content, Jamie nestled against him, pressing her ear to his heart, which beat solidly in his chest. Her own heart was radiant with emotion. She'd tried to close herself off from love, but Rich had made that impossible.

His hand reached for hers. Palm to palm. Heart to heart.

And Jamie felt—finally—like the married woman she was. A wife deeply in love with her husband. A woman deeply loved by a man.

Epilogue

The brightly decorated Christmas tree stood in the corner of Rich and Jamie's spacious new living room, in front of a large bay window that overlooked Puget Sound.

Jamie sat with her swollen ankles elevated while Rich brought her in a cup of tea from the kitchen. He'd insisted on doing the dishes and Jamie hadn't argued. She was tired and crabby and impatient for their baby to be born.

"We really should take down the tree," she said. Christmas had passed several days before.

"Take down the tree?" Rich objected. "We can't do that!"

"Why not?"

"Junior wants to see it."

"Rich," Jamie muttered, her hands resting on her protruding stomach. "I've got news for you. Junior has decided he'd rather not be born. He's hooked his foot over my ribs and says he'd rather stay right where he is."

"You're only three days past your due date."

"It feels like three months." She'd given up any hope of seeing her feet back in October.

"Can I get you anything else?" Rich asked. "A pillow? Your knitting? A book?"

"Stop being so solicitous," she snapped.

"My, my, we are a bit testy this evening."

"Don't be cute, either. I'm not in the mood for cute."

"How about adoring?"

"Maybe...but you're going to have to convince me."

"Perhaps I should try for the besotted look." He crossed his eyes and dangled his tongue out of the side of his mouth, imitating the impression she'd done of him earlier that year.

Despite her low spirits, Jamie laughed and held her arms out to him. "I love you, even if you do look like a goose."

Rich sat on the ottoman facing her. "I love you, too. I must, otherwise I wouldn't be this worried." The humor left his eyes as he leaned forward and placed his hand on her stomach. "Come out, come out, whoever you are."

"Are you really worried?" He tended to hide his anxiety behind a teasing facade, and Jamie had been so consumed by her own apprehensions that she hadn't taken the time to address Rich's.

"I'm anxious." His hands gripped hers and he raised

her knuckles to his mouth and gently kissed her fingers.

"So am I! I want this baby to be born."

"I can hardly believe how much I love him already," Rich whispered, his eyes serious. "At first, the baby was something we talked about. When I learned you were pregnant I was so excited I could've walked on water. Then a few weeks later, we were living together. This summer we sold your condo and moved here. That was only the beginning of all the changes in our lives."

"I know."

"Then Junior started getting sassy, constantly moving around, letting us know he was there."

"He—or she," Jamie said with a grin.

"I'll never forget the first time I felt him—or her—move."

"I won't, either," Jamie said.

Rich smiled that lopsided grin of his that never failed to disarm her. "Everything's changed, hasn't it?" Once again his blue eyes brightened. "This child is part of you and me—the very best part of us both. Every time I think about him, I get all soft inside. I want to hold him in my arms and tell him how much his mother and I wanted him. Or her," he added with a smile. "Enough to go to exorbitant measures."

"Not that it was necessary," Jamie whispered. "Might I remind you that Junior was conceived in the good old-fashioned way?"

Rich leaned forward and reminded her of some other

good old-fashioned methods they'd discovered. She was laughing when she felt the first contraction. Her eyes widened and she squeezed Rich's hand.

"Jamie?"

"I think all my complaining might have done some good. Have you got the stopwatch?"

Rich paled, nodded, then rushed into their bedroom, returning with the stopwatch he'd purchased after attending their childbirth classes.

He knelt in front of her, clasping her hand. "Are you ready, my love?"

Jamie nodded. She'd been ready for this moment for the past nine months.

With a loud squall, Bethany Marie Manning made her way into the world thirteen hours later. Rich was at Jamie's side in the delivery room. When Dr. Fullerton announced that they had a daughter, Rich looked at Jamie, his face filled with wonder and surprise.

"She's a girl?" he asked, as though he wasn't sure he'd heard correctly.

"Do you want to check for yourself?" Dr. Fullerton teased.

Jamie watched her husband, searching for signs of disappointment, but if there were any she didn't see them. The nurse weighed Bethany, then wrapped the protesting infant in a warm blanket and handed her to Rich.

Rich stared down at the bright pink face and smiled. When he looked over at Jamie his eyes shone with unshed tears. "She's beautiful."

"You're not disappointed we didn't have a son?"

"Are you crazy? I always wanted a girl. I just said I wanted a boy to keep you off guard." Very gently, Rich bent down and kissed his daughter's forehead.

Hours later, Jamie woke and saw that Rich was asleep, slumped in the chair next to her hospital bed. His head rested against hers. Smiling contentedly, she rubbed her fingers through his tangled hair.

Yawning, Rich raised his head. "Hello, little mother."

"Hello, proud daddy."

"She is so beautiful. Oh, Jamie, I can't believe how much I love her. And you." He kissed her hand, then held it against his jaw. "I never knew I could feel like this."

Feeling dreamy and tired, Jamie nodded and let her eyes drift shut.

"Don't you worry about a thing," Rich whispered, his face close to hers. "I've taken care of everything."

Jamie's eyes flew open. "What do you mean by that?"

"Ballet classes." He pulled open the drawer in the bedside table and withdrew a Seattle phone book. "I've called two schools, both of whom are sending us brochures. I also talked to a teacher about piano lessons."

"Rich!"

"Just kidding." He lifted her hand and clasped it between his own. "I love you, Jamie."

"I love you, too," she whispered.

They'd come so far, Jamie mused. They'd tried to

manipulate fate, create their own destiny, constrain their marriage with limits and conditions.

Instead, love had caught them unawares.

* * * * *

Paul's Story

in

Stand-In Wife

Prologue

The morning was bleak, the sky, gray and overcast. The phone call from the hospital woke Paul Manning from a sound sleep—his first decent sleep since his daughter, Kelsey Diane, was born seventy-two hours earlier. Because of toxemia, his wife, Diane, had been placed in intensive care as a precaution.

Things quickly got worse, however, complicated by the fact that Diane had been born with only one kidney. Generally the toxins disappeared from the mother's body following birth, but in Diane's case that hadn't happened. Instead they'd attacked her liver and kidney, and before Paul fully realized the seriousness of her condition, she'd slipped into a coma. Paul and Diane's sister, Leah, had held a vigil at her side. After two days Dr. Charman had sent them home, promising to contact Paul if there was any change. Now he had.

"Could you come to the hospital?" he asked.

"What's wrong?" Paul demanded, frightened by the weariness in the physician's voice.

"It'd be best if you came to the hospital. I'll explain everything once you're here."

It wasn't supposed to happen like this.

A half hour later Paul Manning was shouting the words in his mind, but not a sound passed his lips. He was overwhelmed by pain, disbelief, shock—they punched him viciously, knocking the wind from his lungs. Dizzy and weak, he slumped into the hospital chair.

"We did everything we could," Dr. Charman murmured, his voice subdued with defeat.

Women gave birth...but they didn't die from it. Not in this day and age. Not when they were at one of the best medical facilities in the country.

The pregnancy had begun in a completely routine manner; Diane had never seemed healthier. Then, in the eighth month, she'd developed toxemia. Paul hadn't been too concerned, blithely unaware of how deadly her condition would prove to be.

Diane had suffered from toxemia during her first pregnancy, too, and everything had turned out all right. The twins had been born six weeks premature, but the toxemia hadn't been life-threatening to either her or the boys.

"Is there someone you'd like me to call?"

Paul glanced up and shook his head. He didn't want his family just yet. For now he needed to grieve alone. "I'd like to be with her for a few minutes if I could."

Dr. Charman nodded and led the way down the quiet corridor to Diane's room. Paul's heart was pounding savagely, his head whirling, his legs unsteady. He felt as though he was in a nightmare, and he prayed someone would wake him up.

Dr. Charman opened the door and stepped aside. "I'll wait for you here," he said.

Paul nodded, surprised by the sudden calm that enveloped him. He hadn't expected to feel serenity. Not when the grief, the guilt and pain, were crushing his heart.

The first thing he noticed was that all the tubes had been disconnected. His wife's face glowed with a beauty that transcended anything he'd ever known. For a moment he was sure Dr. Charman had made a mistake, that Diane was only sleeping.

He remembered the first time he'd met Diane six years earlier. He'd been in the army, stationed in Alaska, and she'd come up for the summer to work in a cannery. He was nearly thirty and she was barely twenty-one. Paul had taken one look at her, and it was as if his heart had stopped. He'd fallen in love a dozen times before, but no woman had ever affected him the way Diane Baker had. By the end of the summer, she'd decided to drop out of college and marry him.

They'd talked for hours on end, planning their future. Paul's degree was in journalism, but he intended to be a novelist one day. Diane read his work, built up his confidence, convinced him he'd sell his stories. Through the years her belief in him remained unwavering.

Six months after they were married she was pregnant. When she had Ryan and Ronnie, Paul thought his heart would burst with pride. He had a family of his own now. A wife he adored and two sons. Twin sons.

Then, a year ago Diane had decided she wanted a little girl. Paul would've preferred to wait, space out their family, get the boys in school first. But Diane had been adamant. She'd wanted another baby. They'd argued about it, but in the end she'd convinced him. Actually, he used to joke, it was a sheer black nightie that had convinced him. The truth was, he'd never been able to refuse his wife. She was his whole world—and now she was gone.

Paul looked down at her and his heart felt the heaviness of grief. The emptiness. What would he do without Diane? How could he possibly face life without her?

Diane was at peace, but Paul was in turmoil.

The anguish rose in his throat until it escaped in a low moan. Gripping the railing of the hospital bed, he closed his eyes and felt his body rock with grief.

A sound outside the room caught his attention and he turned, recognizing Leah's voice. Leah, Diane's sister.

The two women had always been close, and it didn't surprise him that she was here. Moving from his wife's side, he opened the door to find a stricken Leah pleading with Dr. Charman.

"Paul?" She shifted her imploring gaze to him. "I woke up. Something told me to come to the hospital…right then…not to wait. I'd only been home a few hours."

Paul nodded. He hadn't been asleep long himself.

"I can't believe this," she sobbed. "Not Diane…" She

covered her mouth, and her shoulders shook with the pain of a loss that went soul deep.

Paul opened his arms to her, and Leah walked into his embrace, but he didn't know who was comforting whom.

He needed her and she needed him.

One

Kelsey's weak cry stirred Paul from his light sleep. He blinked and rubbed a hand down his weary face. The midnight feedings were the worst, especially on Friday nights.

Life had fallen into a dismal pattern in the six months since Diane's funeral. He'd never worked harder in his life. Keeping up with the kids and the house and his job left room for little else. The demands seemed endless.

His family had pitched in to help every way they could. Between his mother and his sister-in-law he was managing, especially with his mother taking the kids every weekday, shuttling the boys to preschool and picking them up.

Kelsey cried again, and Paul threw aside his covers and sat on the edge of the bed. Blindly, he searched with his feet for his slippers, then stood and pulled on his robe.

Kelsey's crib was in his room, and he automatically reached for her, placing her against his shoulder.

"Just a minute, sweetheart," he said, walking around the room until he'd located a freshly laundered diaper on top of the dresser.

Bless Leah. He didn't know what he'd do if she hadn't taken over the laundry. With so many extra medical expenses, plus the cost of the funeral, he couldn't afford a diaper service or even disposables, or, at least, not as many as he needed. At night he used the old-fashioned kind, often going through two or three. So every afternoon on her way home from teaching at the college, Leah came by to prepare dinner and start the laundry. He wouldn't have survived the past few months without Leah and his mother.

He deftly changed Kelsey's wet diaper while her bottle was heating in the microwave. He was getting fairly good at this diapering business. Early in his married life, Paul had teased Diane that she could have as many children as she wanted as long as she was the one who dealt with the messy diapers. Now changing diapers, like so many other tasks, had become his alone.

Settling in the rocking chair with Kelsey, Paul carefully touched the nipple to her lips. The baby's tiny mouth parted, and she sucked hungrily.

He brushed the soft blond wisps of hair from her sweet face. How grateful he was that Kelsey had been born healthy. Diane had wanted a little girl so badly. An ultrasound early in the pregnancy had told them that she was to have her wish. Paul hadn't cared one way or the other, but Diane had been overjoyed at the prospect of a daughter.

Paul had been with her when Kelsey was born.

Because there'd been so much concern about Diane's condition, they'd immediately handed Kelsey to him. Despite everything that had happened since, he remembered the surge of love and pride he'd experienced holding his newborn daughter that first time.

It wasn't Kelsey's fault that her birth had cost Diane her life. Not once had Paul thought to blame her. Who was there to accuse? God? Fate? Life?

Paul didn't know. He'd given up looking for answers. There wasn't enough time or energy left in a day. Not when he had to deal with the reality of raising three motherless children, aged four and less than a year.

Once Kelsey had finished the bottle, Paul held her over his shoulder again and rubbed her back. Gently rocking back and forth, he closed his eyes. He'd rest for a few minutes…he told himself.

Just a few minutes…

Saturday morning, when Leah let herself into the house that had once been her sister's, she found her brother-in-law asleep in the rocking chair, his arms cradling Kelsey.

She hesitated, not wanting to disturb him. He'd been so tired lately. They both had.

Too tired to grieve.

Too tired to do anything more than simply function, taking one step at a time, dragging from one day to the next. Moving forward, because they had no choice.

Even now, six months after her sister's death, Leah had trouble accepting the permanence of the situation. More often than she could count, Leah expected Diane to come into the room, bringing her warm smile and effervescent personality. How empty life felt without her. Empty for her.

For Paul.

For the children.

Then some days it was as if Diane was actually there. At the oddest times Leah could almost feel her sister standing beside her, thanking her for helping, for encouraging Paul.

And then there was the dream.

Leah had never told her brother-in-law about it. She'd never told anyone. It had come the night Diane died.

Paul and Leah had been at the hospital with her sister for three days, and there hadn't been any change in Diane's condition. Dr. Charman had insisted they both go home and get some sleep. Nothing was likely to happen for some time yet, he'd told them. Paul had been as reluctant to leave as Leah had, but in the end they'd both agreed.

Leah had gone to her apartment, showered and fallen into bed. She'd slept deeply, and in her dream Diane had come to her, walking through a field of wildflowers. She was barefoot and happy. Then she'd stood under a flowering magnolia tree and looked at Leah. A brilliant white light had settled above her. Diane had smiled into the light, and although Leah couldn't hear what her sister was saying, it had seemed to her that Diane was requesting a few more minutes. She'd then turned from the radiant light and smiled at Leah.

Holding a daisy, plucking at the petals, she'd told

Leah how sorry she was to leave her, to leave Paul and the children. Leah had tried to interrupt, but Diane had stopped her. Her sister had explained how hard she'd battled to live, then said she'd come to understand that there was a greater wisdom in accepting death.

The problem, she whispered, was that she couldn't freely give up her life with Paul and Leah holding on to her the way they were. Holding her back. The strength of their love and their will kept her with them, prevented her from dying. It was the reason they'd been sent home. Once they were gone, she would be free.

Leah had tried to argue with her, but Diane had smiled serenely and shaken her head, claiming there wasn't enough time. She'd spoken quickly, pointing out to Leah that Paul and the children would need her help. Looking directly into Leah's eyes, she'd smiled again and asked if Leah would be willing to take her place. Leah hadn't understood then and wasn't sure she did now, but in the end she'd promised to do whatever was needed.

The next instant Leah had awakened. For a confused moment she'd lain there in bed, certain it had all been a dream. Only a dream. Yes, Diane *was* at the hospital and it *was* true that her condition was serious, but her sister *wasn't* going to die. No one had even mentioned the possibility. Quickly Leah had gotten out of bed and rushed back to the hospital to discover that Paul was already there with Dr. Charman.

Her sister was gone.

* * *

The dream had haunted Leah for months. She'd kept her promise to Diane and was doing everything she could to help Paul with the children, but it seemed so little.

To his credit, Paul was holding up well. He was such a good father. But Leah wondered how much longer he'd be able to continue under the strain. All along, he'd been the strong one, reassuring her, reassuring his children, his parents and everyone else.

Leah didn't know how he did it. But she was grateful. His confidence was the glue that held everything together. It kept them all going—Leah, his family, everyone who was trying to help. Paul's mother took the children during the day. The cost of day care for three preschoolers was outrageous. When Paul told Leah the quotes he'd gotten from several child-care facilities, she'd thought he was joking. He couldn't survive financially paying those fees.

Because Paul's hours at the newspaper often stretched past six o'clock, Leah had gotten into the habit of picking up Kelsey and the boys at his mother's place on her way home from the college, where she taught math. Since the kids were invariably hungry, she'd start dinner. She'd also run a load or two of laundry and do whatever else she could to lighten Paul's obligations.

For six months they'd all worked together, more or less coping with everything that needed to be done. Leah, however, was growing concerned. Elizabeth Manning was a wonderful woman, but she hadn't been responsible for small children in many years, and the demands of caring for three of them were beginning to take their toll. Not only that, the older Mannings had been planning a trip to Montana to visit Paul's two sisters. Christy was pregnant with her first child, and Elizabeth Manning was hoping to be with her youngest daughter for the birth of her child.

Paul was as concerned about the situation as Leah was. Even more so. But she didn't know what he intended to do. The problem was, he probably didn't, either.

What *could* he do?

"Mommy!" Four-year-old Ryan, the older—by ten minutes—of the identical twins, came out from their bedroom, sleepily rubbing his eyes. He dragged his security blanket on the carpet behind him.

"Good morning, sweetheart," Leah said, lifting his warm little body into her arms.

"I want my mommy." Ryan's arms clasped her neck tightly.

"I know." Her voice caught as she spoke.

"When's she coming home?"

"Your mommy's in heaven now, remember?"

"But when will she come back?"

Unexpected tears filled Leah's eyes. "She won't.... Don't you remember what your daddy said?"

"But I *want* her to."

"I do, too." It was difficult to make Ryan and Ronnie understand, difficult to understand herself. And it didn't seem to be getting any easier.

Diane had had a husband, children, responsibilities.

Her sister had been full of life and laughter. Her death made no sense to Leah. None.

Diane was blond, pretty, animated, energetic. Leah was tall and ungainly, and she lacked Diane's confidence and vivacity. At five-eight she was a full five inches taller than her younger sister had been. Her hair was a pale brown, and unlike Diane's beautiful blue eyes, hers were an indeterminate color, somewhere between green and brown depending on what she wore. Diane had been the striking one in the family.

Diane had also been the only family Leah had. Their parents had divorced when they were young, and their mother had died several years ago. They'd lost contact with their father in their teens. Any aunts, uncles, cousins, had long since faded from view.

"Are you hungry?" Leah asked Ryan, turning the conversation away from the painful subject of Diane.

Ryan's head was buried in her shoulder. He sniffled and nodded. "Can you make Egg McManning the way Mommy did?"

"Ah…" Leah hesitated. She had no idea what Egg McManning was. "Sure, but you'll have to show me how."

"Okay." Ryan brightened a little. "First you cook eggs and cheese and muffins, then you put everything together and eat it."

"Oh…" Leah was going to need a few more instructions than that. Diane had had an active imagination. She could make the most mundane chores fun and the simplest meal a feast.

"I'm hungry." Ronnie wandered out of his bedroom and into the kitchen. With both hands, he pulled out the kitchen chair, then climbed up onto the seat. He stuck his thumb in his mouth.

"Aunt Leah's making Egg McManning," Ryan told him.

"Good." The thumb left his mouth long enough to say that one word.

Until Diane's death Ronnie had given up sucking his thumb, but he'd started again. Leah hadn't suggested he stop and wouldn't for a while. Life had already landed him a harsh blow; she wasn't about to chastise him because he needed a little extra comfort.

"Did I hear someone mention Egg McManning for breakfast?" Paul stood in the kitchen doorway, Kelsey on his shoulder, sleeping soundly.

"Aunt Leah's making them for us," Ryan explained solemnly.

"I hope you'll share the recipe with me," she muttered under her breath.

"Toast English muffins," Paul said between yawns, "add some scrambled egg, a slice of cheese and voilà." He pressed his free hand to his mouth, stifling another yawn. "How long have you been here?"

"Only a few minutes." Leah had her back to him, searching the contents of the refrigerator for a carton of eggs.

"I thought you couldn't come until noon today."

"I lied," she said over her shoulder, giving him a quick grin. "I cleaned up my place last night and figured I'd get a head start with the kids this morning." She set the eggs, muffins and cheese on the counter. "I thought Ryan and Ronnie might enjoy a trip to the zoo." Out of the corner of her eye she watched for the twins' reaction.

"The zoo?" Ronnie asked excitedly. "With lions and tigers and bears?"

"Didn't you have a date last night?" Paul asked, frowning.

"I was too tired to go out." She grabbed a skillet that had been left to dry in the rack next to the sink and set it on the stove.

"If you were so tired, where'd you find the energy to clean house?"

Paul was like that sometimes. Leah guessed it was the reporter in him. He'd prod until he got the answer he already knew to be the truth.

"If I were you," she said, waving a spatula at him, "I wouldn't look a gift horse in the mouth."

"I know what you're doing." Fierce pride brightened his blue eyes.

"So do I," she countered smoothly. "I'm cooking breakfast for two hungry little boys."

Kelsey woke and started whimpering. Leah got the impression that Paul would've preferred to continue their conversation, but didn't know which to do first, deal with his daughter or talk to Leah. "But—"

"I'll heat her bottle for you," she offered, cutting off his reply.

Paul looked haggard. She'd purposely come to the house early so he could have part of the day to himself. The guy was exhausted. They all were. But for Leah there was an escape. At the end of the day she went home to her apartment, free from the demands of three small, needy children. A place of her own where she could find peace and privacy. Paul had no such deliverance.

Breakfast was ready when he returned with a freshly diapered Kelsey. He'd taken the time to dress in jeans and a sweatshirt, Leah saw, glancing in his direction.

She set three plates on the table and reached for Kelsey, tucking the baby in her arms and smiling as she eagerly began to gulp down her formula.

"You're ruining your social life," Paul said, biting into the muffin as though it had been days since his last meal.

"No, I'm not." There wasn't any social life to ruin, Leah thought. She only dated occasionally. Rob was a friend and would never be anything more. They had a good time together, but canceling an evening with him wasn't a big deal.

"You should've gone out last night," Paul said stubbornly.

"I wasn't in the mood." She stroked the side of Kelsey's face, her heart constricting as she noticed her resemblance to Diane. The little chin, the shape of her ears...

"Leah, please don't."

The earnestness in Paul's voice caught her attention. Slowly she lifted her eyes to his.

"I feel guilty enough knowing what this is doing to my parents," he said. "Please, don't you sacrifice yourself for me, too."

"It's not for you," she told him. "It's for Ryan, Ronnie and Kelsey. And it isn't a sacrifice. If the situation were reversed, Diane wouldn't think twice about doing the same for me. She'd *expect* me to help."

Paul closed his eyes and nodded, his face grim. "I still don't feel good about it."

"I know." Leah did; she knew it went against Paul's pride to rely on his family so much. He didn't have any choice, but he didn't like it.

Not one bit.

Paul was in an angry, unreasonable mood. If there was anything to be grateful for, it was that Leah had taken the boys to the zoo and Kelsey was napping.

He would've liked nothing better than to sit down at his computer. He was five chapters into a book, but he hadn't written a word since Diane's death. How could he? There hadn't been a moment he could call his own. Not that he'd been in the state of mind that would allow him to get absorbed in his novel anyway. But he wanted to try, as much for Diane, who'd loved this story, as himself.

His two younger brothers had asked him to join their softball team. He felt a bit guilty for spurning Jason and Rich's efforts to divert him, but feeling like a charity case was worse.

In any event, there wouldn't have been time for softball this Saturday, since a dozen chores around the house needed to be done.

One of the twins had pulled the towel rack off the bathroom wall. When he'd asked who was responsible, both Ryan and Ronnie had claimed, "not me." *Not me* seemed to have a lot to answer for lately.

Once he'd finished the bathroom repair, Paul moved into the twins' bedroom, where the closet door was off the track. Setting it back in place wasn't a simple task. Again and again he struggled to fit it onto the narrow groove until it was all he could do not to rip the door out in his frustration.

"You're losing it, old boy," he said, forcing himself to step back and take several deep breaths. Calmer now, he finally succeeded in fixing it.

From there, Paul moved to the garage. His car needed an oil change, and although he'd gotten in the habit of going to a twenty-minute lube place, this time he decided to do it himself, hoping to save a few dollars.

Tinkering in the garage, he realized he needed a few things from the hardware store. No big deal. He'd be back in fifteen, twenty minutes tops. It wasn't until he'd gone a block down the road that he remembered Kelsey.

He tore back to the house like a madman and raced inside the front door, his heart pounding so hard it sounded like thunder in his ear.

Kelsey was sleeping soundly, completely unaware that her own father had actually forgotten her.

Slumping into the rocking chair, Paul clenched his fists, resisting the urge to plow one through the wall. Paul had never been a violent man, and he was horrified by the rage that surged through him.

Leah's timing couldn't have been worse. The boys exploded through the front door, happy and excited. Ryan and Ronnie were each clutching a bright red balloon in one hand and an ice-cream cone in the other.

"Daddy! Daddy, guess what we saw?"

Paul didn't answer, but that didn't seem to dampen Ryan's enthusiasm.

"There was an eagle, a great big one with wings as long as…as an airplane and claws like this." He formed his small hand into the shape. "Bigger even."

"Paul, what's wrong?" Leah's soft voice came to him. If he closed his eyes, he could almost believe it was Diane speaking to him—only it wasn't.

"I left the house to do one small errand," he said in a low voice.

"Yes?"

"I went without Kelsey. I left her in the house alone," he said. "Anything could've happened, don't you understand? I left my own daughter behind...I completely forgot about her."

"Nothing happened. It's not the end of the world."

"Isn't it?" he shouted.

Leah steered the boys toward the kitchen. "Finish your ice cream at the table, then wash your hands," she told them calmly. "After that, it's time for your nap."

"Ronnie, get your thumb out of your mouth," Paul yelled. "You're too old to be sucking your thumb."

The boy raised stricken eyes to his father and rushed into the other room.

"Take a few minutes to relax," Leah told Paul, "and I'll bring you a cup of tea."

"I don't want any tea."

"I know," she said. "You want Diane back. We all do."

"A cup of tea isn't going to help."

"Perhaps not, but we need to talk, and anytime Diane had something important she wanted to discuss, she did it over a cup of tea."

Paul didn't need his sister-in-law to tell him about his dead wife's habits. For an instant he wanted to lash out at her, the same way he had at Ronnie. But the guilt he felt at his irrational anger compounded as he followed Leah into the kitchen. Ryan and Ronnie were sitting at the table. Their excitement was gone, their shoulders hunched forward. Paul leaned over and kissed Ronnie's cheek. "I'm sorry I snapped at you."

"I won't suck my thumb anymore," the four-year-old promised tearfully.

Ryan scooted off the chair and raced to their bedroom, returning with his yellow blanket, which he indignantly handed Paul. "If Ronnie can't have his thumb, then I don't want my blankie."

"You're sure?" Paul asked. Ryan hadn't slept without his blanket since Diane's death.

"Yes."

"If you're finished, go wash your hands," Leah told the boys. "Naptime."

Paul expected an argument. The boys rarely went to sleep without a fuss these days. They seemed to feel that if they were old enough for kindergarten in September, they were old enough to forgo afternoon naps. To his surprise neither one voiced a protest.

He was left alone in the kitchen as Leah walked the boys down the hallway. She returned a couple of minutes later and poured them each a cup of hot tea.

She was about to sit down when Ryan stalked back into the kitchen, glaring at his father. Here it comes, Paul thought. The argument about naptime.

"What is it?" Paul demanded impatiently.

Ryan blinked, pointing at the blanket on the chair next to Paul. "Ronnie's got his thumb in his mouth so I want my blankie back." He grabbed the tattered yellow blanket and raced to his bedroom again.

Leah was smiling, and if he'd been in a better mood, Paul would've found humor in it, too.

"So you had a good time at the zoo?" he managed to ask politely.

"Yes. The boys were great." She stared down at the delicate teacup in her hands. "Listen, Paul, I've been doing some thinking about the situation here, with you and the kids, and it seems to me we need to come up with some solutions."

"*We?* This isn't your problem."

"Yes, it is, although I hesitate to call it a problem."

"Then what would you call it?"

"An opportunity."

"An opportunity for what?" he asked, hating the way he'd raised his voice. The anger he felt simmered just below the surface, and seemed ready to burst forth at the slightest provocation.

"I've given a lot of thought to what I'm about to propose."

"Leah, listen, forgive me, I'm in a foul mood. Not good company. I don't know what's wrong with me, but—"

"I know what's wrong. What's wrong with all of us. Why Ronnie's started sucking his thumb again and why Ryan can't get to sleep unless he's got his blankie."

"It's Diane…."

She nodded. "We all miss her, we all need her, but she isn't here and we have to adjust. It's going to take time and patience."

"I've run out of both," Paul admitted wryly.

"So have I," she acknowledged, surprising him. "That's why I want to give my notice at the college and move in with you and the kids."

Two

"I won't hear of it," Paul said bluntly, emphatically.

Leah had expected an argument. Paul was proud. Being forced to accept her help, or anyone's for that matter, conflicted with his independent nature. He'd been forced to rely on her and his parents for the past six months, which was difficult enough.

"I've considered this very seriously," Leah said.

"I appreciate the offer, but I can't allow you to do it." Paul shook his head. Others might have buckled under at the obstinate look in his deep blue eyes, but Leah had come to know her brother-in-law too well to surrender that easily.

"The boys aren't adjusting."

"Leah, I said no," he returned firmly.

"Ryan can barely leave the house without his blanket. We both know he has trouble going to sleep without it."

"In time he'll give it up."

"And Ronnie's taken to sucking his thumb again," she continued undaunted. "In case you haven't noticed, he's become ambidextrous, although he continues to favor his right hand."

"Both thumbs?" Paul didn't bother to disguise his shock. His eyes hardened as he said, "In time the boys will learn to adjust."

"They need stability and security."

"I'm trying," Paul said, inhaling sharply. "I'm doing everything I can."

"No one's blaming you."

"I can't do everything."

"And that's my point," Leah told him quietly. "No one expects you to. My moving in will only be temporary. It'll give the boys a chance to adjust to Diane's loss without all the upheaval they're going through now. It'll help regulate Kelsey's schedule, too."

"What's wrong with her schedule?" Paul demanded.

Leah didn't want to sound critical of his efforts, but, in fact, Kelsey didn't *have* much of a schedule.

"It's…erratic. Especially at night."

"But she wakes up and—"

"You *expect* her to wake up and you're so attuned to the slightest noise that when she does, you spring out of bed instantly."

"I had to put her crib in my room," he said, "otherwise I didn't hear her."

"I'm just explaining that you need to move her into her own room and start regulating her eating schedule a little more." She paused. "I can help you do that."

He sighed wearily but didn't respond.

"It'd only be for a few years," Leah murmured.

"You don't really think I'm going to agree to this, do you?"

"Just until the boys are in school full-time and Kelsey's in preschool. By then the kids won't need me as much and I'll be able to resume my teaching career."

Paul didn't say anything for several minutes, weighing her words. "No," he finally said. "I appreciate this more than you'll ever realize, but I can't let you do it. It's too much of a sacrifice."

"Diane was my sister," Leah said softly, hoping to hide the pain that surfaced whenever she mentioned her sister's name. "Her children are the only family I have left. It wouldn't be a sacrifice—it would be something done willingly and out of love. The twins need me and so does Kelsey."

"But it's not fair for you to give up your life."

"Give it up?" she repeated with a short laugh. "You make it sound like I'm offering to leap into a volcano to appease some ancient god. I'm going to take a leave of absence from teaching. That's all."

"You won't be spending your time traveling or studying, though, will you?"

"No, but I'll gain more from the experience than you think. I love the children. I really want to do this."

"What about money?"

It went without saying that finances were currently tight for Paul. He couldn't pay Leah, nor could he offer to reimburse her for lost wages, but she'd taken all of that into account.

"I'll be giving up my apartment, so I'll be saving on

rent. Plus, I have a small trust fund from my mother and grandmother. It isn't a lot, but it's enough for the next couple of years."

Paul hesitated, his jaw tensing before he slowly shook his head. "Your offer touches me deeply, but I just can't let you do it."

Leah knew it would eventually come down to this. She knew she'd have to bring up the subject of Eric and Elizabeth Manning.

"What about your parents?" Although Leah preferred not to drag them into the discussion, she had no choice. Paul's parents had retired several years before and enjoyed traveling in their motor home. But since Diane's death they'd stayed in Seattle to help Paul with the children. She'd been unable to visit Taylor, her oldest daughter, when little Eric was born. Now Christy was pregnant and it looked as if, once again, Elizabeth wouldn't be there for the birth of a grandchild.

"I've been checking into having someone from church watch the kids while Mom and Dad are away," Paul informed her stiffly.

"Strangers?" Leah raised her eyebrows.

"What else can I do?" he flared.

"Let me move in with you. It's the obvious answer. The kids love me and I love them. They'll be in their own home, with their own toys. They've had enough disruption in their lives already. I know how hard this is for you, Paul, but you can't let your pride stand in the way of what's best for your children."

He stood abruptly and walked to the far side of the kitchen. "It seems so unfair to *you.*"

"But I'd consider it a privilege. I don't expect there'll be many other opportunities in my life to do something like this for those I love. My being here with the kids can make a difference. It can help them adjust to the loss of their mother. Please believe me, it isn't a sacrifice, it's an honor. Years from now I'll be able to look back and feel good about the contribution I made to shaping my sister's children, to helping them through this difficult time."

Paul rubbed his face with both hands. "I don't know."

He was weakening—Leah could see it, although he was still struggling with his pride, his natural inclination to carry everything on his own shoulders.

"It won't be for more than a few years," she reiterated.

"What about you and Rob?"

Leah smiled to herself. She'd been dating Rob Mullins for three years. They were both members of the math department at Highline Community College and shared a number of interests. Above all, they were friends. If they were going to marry, they would have done so long before now. "What about him?" she asked.

"What does he think of this?"

"I didn't ask him."

Paul's eyes widened.

"Rob'll understand," she assured him. Leah didn't feel it was necessary to go into the intricacies of their relationship. They dated more for the sake of companionship and convenience than romance. Rob was divorced and had been for fifteen years. If he wanted to remarry, he would've brought up the subject long ago.

"How can you be so sure he won't mind? If I was dating Diane right now, I can tell you I wouldn't take kindly to her moving in with her brother-in-law—no matter what the circumstances."

"You're not Rob. And I'm not Diane…."

"He'll care."

Leah ignored his concern. "There's only a couple of weeks left in the term, and I've already talked this over with Dean MacKenzie. I told him there's a strong possibility I wouldn't be returning for at least a year. But he needs to know for certain."

Paul didn't say anything for several minutes. He walked over to the teapot, carried it back to the table and refilled their cups. "I don't have a good feeling about this."

"But you'll agree to let me move in with you?"

He nodded slowly. "And I'll thank God every day for a sister-in-law as unselfish as you."

"What's this?" Ryan asked, lifting a textbook from one of the boxes neatly stacked in the corner of Leah's closet.

Each of the four bedrooms was now in use. Leah took the one across from the nursery and next to the twins' room. The master bedroom, where Paul slept, was at the far end of the long hallway.

"A book," she said as she unpacked her suitcase. She hung up one item at a time as the boys investigated several of the heavy cartons she'd brought with her. Most of her furniture had gone into storage, but she hadn't been able to part with some of her precious books. She probably wouldn't have the time or the energy to explore propositional calculus in the next couple of years; nevertheless, she'd hauled several boxes of books from her office.

"I like books," Ronnie said, taking his thumb out of his mouth long enough to tell her. He sat on the carpet next to his brother, tucking his legs beneath him. Ryan held his tattered yellow blanket under his arm as he leafed through the text, carefully examining each page as though he understood the concepts. Leah didn't have the heart to tell him he was holding it upside down.

"After dinner I'll read you a story," she promised them.

"Mommy used to read to us."

The memory of Diane sitting with her sons flashed into Leah's mind. She remembered her sister sitting on the living-room couch with the twins on either side. A large book of nursery rhymes was spread open across her lap as she read aloud. The boys nestled against her, half-asleep.

The injustice of her sister's death, the heartlessness of it, struck an unexpected blow. Leah paused in her task, holding a silk blouse to her stomach until the disturbing image passed.

"Are you going to be our mommy now?" Ryan asked, looking up at her with wide blue eyes. Paul's eyes. Both boys had been blessed with the same incredibly blue eyes as their father. Leah wasn't sure she'd ever seen eyes that precise color. It was the first thing she noticed whenever she met any of the Manning family.

"Mommy's in heaven," Ronnie said, poking his brother with his elbow.

Ryan went still for a moment and shut his eyes tightly. "Sometimes I forget what she looks like. I have to try real hard to remember."

"Here," Leah said, sitting on the end of the bed, eager to prompt the boys' memory. She reached for her purse and withdrew her wallet. Inside were several pictures of Diane, Paul and the twins. She took them out of the plastic case and handed them to the boys, who'd gathered beside her.

"How come she's so fat?" Ryan asked, pointing to the first picture.

Leah smiled. "That's because you and your brother were growing inside her tummy," she explained, ruffling Ryan's blond hair.

"I don't 'member that."

"I don't suppose you do."

"Kelsey was inside her tummy, too."

"Yes, she was," Leah said, picking up Ronnie and settling him on her lap. "Here's a picture of the two of you when you were born." They were dressed in white T-shirts with protective cuffs over their tiny hands. A small blue ribbon was taped in each baby's fuzzy blond hair.

"Which one's me?" Ryan asked.

"That one." Leah pointed to the infant on the left, although she didn't actually know.

"What's this picture?" Ronnie asked, pulling the bottom one free from Leah's hand. She had to look herself before she could say.

"That, my young man, was taken at Easter a few

years ago." She grinned, remembering how the candy-filled baskets she'd brought the boys had been bigger than they were. Ryan and Ronnie were toddling toward her when she'd snapped the picture. It was one of Leah's favorites.

She shuffled through the other photographs, and paused as she came upon one of Paul and Diane together. Paul's eyes held Diane's, and it was clear how much in love they were. Leah's heart constricted. It seemed so unfair that Paul should lose Diane. Six months after her death he was still grieving as though it had happened only yesterday. But then, so was she.

Leah often had questions about Diane's death. Not medical questions, but…spiritual ones. She didn't know what other word to use. She'd never told Paul, never told anyone, about the dream.

In some ways it was what prompted her to suggest she move in with Paul and the children. It was during the dream that Diane had asked Leah to take her place.

In retrospect Leah wished she'd questioned Diane, argued with her, convinced her to stay. Even after all these months, that vision of Diane haunted Leah. Sometimes she believed it was a product of her own imagination. Other times, she was sure it was real.

At any rate, Leah had kept her word. She'd moved in with Diane's family and was taking her sister's place—as a mother, but certainly not as a wife. Even with the kids, she felt woefully inadequate.

Leah didn't know how she, a single woman, a college-level math professor, was supposed to deal with three small children on a daily basis. She didn't have all the answers, only the determination to keep her promise to Diane.

There was bound to be a period of adjustment for them all, Leah realized. Paul was grateful for her help, but at the same time resentful that he needed her. And he *did* need her, no question there. Still, it would take a while for him to get over that.

Leah respected Paul. He'd loved her sister, still loved her, and was a good father. Although she didn't have much in common with him, other than their love for the children, for now that was enough.

"Tell you what we'll do," Leah said, tucking her arms around the children and bringing them close to her side. "We'll find some pictures of your mommy and put them up in your room, so you won't forget what she looks like. How does that sound?"

"Can we put up a picture of me, too?" Ryan asked. "So Mommy won't forget what *we* look like?"

"Yes, sweetheart, we can," she whispered, kissing the top of his head.

"Where is everyone?" Paul's voice came from the kitchen.

Leah glanced at her watch. She'd been so busy unpacking, the time had slipped away from her. Before she could get off the bed, Paul was standing in the bedroom doorway.

He wore his trench coat, a gift from Diane when he'd been hired by the Seattle daily paper. What decent journalist didn't own a trench coat, she'd teased.

"Ah-ha, here you are," Paul said, crouching down and holding out his arms to his sons. Ryan and Ronnie ran across the room to hurl themselves into their father's embrace.

With a growl Paul stood, lifting both boys off the floor and hugging them close.

"Where's Kelsey?" he asked, lowering the boys.

"Napping." Although now that Leah noted the time, she realized Kelsey was probably awake. She moved into the nursery, and sure enough, the little girl was lying on her back, her hands fluttering gaily. Leah picked her up.

"I see you got everything moved in all right," Paul said, following her into the nursery.

"Almost everything. I'll need to make one last trip in the morning, but that should do it."

"You've got enough room for everything?"

"Plenty," she assured him. Enough room in her heart to nurture these precious children. And what else really mattered?

"Dinner's just about ready," Leah said as she set Kelsey on the changing table and began to remove her soggy diaper.

"I can do it," Paul said, taking over. "You must be exhausted."

"I'm fine, really." But she didn't protest. Giving him some time alone with his daughter, Leah walked into the kitchen.

It was even more difficult for Paul to accept her help now that she was living in his home. She hoped he'd grow accustomed to her being there and wouldn't feel the need to repay her for the "sacrifice" she'd made. Although she'd tried repeatedly, she couldn't make him understand that she didn't consider this an imposition. It was her idea, after all, as she'd reminded him more than once.

Dinner was on the table a few minutes later. Leah had never been much of a cook. There'd been no reason to develop that skill when the only one she was feeding was herself. Until recently, she'd survived on frozen entrées and fast-food dinners. Diane used to claim her unhealthy eating habits would be the end of her. But it wasn't Leah who'd left behind an anguished family.

When they were finished with dinner—a basic chili and an uninspired salad—Paul cleared the table while Leah stacked the dishes in the dishwasher. Wordlessly they worked together while Ryan and Ronnie entertained their sister.

"I wish you'd let me do that," he said as she scrubbed a pot.

"I don't mind." There were only a handful of dishes that needed to be washed by hand, and she'd be done in a few minutes.

"Perhaps *you* don't mind, but *I* do," Paul said, his words taut.

The stark tone of his voice surprised Leah. It wasn't going to be easy, the two of them adjusting to each other's presence.

"All right," she agreed amicably enough. She didn't know what Paul thought of her. She wondered if he had any feelings toward her, one way or the other.

They'd worked together, talked occasionally, grieved together, wept in each other's arms—but when it came to defining their relationship, Leah was at a loss.

She turned off the water and dried her hands. Replacing the dish towel on the wire rack, she glanced over at Paul, her eyes skimming his. In that one brief glance, she saw so much. His fatigue. His pain. His regret.

She was about to leave the room when Paul caught her by the arm. He dropped his hand almost immediately, and for a moment he said nothing. But his meaning was clear.

He was sorry for speaking harshly to her. Leah knew that as surely as she'd ever known anything. Something deep inside her longed to comfort him, assure him that she understood.

The days might pass. But the pain didn't.

"I didn't mean to snap at you," he said.

"I know."

"It's just that…"

"I *know,* Paul. You don't have to explain. You're grateful I'm here and at the same time you wish I wasn't. You aren't going to hurt my feelings. I understand."

Leah did understand; nevertheless his words a few minutes ago had hurt. She knew Paul hadn't meant to be insensitive, and he wasn't unfeeling. But his response to her being there, performing the tasks that had once been his wife's, left her feeling unwanted. Diane was the one he wanted, not Leah.

His reaction stirred once-forgotten inadequacies and brought to life deeply buried resentments, not toward Diane, but toward their mother. Diane had been the beautiful child; Leah was plain, inept. While Diane had been a high school cheerleader, Leah had been shy, studious, a plain Jane. Leah knew she'd embarrassed her mother. Diane was her golden girl, Leah ordinary and unattractive.

The way their mother had favored one sister over the other had hurt Diane more than it had Leah. Leah had worked hard at her studies, received a full scholarship to the University of Washington and graduated with honors. By then their mother was gone, but Diane had been there to cheer her success. She'd always been there to boost Leah's self-confidence.

But she wasn't there anymore.

Later that night, after the boys and Kelsey were asleep, Paul brought Leah a cup of coffee. She was sitting in front of the television mindlessly watching some sitcom, too tired to move. She was physically and mentally exhausted.

For months Paul had carried all responsibility for these children. Leah didn't know how he'd managed for so long.

"Thanks," she said, accepting the steaming mug.

"You look beat."

"I was just wondering where the boys get their energy."

"They're a handful, aren't they?" His smile was filled with fatherly pride, and Leah found herself responding with a smile of her own.

Paul settled on the recliner across from her. He was a good-looking man. His features were imperfect, rugged, but nevertheless appealing. Or maybe appealing *because* of that. It was easy to understand why Diane had fallen in love with him.

Leah would never forget the day Diane had called her from Alaska nearly seven years ago. She'd phoned to tell her she'd married Paul Manning. Leah had been aghast. She'd never met Paul, and her sister, after an all-too-brief courtship, had decided to marry him. Leah was, to say the least, shaken.

They'd always been close. It had hurt that her sister would marry this man without even talking it over. For a time Leah had been furious. Meeting Paul had only partially appeased her. Eventually, though, she'd seen that despite Diane's age, it was a solid marriage. The fact that Paul so obviously loved her had gone a long way toward reassuring Leah.

"You'll get used to the boys' antics," Paul said, interrupting her thoughts.

"Does Ryan usually take his stuffed animals in the bathtub with him?"

Paul grinned. "Not usually."

"I see. So what happened tonight was in my honor?"

"Don't worry, they'll dry. A little the worse for wear, but they will dry."

"What about his blankie? We can't wash it?" Leah hadn't been able to persuade Ryan to let go of it for even an hour to run it through the washing machine. Whenever she suggested it, the four-year-old clung to his stained, torn blanket as if she'd proposed burning the thing—which might not be such a bad idea.

Paul rolled his eyes. "At least Ronnie's thumbs are clean."

Leah chuckled, but she worried about the boys and their unabated need for reassurance.

"We're going to be all right," Paul said, closing his eyes and leaning his head against the back of his chair.

"There were days I wondered but now, for the first time since the funeral, I believe it."

"Me, too."

Paul sighed, straightened, then took a sip of his coffee. After a moment he stared blankly at the television screen.

"I miss Diane most right about now," he said, his voice low. "We used to sit and talk every night after the boys were asleep. She'd tell me about her day, and I'd talk to her about mine. I'd hold her in my arms and we'd relax together, on that sofa you're sitting on now." He shook his head. "I've tried a hundred times to remember the things we said, to resurrect the good feelings I had holding her in my arms. But you know, I can't remember a single word of our conversations."

"It was just having her there, listening, that was important."

Paul nodded. "I suppose you're right." But he didn't sound convinced.

They didn't often talk about Diane. She guessed it was natural that it would happen tonight, her first night in his home.

"You know what *I* miss about her most?" Leah asked.

"No."

"Shopping at the mall."

Paul chuckled. "I should've guessed. I've never been able to understand what it is about shopping that intrigues you women."

"Diane had an incredible knack for finding a bargain."

"You mean she had an incredible knack for spending money, don't you?"

Leah folded her legs under her and smiled. "It wasn't so much the shopping, but the time we spent laughing when we tried on clothes and ordered cheesecake for lunch and then, because we felt guilty, salad for dessert."

Leah's stomach tensed at the pain that came into Paul's eyes. A look that was reflected in her own.

It was supposed to get easier, but she'd never missed her sister more than she did at that moment. Missing Diane hurt so much. For months, Leah had kept the ache of loneliness to herself, not daring to discuss it with Paul, knowing that he, too, was overwhelmed by pain. It was oddly freeing to release some of her own anguish now. To reveal it to the one person who'd completely understand.

"We're going to be all right," Paul said again.

"Yes, I think we will," she murmured.

In their own ways they were coping. How well remained to be seen.

For a long while Paul said nothing.

Neither did Leah.

Paul finished his coffee, then set aside his mug, closing his eyes, visibly relaxed.

Leah finished her coffee too, knowing that if she didn't go to bed immediately, she'd fall asleep right there on the couch.

The day had been even more tiring than she'd realized. Her bones ached from the exertion of moving.

From the fatigue of dealing with the unending demands of two preschoolers and an infant.

"Good night, Paul," she said, unfolding her legs and standing awkwardly. Her feet didn't seem to want to cooperate.

"'Night, Diane."

Three

Diane.

Paul's eyes shot open. For a moment it had almost seemed as if Diane was in the living room with him. As if he were chuckling over Ryan's mischievous nature with his much-loved wife. Then…a slip of the tongue had nearly crippled him with grief.

For an agonizing moment he was at a loss for words. It had been a natural mistake, he supposed. Under the circumstances an understandable mistake. Certainly a forgivable one.

"I'm sorry," he said, looking at Leah, hoping he hadn't offended her.

"No problem," she reassured him with a smile. She headed toward her bedroom.

Paul reached for his coffee and saw that his hand was shaking as he raised the mug to his lips.

Diane.

Sometimes he wondered if the ache of her loss

would ever ease. She'd been gone half a year, yet his grief was as powerful now as it had been that night, the night of her death.

In the time since her funeral, Paul had experienced the full range of emotions. Unleashed fear. Burning anger. Intense sadness. And occasionally a sort of acceptance. Just when he felt he'd moved beyond the pain, something else would happen, and he'd have to deal with each series of emotions all over again, as if facing them for the first time.

He was grateful to Leah, although he hadn't been nearly as gracious as he should've been when she'd offered to move in. He liked Diane's older sister. She was a generous woman, and he'd always be grateful to her for the commitment she'd made to him and the children. Frankly Paul didn't know what he would've done without her.

He recalled the first time he'd met Leah, and how surprised he'd been. He'd expected another Diane. Someone so full of life and laughter that her smile rivaled the brilliance of the sun. He'd imagined she'd be as blond and pretty as his young wife.

Leah was none of those things.

She wasn't unattractive; he wouldn't even describe her as plain. As a writer he should be able to find the right words, yet each one that came to him, he ended up discarding. At one time he'd thought of her as nondescript.

He'd since changed his mind.

There was a subdued radiance to her, a joy that broke through her restraint every so often when he wasn't expecting to see it. It never failed to charm him.

She'd always been Ryan and Ronnie's favorite relative. It had been Leah who'd comforted them when they learned about their mother. It had been Leah who'd encouraged them when Paul had no encouragement to give. It had been Leah who'd cheered them when he didn't know if he'd ever have the strength to laugh again.

That afternoon had been a good example. He'd returned from the office to find her in her bedroom, with the boys gathered around. When he'd walked in, she'd looked up and smiled…and for a moment, the briefest of moments, Paul had felt whole again.

Over coffee that evening he'd experienced that same sense of wholeness, as though the crushing weight he'd been carrying since Diane's death had been eased. Not by much, but enough for some of the numbness to leave his heart.

He owed Leah a debt he couldn't repay in several lifetimes. Although he didn't want to admit it, he was glad she was there with him and the children. He'd promised himself he wouldn't take advantage of her generosity. He'd make sure she had time to herself, time to get away, socialize—do whatever she needed to do to keep her sanity during the next two years.

Her sanity, after all, was essential to his.

A month passed, the easiest weeks for Paul since Diane's death. Each day he felt less embittered, less confused, less depressed. He'd even started thinking about working on his novel again. The anticipation cheered him.

The transition from college professor to house-keeper–mother must've been hard for Leah, but she was managing exceptionally well. Paul was proud of her, proud of the progress she'd made. Her efforts around the house had made a tremendous difference. She'd begun some of the yard work, too, and with Ryan and Ronnie's "help" was planting a garden.

All three children were thriving under her attention and care. Paul couldn't believe the difference in his sons. Ryan actually forgot his blankie sometimes. He was watching cartoons without it one afternoon when Paul had arrived home from work. Ronnie was beside him, and for the first time in recent memory, his son's thumb wasn't in his mouth.

Paul had praised Leah, but she'd quickly dismissed his compliments, claiming the changes in the boys' behavior weren't due solely to her. Although the boys were more secure now that she was there to take care of them, attending the preschool with their neighbor-hood friends had helped, too. And the summer sunshine, she said, had also contributed.

Although Paul didn't really agree with her, he'd let it pass. He definitely attributed the boys' improvement to Leah, but he knew she wasn't comfortable with his appreciation.

He used to think of her as quiet and unassuming. But in the past few weeks he'd realized she was more than that. She was sensitive and loving, and her gentleness was a balm that was healing them all.

The phone on his desk rang, and Paul reached for it.

"Hi there, big brother," a deep voice greeted him.

"Rich, hello." Paul hadn't heard from his brothers much lately. Mostly it was his fault. He'd rejected their efforts to draw him out after Diane's death. Both Rich and Jason were on a softball team and they'd wanted him to join them in a summer league. Paul had nearly laughed out loud. There wasn't time for sports in his life. And the thought of playing softball had seemed ludicrous, considering the loss he'd endured. Paul understood that Rich and Jason were only trying to help, but he hadn't been ready.

"Rich, it's good to hear from you," Paul said, meaning it.

"You might have called me," his brother responded. "I've left you enough messages."

"I know. I'm sorry."

"You're fortunate I'm willing to let you make it up to me."

"I figured you would."

"I'm calling to ask sort of a favor." Some of the teasing left Rich's voice.

"Oh?"

"One of the guys on the softball team, John Duncan— you remember John, don't you? The mechanic from the garage off Seventy-sixth?"

"Yeah." Paul vaguely recalled meeting the guy. "What about him?"

"He has to miss the next two or three games. Jason and I were talking it over and we thought…since Leah's taking care of the kids now, maybe you could get away for a couple of Saturday mornings. If you have to bring the twins, that'd be okay, too. Jamie always comes to the games and I'm sure she wouldn't mind looking after them."

Despite himself, Paul chuckled.

"What's so funny?"

"Richard, Richard, haven't you learned yet?"

"Learned what?"

"Not to volunteer your wife for something until you've checked with her first."

"Oh…right. Listen, the team's desperate. John's a good shortstop, but not as good as you."

"Do you suppose buttering me up's going to help?"

"I was hoping it would," Rich admitted honestly. "Can you do it?"

"Let me get back to you."

"When?"

"This evening," Paul promised.

He was tempted. Leah would encourage him to do it; he knew that without asking.

Maybe he would, Paul decided. Maybe he would.

"You're positive you don't mind?" Paul asked for the third time the following Saturday morning. He couldn't help feeling guilty about abandoning Leah with the kids while he went off to play softball.

"Paul," she chided, smiling up at him. "Go, before I push you out the door. Don't worry about us. The boys and I will have lots of fun."

"Planting a garden sounds more like work to me." A half dozen egg cartons cluttered the kitchen counter. Leah and the boys had been enthusiastically working on this project for weeks.

Somehow they'd gotten him involved. Two week-ends before, he'd found himself spading up a section of the yard for them to use. When he'd finished, Leah and the boys had dumped topsoil and fertilizer on the rough earth, spreading it out as evenly as they could.

Then the eggshells started turning up. One afternoon the three of them had been engrossed in filling halves of eggshells with potting soil and then inserting a single seed. Now the tiny zucchini, cucumber, radish and let-tuce sprouts poked out of the shells.

The seedlings, Leah declared that morning, were now strong enough to be planted outside.

Paul's sons had been delighted with the idea. More than once he'd seen the two of them peering over the kitchen counter, as if they were hoping to catch the seeds bursting instantly into full-grown plants.

"I could bring Kelsey with me," he offered.

"Then she'll go down late for her nap and be crabby. You don't need that." She carried the boys' empty cereal bowls to the sink. "Now, hurry or you'll be late."

Paul drank the last of his coffee. As she strolled past, Leah grabbed the bill of his baseball cap and pushed it down, past his eyes. "Have fun, Mickey Mantle," she teased.

Paul laughed, straightened the cap and grabbed his mitt. It wasn't until he was outside starting his car that he realized he hadn't felt so lighthearted in a long time.

Paul's softball skills were a bit rusty, but he made a diving catch and caught a ground ball that turned the tide of the game. His brothers and temporary teammates slapped him on the back and ran off the field with him.

It felt great to get out like this. To laugh. Strangely, perhaps, he didn't feel guilty about having fun. It felt right to be with his brothers.

Jamie, Rich's wife, had packed a picnic lunch for after the game. She invited Paul to join her, Jason and Rich, but he declined, anxious to return home. Jamie and Rich's little girl, Bethany, was spending the day with Jamie's mother, so they were free to enjoy an all-adults afternoon.

Jason had eagerly accepted their invitation, and Paul was glad to see it—his two brothers together—his sister-in-law so pleasant and kind. Although Jamie had been part of the family for almost two years, it never ceased to surprise him that his play-the-field brother had married her. Of the three of them, Rich had been blessed with the best looks. His tall, compelling presence had garnered him attention from the opposite sex since high school. In fact, that was where he and Jamie had become friends. Good friends. And their friendship had eventually led to marriage.

Paul liked his sister-in-law a great deal. Compared to Rich's other girlfriends, she seemed so…unpretentious, even a little ordinary. In many ways she was like Leah.

He sighed as he thought of Diane's sister. Leah, ordinary? There was nothing ordinary about her! And, to be fair, Jamie was pretty special, too. Maybe it was that still-waters-run-deep thing, but these were self-confident, compassionate women, both of them.

A grateful tenderness took hold of him as he considered the changes Leah had brought to his life in the past month. The changes she'd made in his children's lives. Her warmth had largely gone unnoticed by him until she'd moved in. Her optimism. Her smile, too.

There was something about her smile that defied description. The way it subtly lifted the corners of her mouth and then made its way into her eyes. He'd always thought Leah's eyes were plain, an unremarkable hazel. Now he knew better, and he found her eyes, with their changeable color, fascinating. If she wore green, her eyes seemed green. If she had on a blue sweater or shirt, her eyes showed hints of blue. If she wore something dark, the brown highlights revealed themselves.

Her eyes were a lot like Leah herself, Paul decided. Adaptable. Multifaceted.

He'd come to know Leah in the past month. Really *know* her. Appreciate her and her quiet ways. He'd tried to analyze what had happened to him since her arrival in his home, but he couldn't quite figure it out. When she'd first arrived, he'd been consumed with his grief, almost afraid to let go of it. What was left for him if he didn't have his grief? Emptiness? A looming black hole of *nothing*.

After the first week with Leah, he noticed there'd be periods of time without the harsh pain. He'd feel almost free. Then something would remind him of Diane, of how lonely he was without her, and the pain would return full force. He thought about this new emotional pattern.

Pain.

No pain.

Pain again, but not as intense as before.

Then gone again.

Paul found it curious that Diane's sister could have brought about so dramatic a difference. More curious still that someone who was practically a stranger to him could ease his misery.

He pulled into the driveway of his home, eager to see Leah and the children. Eager to see their progress with the garden. He put his softball mitt in the hall closet and grabbed a cold soda from the refrigerator. He was tasting his first swallow when he happened to look out the sliding glass door.

And froze.

The can was poised in front of his mouth as he watched the scene in the garden. Kelsey was sitting in her stroller, small arms stretched upward, attempting to catch a butterfly. The boys were digging with hand shovels, intent on their task, with Leah looking on, laughing at something one of them said.

The sound of her laughter drifted toward him, and Paul swore he'd never heard anything more beautiful in his life.

She was wearing faded jeans and a short-sleeved green shirt. She'd left the last two buttons unfastened and knotted the tails at her waist. Her hair was caught by the breeze, and the sunshine cast an iridescent glow through the fine strands.

Paul's heart constricted, but not with the pain he was accustomed to feeling. He almost wished it *was* pain. He knew how to deal with that, how to react. But it wasn't pain he felt now.

It was desire.

A desire so gut-wrenching it took his breath away.

It wasn't anything as simple as sexual need. He'd never thought of Leah in those terms, never considered making love to anyone other than his wife, who was seven months in the grave. What he was feeling was an emotion totally outside his experience. Bigger than mere desire, bigger than the contentment of companionship or the sharing of grief. Bigger than Leah and him.

Strange as it seemed, he felt an overwhelming urge to sit down and weep. Tears burned for release, tightening his chest, stinging his eyes. With effort he was able to hold them at bay.

Hours later Paul still wasn't sure what it was about that scene that had struck him so hard. Perhaps simply the beauty of those moments. The sky had been bright blue, the sunshine beaming down like God's smile on those he cherished most. His children, who were quietly happy as they scrabbled in the dirt or grasped at butterflies. And Leah…

It came to Paul then, as he sat at his desk, looking over some bills and bank statements. He understood now. What had affected him so strongly was…life. How glorious life could be. How beautiful. How precious.

For months he'd been in the dark, lingering in the coolness of the shadows. The sudden contrast between light and dark seemed so profound.

When Leah had first come to his house, Paul had been dying. He'd wanted to die with Diane. A month had passed and he'd discovered, much to his surprise, that he wanted to live.

* * *

Leah's shoulders ached. She'd spent most of the morning working in the garden with the boys. Not used to that kind of physical exercise, she supposed it was little wonder that her muscles were rebelling. After lunch, she'd taken a long, hot shower and changed her clothes. The boys were tired; they'd gone down for their nap with hardly any complaints.

The house was quiet. Paul was working in his den, the boys and Kelsey were asleep, and Leah settled in a living room chair with her library book. Reading for pleasure was something she'd missed over the past few years. But no more than five minutes into the first chapter, her eyes kept drifting shut.

She woke shortly after three, puzzled to find a blanket draped over her shoulders.

"Good afternoon, Sleeping Beauty," Paul teased when she opened her eyes.

Sitting up, disoriented, Leah glanced around. The last thing she remembered was setting aside her book and resting her eyes. Only for a moment, she'd promised herself.

"The garden looks great," Paul was saying.

Leah's smile was filled with pride. "Thank you. The boys and I worked hard."

"I can tell. They're awake, by the way."

"And hungry, too, no doubt." She began to fold the blanket, ready to get up and meet the demands of her nephews.

"Don't worry about it. We walked down to the store for ice-cream bars. Kelsey went along for the ride."

"Is Leah awake yet?" Ryan asked as he bounded into the living room. He sent her a wide grin when he saw that she was. "Did you tell her about the surprise?" he asked, looking up at his father.

"Not yet."

"What surprise?"

"It's nothing big," Paul explained. "We brought you back an ice-cream bar. I hope you like double fudge."

"I love it. Thank you, Paul." She smiled up at him and, closing her eyes, stretched her arms high above her head and yawned.

When she'd opened her eyes, she saw that he was still watching her. He was frowning, though, which she hadn't seen him do lately. He turned abruptly and hurried into the kitchen.

Leah followed. Ronnie and Ryan dragged a chair over to the fridge and both of them stood on it, squabbling as they opened the freezer. They took out the ice-cream bar they'd bought for her and carried it over to her, each holding one end. Sitting at the table, she opened the small box. The ice cream had melted a little on the walk home.

Paul pulled out a chair, turned it around and straddled it, resting his arms along the back. "When's the last time you talked to Rob?" he asked unexpectedly.

"Rob?" she repeated, wondering why Paul would ask about him. "I don't know. I haven't thought about it."

"Don't you think it's time the two of you went out?"

"No." Contrary to what Paul seemed to believe, her relationship with Rob didn't involve any real commitment. Which must seem strange to someone like her brother-in-law, who felt so deeply about people and things.

"Shouldn't you call him, then?"

"Not really."

Paul frowned again. "Don't you care about him?"

She shrugged. "Yes, but…"

"Then call." He moved off the chair, got one of the portable phones and handed it to her.

"All right, all right," she said with a resigned sigh. She didn't know why it was so important, all of a sudden, for her to call Rob, but in an effort to appease Paul, she'd do it.

As it turned out, Rob sounded pleased to hear from her and suggested they go to a movie that evening. When she mentioned it to Paul, he seemed pleased. More than pleased—relieved.

She found his response odd, but shrugged it off.

"You look nice," he told her when she'd changed for her date several hours later. He was reading the paper, the very one that employed him, when Rob arrived.

Rob, in his mid-forties, had never been what Leah would call her "heartthrob." She doubted that he'd ever been any woman's heartthrob. Tonight he wore a gray cardigan—the same one he'd worn every time they'd gone out, other than to faculty dinners, for the past three years.

Leah introduced the two men. Rob stepped forward and shook Paul's hand, but he seemed a bit nervous, Leah noted, which she hadn't expected.

The boys each wanted a hug, then started to follow

her to the door. Paul distracted them and she was able to leave without giving them a chance to ask Rob a lot of questions.

The evening was clear and bright. June weather was generally mild in the Pacific Northwest, and this June was no exception.

"It's good to see you again," Rob said as he helped her into the car. He'd always been a gentleman, and it was the small touches, the old-fashioned manners, that made him so endearing. No one was going to define sex appeal using Rob Mullins as an example, but he was considerate and kind.

"It's good to see you, too," she said with a slight smile.

He walked around the front of the car and joined her in the front seat. "The college seems lonely without you."

"Summer term's pretty slow anyway," she said briskly, not wanting to make too much of his words.

"True, but I always knew you'd be back come fall. It's not going to be the same without you, Leah."

He surprised her by blushing. This was probably the most romantic thing he'd said to her in the three years they'd been seeing each other.

Rob seemed flustered as he inserted the key in the ignition. Leah fastened her seat belt and as Rob backed out of the driveway, a movement in the front window caught Leah's eye.

The twins, grubby hands pressing against the pane, were staring at her. She smiled and waved.

Ryan waved back. Ronnie didn't.

Instead, his thumb went into his mouth.

Leah sighed. Ronnie hardly ever sucked his thumb these days.

Her eyes were still on the window when Paul appeared, standing behind his sons. His gaze connected with hers, and something indefinable passed between them. The power of that moment left Leah breathless.

Her pulse burst into a rapid-fire speed.

Could it be regret she read in Paul's eyes? That made no sense. Maybe he was only reliving his early carefree days with Diane. Or—maybe—he still felt guilty about interfering with what he persisted in calling Leah's "social life." Anyway, the moment was too brief to be sure of what he might have meant.

What it was, if it was anything at all, Leah couldn't say. By then Rob had driven past the house and the moment was lost.

Leah dropped her gaze to her hands, tightly clenched in her lap. Could it be that Paul *hadn't* wanted her to go out with Rob? That was ridiculous. He'd practically arranged the date himself.

She and Rob had a pleasant enough evening, watching a popular new romantic comedy, but that look she'd exchanged with Paul was never far from her mind.

Although it was shortly after ten when Rob drove her home, the house was dark and quiet.

"Would you like to come in for coffee?" she asked.

"Not tonight, thanks."

Leah hated to admit how grateful she was. They hadn't had much time to talk, thanks to the movie. But although Rob hadn't said much, Leah knew he felt uneasy about her living situation. He didn't ask her any direct questions about Paul, but he'd hinted that he feared something romantic might be developing between Leah and her brother-in-law.

She'd let his insinuations go unanswered. To deny anything would have invited argument. If it hadn't been so completely ludicrous a suggestion, Leah might have laughed.

Paul had loved Diane. Her sister had been beautiful and vivacious; Leah was neither. Diane had been witty and charming; Leah lacked both skills. After loving Diane, there was little chance Paul would ever feel anything more than gratitude for Leah. Deep, heart-felt gratitude, to be sure, but just gratitude nonetheless.

"Could I see you again soon?" Rob asked her, sounding a bit flustered.

"Of course."

"Next week?"

"That would be fine."

Rob grinned. "I'll give you a call, then…say, Monday evening?"

"I'll be here."

He climbed out of the car and walked around to her side to open the door. He offered her his hand, which she accepted, and escorted her to the front door. Once again he seemed a little ill at ease. Was he planning to kiss her good-night? she wondered. They'd only kissed occasionally. Light kisses. Nothing urgent and certainly nothing close to passionate.

Rob put his arms around her waist and pulled her

closer. He gave her the opportunity to object and, when she didn't, he brought his mouth down to hers. It was by far the most ardent kiss they'd ever shared. But Leah had the feeling that he was testing her with it, trying to ascertain whether there was anything romantic between her and Paul.

He broke off the kiss and stared down at her, as if reading her expression.

"Good night, Rob," she said, breaking free of his crushing embrace. "I'll talk to you next week."

Rob released her immediately. "Okay," he said breathlessly. "I'll phone you Monday."

Leah let herself in and, leaning against the door, she sighed. Not with pleasure, but with relief. The movie had been entertaining, and Paul was right—it probably did her good to get away for a few hours. But she hadn't enjoyed herself as much as she'd thought she would.

There hadn't been a lot of opportunity for conversation, of course, but she'd been rather bored with what there was. Rob had seemed—she hated to say it—dull. If he wasn't hinting at a romance between her and Paul, he was making her sound like a martyr for moving in with Paul and the children. It had made Leah uncomfortable.

She saw a sliver of light from under the door to Paul's office and was half-tempted to politely tell him she was home.

Before she could make up her mind, Paul came out.

"I thought I heard you," he said, greeting her with a warm smile. He smiled more often these days, and she marveled at how it changed his whole face—although it never quite seemed to cut through the pain in his eyes.

"I'm home," she announced, feeling slightly nervous and not knowing why.

"How was it?"

"Fine. We went to a movie." She told him which movie they'd seen and added a comment about the lead actors.

Paul nodded and buried his hands in his pockets, striking a relaxed pose. "I'm glad you got out of the house for a few hours."

"You're just feeling guilty about playing softball with your brothers this morning," she said with a slight laugh. "Would you like some coffee? I can make decaf."

"Yeah," he said, following her into the kitchen, "I would."

"Instant okay?"

"Sure."

Leah filled two mugs with water and stuck them in the microwave.

"You should've invited Rob in."

"I did," she said, her back to him as she punched the buttons on the microwave.

"So why didn't he come inside?"

Leah shrugged. "I don't know."

"Because of me?"

"He didn't say." She turned around and folded her arms, waiting for the timer to go off so she could add instant coffee to the hot water.

"You'll be seeing him again, won't you? Soon?"

Four

"**Y**es," Leah confirmed, frowning. It bothered her that Paul seemed so eager to have her out of his home. "Rob and I will be going out again soon."

Paul nodded. "Good idea."

"Good idea?" Leah laughed as she finished stirring decaffeinated instant coffee into the hot water. "Why?" she asked as she handed Paul a mug.

He led the way to the kitchen table and pulled out a chair for her. "It eases my mind."

His answer made no sense to Leah. He must've read the question in her eyes, because he elaborated.

"There's nothing I can do to reimburse you for everything you've done, Leah. I can't afford to pay you."

"Paul…"

"I don't own anything valuable enough to give you."

"But Paul—"

"It seems like such a little thing to encourage you to

get out every once in a while. I want to be sure you have ample opportunity to do so."

Paul lowered his gaze to his coffee, his hands enclosing the mug.

"It hasn't been so bad." Leah wished she knew of some way to reassure him. Yes, it had taken her a few weeks to work out a schedule for the children, and yes, she was usually exhausted by the end of the day. But she wasn't making some noble sacrifice, as Paul and Rob were implying. Mothering these children was something she *wanted* to do. Already she was reaping rewards beyond anything she'd imagined.

"I want you to have fun," Paul said emphatically.

"Oh, Paul," she breathed. "Don't you think I am? Kelsey, the boys and I had a marvelous time today planting our garden. I'll have those memories all my life. This morning with the children was the most wonderful part of my day—not my date with Rob."

"You should slow down, then," he continued gruffly. "There's no need to keep the house and yard spotless. I feel guilty enough as it is without you working all hours of the day and night."

If Leah had ever heard an exaggeration, this was it. Her housekeeping skills could best be described as adequate. Her interest in planting a garden had come about as the result of a project the boys had brought home from preschool—a seedling inside a Dixie cup. She'd worked hard on the garden, yes, but it was a labor of love.

She couldn't, *wouldn't* slow down. It was partly because of her sense of duty, partly her need to keep busy. Other than summer holidays, this was her first work experience outside a classroom since she was five years old. There was a whole lot for her to learn, to explore.

"I'm enjoying myself."

Paul looked as though he didn't quite believe her.

"I am, honest." She leaned forward and placed her hand on his forearm in an effort to convince him. The action had been instinctive, but the instant her hand touched Paul's arm, Leah realized it was a mistake. She wasn't sure why, except that her heart leapt.

Even hours later, as she lay awake in bed, her mind refused to let go of that moment. She'd removed her hand immediately, and the conversation had continued, but something had changed.

Only Leah didn't know what it was.

She wasn't good when it came to relationships. She'd never been good with them. She recognized love; love was easy. Her feelings toward Kelsey and the twins were as strong as any mother's. Diane might have given birth to the children, but Leah was the one taking care of them now, and her protectiveness toward them was fierce.

In some ways she supposed she loved Paul, too. But on a different level. One that was less clear, less straightforward.

They'd bonded. That was the only logical explanation for what had happened to her when she touched his arm. They'd been through so much together. The trauma of Diane's death. Her funeral. And now the

314 Debbie Macomber

raising of the children. Naturally that had created a bond between them.

This bonding phenomenon, this closeness they now shared, would explain the physical response she'd felt when she touched him. It wasn't a sexual response. Or was it? Leah didn't know. If she'd had more experience with relationships, she might be able to define it better.

Rob had touched her that night, too. His kiss had been probing and urgent. She hadn't liked it, had wanted to rub her lips and erase it when he'd finished.

But with Paul, her senses had leapt to life, and she'd been intimately aware of him. Their eyes had met, and his had stared relentlessly into hers.

Rob had kissed her, and she hadn't felt a fraction of the sensation she had when she'd briefly touched Paul's arm. It was Rob she was dating, though. Rob she'd be spending time with. Rob who'd asked her out.

Now that she had time to think about it, Leah realized she'd prefer it if Rob didn't phone her next week. His insinuations about her and Paul had insulted her. And yet…maybe there was some truth to them, although she hardly dared to express it. If it *was* true, that bothered her even more. It just seemed…wrong.

Leah felt trapped.

Rob seemed eager to continue their relationship while she felt content without him, satisfied to put everything between them on hold. True, she'd been the one to contact him, but only because Paul had insisted.

It was obviously important to Paul—a matter of pride, even—that she continue to see Rob. As though this was the one thing he could do to ease her load.

Nothing she'd said had persuaded him that she was pleased with the status quo.

Her inability to describe her feelings adequately frustrated Leah. For the first time since Diane's death, she felt that her anguish had begun to lift. The children had raised her spirits, returning to her the gift of laughter. It felt so good to wrap her arms around them, to let go of her grief.

Leah smiled to herself in the dark. She hadn't thought of it in those terms before. Being with the children meant she was absorbed by *their* needs. And because she had to consider their feelings ahead of her own, she found herself grieving less. Not that she didn't miss Diane just as much, but that loss no longer felt like an open wound.

Leah couldn't be around the children and continue the melancholy patterns that grief had brought into her life. *She* was the one who'd benefited from coming to live with them. Now if only she could make Paul understand that….

As he'd promised, Rob called Leah Monday evening, right after she'd finished clearing the dinner dishes. Paul answered the phone and, without a word, handed her the receiver. Although he left the kitchen to give her privacy, she couldn't shake the feeling that wherever he was, he'd be able to listen to her side of the conversation.

"Hello, Leah."

"Hi, Rob."

"How are you?"

"Fine, thanks. You?"

"Good."

She wondered if their conversation could get any more banal. "I'm glad to hear it."

"Will you be free Saturday evening?"

"Ah…yes. I shouldn't have any problem getting away." Paul would make sure of that.

"Great. What about a poetry reading in Blaine? I know it's a bit of a drive, and we probably won't get back until late, but I think the effort will be worth it."

"That sounds…nice." It sounded boring, but Leah didn't feel she had any other option. If she made an excuse, Rob would be convinced there really *was* something between her and Paul. And Paul seemed to find it vitally important that she date Rob.

Leah didn't have a lot of friends. Her best friend had always been her sister, and her only other really close friend, Linda Potter, was traveling in Europe this summer. Getting out with Linda occasionally might have eased Paul's concern, but since she was away, Leah was stuck with Rob.

"Wonderful. I'll pick you up around six, then," Rob said.

They spoke for a few more minutes, the same insipid comments that had marked the beginning of the call. Leah hung up, wondering what it was about Rob that had ever interested her. Instinctively she realized they were destined to be no more than casual friends. She also realized it wasn't Rob who'd changed, but her.

No sooner had she ended the conversation than Paul entered the kitchen, his eyes searching hers.

"That was Rob," she explained unnecessarily.

"I gathered as much," he said, revealing no emotion.

"We're going out again on Saturday evening." She didn't have the courage to tell him it was to a poetry reading for fear Paul might laugh, and then she would, too. And laughter between them would be so intimate.

The doorbell chimed just then, and Paul, looking as though he meant to say something else, left to answer it. Leah didn't know if she should be grateful for the interruption or not.

She was arranging the last of the plates in the dishwasher when Elizabeth Manning walked into the kitchen, smiling affectionately when she saw her.

"Hello, Leah."

"Hello!" She greeted Paul's mother warmly, drying her hands on a kitchen towel. Before Diane's death, the Manning parents had been mere acquaintances, but over the past few months Leah had come to love and appreciate them. "When did you get back?"

"This morning."

At the sound of their grandmother's voice, the twins raced out of the back bedroom and hurled themselves at Elizabeth's legs, shrieking with excitement.

Elizabeth laughed and reached down to hug her two grandsons.

Leah smiled at the boys' glee. They'd missed their grandparents. After she'd come to live with Paul, the older Mannings had taken a two-week trip down the Oregon coast in their motor home.

"There's coffee made," Leah said, getting four cups while Elizabeth gave the twins two giant seashells she'd brought back for them. Ryan and Ronnie were thrilled with their gifts. They dragged their grandmother down the hallway to show her the picture of their mother that Leah had put up on the bedroom wall.

When she'd finished pouring the coffee, Leah carried the tray into the living room, where Paul was sitting with his father. He glanced up and smiled at her.

Elizabeth returned with the twins and they all sat down. Elizabeth and Eric were on the couch, with the boys at their feet. Paul was in his recliner and Leah across from him. Kelsey was crawling around on the floor, and after a moment Elizabeth picked her up. Kelsey struggled momentarily, but settled down in Elizabeth's lap to investigate her necklace and then taste it.

"It's good to be home," Eric was saying to Paul. "I suppose we should've phoned first, but we were eager to see how everything was working out for you."

"We're fine, Dad." Paul's eyes drifted to Leah.

It *had* been going well, better than either Paul or Leah had expected. There'd been adjusting on both their parts, but they'd created a comfortable routine. The children were thriving. For a long moment Leah and Paul simply stared at each other.

Leah suddenly realized she needed to say something to break the silence. "Everything is going just great," she confirmed, clearing her throat. She was grateful when Ryan clambered onto her lap. Not wanting to be outdone by his brother, Ronnie joined him. Leah had to peek out from behind the boys' backs. "The twins and I visited the school earlier this week and registered for kindergarten classes."

"We went to the big kids' school," Ryan said eagerly.

"Since the boys have summer birthdays, I was a little concerned about whether they'd be ready for kindergarten," Leah explained.

"But Leah had them tested, and it looks like everything's a go," Paul said, sounding pleased.

"Although I did request the morning session," Leah added. "The boys still need their naps."

"We do not," Ronnie denied righteously. "I'm almost five." He held up his hand, splaying his fingers. Ryan quickly imitated his brother.

"I remember when my boys were that age," Elizabeth said, smiling broadly. "Your daddy felt the same way. 'Five's too old to nap,' he insisted, but I put him down every afternoon because I needed the peace and quiet myself."

"I'm thirty-six years old," Paul said, looking at Leah, eyebrows raised, "and my mother still tells tales about me."

"I always will," Elizabeth told him. "It doesn't matter how old you are, you'll always be my little boy."

Paul's parents left an hour later, after relaying a few of their adventures along the Oregon coast. The visit was a good one.

Leah envied Paul his family. He was close to his siblings and parents. Leah and Diane only had each other. Their mother suffered from a personality disorder, and their father had abandoned the family when the girls were barely old enough to remember him. Leah's grandparents lived on the other side of the country, and she could recall visiting them only once. They'd died while she was in her teens.

Diane had loved Paul's family, too. She'd never complained about problems with her in-laws, and made a point of giving Paul ample opportunity to do things with Jason and Rich, his two younger brothers.

Leah wasn't well acquainted with Paul's siblings, but she knew they'd all pulled together—particularly the boys who, unlike the sisters, lived in Seattle—to help Paul after Diane's death. Paul's pride had stood in the way, and he'd systematically rebuffed their efforts. He'd grudgingly accepted hers, Leah realized, because he'd had no other option.

Things were better now. They'd all begun to adapt. The changes that were taking place in their lives were positive ones and for that, Leah was grateful.

The following Saturday, Paul was in a foul mood— and he didn't know why. The day had started well, but by evening it had deteriorated. Leah's date had arrived shortly after dinner, and Paul had barely been able to look at the man.

Ryan had wanted ice cream sometime later, and for no reason at all, Paul found himself saying no. The boys had looked shocked when he snapped at them and quickly retreated to their bedroom.

Feeling guilty, Paul had gone in after them, apologized and then together they'd dished up huge bowls of ice cream. The boys had put on their own toppings and smeared chocolate syrup all over the counter. Paul had conscientiously cleaned up the mess.

He didn't want Leah coming home from her night on the town to find the kitchen a disaster.

He thought back over his day, which had been a good one. That further confused Paul. If he'd had to cope with one frustrating event after another, he might be entitled to a foul mood. But he hadn't.

That morning he'd played softball with his brothers. He'd forgotten how much he enjoyed sports, and was disappointed that John Duncan would be returning the next week.

Leah and the kids had surprised him by coming to the park to watch the last couple of innings. It felt great to hear Leah cheering him from the stands. In all the time he'd known his sister-in-law, he'd never heard her raise her voice. He'd played his best when Leah and the kids were there, and afterward, for a treat, he'd taken everyone out to McDonald's.

The afternoon didn't explain his rotten mood, either. He'd repaired the screen in Kelsey's bedroom without a hitch. He'd even had time to mow the lawn. The twins had followed him with their plastic mowers, blowing bubbles into the bright June sunshine.

Leah was in the backyard with Kelsey, planting the herbs she'd picked up at the local nursery. She'd never grown them before and wanted to see how well they did. He'd teased her about having a green thumb, and the sound of her laughter had lingered long after he'd gone into the house.

Before he knew it, dinner was on the table and Leah was getting ready for her date with Rob Mullins. Paul had tried to act nonchalant. He was happy she was going out, wasn't he? Hell, making sure her social life continued was the least he could do. He had to give her a chance to get away from the daily grind of looking after the house and the kids.

Rob seemed like a decent enough guy. A bit on the boring side, but then he hadn't expected a math professor to be a stand-up comedian.

Once the kids were asleep, Paul went into his den and turned on the computer to work on his novel.

He should be thrilled about the opportunity. Overjoyed.

But he wasn't.

His attention span was short, his thoughts on everything but his novel. He worked late, forcing himself to review the five chapters he'd written before Diane's death, making a few changes and corrections as he went.

It was well past eleven when he finished reading. The novel was good. At least he thought it was, but what did he know? Not much, he decided.

He had no reason to delay going to bed, but was strangely reluctant to do so. The boys would be awake before six; he'd told them to crawl into bed with him when they woke up and let Leah sleep.

He checked on the kids, who were sleeping soundly, and glanced at his watch, wondering how much longer Leah would be out. She hadn't told him what time she'd be back, and he hadn't asked. Not that it was any of his business…

He sat down in the living room with a novel he'd been wanting to read, but his mind kept wandering. The image of Rob taking Leah in his arms and kissing her sprang, fully formed, into his mind.

Without understanding why, Paul was furious. He slammed the book shut and stood abruptly, his chest heaving with exertion. If Rob was kissing Leah, it had nothing to do with him.

Clenching his fists, he sank back into the chair and opened his book. It didn't make any difference. The anger simmered just below the surface, looking for an excuse to erupt...but there wasn't anyone to pick a fight with. Except himself.

He was going to stay awake and wait for her, Paul decided. He didn't care how late she was; he was going to sit right in this chair until she was home. If she didn't come home...well, he'd deal with that when the time came. He'd have to do some serious thinking about the situation if it turned out Leah spent the night with Rob Mullins. He didn't want an immoral woman raising his children, he thought heatedly.

Leah? Immoral? *Come on!* Paul wanted to kick himself. He'd never known anyone more forthright and honest.

He heard a car door closing, and his heart went into a panic. He leapt off the chair as if he'd been doing something illegal. If Leah invited Rob inside, he didn't want them to think he was waiting up for her.

Hiding in his bedroom and turning off the lights wouldn't work, either. They would've already noticed the lamp on in the living room.

Thinking quickly, Paul dashed into Kelsey's room. Carefully, so as not to wake her, he scooped her up from the crib and hurried back to his chair, holding his small sleeping daughter in his arms.

He'd been seated no more than a couple of seconds when Leah slipped quietly inside the house. She paused when she saw him and Kelsey, her expression immediately worried.

"Is she sick? I knew I shouldn't have left her when she was teething." The concern in her voice eased Paul's loathsome temper. He glanced down at the slumbering infant. If Kelsey's teeth were bothering her, he hadn't known it. She'd been a perfect baby all evening.

"She's been fussy this week," Leah said, looking guilty. "I'm sorry I—"

"Kelsey's fine...now," Paul said, gently placing his daughter against his shoulder and patting her back. He felt like a fool playing this game with Leah—a fool and a jerk—but he didn't have the courage to tell her the truth. "I was just going to put her back to bed."

"Was she up all evening fussing?"

"Not all evening," he said, hating himself for the deception.

"I could use a cup of tea," Leah said, hanging her sweater in the hall closet. "How about you?"

"That sounds good," he answered in a whisper. He carried Kelsey back to her bedroom and put her in the crib.

When he returned to the kitchen, Leah had set the kettle on the burner and was getting two mugs.

She looked lovely this evening, Paul mused, shoving his hands in his pockets as he watched her graceful movements. She looked...he searched for the right word. *Beautiful,* he decided. For reasons he couldn't explain, he'd never thought of Leah as beautiful before.

She turned to smile at him and he was lost. Lost in her wistfully intriguing smile.

Leah swallowed and glanced away.

Paul shook himself out of his trance and walked to the other side of the kitchen, opening the refrigerator and taking out the milk. He didn't drink his tea with milk, but he needed an excuse to leave her and that one conveniently presented itself.

"I was thinking," he said, setting the milk carton in the center of the table.

"Oh?"

"You should marry Rob." Paul wouldn't have surprised himself more had he suggested they jump off the Tacoma Narrows Bridge together. It was the last thing he wanted. It would be disastrous to the children if Leah left now. Disastrous to him, too.

"Marry Rob?" she echoed, astonished.

"He seems okay." That sounded like faint praise, but he'd sound like a fool if he said the suggestion had been a joke. Given no other option, he took his own stupid idea even further.

"Rob's not the marrying kind," she said.

"Why not?"

She shrugged. "He was married before, and apparently it was a bad experience."

"What about you, Leah?" Paul didn't know why he couldn't leave the subject alone. He didn't know why he felt the need to pursue it again and again, when it was the very thing he dreaded most.

"What *about* me?"

"You should be married." For reasons he couldn't

begin to explain, he felt strangely relieved bringing the subject out in the open. He'd never understood why Leah hadn't married. She was generous. Unselfish. She had a sense of humor and she was easygoing—and she loved kids. He'd watched her with the children all these months, and thanked God with every breath he drew that she was there with him.

Leah frowned at his remark. "I guess I'm a lot like Rob. I'm not the marrying kind."

"I don't believe that."

She carried the pot of tea to the table and filled their mugs. Pulling out her chair, she sat down. "I've never been in love."

"Why not?"

Leah laughed. "I don't know. It just never happened."

"How *do* you feel about Rob?"

She shook her head. "I can't see myself in love with him. He's too self-involved. We'll never be anything more than friends."

"Did you have a good time this evening?"

"Fair." She lowered her gaze, and Paul thought he might have detected a blush. "I…I don't think I'll be seeing Rob again." She said it as if she expected an argument from him.

"Why not?"

"Because…I have my reasons. Do you mind if we discuss something else?"

"Sure, I mean…no, I don't mind. I don't mean to pry." Mysteriously, the dark mood that had been weighing down on him all evening suddenly lifted. Paul didn't want to analyze his feelings. He hadn't said anything to Leah earlier, but he wasn't all that impressed with Rob. Asked for specifics, he couldn't have defined his feelings, other than to say he simply didn't feel the other man was right for Leah.

"How'd everything go with the kids tonight?" she asked in a blatant effort to change the subject.

"Good. They all went down without a problem."

"Did Ryan take his blankie to bed with him?"

Paul chuckled. "He made a gallant effort to go without it, but in the end he succumbed."

Leaning back in her chair, Leah took a sip of her tea. "I suspect if Ryan took his blankie to bed with him, then Ronnie figured he had every right to suck his thumb."

"Naturally." Paul smiled and drank his own tea. "I worked on my novel this evening," he said almost shyly. He wasn't sure why he'd even mentioned his book to Leah. He'd given up analyzing the things he said; he only knew it was something he wanted to tell her.

"How's it coming?"

"Better than I thought."

"How far are you into it?"

"Five chapters—a hundred and ten pages, to be exact. I've been doing a bit of revising."

"What's it about?"

Her interest seemed genuine; otherwise Paul wouldn't have bored her with the details. The story had begun to take shape in his mind long before he'd decided to write it down. It was a thriller with an ex-military hero, a reporter heroine and a plot that involved the illegal arms trade, the Russian mafia and the Middle East.

Leah listened intently, then asked him several

thought-provoking questions. Paul answered them as best he could, amazed at her insight. Grateful, too, because she'd pointed out a major plot weakness he'd overlooked.

The next time he glanced at his watch it was nearly one. Paul was astonished by that. They'd been talking for an hour and a half.

"My goodness," Leah said, looking at her own watch. "I had no idea it was so late."

"Me, neither."

They both stood and walked toward the sink. Leah set her cup down first, then Paul followed with his. But when she turned, apparently she didn't realize he was directly behind her. To keep from colliding with him, she jerked back.

Paul's arms instinctively reached out to steady her. His hands closed over her shoulders.

They both froze.

For a long moment neither moved. Paul's eyes drifted slowly over Leah's flushed features. Her arms were raised, her hands braced against his chest. Her breasts—

Stop! Paul chastised himself. He shouldn't be thinking such things. Not about Leah.

"Are you all right?" he asked once he found his voice. He could hardly breathe, hardly think. All he seemed capable of was feeling.

"I'm fine." Her words were scarcely audible, and she was slightly breathless. Her eyes continued to hold his.

Paul knew he should release her. He knew he'd held

on to her much longer than necessary. He knew…he knew he was going to kiss her.

Before he could stop himself, before his control slipped back into place, Paul lowered his mouth to hers.

Five

Paul felt as though someone had carved out his insides. He felt empty…no, it wasn't emptiness he was feeling, but he couldn't identify the intense, unfamiliar emotions that raged through him.

He abruptly dropped his arms, letting go of Leah. Wordlessly they stepped away from each other. He saw how swollen her lips were. Her beautiful eyes, more green than brown, were wide and staring up at him.

He wanted to tell her he was sorry, beg her forgiveness, but he couldn't make himself do it. She looked at him unblinking, her face devoid of color.

Then, just as he found the courage to talk to her, she edged her way past him and hurried down the hallway to her bedroom. She closed her door with a resounding bang—which told him how upset she was, otherwise she would never have risked waking the children.

Paul considered going after her, to explain, only he didn't know what he could say that would excuse what he'd done. He waited a few minutes until he could control the trembling in his hands, then turned off the lights and headed down the hallway to his room.

But he hesitated outside Leah's door. Clenching his fists at his sides, he silently berated himself.

He could've stopped himself from kissing her, yet he hadn't. He'd given in to the impulse, knowing full well he'd be faced with regrets later. None of that had mattered at the time. He'd wanted to kiss her. He'd *needed* to kiss her.

He'd pulled her into his arms, touching every inch of her body with his own, adding to his excitement.

Adding to his guilt.

Her right hand had moved from his chest to caress his face. How warm her fingers had felt against his skin. How smooth.

How right.

It was then that he'd deepened the kiss and she'd given a small gasp—Paul didn't know if it was in pleasure or surprise.

Whatever control Paul possessed, which admittedly was darn little, had been lost at that moment. He'd thrust his hands into her hair and hungrily slanted his mouth over hers. Leah's response was undeniable.

He couldn't make himself break away. Couldn't make himself *want* to break away. Her tongue had shyly darted forward, and the kiss became even deeper.

Paul knew he had to end it now. Before they went beyond kissing…

He tore his mouth from hers. They were both gasping

for breath, their shoulders heaving. The look on Leah's face would haunt him to the grave.

He saw her shock. Her confusion. But what hurt the most was the self-loathing he could see in her eyes. Perhaps it was just a reflection of his own. Paul didn't know anymore.

Defeated, he moved past her bedroom door, taunted by the twin demons of guilt and desire. It hurt to walk away from Leah. It'd been nearly nine months since he'd experienced the ecstacy, the physical release of a woman's body. Nine agonizing, grief-filled months.

But that was no excuse. He wasn't some teenager overwhelmed by hormones. He was fast approaching forty; by now he should have his libido under control.

But was it so wrong to feel again? he asked himself as he readied for bed.

Yes, came the immediate response. When Diane died, he'd known, had accepted, that the sexual part of his life was over. Gone forever. He'd had a healthy, active sex life with Diane, and when she died he couldn't imagine himself ever wanting another woman. He'd felt so certain of that, so sure that being with anyone else would amount to a betrayal of the wife he'd loved.

But perhaps he'd been shortsighted. Perhaps he'd been foolish. He was still alive, after all. He still had needs, desires, the kind a man felt for a woman.

But Leah? His wife's *sister?*

She'd felt so warm. She'd tasted so sweet…so womanly.

He felt trapped.

Diane was gone. Dead. He was alive. But was he?

He felt caught somewhere between life and death. One foot in the present, the other in the past.

Diane and Leah.

They were sisters. He was *related* to Leah. How could he feel the way he did about her? It was wrong.

A crystal-clear memory of his wife came into his mind. It was the day she'd learned she was pregnant with Kelsey. She'd planned a surprise celebration for when he returned home from work. Leah had taken the boys to the movies, giving him and Diane several uninterrupted hours. They'd made love, then sat up in bed eating ice cream and pickles. The memory of the teasing and the laughter would always stay with him. He'd loved Diane. Loved her more than life itself. But *he* was the one who'd been left behind.

The image of Diane sitting in their bed, ice cream smeared across her mouth, faded. Paul shut his eyes as tightly as he could, trying unsuccessfully to bring her back. Instead it was Leah who drifted into his mind. Leah, crouched in the sunshine as she worked in the garden. The children were gathered around her, Kelsey trying to catch a gold-winged butterfly, his sons busy digging in the dirt.

What had he done? The fact that he'd inflicted himself on Leah filled him with disgust. Heaven only knew what he was going to say to her in the morning.

What *could* he say? He didn't have a single excuse to offer her, not a single explanation to give. Needing her like this, using her like this, had been selfish and wrong.

But it *felt* right, his mind countered. Nothing had ever felt more right.

"No!" he muttered. It was wrong, wrong, wrong.

He was so confused. His thoughts were tangled, contradictory, uncertain.

He didn't know what to do.

Leah couldn't sleep. She lay on her back staring up at the ceiling in the darkened room. Silent tears slipped from the corners of her eyes, rolling into her hair and onto her pillow. She let them fall.

She hadn't known a kiss could be so good. She hadn't known desire could burn so hot. She'd always been sensible when it came to men and relationships. In charge of every situation. Always in control.

Until Paul kissed her. One kiss, and her body had felt as if it were on fire.

Her heart was still beating much too fast, its cadence echoing in her ear. Her body throbbed with pleasure.

With shame.

With need.

If only Paul had said something. But she'd seen the stricken look in his eyes, seen for herself his tortured regret. His reaction had hurt her more than anything since Diane's death. Unable to bear it, Leah had turned, with as much dignity as she could muster, and retreated to her bedroom.

But her dignity was cold comfort.

If only she understood what had prompted Paul to kiss her. Had she, without realizing it, done or said something to lead him on, sent inadvertent messages, seeking his touch?

She must have; otherwise, she wouldn't have gone so eagerly into his arms. Otherwise, she would've broken away. It was all too clear how willingly she'd accepted his embrace.

Mortified by the thought, she covered her hot face with both hands.

Shivering, Leah remembered the blatant way she'd responded to him. She'd opened up to Paul. Opened her arms. Opened her heart. And...her face grew hotter still. She'd been looking for more. Much more.

She'd lost herself in his kiss, responding to him as she never had to any other man. She'd actually pressed herself against him....

The kiss had gone wild, and demand had shot through her veins. For the first time in her life, Leah had felt completely out of control with a man. She'd wanted him so badly. Wanted to feel his arms around her. Wanted his kiss. Wanted to experience the welcoming touch of his tongue...

She'd wanted her sister's husband.

Leah closed her eyes and waited for revulsion to attack her. Waited for guilt to bury her.

She waited. And waited.

But it didn't come. Not the revulsion or the guilt.

Yet in her heart of hearts, Leah experienced such regret it all but consumed her. Regret because of the way he obviously felt about their kiss. It seemed to her that *he* was feeling the revulsion and guilt she wasn't. That, too, was a painful reality—Paul's disdain for her because of what they'd done. What *she'd* done.

Was she falling in love with him? Leah asked herself.

She couldn't answer that any more than she could answer any of the other questions that tormented her.

Her fingers touched her still-swollen lips. They felt bruised—just like her heart. The memory of that moment in his arms returned, bringing with it all the fever, all the madness, all the fury, of their kiss.

She shouldn't be feeling these things, she chastised herself. It was wrong.

How was she going to look Paul in the eye the next morning? How was she going to pretend nothing had happened?

Around her the night breathed. The dark closed in. The rain, which had been threatening all evening, tapped against the windows.

It was a long time before she fell asleep.

Leah woke the next morning, feeling as though she hadn't slept at all. The boys were awake; she could hear them in the kitchen. Apparently Kelsey was up, as well. She turned onto her side and glanced at her clock radio. It was nearly nine. How Paul had been able to keep the kids from waking her was a mystery. Throwing back the covers, she got out of bed and quickly dressed for church.

"Leah," Ronnie cried when she walked into the kitchen, "Ryan got the prize in the cereal box. Tell Daddy it's my turn!"

"I don't remember whose turn it is," she told him, surprised to see that the boys and Kelsey were already dressed.

"It is so my turn," Ronnie insisted.

"Ryan can share." Paul's gruff voice didn't make her feel any better. So far Leah had been able to avoid looking at him, but she wouldn't be able to keep that up for much longer.

He hadn't spoken directly to her, which did nothing to ease the tension between them. Leah could feel the strained nervousness as intensely as she'd felt his touch the night before.

She poured herself a cup of coffee and hurried into the bathroom, where she applied her makeup. By the time she'd finished, Paul had set the breakfast dishes in the dishwasher and wiped the table.

Leah half expected him to make an excuse to skip church that morning. She was half hoping he would. But apparently he didn't plan to stay home, much as she would've preferred it.

They didn't exchange a word on the short drive to the church. Even the children were strangely quiet.

Once they arrived, Leah brought Kelsey to the nursery, while Paul escorted the boys to their Sunday school class.

When Leah entered the church, she saw that Paul's parents had arrived and, sighing with relief, went to sit with them. Rich and Jamie sat in the pew directly in front of Eric and Elizabeth. Being surrounded by Paul's family comforted Leah, made her feel welcome and accepted.

As Paul slipped into the seat next to her, she noticed that he maintained a safe distance between them.

The service passed in a blur for Leah. Her head was so full of what had happened between her and Paul, she couldn't concentrate on the sermon.

When they stood for the closing hymn, Elizabeth

Manning leaned toward Leah and whispered, "Are you feeling all right?"

Leah quickly nodded.

"You're looking pale." She paused. "So is Paul."

"I'm fine." But Leah's heart was hammering. She was a little taken aback by how easily Elizabeth had detected the tension between her and Paul. She could only pray that her alarm didn't show in her eyes.

As they finished singing the final verse of the hymn, Leah felt Paul's gaze. Everything in her wanted to turn and look at him, but she lacked the courage. Eventually they'd need to speak to each other. Eventually they'd have to discuss what had happened. But she wasn't ready now and she didn't know how long it would take before she was.

Leah met Jamie, Rich's wife, on her way into the nursery to pick up Kelsey. "You're coming, aren't you?" she asked. At Leah's blank look, Jamie elaborated. "Mom wants all of us to come over for brunch. Paul must've forgotten to tell you."

"Ah…"

"Typical man," Jamie said with a smile. "How's everything working out?"

"Great," Leah responded with a too-bright smile. She'd only talked to Paul's sister-in-law a handful of times, but she liked Jamie. Bethany, Jamie and Rich's little girl, was nearly eighteen months old and, from something Paul had said, it looked as if the couple would be having a second child soon.

Paul met Leah in the hallway outside the nursery.

"Mom and Dad invited us to brunch," he said brusquely. "Is that all right with you?"

"It's fine."

These were the first words they'd spoken all morning.

"If you'd rather, I could drop you off at the house and take the kids over myself."

The suggestion hurt—he was trying to avoid her—but she tried not to let it show. "It'd…only raise questions if I didn't come."

"You're sure?"

She shifted a squirming Kelsey in her arms. "If you'd prefer me not to be there, just say so." Her eyes defiantly met his.

"I want you there," he admitted, then turned and left her.

In retrospect Leah realized she should've taken Paul up on his offer to drop her off at the house. The brunch at his parents' was trying for both of them. Although they'd attempted to disguise the tension, Leah knew they hadn't succeeded.

After she and Paul had gathered up the kids, Eric and Elizabeth walked them out to the car. They didn't say anything; they didn't have to. Their concern was all-too-apparent in their worried expressions and the lack of conversation.

All three children fell asleep in the car on the ride home. Leah carried Kelsey, while Paul dealt with the boys. She was on her way out of the baby's room, headed to her own room for a nap, when Paul stopped her.

"We have to talk," he said starkly.

Leah nervously shifted her weight from one foot to the other, her heart pounding with dread. She wasn't ready for this. Yet she knew they couldn't delay a confrontation much longer.

"I'm not sure where to start," he said after an awkward moment.

Leah said nothing. She didn't know where to start, either. But she felt a heady sense of relief that he was willing to bring everything out into the open.

"I didn't mean for it to happen," he said, his anger close to the surface. "I certainly didn't plan it."

"I...realize that."

"I know I frightened you."

"No." She couldn't very well tell him that their kissing was one of the most beautiful experiences of her life. She couldn't admit that she'd never felt in any man's arms the things she had with him.

"I didn't?" He seemed surprised to learn that. He hesitated, then turned abruptly and moved away from her. "I...I don't know what came over me. I love Diane...I haven't been with a woman since..."

At the mention of her sister's name, Leah went stiff. The implication nearly choked her. "In other words, I just happened to be handy."

"No!" he practically shouted. "That wasn't it at all."

"Then what was it?"

"If I knew that, do you think I'd be putting us through this hell?" he demanded. "I didn't kiss just any woman. It was you. I'm attracted to *you,* Leah." It sounded as though he was confessing to some particularly shameful crime. "I have no idea when it happened, or even how.

I suspect it's only natural, the two of us living together under one roof."

"I don't buy that."

"Why not? I'm being as honest and as objective as I can."

"I know," she breathed softly.

"Then what don't you buy?"

When it came right down to it, Leah couldn't believe that Paul could possibly find her attractive after having loved Diane. Leah knew her own skills and assets, and captivating men wasn't one of them. She'd discovered early in life that she couldn't compete with her sister. She hadn't wanted to. She'd loved Diane.

Paul had loved Diane, too. And having loved a woman who was laughter and sunshine and beauty, it wasn't likely he'd be interested in one who was sensible and plain and dull.

But she couldn't find the words to explain this to Paul. The uncomfortable silence grew.

"I...think it might be best if we both put the incident behind us," she finally said.

"That doesn't answer my question."

"I don't want to talk about it," she insisted, raising her voice.

Her fervor seemed to surprise him. "So you'd rather forget it ever happened?"

"Yes."

He eyed her skeptically. "Can you?"

"Yes," she lied. "Can't you?"

He hesitated, then nodded. "And it goes without saying that it won't happen again. You have my word on it."

* * *

Paul knew he'd blundered badly in his conversation with Leah. Seeing her that morning, watching the way her eyes avoided his, was agonizing. He wanted to take her hands in his and plead for her forgiveness. But when he'd built up the courage to confront her, he'd done it all wrong. He'd made it seem as if he'd kissed her because he'd gone nearly a year without sexual gratification and she was available.

He hadn't even told her how sorry he was.

But was he?

Paul didn't know anymore. He'd woken and his arms felt empty without her. For long seconds he lay there, his heart racing.

He waited for the guilt to kick him in the teeth. For Diane's image to appear and damn him for his weakness. For God to intervene and save him from himself.

It didn't happen.

All he could think about was how much he wanted to kiss Leah again.

Her reaction in the morning had quickly convinced him that his actions had betrayed a basic trust between them. She was embarrassed, perhaps even frightened. He'd known that he'd need to reassure her. He should've done it immediately, as soon as she'd entered the kitchen. But he'd waited, telling himself he'd do it right after church. Then they'd ended up at his parents' house, and that second delay had only made it more difficult.

During the ride home he'd rehearsed what he planned to say. It had sounded good in his mind, but the minute he'd tried to voice his thoughts, he'd botched everything.

What else could he do but promise never to touch her again? It was obvious that he'd offended her. His need had repulsed her.

Leah napped well into the afternoon. When she woke, Paul was in his den, presumably working on his novel. He didn't come out until dinnertime, and then only long enough to eat before he returned to his private refuge.

After their baths Leah read to the boys until they were sleepy and her voice had grown hoarse. Once the kids were tucked in their beds, she withdrew into her room and read late into the night.

By the time she woke in the morning, Paul had already left for the office.

The boys requested Eggs McManning for breakfast. By now Leah was quite proficient at creating the family favorite. She was standing in front of the stove, the spatula in her hand, when her eyes suddenly filled with tears. They came so unexpectedly that she was caught completely unawares. She brushed them with her forearm, hoping the twins wouldn't notice.

Why was she weeping, anyway? Was it because she was falling in love with a man who could never love her back? Because she lay awake nights remembering how hot and urgent his mouth had felt on her own? Because she dared not look him in the eye for fear he'd know what she wanted?

There was an even more pressing question: How

could she go on, living in his house, caring for his children, as if everything was still the same?

Paul let himself in the house and was immediately met by the enticing aroma of dinner. He walked unnoticed into the kitchen and stopped, mesmerized by the sight of Leah at the stove. He'd purposely avoided her that morning, left early just so he wouldn't have to smile and pretend nothing had changed between them. He'd never been much good at pretending; his expertise was in escape, which was why he'd gone to work early. Now he doubted the wisdom of his actions.

The impact of seeing Leah, of being this close to her after nearly twenty-four hours, hit him hard. It was like being punched in the chest, his lungs emptied of air.

He must've made some kind of noise because Leah turned to face him. "I didn't hear you come in," she said, sounding as normal as always.

Paul was slowly going out of his mind, and there she stood, frying pork chops as if nothing was wrong. He had to marvel at her ability to pretend. To him, the tension was thick enough to slice into bite-sized pieces.

But…maybe it was all him. Maybe she *didn't* feel it. Maybe he was the only one.

That thought, somehow, wasn't comforting.

Paul didn't realize his mistake until they were finished with dinner. Leah had said very little. She'd been careful not to look at him even when he asked her a question, which she'd made a point of answering as tersely as possible. The boys were cranky; Paul blamed it on the tension between him and Leah—a tension that proved her emotions were no less involved than his. She'd almost fooled him, though, almost convinced him. She'd certainly given a performance worthy of an Academy Award.

Yet he said nothing. How could he? Like her, he was trapped. He had to continue pretending.

It rained again that night, beating against his window in a relentless rhythm. For the third night in a row, Paul found it difficult to sleep. The howling wind wasn't helping.

He considered getting up, drinking a glass of milk. Maybe reading for a while. Of course, he could revert to pacing away the long hours until morning, the way he'd done the first few months after Diane's death.

What really kept him awake was Leah. Knowing she was so close. Only two doors away...

Night. Wind. Rain. Wanting Leah. Loving Diane. Suddenly it was all too much for him, and he tossed aside the blankets and climbed out of bed. Bare-chested, he walked into the kitchen and opened the refrigerator to pour himself a glass of milk, which he gulped down. Rinsing out the glass, he set it in the sink, then headed back to his room.

A movement in the shadows startled him.

"Leah?"

"Paul?"

"What are you doing up?"

"I—I couldn't sleep. I was just going to get myself some milk."

His eyes quickly adjusted to the dark. As soon as they did, Paul wished they hadn't. She stood in the shadows, but the pale light coming from the night-light in the twins' bedroom silhouetted her slight form, highlighting her breasts and the slimness of her waist and hips. He already knew how she felt in his arms and— Paul shook his head and nearly groaned out loud as he deliberately chased the memory from his mind.

"Why are you up?" she asked breathlessly.

"I couldn't sleep, either." His heart was pounding so hard he was afraid she could hear it.

The silence lingered, grew embarrassingly long, yet neither moved.

"I…had a glass of milk, too," he offered when the silence seemed to stretch to the breaking point. He was surprised by how difficult it was to speak coherently.

The desire to touch her was suddenly so strong he had to clasp his hands behind him in order to resist reaching for her.

"The storm…kept me awake." Leah's voice was barely a whisper. She looked up at him, her eyes wide and imploring.

Waiting. Wanting.

Still neither of them moved. Neither breathed.

Paul groaned inwardly. Wasn't she aware of the signals she was sending him?

Apparently not. His control was almost at its end. But he held on to it, because the truth was, he suspected she didn't actually know what she was doing, staring up at him like that.

"I should be getting back to bed," he muttered.

"Yes."

They were so close her breath fanned his face. Then

Leah lifted her head and their lips were mere inches apart. Their breathing was erratic, and he shut his eyes, concentrating on her scent, relishing the feel of her breath on his face.

"Leah…" His voice came from deep within his throat. "Stop me," he groaned.

He was seconds away from taking her in his arms and breaking his promise to himself. His promise to the memory of his dead wife, his promise to God, but most important, his promise to Leah.

Six

Paul didn't know how he managed to avoid kissing Leah. He stumbled back to his room and literally fell across his bed. He heard her return to her bedroom, and only then was he able to breathe easily.

He'd expected to encounter all kinds of problems when Leah moved in with him and the children, but this wasn't one of them. Having to fight a sexual attraction to her hadn't once entered his mind.

Who would've believed this could happen? Not Paul.

It had all started with a simple kiss. An anything-but-simple kiss, he amended. He would gladly surrender everything he owned not to have touched her that first time. Not to have tasted her sweetness, felt her willingness.

One kiss had brought him past the point of pleasure; it had opened a Pandora's box of hungry need.

His desire for her was shameless. Just a few minutes ago, it had taken all the control he possessed to walk away from her. He wasn't sure he'd have the strength to do it again.

Where did that leave them?

Paul couldn't explain what had come over him the past few days. Although he was nearly thirty when he married Diane, he hadn't had an extensive history of sexual experience. His army buddies had bragged about their sexual conquests and playfully joked with Paul, claiming he was the only man they knew who was more interested in a woman's mind than her body.

Not with Leah. He'd been fighting erotic fantasies about her for days, doggedly pushing them out of his mind and then damning himself for his thoughts.

For years he'd prided himself on his self-control, his discipline, but lately that discipline was breaking down. In fact, it was going to hell in a hand basket, as the saying went.

Although his breathing calmed, the frightening excitement didn't lessen once Paul was in his own room; if anything, it increased. Every time he closed his eyes, Leah was there, looking up at him, her beautiful eyes languid with desire. Every instinct he had told him to take her in his arms and hold her tight. He longed to curve his hands around her waist and nestle close to her softness.

What was he going to do? He'd already discovered he couldn't ignore her. He couldn't be in the same room and not react to the tension between them. No matter how hard he tried, he couldn't keep the memories of the night he'd kissed her from bombarding his mind. No more than he could repress the guilt those same memories occasioned.

Paul didn't know how Leah managed to pretend that this strained awareness didn't exist. She did a masterful job of it, but that ability was beyond him.

He could do what he'd done that morning—leave for work early in order to avoid any contact, verbal or otherwise, with Leah. But the problem with that was his children. He couldn't escape her without depriving himself of what little time he had with them. In the end he'd only be cheating himself.

The one other option that presented itself was an open, honest discussion. However, he'd attempted that once and made a mess of it.

Paul sighed wearily. The situation was even worse than he'd thought. Quite simply, he had no idea what to do now.

"Your parents phoned." That was how Leah greeted Paul when he returned home from work the next evening. Just the way she said it told him she'd had a bad day. He was almost glad. His own had been a disaster, and if she was miserable, too, he figured that was only fair.

His mood lightened considerably.

"What's up with them?"

Leah shrugged, keeping her back to him—an irritating habit of late. "They asked if they could come visit."

"What did you tell them?"

Hearing his father, Ryan ran in from the backyard, and Paul lifted his son into his arms, hugging him briefly.

"What *could* I say?" Leah continued, turning to face him. "I told them they were welcome anytime."

Ronnie raced in behind his brother, looking for the customary hug. Paul absently complied, then bent over and kissed Kelsey's cheek as she gleefully pounded away on a pan with a wooden spoon.

"They wanted to be sure we were both going to be home."

Paul straightened slowly. "That sounds ominous."

"I…think it might be." Leah turned back to the counter, where she was grating cheese for a taco salad.

Paul reached over and stole a black olive from the bowl of lettuce. "Why do you say that?"

"I know your mother sensed something was wrong… between us Sunday morning," she explained.

"So?" Paul was surprised that he could act so nonchalant, since he felt anything but. Not that he was worried about his parents' visit, of course. No reason he should be.

"So…it worries me."

"Why?"

She whirled around and glared at him, and it was all Paul could do not to clap his hands and cry out, "Hot damn!" Finally. Finally. Leah Baker was showing some emotion. She couldn't pretend anymore. She couldn't ignore him any longer. Couldn't continue this maddening game of make-believe.

His parents arrived at seven-thirty. The kitchen was clean, and the boys were outside playing on the swing set in the still-bright sun. Kelsey had been diapered and put to bed for the night. Paul had to marvel, not for the first time, at Leah's efficiency.

The minute his father stepped into the house, his gaze sought out Paul's. There was something on his mind, all right. Paul knew the look. The last time Paul could remember seeing that particular expression was when Christy had announced she was married to Cody Franklin. The news came as a shock, especially since she'd been engaged to James Wilkens at the time. Leave it to his youngest sister to marry one man while engaged to another.

"So, what's bothering you, Dad?" Paul asked.

"I'd like to talk to you."

"Sure."

Eric sent Leah an apologetic look. "Privately, if you don't mind?"

"Of course not." Paul sent Leah a glance, too. Her eyes met his, and she looked so uncertain, so dubious, that he had to resist an urge to tell her there was nothing to worry about. But he didn't say anything, because he wasn't sure himself.

"And while you two are chatting, Leah and I can have some time to ourselves," his mother said conversationally. Except that Paul wasn't fooled. He recognized her concerned tone of voice. When he was a teenager, that concern had often led to having the car keys taken away, or being grounded—until he saw things the same way his parents did.

Whatever was going on seemed worrisome. Leah, who'd apparently recovered, cast him a prim I-told-you-so look and led his mother into the kitchen.

Whatever this was all about, Paul was pretty sure he didn't like it. His parents were wonderful; the first six months after Kelsey was born, Paul couldn't have survived without their encouragement and support. But he was thirty-six years old, far past the point of being reprimanded by them.

Leah claimed his parents had sensed that things had gone awry, although Paul doubted it. Yes, the mood had been a bit tense and his family might've read something into it, but surely that hadn't brought about this unexpected visit.

Paul preceded his father into his office and closed the door. The room wasn't large, but adequate for his needs. The desk, with his computer, took up one wall. Two more walls were dominated by bookshelves. Paul gave his father the desk chair and took the stool for himself.

"What's wrong, Dad?"

"Nothing." As he spoke, he slowly raised his eyes to meet Paul's. "At least I hope not."

Paul smiled benignly and waited.

"As you know, your mother and I are leaving next week for Montana. She's got her heart set on being with Christy for the birth of this baby."

"Yes, I know. You don't need to worry about the house. Jason, Rich and I will look after the old homestead for you."

"It's not the house I'm worried about," Eric said gruffly.

"Then what is it?"

"It's Leah."

Paul went stiff. So much for all the reassuring things he'd been telling himself. His father was staring at him as though he expected Paul to leap up and announce that he was lusting after Leah. Not that it was exactly a lie.

"What about Leah?" Paul asked once he could trust his voice not to betray his uneasiness.

"I'm concerned about her."

There was no question that Leah worked too hard and didn't take enough time for herself. Diane had been far more social than Leah, more outgoing. Leah's idea of indulging herself was reading a good book.

"The family realizes that everything's on the up-and-up between you two."

"On the up-and-up?"

"That the two of you aren't sleeping together," Eric explained bluntly.

His father was entering territory Paul considered off limits. "Dad, listen, I know you mean well, but I don't think—"

"Paul, I hate to broach the subject, but there've been rumors. It's only natural, I suppose. I'm well aware that men and women live together without benefit of marriage all the time. Sadly it's a matter of course these days."

"Dad, I don't care what other people think." There'd always be those who believed whatever they wanted to, no matter how innocent the situation.

His father folded his arms over his chest and nodded. "Perhaps not, but how does Leah feel?"

Paul was stunned. He hadn't given Leah's reputation a moment's thought. She was the one who'd suggested moving in with him, after all. He'd assumed, perhaps erroneously, that whatever talk there was didn't concern her. Now, imagining anyone daring to criticize Leah sent hot fury racing through his veins. He wasn't a man to get angry often, but he was now.

"Who's been gossiping about us?" he demanded of his father. "What did they say?"

"That's not important."

"The hell it isn't! I want to know who—"

"There are a few other, more important issues you should be considering," his father interrupted.

That worried Paul even more. Had the rumors turned vicious? "Such as?"

"When Leah moved in with you—it's been what? Six, seven weeks?"

He nodded brusquely. Her coming had changed his life. For the first time in nearly a year Paul wasn't suffocating under the burden of emotional pain, suffocating under the strain of nurturing his children alone. Leah had provided much more than child care, though. She'd cheered his grief-stricken heart, given him a reason to wake up every morning, brought him into the sunlight.

"What about her health insurance?"

"Her health insurance?" Paul exploded. First his father said Leah's reputation was on the line and now he was worried about her health insurance.

"When you said she'd be moving in with you for the next couple of years, I wondered," his father continued. "From what I understand, the college benefit program will only carry her for a few more months and then she'll be canceled. In this day and age, no one can risk going without medical insurance."

"I...hadn't thought of that." Now that he'd simmered down, Paul felt like a selfish jerk. He'd never bothered to ask Leah about her medical coverage. He'd been so grateful for her help he hadn't stopped to fully consider the cost of her sacrifice.

"What about her other benefits? Will she be losing those, as well?"

"I don't know."

"While we're discussing Leah, let me bring up something else. Have you had your will altered?" his father asked.

"My...will?"

"Your legal affairs need to be in order, son. If anything were to happen to you now, what would become of the children? With Diane gone, they could be made wards of the state unless there's some provision for them in your will."

Paul was stunned by his lack of foresight. "I didn't realize." He slowly expelled his breath and rubbed a weary hand down his face. "I'll make an appointment with James first thing in the morning." Although Christy had broken her engagement with James Wilkens, the attorney remained a good family friend.

"You need to do more than that," his father said emphatically.

"I do?" Paul could only guess at what else he'd let slide.

Eric Manning hesitated. It wasn't often Paul saw indecision in his father's face. "You might not like what I'm about to say. You can tell me it's none of my business, and you'd be right, but since you asked, I'm going to tell you. I think you should marry Leah. The sooner the better."

* * *

"Would you like some iced tea?" Leah asked Paul's mother, trying to disguise her nervousness.

The sliding glass door to the backyard was open, and she kept her eye on the twins. Only that morning she'd found them weeding the garden; unfortunately they'd yanked up all the herbs she'd planted with such care.

"No, thank you, my dear." Elizabeth pulled out a kitchen chair and sat down.

Elizabeth lowered her eyes to her hands, folded atop the table, as though she, too, felt on edge. "I've been meaning to have this talk with you for some time, Leah. I probably shouldn't have waited this long."

Leah's heart seemed to stop. Paul's mother *knew*. As hard as Leah had struggled to hide it, Elizabeth had read the love in her eyes. And if she'd recognized that, then surely she'd seen the guilt and the confusion.

Leah sank into the chair across from Paul's mother. It was all she could do not to cry out that she'd never meant for Paul to kiss her.

"Our family is deeply indebted to you, Leah," his mother began.

"Nonsense."

"No," Elizabeth said firmly. "We're grateful for the way you've stepped in and helped Paul and the children. You've made a world of difference to their lives, and ours, too.

"I was terribly worried about Paul after Diane died, you know. I thought he might need counselling, but he gradually worked through his grief."

"We both have." Learning to deal with her sister's death had been a painful process for Leah, too.

"The twins are doing so much better," Elizabeth went on. "You were right, they needed their own home and their own toys and familiar friends. These last two months have been good for Ryan and Ronnie. There's color in their cheeks and they're laughing again. And Kelsey's growing like a weed."

"I found her standing up this morning. That little rascal's going to be walking soon." Leah had difficulty keeping the pride out of her voice.

Elizabeth beamed. "That's a perfect example of what I mean."

"You give me more credit than I deserve."

"I doubt it." Elizabeth's smile slowly faded, and her blue eyes grew serious. "I believe you told Paul you'd be willing to stay with him and the children until the boys were in school full-time and Kelsey's in preschool?"

Leah nodded. "He won't have to deal with three pre-schoolers a couple of years down the road. By then, he'll be able to deal with the situation a lot better."

"What do you think will happen to the children after you leave?" Elizabeth asked candidly.

"I—I don't understand."

"How do you think the twins and Kelsey will react once you move out?" she elaborated.

"That's several years away. There's no way of knowing how they'll feel."

"I think there is. The twins have already lost their mother, and we're both aware of how deeply Diane's death affected them."

Leah said nothing, her heart growing heavy with doubts.

"As for Kelsey…you're the only mother she's ever known."

"Oh, dear," Leah breathed. "I never thought…I just didn't realize…" She'd been so stupid, so blind. She'd hoped her moving in with Paul would be a solution; instead it was creating more problems. The time would come when she'd have to go. She couldn't continue living with Paul indefinitely.

"What should I do?" she asked, her eyes pleading with Paul's mother. "I can't leave the children now—I love them so much." A panicky feeling washed over her. She'd been foolish and thoughtless, but it was too late to change that now.

"I know how you feel about the children."

That was something else Leah had failed to consider—her own feelings. She loved these children as much as if she'd given birth to them herself. Walking away from them would be agony—unbearable agony.

"There *is* a solution." Elizabeth's voice came through the haze of regrets in Leah's mind. "Although you may not completely agree with me…"

Leah raised her eyes to Elizabeth's, her heart in turmoil. "Solution?" she whispered.

"Leah, I've upset you."

"No…no." She reached for Elizabeth's hands. "You've pointed out some things I should've considered. I can't believe I was so…thoughtless."

Elizabeth nodded and, looking a bit uneasy, asked, "I hope you won't feel I'm prying—but how's your relationship with Paul?"

Leah could feel the color rise to her cheeks. "We get along…just fine. We always have. He's wonderful with the children, and I've always liked and respected him." She knew she was talking too fast, but couldn't make herself slow down.

"So, the two of you are compatible?"

"Oh, yes—we haven't had a single disagreement." She didn't think she could count a kiss as a dispute. Perhaps if they were at odds more often, she wouldn't feel this growing attraction to him.

"I hear from Paul that you're dating a fellow professor."

"Sort of…yes. His name's Rob Mullins, and we've gone out a couple of times in the last few weeks." She didn't mention that she wouldn't be seeing Rob again.

Elizabeth hesitated, and Leah had the impression she found this part of the conversation disconcerting. "Do you have…feelings for Rob?"

Leah frowned, not sure where Elizabeth was going with this. "Not exactly—we're friends."

Elizabeth seemed relieved at that. Her smile broadened, and she gently squeezed Leah's fingers. "As I said earlier, I think Eric and I may have come across the perfect solution. We talked about it at some length and although we're well aware that what happens between you and Paul is none of our concern, we felt we needed to speak up."

"Of course."

Elizabeth made a shallow attempt at a smile. "Have you ever thought of marrying Paul?"

Marrying Paul?

For some reason Leah recalled the night before, when she'd been unable to sleep and had left her room, hoping a glass of milk would help. She hadn't known Paul was up. If she had, she would never have ventured into the hallway. Would never have opened her door.

By the time she noticed her mistake, it was too late. Although she'd plastered herself against the wall in the hallway, willing him to pass and return to his own room, he'd stayed where he was, his eyes meeting hers in the dim light.

Before she could stop herself, Leah had realized they were only inches apart. She'd so desperately wanted his touch that she'd nearly swayed into his arms.

How they were able to break away from each other Leah didn't know. She hadn't realized it was possible for two people to come so close to making love without even touching.

"Leah?" Elizabeth's voice broke into her thoughts.

"Yes?" Startled, she looked up, surprised to find that Paul and his father were in the room.

"I believe we've given these two something to think about," Eric Manning was saying. "We should leave now and let them discuss it in privacy."

Elizabeth stood and Leah did, too, impulsively hugging Paul's mother. She closed her eyes for a moment, wondering how to rectify what she'd done. These past few weeks had been among the happiest of her life. For the first time since childhood, she felt as though she belonged, as though she was needed and loved. But in her ignorance she'd overlooked what should've been obvious. Worse, she didn't know what to do about it. Elizabeth's suggestion would never work. Paul wouldn't want to marry her. Nor should he have to.

Paul and his father exchanged handshakes, and then Paul escorted his parents to the front door. Leah set her iced tea glass in the sink.

When he returned to the kitchen, Leah was staring down at the kitchen table. Then, seeking his reassurance, she slowly raised her eyes to his.

"Tell me about your health insurance!" Paul said, sounding angry.

"My…health insurance?"

"Yes." It was so rare for Paul to raise his voice that he'd shocked her.

"I could be ruining the children's lives, and you're worried about my *health insurance?*"

"What?" He shook his head. "You've been canceled, haven't you?" he demanded.

Leah shrank from the cold fury she saw in him. "I don't know…. Is it important?"

"Yes. And what did you mean you've 'ruined the children's lives'? You've been our salvation!" He rammed both hands through his hair. "I'm the one who's been selfish." He walked away from her, then pivoted sharply. "Why didn't you say something?"

"About my health insurance? Trust me, Paul, I was dealing with more important matters."

"Like planting a garden?"

"Yes, like planting a garden." She didn't understand his anger. It was so unlike him. She turned away, fighting tears. "If it'll make you happy, I'll see to it tomorrow morning. Why are you acting like this?"

"My father pointed out a few home truths." He grimaced. "I can't believe I've been so obtuse. I should never have allowed you to move in."

Leah thought she might be physically sick. Paul was going to send her away. For all the reasons his mother had mentioned.

"No!" Her cry came straight from her heart. "I won't let you do it."

"Do *what?*"

"Send me away. I'll fight you. I'll even fight your parents, but I refuse to leave Kelsey and the twins." *And you,* she added silently.

"Send you away?" Paul repeated, aghast. "I shouldn't have let you come, but now that you're here, I'd never make you go…." He hesitated, suddenly pale. "Unless that's what you want."

Tears of release and relief filled her eyes. She brushed them aside, not wanting Paul to know how badly she'd needed his assurance.

"Do you *want* to leave, Leah?"

She glared at him, her eyes defiant. "No! I just got done telling you that."

He sighed and took one step toward her, then stopped, his look intense. "Did my mother suggest the same solution to you as my dad did to me?"

Leah watched him closely, hoping to read his reaction. "She…thought we should get married."

"And?"

"And…I haven't had time to think about it. But it

seems…above and beyond the call of duty for you to marry me."

Paul's eyes narrowed as he studied her. Apparently he didn't understand.

"I already explained I'm not the marrying kind," she added, trying to salvage what remained of her pride.

"I never have understood that attitude. You're a warm, gracious, generous woman. What makes you think you're unmarriageable?"

Leah laughed nervously. She'd never received much attention from the opposite sex, not even when she was younger and prettier. She was too bookish for most men. Too serious. She hadn't fallen in love in her twenties, and by the time she was thirty, she'd ruled out any possibility of marriage.

"I mean it." Paul sounded angry again.

Leah hesitated. Her heart was racing with hope. For the first time in her life she had a chance at real happiness, a promise of something more than she'd ever dared dream. A family. Home. Love. Yes, it had all belonged to her sister, but Diane had come to her in the dream. Diane had sent her to Paul and the children.

"Are you saying you'd be willing to marry me?" she asked in a rush.

Paul buried his hands in his pockets. "Yes. If it wasn't so unfair to you."

"Unfair?"

"Leah, look around you! I'm raising three motherless children. I'll be paying Diane's hospital bills for the next two years and—"

"I know all that."

"I don't have anything to offer you."

Only a wealth beyond her wildest dreams—a wealth that had nothing to do with material things. He was offering her more love than she'd ever thought to find.

"What about the children I love? A home? A family?"

When Paul's gaze connected with hers, he looked uncertain. "That would be enough for you?"

Leah nodded.

His voice was gruff with emotion when he spoke. "Will you marry me, Leah, for all our sakes?"

In a heartbeat. "Yes," she whispered. "Yes, I'll marry you, Paul."

Seven

"We're mature adults," Leah said as solemnly as she could. "We both realize this isn't a love match."

"We're going into this with our eyes wide open," Paul agreed.

"Exactly." The relief she felt knowing she wouldn't be forced to leave the children was so great that Leah slumped in the kitchen chair, holding up her head with both hands. She brushed loose strands of hair from her forehead and smiled weakly up at Paul.

"There is love involved, though," Paul said pointedly, studying her.

She'd never been more aware of a man's look. Engrossed in it. Absorbed. Since the night they'd kissed, she'd noticed that the way Paul looked at her had changed. Once again she wished she was more experienced in relationships, because she couldn't say exactly *how* it had changed—or what it meant. He seemed to watch her more closely, his gaze bolder, less veiled. She glanced up to see that he was still waiting for her to respond to his statement.

"Naturally there's love involved," she said, speaking too quickly. "We both love the children," she added, hating the breathless quality of her words.

Paul pulled out a chair and sat across from her. "The children are a vitally important part of this, but there's more involved here. I want to know what you feel for me."

Leah had come to know a directness about Paul that she loved...and feared. Her own manner was more subtle and she tended to think more slowly and methodically. To her, every aspect of a problem needed to be analyzed and then logically examined. It was the way she lived her life.

Paul, on the other hand, had neither the time nor the patience to mull over any issue. He wrote to a deadline, and believed that it shouldn't take more than five minutes to think through a situation.

Defining feelings seemed to come more easily to him, as well. Leah had always found that difficult.

"Leah?" Paul prodded when she didn't answer right away.

"I...I don't know what I feel for you." It was an honest answer...as honest as she dared. She was afraid to love him, and even more afraid that she already did. He made her experience emotions, physical desires, that she hadn't known she was capable of feeling.

"What do you expect from this marriage?" Paul asked her next.

"I don't know that, either. I haven't had time to

think about it." Then it struck her, something she should've considered much earlier. "What exactly do *you* expect?"

"A wife."

He left it at that, left it for her to fill in the blanks. "I…see."

"Do you, Leah? After we're married, I'll want you to move into my bedroom, share my life and my bed." He hesitated as though he expected an argument. "I realize you don't love me now, but I'm hoping you will in time. Do you have a problem with that?"

Talking so openly had always made Leah uneasy. She lowered her eyes. "No…but do you honestly think we can make a marriage work?"

"Of course. Otherwise I'd never agree to it, and neither would you."

"I've been so obtuse," she said, recalling her conversation with his mother. "I can't believe I was so inconsiderate. I really hadn't given any thought to how the children would feel after I moved out."

"I wasn't thinking too clearly myself."

"It's so unlike me."

"I know. Me, too."

"Why did it take your parents so long to say something?" The concerns Elizabeth raised were valid and should have been voiced sooner, in Leah's opinion.

"I asked my dad the same thing," Paul told her. "He said they'd just thought of all this."

"Well, I'm glad they did—for the children's sake."

Paul merely nodded.

* * *

Paul glanced nervously at his watch. He only had an hour for lunch and Leah was already five minutes late. He knew something must have detained her, since she was as punctual as she was honest.

Pacing the hallway outside the licensing office in the King County Courthouse, he thought over the changes of the past two days. For the first time in nearly a week, he'd slept soundly. The erotic fantasies centering on Leah that had cost him several nights' sleep had eased. When he went to bed, he closed his eyes, half-fearing she'd stroll into his mind. A vision of her had made nightly appearances since he'd kissed her. She'd smile seductively at him, and then his imagination would take over, tormenting him for hours on end.

But it hadn't happened since Leah had agreed to marry him. Perhaps that was because he knew it was only a matter of time before he made love to her. He'd made sure the night of his parents' visit that Leah understood theirs would be a real marriage.

There'd been a time, not all that distant, when he would've pleaded with God to help him, pleaded with Diane to forgive him and wallowed in guilt for even thinking of making love to his sister-in-law. He felt an acceptance now, an inevitability.

He *needed* Leah. Not for the physical release her body would yield him, although that was part of it. He needed her the way a man needs the substance of life. Air. Water. Food. Just as she was vital to his children, Leah was vital to him. He woke in the morning, and his first thoughts were of her. During the workday he often found himself looking at his watch and calculating how long it would be before he could go home—to her and his children. He wasn't sure when all this had started to happen or even if it was a good thing. All he knew was that it *was* happening.

Did he love Leah?

Paul didn't know. Certainly what he felt for her was unlike his love for Diane. In the months since her death, Paul had become more objective about his marriage to Leah's younger sister. He loved Diane, heart and soul. He'd never experienced deeper grief than when he'd lost her. She was an unselfish woman, and he knew she wouldn't have wanted him and the children to live alone. He genuinely believed Diane would have approved of his marrying Leah. Of Leah raising her kids.

To Paul's way of thinking, if he were to marry a second time, Leah was the perfect choice. For the obvious reasons, yes, but for less obvious ones, too.

In marrying Leah, he'd still be able to hold on to Diane, remain emotionally faithful to her. The two sisters would be forever linked in his mind, his heart. Leah shared his love for Diane, and that alone averted the potential resentments and problems of a second marriage. Leah wouldn't make unreasonable demands in an effort to force Diane out of his life.

Less than a month ago, if anyone—his father or any of his brothers—had suggested he remarry, Paul would've resisted it, regardless of the proposed partner. Even Leah. He hadn't been ready, emotionally or in any other way.

"Paul!" Leah hurried down the courthouse corridor. "I'm so sorry I'm late."

She looked nice, Paul observed. Her hair was held back on either side by silver clips, and she wore a simple linen dress that skimmed her figure.

"I hope I haven't kept you waiting," she said.

"No more than five minutes. Don't worry about it."

"The babysitter was late, and then I couldn't find a parking place and—"

"You're here now and that's all that matters."

She placed her hand over her heart as though to calm its pounding, and Paul ignored the urge to put his arm around her. He found himself looking for excuses to touch her, but so far had managed not to. His fear was that once he did, he wouldn't be able to stop. A touch would lead to a kiss and a kiss would lead...who knew where.

"We apply for the marriage license over here," he said, directing her through a pair of doors.

She nodded, then paused before entering the office. "You're sure you want to go through with this?" she whispered without looking at him.

If either of them was going to entertain second thoughts, the time was now. Yet Paul didn't hesitate. He knew what he wanted; he wanted Leah. "Positive. What about you?"

Her smile was sweet. "I'm here, aren't I?"

Applying for the marriage license took barely five minutes. Paul was glad that Leah had left the kids with a sitter. For the first time since she'd moved in with him, he had uninterrupted time alone with her—away from the house.

"How about lunch?"

His invitation seemed to surprise—and please—her. "I'd like that."

There was a popular bookstore off First Avenue with a small restaurant in the basement. Paul ate there often and enjoyed the feel of the place. It wasn't fancy, or even close to fancy, and it certainly wasn't where a man would take a woman he wanted to impress. But it was a restaurant Paul knew Leah would love.

They stood in line to order, then found a table at the back, next to an old brick wall hung with bookshelves and pieces by local artists.

"This is perfect," Leah said, glancing eagerly around.

"I thought you'd like it."

She smiled shyly. "I have some exciting news."

"Oh?"

"Kelsey took her first step this morning!"

Leah looked as proud as if his daughter had flown to the moon and back on her own power.

"I've been expecting it any day," he said, smiling back at her.

"The boys were as excited as I was."

"I remember when Ryan and Ronnie were that age."

A waitress delivered their chicken pot pies and hot coffee.

Leah reached for her fork. "Who walked first, Ryan or Ronnie?"

"Ryan. He wanted his blankie, and since I was holding it out to him, the most expedient way to collect it was to take a few steps in my direction. As I recall, Ronnie refused to allow his brother to outdo him and walked almost immediately afterward."

"It's hard to remember the boys at a year old," Leah said with a happy sigh.

Paul nodded, then said, "Leah, let's not talk about the children."

Her gaze shot up, and her eyes, which were a vibrant green today, reflecting her pale green dress, revealed her bewilderment. "Why not?"

"Because we're going to be married soon."

"You…want to discuss that?" She sounded worried.

"No. But at some point in the future the children will be gone and there'll be only the two of us. We both love the children. That's a given. We've agreed to get married for our own individual reasons, but in the end it'll come down to the two of us. We need to build a relationship."

"A relationship," she repeated, as though the words felt awkward on her tongue.

"If you prefer, we could call it a friendship."

Leah nodded. "You're right, of course.… It's just that I'm not very good at this sort of thing. You'll probably need to help me."

Her confession touched him. After all that Leah had done for him and the children, it gladdened his heart that he could assist her in some small way. He'd make this as easy on her as he could, guide her whenever possible, encourage her to feel confident in her own emotions. If he'd been forced to identify any fault of Leah's, it would be her stubborn self-reliance. He recognized it because he was fiercely independent himself. As the oldest of five children, he'd learned early in life that he had to be.

"What shall we talk about?" Leah asked softly.

"Anything we like."

An earsplitting silence followed. They'd lived together for nearly two months. They'd agreed to marry. They planned to spend the rest of their lives together. Yet when Paul took the children out of the conversation, they had nothing to say.

"Oh, dear," Leah said, her eyes filled with alarm. She set down her fork. "This is more difficult than I realized."

"Do you want to tell me about your garden, Mary, Mary, Quite Contrary?"

Her eyes brightened, but after a moment the enthusiasm drained away. "What's there to tell you? It's growing nicely."

"My parents keep a garden," Paul volunteered.

"Do they grow herbs?"

"Not to my knowledge."

"What about zucchini?"

"Enough to feed the entire state," Paul said. His dad routinely dropped off huge quantities of the vegetable. Paul hadn't the heart to tell him he'd rather eat gravel than zucchini. At least Diane had found a recipe—zucchini chocolate cake—that made it tolerable.

Their conversation got off to a slow start, but by the end of the hour, Paul felt they'd made some real headway.

When they'd finished their lunch, Paul walked Leah back to where she'd parked the car. Although he was late getting back to the office, he found himself reluctant to leave. He'd be home in a matter of hours, but he wanted to hold on to this time alone with her.

Leah didn't seem eager to leave, either. She held her

car keys in one hand, glancing down at them periodically.

Suddenly he felt an impulse to kiss her. But it wasn't the kind of thing he was comfortable doing on a busy Seattle street. He knew any public display of affection would only embarrass Leah. Diane would've spontaneously thrown her arms around his neck and kissed him regardless of where they were or who was watching.

But it wasn't Diane he was marrying; it was Leah.

Leah woke on the morning of her wedding day to bright sunshine. Paul had contacted a minister acquaintance who'd agreed to perform a private ceremony at his office, with the minister's wife and his youth pastor serving as witnesses.

They'd arranged everything quickly, quietly. They hadn't said anything to Paul's family. Leah wasn't sure Paul intended to say anything until afterward, which suited her fine. Being hovered over by his mother would've made Leah more nervous than she already was.

She didn't doubt that she was doing the right thing in marrying Paul, but she preferred to do it without formalities. His family would've insisted on making a production out of it, which wasn't at all what Leah wanted.

She'd purchased a white linen suit for the ceremony. Normally she didn't wear a hat, but she'd found one she rather liked. The salesclerk had been very helpful, and Leah was grateful for the extra touch of style.

Diane had always gone with her when she needed to buy something for a special occasion. How ironic that

Leah had never craved her sister's opinion more than she had while trying to choose what to wear when she married Paul.

The ceremony itself took only minutes. Filling out the marriage license had been more complicated than the wedding itself. They'd decided on plain gold bands and Paul's eyes, warm and reassuring, had held hers when he'd slipped the ring on her finger.

It had seemed appropriate to have the children with them; Kelsey stood between the two boys who held her hands, and all three stared wide-eyed as their father married Leah.

Afterward Paul kissed her briefly. Although his mouth had barely grazed hers, a riot of sensations came rushing at Leah. She trembled in his arms and prayed he hadn't guessed how strong her response had been.

When they left the church office, Paul suggested they visit his parents.

Leah agreed. The children would need their afternoon naps soon, but there was time for a short visit.

Elizabeth looked mildly surprised when she opened her front door. "Paul, Leah," she greeted them cheerfully, holding the screen door. "Come in, please." She took Kelsey from Paul's arms and set her on the carpet. "I hear she's walking now."

"Just watch. This kid's headed for the Olympics at the rate she's going," Paul said, smiling.

"Paul." His father strolled into the living room, looking delighted by their unexpected arrival. "Sit down, sit down."

Leah sat on the couch and Paul joined her. The boys

hurried to the kitchen and stood by the counter, waiting for their grandmother to offer them the cookie jar.

Elizabeth complied with a smile, then walked into the living room. If Paul's parents noticed that he and Leah were overdressed for an early Saturday afternoon, neither commented.

Paul reached for Leah's hand, squeezed her fingers with his own, then looked at his parents. "Leah and I stopped by to tell you we've taken your advice. We were married about an hour ago."

"Married!" his mother cried.

"Married!" his father boomed, vaulting to his feet.

Perplexed, Leah turned to look at her husband. Perhaps they'd misunderstood. Perhaps that *wasn't* what his parents had meant. But Leah had been so sure....

Elizabeth started to weep softly.

"Mom?" Paul made no effort to disguise his confusion. "Good grief, I'd think you'd be happy."

"I am."

"Then why the tears?"

"Because you're just like Taylor and Christy."

"Don't forget Rich," Eric snapped.

"What do the girls have to do with Leah and me?"

"First, Taylor married Russ in Reno. She didn't have a single family member there. Not one. Your father and I could've flown there in less than two hours. Out of the blue she marries a cowboy she's known less than three months."

"Then Christy married Cody," Eric went on. "In Idaho, no less. She flies to a neighboring state to get married for fear her family might find out about it."

"If you'll recall," Paul added wryly, "she was still engaged to James at the time. She felt she had no other choice."

"She didn't even let Taylor in on what she was doing, not until much later." Elizabeth wiped the tears from her face. "If it wasn't bad enough that your sisters married without family present, Rich had an ordinary judge marry him and Jamie."

"That's because they were planning their divorce shortly afterward," Paul said, defending his brother. "Besides, we were married by a minister, not a judge, if that's any consolation."

"Wait. He was planning a divorce?" Confused, Leah whispered the question in Paul's ear.

"I'll tell you later," he promised.

Vaguely Leah remembered Diane describing the details of Rich's marriage to Jamie Warren. As she recalled, the couple had originally gotten married for the purpose of having a child. Diane had explained that they'd planned for Jamie to be artificially inseminated, but when she did become pregnant, there hadn't been anything artificial about it.

"You're upset because we didn't invite you to the ceremony?" Paul asked his parents, who shared an incredulous look.

"Yes." His father's loud voice echoed through the house. "What is it with you kids? Don't you have any idea how badly your mother and I want to attend a wedding in this family? We have five children, four of them now married, and we've yet to be invited to a single child's wedding."

"Dad, Mom, I'm sorry," Paul said, sounding genuinely contrite.

Leah felt terrible. She should've encouraged Paul to mention their decision to his family. She hadn't done so for selfish reasons. She was afraid Elizabeth would make a fuss, something Leah had wanted to avoid.

"I apologize, too," Leah said meekly.

"It's done now," Eric said, tight-lipped. Then he made an effort to relax. "But you're making a habit of this, son," he muttered, referring to Paul's first wedding in Alaska.

"I promise if I ever get married again, I'll make sure you and Mom are there for it."

Although she knew Paul was joking, Leah felt a small twinge of anxiety and possessiveness.

"Jason's our last hope for a family wedding," Elizabeth said, dabbing her eyes with a tissue she'd taken from her pocket.

"Jason," Paul repeated, barely holding back a laugh. "I hate to disappoint you, but I can't see Jason ever getting married. He's too set in his ways."

"God's going to find that son of mine a wife," Elizabeth said. "I can't believe the good Lord would give me five beautiful children and then cheat me out of the pleasure of putting on even one wedding."

"I'm sure everything will work out for the best," Paul said in a soothing voice.

The boys started squabbling, and Leah knew it was because they were tired and hadn't had their lunch. Kelsey was about to fall asleep, as well.

"We should be going," Leah said, turning to Paul. "I

feel really bad that we disappointed you," she added to the Mannings. "I hope you'll forgive us for being so thoughtless." She stood, reaching for Kelsey. The little girl laid her head against Leah's shoulder and yawned sleepily.

"Where are you two going for your honeymoon?" Eric asked.

Paul and Leah exchanged shocked glances. "We hadn't planned a honeymoon," Paul replied.

"I certainly hope you intend to get away for the night, at least."

Paul frowned apologetically at Leah. "Actually I...we hadn't discussed it."

"That's no excuse," Elizabeth said immediately. "Leave the children with your father and me, and the two of you take the rest of the day and tonight for yourselves."

Leah wanted to object, but was immediately cut off. "But—"

"There's no but about it. You're family now, although I've always considered you part of our family anyway. Now it's official. And I won't allow this cantankerous son of mine to deprive his bride of a honeymoon."

"What about the children's things?"

"You can bring them over later. I'll give them lunch and put them down for a nap and everything will be just fine, won't it, boys?"

Spending time with their grandparents had always been a special treat, and the twins were eager for the opportunity.

"You're positive this isn't too much trouble?" Leah murmured. Since Kelsey was already asleep, Leah carried her to the crib set up in the Mannings' spare bedroom.

"No problem whatsoever," Elizabeth insisted. "You and Paul go and have a nice uninterrupted day. I'll drop the children off after church in the morning."

"This is so nice of you."

"Nonsense." Paul's mother hugged her. "I'm so happy for you and Paul. I couldn't imagine him finding a better wife."

Leah had no illusions about her marriage. As she and Paul had discussed earlier, theirs wasn't a love match— although Paul had made sure she understood she'd be sharing his bed. But for all intents and purposes, it was a marriage of convenience.

Convenient for him. Convenient for the children. Convenient for her.

"Thank you again," Leah said when Paul's mother escorted her to the front door.

Paul helped her into the car. The twins and their grandparents stood on the front lawn and waved as he started the car and they drove away.

Paul was quiet for several minutes, and without the children as a buffer, Leah felt awkward and ill at ease.

"I'm sorry, Leah," he finally said.

"For what?"

"For cheating you."

"Cheating me? I don't understand." She didn't feel the least bit slighted. Her wedding was exactly the way she'd wanted it. Intimate, with only the children present.

"Mom and Dad were right. I should've planned a honeymoon trip for us. It was inconsiderate of me."

"I don't want a trip."

"Perhaps not, but you deserve one. You deserve a whole lot more than I'm giving you." He sounded angry, but his disappointment was obviously directed at himself and not at her.

"Stop right this minute, Paul Manning."

"Stop? We're on the freeway."

She sighed. "I was speaking figuratively."

"Oh."

"It's not your job to read my mind. If I want something, I'll ask for it. All right?"

"All right."

A few minutes passed. "What about our wedding night?"

"What about it?" Leah felt uneasy discussing the subject.

"Do you want to go to a hotel?"

"No." Her response was immediate. A hotel would only make her more nervous than she was already.

"Why not?"

"Well…because…you might feel pressured to make love to me."

"Feel pressured?" She thought she detected a note of humor in his tone.

"I…I think our marriage would be better served if we delayed the…physical aspect of our relationship, don't you? I mean…what I'm trying to say is that, well, we hardly have anything to talk about without the children. Remember what it was like at lunch the other day? It makes sense to me that we should develop a solid friendship before we…you know."

"The term is make love," Paul returned impatiently.

"Right...before we make love." It was difficult for her to speak so openly, but she made the effort because too much was at stake. They had their whole lives before them. It seemed to her there was plenty of time to become comfortable with each other before beginning the sexual part of their marriage.

"You agree, don't you?" she asked timidly.

Paul didn't answer right away. "We'll sleep in the same bed."

He left no room for doubt. "If you want," she said.

"I certainly do."

"I'm agreeable to that." Leah found herself wishing they'd discussed this earlier.

"What about tonight?" he demanded. "If you don't want to go to a hotel, how do you suggest we spend the night?"

Leah hesitated. "Would you mind if we just stayed home?"

Eight

"You want to stay home." Paul was sure he hadn't heard her right. Not only had she chosen to skip a honeymoon, but she also wanted to ignore their wedding night. If it was what she really wanted, then fine, he could accept that. He didn't like it, but he could accept it. But staying home, that was another matter entirely.

"There's so much to do," she was saying.

"Like what?"

"I…thought I'd use this afternoon to move my stuff into your bedroom."

"Good idea. But what about tonight?"

"Tonight?" she echoed, her voice slightly raised with what sounded like nervousness.

"We should do something special."

"I thought…we already decided…not to, you know…haven't we? We'd agreed to hold off on the—"

"I was thinking more along the lines of going out to dinner."

"Oh."

The silence between them was filled with tension.

"Don't worry, Leah, I'm not going to ravish you." Paul didn't know how this marriage was going to survive with Leah's current attitude. He'd only kissed her twice. The first time had been one of the most sensual experiences of his life. The second had been at the end of their wedding ceremony, and although it had been little more than a brushing of lips, Paul had felt a hot current of need surge between them. She could deny it if she chose, but he wasn't going to.

Yet, despite the intensity of their attraction, Leah seemed determined to follow through with this self-imposed abstinence. Paul didn't really understand why, and it frustrated him.

When his parents had offered to take the children, Paul had entertained thoughts of bringing Leah home, carrying her over the threshold and directly into his bedroom. He'd envisioned an afternoon of introducing her to the physical delights of marriage. After dinner, he'd introduce her all over again.

He pulled into the driveway, turned off the engine and sat for a few minutes, trying to collect his thoughts.

"We can go out to dinner, if you like," she said weakly.

He nodded. Starting their marriage with an argument wasn't a healthy sign, especially since they'd never spoken crossly to each other before. Apparently they'd been saving all their arguing for the so-called honeymoon.

Paul went around to open her car door, and Leah

smiled tremulously up at him. Try as he might, he couldn't resist her and returned the smile.

So she wanted to build a solid relationship before they made love. He supposed he could understand that. He himself tended to see physical love as part of developing a relationship, but he realized she didn't. For her, that came later, after common ground had been established between them.

Okay, he could live with it.

He prayed he could live with it.

Once inside the house, they moved into their separate bedrooms and changed clothes. As Paul loosened his tie, he wondered just how long Leah felt they should hold off. He walked over to the closet and stood there, staring blankly at the row of clothes.

Would she make him wait a week? He could endure a week.

What about a month? Nope. Out of the question.

He removed his shirt, then, sitting on the end of the bed, he untied one shoe and slipped it off his foot.

He didn't realize he'd been there so long, mulling over the situation, until he heard Leah outside the bedroom.

"Paul?"

"Yes."

"I'm ready to bring in some of my things."

"Just a minute." He finished changing in record time, then opened the door. She stood there in a loose shirt and faded jeans, holding a load of clothes in her arms. Paul took them from her and carried them to the bed.

"I was thinking I could move my things, and you could take the children's stuff over to your parents'."

"Sure," he said amicably enough. He wasn't eager to leave her, but it might be for the best. He'd put the time to good use, ponder what he was going to do about this nonmarriage-marriage.

"Do you want some lunch before you go? You must be starved—you didn't have anything to eat this morning, did you? I know I didn't."

"No, thanks." He shoved his car keys into his jeans pocket.

"But aren't you hungry?"

His eyes found hers. "Yes, Leah, I'm hungry," he informed her. "I'm starving to death."

His exit made for excellent drama, but it didn't do anything to improve his mood.

They were married. He had the legal document to prove it. And yet he couldn't enjoy the rights and privileges of marriage....

Paul hadn't come to any conclusions by the time he returned to the house. His poor parents must be wondering what was going on. He'd parked in their driveway, gotten out of the car, walked to the door, waited until his mother answered, handed her the clothes Leah had packed for the kids and a fresh stack of diapers for Kelsey, turned around and left.

He thought he might've heard his mother call after him, but if that was the case, he'd ignored her. He also thought he might've heard his father chuckling, telling Paul's mother she should recognize a man in a hurry when she saw one.

Paul was in a hurry, all right, but he didn't have anywhere to go.

Back at the house, Leah had emptied her bedroom and transported her clothes, books and assorted paraphernalia into his. A lot of good sleeping in the same bed was going to do them.

"I…fixed you some lunch."

"Thanks." He made the effort to smile as he walked into the kitchen.

She followed but stayed several feet behind. What did she think, he was going to attack her?

"You're angry with me, aren't you?" she asked, folding her hands.

"No."

"You are. I can tell.… I told you I'm not good at these things. Di— My sister was always so much better at dealing with emotions… Dealing with men, too. You regret marrying me already and…"

She sounded close to tears. Whatever anger or frustration Paul was experiencing died a sudden death. He walked over to her and took her in his arms, wanting to ease her distress.

"I'm sorry," he breathed into her hair, loving the feel of her in his arms. With his finger he brushed a strand of hair from her face.

"I feel like a total failure as a wife and we haven't even been married a day. I'm sorry…." He heard the tears in her voice and he felt like the biggest jerk who'd ever lived. He'd behaved like a little boy who'd had his candy taken away from him. If anyone was to blame, he was the one.

"No, *I'm* sorry," he whispered.

"You?" She lifted her head and looked up at him. "Why?"

"Because I've acted like a major jerk."

"You're disappointed because I wanted to wait before we…made love?"

He nodded.

"I…I didn't think you'd want me. Not really."

"Not want you?"

She lowered her eyes and went completely still. The only movement was the rise and fall of her chest as she breathed. "I'm not very pretty."

"Leah, for heaven's sake, you're so beautiful you take my breath away!"

"Please don't lie to me. I know my assets and my weaknesses and—"

Paul reacted instinctively, framing her face in his hands, his eyes on hers. Whatever else she'd intended to say disappeared as his mouth claimed hers. He'd obviously caught her off guard. Leah braced her hands against his chest and, after a moment of surprise, parted her lips to him.

Paul groaned. He hurt. He ached. He wanted her so badly….

Leah groaned, too, and he took her mouth again, this time long and slow instead of hungry and demanding. Paul found himself drowning in hot sensation. He had to touch her….

Leah groaned anew.

"Am I hurting you?"

"No."

"Frightening you?"

"Yes."

He started to move away.

"No," she pleaded, clutching his wrist. "What frightens me are the wonderful things you make me feel."

Paul kissed her again. And again. He kissed her softly. Then quickly. Teasingly. Slowly.

Leah's eyes fluttered open with disappointment when he stopped. They were brown-green now and hazy with passion. "Paul?"

"Hmm…"

"I…"

"You're beautiful."

She stiffened, but Paul continued to hold her. "I love the color of your eyes. They intrigue me, the way they change. So many shades of color, of meaning…"

She blushed, but Paul hadn't even begun to tell her everything he found exquisite about her. "You have no idea how beautiful your hair looks in the sunlight." He wanted to tell her about the afternoon he'd watched her working in the backyard with the children around her, but he couldn't find the words.

"I love your mouth."

He kissed her to prove it.

"Paul." She sighed.

"But most of all," he said, "I love your laugh."

"Oh, Paul."

"So don't you dare tell me you're not beautiful."

"You make me want to cry."

Paul smiled. "You've helped dry *my* tears, Leah." He paused. "I want you so much."

"You do?"

"Are you sure you want to wait?" Paul whispered.

"Uh…I'm not sure of anything at the moment."

His fingers were busy unfastening the buttons of her shirt. "What about this?" he asked. "Maybe…"

How or when they made it from the kitchen to the bedroom, Paul didn't know.

They collapsed onto his bed together. As they cuddled there, kissing, she suddenly began to squirm. "We can't," she said breathlessly.

"Why not?"

"Because…because there's someone…here."

Only then did Paul hear the persistent peal of the doorbell. "What the hell," he said, bolting off the bed. He didn't bother to put on his shirt as he marched out of the bedroom and to the front door.

He jerked it open to see Jason—baseball cap on his head and bat in his hand.

"What do you want?" Paul snarled.

"Paul," Leah said from somewhere behind him, her voice the cool mist of reason.

"It's Jason," he said, turning around to face her.

"Don't you think you should invite him in?"

"Frankly, no."

Jason, however, didn't wait for an invitation and strolled boldly into the house. He paused in the middle of the living room and seemed to notice Paul's disheveled state for the first time. Leah was quickly buttoning her shirt, gazing up at his brother with reddened cheeks, clearly wondering why she'd ever left the bedroom.

"I don't suppose I've dropped in at an inauspicious time, have I?" Jason asked, grinning from ear to ear.

* * *

Leah had never been more embarrassed in her life. Her face felt fiery hot.

Jason didn't seem at all disturbed. Paul looked just plain angry.

Both men, however, were staring at her as if *she* should be the one to explain. "We're married," she said after an awkward moment.

"Married." Jason's already broad smile widened. "When did this happen?"

Paul looked at the living room clock. "Three and a half hours ago. You just interrupted my wedding night, so to speak. This better be good."

"Anyone else know?" Jason leaned indolently on his baseball bat, crossing his ankles.

"Mom and Dad."

"They've got the children," Leah said as she turned away. Her shirt was misbuttoned. She hurried to the master bedroom and searched for her bra. By the time she returned, properly dressed, she'd managed to compose herself somewhat.

Jason had plopped himself down on the couch, resting his ankle on his knee. He was completely at ease, arms stretched out on either side.

"So you're married."

"You want to see the proof?" Paul asked.

Jason's gaze meandered over to Leah. "I already have."

Paul's arms circled her waist, bringing her close. "I take it this unexpected visit has a purpose."

"Yeah. But I'm having so much fun watching Leah blush, I thought I'd delay getting around to it a bit longer."

"If you value your neck, little brother, you'll get to the point right now."

Jason rubbed the side of his jaw. "As I recall, Rich interrupted Christy and Cody's wedding night, too. Must be a family habit."

"Jason!"

Paul's brother chuckled and uncrossed his legs. "Actually, it's a bit of a bad-news/good-news story."

"Give me the bad news first."

"John Duncan, the shortstop you replaced, was hurt this afternoon."

"Playing ball?" Leah hadn't realized softball was so dangerous.

"No," Jason assured her. "He tripped over something in the parking lot and sprained his ankle. Looks like he'll be out for the rest of the season."

"What's the good news?" Paul asked suspiciously.

"The team has elected you as a permanent replacement."

Leah's heart swelled with pleasure. Paul loved softball. The two weeks he'd played on his brother's team had done him so much good. He'd come home enthusiastic and happy. She couldn't understand his hesitation now.

"What's the matter?" Jason asked. "I thought you'd be pleased."

"I'm a family man."

"So?" Jason argued. "Rich has got a family, too, and he plays."

Slowly, his face devoid of expression, Paul turned to Leah. "What do you think?"

She nodded eagerly. "I think it'd be wonderful."

"You won't mind?"

"Of course not!"

"Then it's settled," Jason said, springing effortlessly to his feet. "I'll go now and let the two of you get back your…honeymoon." He paused when he reached the front door. "This isn't supposed to be a secret, is it?"

"No." It was Paul who answered.

"Good. Then it's okay if I tell a few choice folks— like your brother, for instance. Rich? Remember him? And his wife?"

A smile appeared on Paul's face. "It's fine with me." He glanced at her. "Leah?"

She nodded.

"Great. See you two lovebirds later."

Lovebirds. The word leapt out at Leah. If Jason hadn't arrived when he did, she and Paul would've made love. Despite all the very good reasons she'd assembled in her mind. Despite the fact that they weren't in love. Despite the fact that she wasn't emotionally ready to deal with the complexities of a sexual relationship. Despite all that, they would have made love.

Leah walked into the kitchen and stood by the sink, staring out at the backyard.

Paul followed her.

"I know what you're thinking," he said, standing behind her.

Leah doubted it. "What?"

"You'd still prefer if we waited before we make love."

"Yes!" She whirled around to face him. "How'd you know that?"

His smile drooped. "Because I'd prefer to wait, too."

Paul changed his mind fifteen times in the next fifteen minutes, and a hundred more times as the evening progressed. Jason calling them *lovebirds* was what convinced him Leah had been right about holding off on the lovemaking.

The word had the same effect on him as a punch to the stomach. Did he *love* Leah? Paul didn't know. He was physically hungry for her. He admired and trusted her. He was grateful to her. He appreciated her. He found her generous and sweet.

But did he love her?

That was the one question Paul couldn't answer. He loved Diane. He could never stop loving her. But if he loved Diane, was it possible to love Leah at the same time?

This was another question for which Paul didn't have an answer.

Although he'd rationalized marriage and a physical relationship between them—Diane wouldn't have wanted him to be alone—he discovered the justification no longer eased his mind. He had no way of really knowing what Diane would've wanted.

Diane had been his wife. But now he was married to Leah. Where did that leave him?

Married to one.

Devoted to the other.

That was where it left him. Exactly where he'd been

weeks earlier. One foot in the present, the other in the past. Torn between two sisters.

One alive.

The other dead.

Married to both.

Paul took Leah out to dinner that night. A fancy restaurant. Expensive, elegant. He'd already robbed her of so many of the things a wife was entitled to. A courtship, for one.

Leah was a beautiful, generous woman, but she'd been the only one giving in their relationship. It angered Paul that he'd been so oblivious to her needs.

Not only had Leah been deprived of a courtship, but she hadn't even had a decent wedding—a ceremony with flowers and music, family and friends. Instead he'd rushed her to a preacher friend, not even the minister at the church they attended. He'd married her before strangers, as though he was ashamed.

As the evening went on, Paul felt even worse. He'd cheated this warm, gracious woman out of so much. He wondered how long it would take him to make it up to her. He knew one thing. He'd do it before he made any physical demands on her.

Leah deserved that much.

Leah wasn't sure what she should expect of married life with Paul. After the first week, she was more confused than ever. Other than that first afternoon, Paul had hardly touched her. He kissed her cheek before he left for the office and again when he came home. But that was the extent of their physical contact.

Yet he'd never been more generous. He frequently brought her small gifts. A red rose on Monday. Bubble bath on Wednesday. A huge chocolate-chip cookie on Friday.

Leah didn't know what to make of the changes in him. He was patient and gentle. Tender in ways she hadn't expected. He praised her efforts, complimented her on her meals and on how clean the house was or how happy the children seemed. He complimented her, too, on her appearance—her hair, the clothes she wore, her eyes.

This was all well and good. But Leah longed to be a wife. A real wife. Not just a stand-in wife and mother, a replacement for her sister.

And she wanted all this even though she'd told him she'd prefer to wait.... She was embarrassed by her contradictory response to him. Yes, she felt that a sexual relationship shouldn't take place until they knew each other well. And yet... And yet...

Nights were the worst for Leah. After dinner Paul generally worked on his novel. He did this once the children were in bed—he always helped her with the twins and with Kelsey. But as soon as they were down for the evening, he retreated to his den.

Although he'd never said as much, not that he ever would, Leah was convinced his sudden focus on the novel was a convenient way to avoid being alone with her.

It might not have hurt so much if he hadn't kissed her and loved her so sweetly the first afternoon they were married. If he *hadn't* kissed her and told her how beautiful she was to him, she might never have known what she was missing.

But she did know.

She couldn't tell him, though; she just couldn't. And she certainly couldn't *ask* him to make love to her. Maybe some women could, but not Leah.

They slept in the same bed, but they might as well be in different countries for all the space Paul maintained between them.

All three of the children could have slept comfortably between them. And sometimes they did.

Ryan and Ronnie were pleased that their aunt Leah was now their daddy's wife. Leah wasn't convinced they understood the implications, except that she'd moved into the bedroom with their dad and they could have their playroom back.

Nearly two weeks after their wedding, Leah was absolutely sure Paul never intended to make love to her. She was busy arranging a vase of cut flowers after dinner on Friday evening when he came into the kitchen. The kids were asleep, and the night was gently warm.

Paul poured himself a cup of coffee.

"How's the writing?" she asked, keeping up the facade.

"Slow."

"Do you want to talk about the scene?" They did that sometimes.

"No."

His refusal hurt a little. If he hadn't been so loving toward her in so many other ways, Leah would've felt even worse. She gave him a smile of encouragement and returned to her task.

A half hour later she was leaving the bathroom—her

hair damp, wearing a cool cotton gown—just as Paul came into the hallway. He stopped when he saw her. His blue eyes looked wild.

Neither moved.

Leah could see every breath he took. She watched the pulse hammering in his neck and felt the tension that seemed to throb through his body.

Right then Leah sensed that he wanted her. It wasn't tension she saw in him but desire.

"Paul," she whispered, holding out her hand. "I…I want to be your wife." Her voice was shaky; she couldn't help that. This was as close as she could come to asking. His reaction to her was an invitation; she knew that. An invitation she was going to accept.

He closed his eyes. "You're…ready?"

She nodded. "I'm ready."

"There'll be no turning back."

"I know."

He took one step toward her and she met him half-way. He wrapped his arms around her waist and lifted her from the floor until her mouth was level with his own. Then he kissed her with an urgency that stole the breath from her lungs.

Nine

Leah had finally, finally given him the signal he'd been waiting for. Hoping for.

In the past two weeks Paul had tried to court her, show her how grateful he was to have her in his life. He'd brought her small gifts. But they seemed insignificant and couldn't begin to express everything that was in his heart. If anything, the gifts seemed to embarrass her more than they pleased her.

He wanted to talk openly with her, explain what was on his mind, but found it impossible. To his credit, during the first week of courting her, his motives had been pure. It was torture sleeping with Leah beside him without touching her. No small feat, he realized, particularly now that he held her in his arms.

The second week, his vision of what he'd hoped to accomplish had blurred, his original objective obscured by his growing frustration. Soon he'd lost track of just about everything, except what he was denying himself. At night he closeted himself in his home office, because being alone with her and not touching her was just too difficult.

Now that she was voluntarily in his arms, Paul wanted no room for misunderstanding. This time, what they started, they would finish. Like he'd told her, there was no turning back.

His hands were eager as he carefully pulled off her cotton nightgown. She must have sensed his excited perusal. Her gaze skirted shyly past him as she smiled. Paul reached out and placed his hand against the side of her face. She pressed her own hand over his.

"Second thoughts?"

Her gaze dropped as she shook her head. "None."

"Good." Which had to be the understatement of the century.

All that was left between them was the richness of their desire. All that was left was a beauty that overwhelmed him. A radiance that transcended them both.

"Oh, Paul," she whispered afterward, her eyes bright with tears. "I never realized it could be so beautiful." She combed her fingers through his hair and brought his mouth back to hers. "I didn't think you'd ever want to make love to me."

"Me not make...not want...never..." The words twisted themselves around the end of his tongue. "I've been doing everything but cartwheels in the garden trying to get you to notice me. What do you need, woman, smoke signals?"

Leah chuckled softly. "I doubt it would've done any good."

"Why not?"

"Because I've discovered that, for all your brilliance, you can be pretty dense."

"Who, me?"

"If anyone needed to send smoke signals, it was me."

Paul was floored. "Are you trying to tell me you—"

She nodded. "I wanted to say something…but I couldn't. I didn't know how. Anyway, you kept avoiding me."

"Avoiding you?" He couldn't believe his ears. "I had to escape because I didn't trust myself alone with you. Leah, I've been crazy for you since before we got married."

"You have?"

It shocked him that she was genuinely surprised to hear it. "You've kept me waiting nearly two weeks."

"I'm…not very good at letting you know my feelings, am I?"

He smiled down at her. "Remember, I'm not a mind reader. You're going to have to tell me what you want."

She nodded—and kissed him again.

At work Paul's mind wandered. There was probably a word for what was happening between him and Leah; he just didn't know what it was. Not long ago, they'd only communicated about the children or the household or occasionally his book. Now they were profoundly, intimately, attuned to each other.

Simply put, he *needed* Leah. He felt a sense of freedom in making love to her. Freedom and joy. A joy so great it all but sang from his heart. He expected to feel remorse and guilt, and had been almost giddy with relief when he felt neither. The first night he'd made love to her he'd lain awake and waited for the guilt to come crashing in on him. It hadn't.

He wasn't certain exactly what he *should* be feeling. If not guilt, then what?

He had loved Diane. He loved her still. That confused him even more. If he cared so deeply for Diane, then how was it possible to love Leah as much as he did?

For the first time in months, Paul was feeling something other than emotional pain, and it felt good. He didn't want to do anything that might threaten the happiness Leah had brought him.

Just thinking about his wife, at home waiting for him, made Paul rush out of the office. He found he did that most evenings now, eager to get home to his family. He'd hug his children and then bide his time until he could be with his wife, with Leah, alone.

Tonight he could hardly wait for the kids to go to bed after dinner. When they protested, saying it was still light outside, Paul appeased the twins by reading them a story. He tucked them in and within minutes they were asleep.

Then he walked into the kitchen, where Leah was cleaning up after bathing Kelsey and putting her to bed. She glanced over at him and smiled shyly.

There was a sweet innocence about her that got to him. He'd look at her a certain way, and she'd blush. He'd discovered that he loved to make her blush. She was very different in that regard from Diane and it entranced him.

"Leah." He moved up behind her and slipped his arms around her waist. He nuzzled her neck. "Let's go to bed," he whispered.

She turned slightly. "Paul, I think we should talk."

"Later," he promised, kissing the side of her face. "We'll do all the talking you want later. I promise."

"The boys...they just went down."

"They're asleep. I made sure of that."

"But..."

He was surprised by her resistance. Not once since that first night had she offered even a token protest.

"All right," he said, dragging in a deep breath. "What's wrong?"

"I...don't know."

"Obviously something's bothering you."

"Yes..." She stayed where she was, her back to him. "What about Diane?" she said in a low voice.

"What about her?"

"Do you...do you pretend—"

"No." He didn't allow her to finish because he knew what she was going to ask. "Not once have I made love to you and thought of her. Not once." He said it emphatically, so there'd be no doubt in her mind.

"Then...then what *do* you think about?"

He said the first thing that came to him. The truth. "How much I want you, how much you satisfy me. How grateful I am that you're in my life—and in my bed."

She turned to face him and slowly raised her eyes to his, studying his expression, seeking some outward sign that he was telling her the truth.

He reached for her hand and brought it to his lips. "It's true, Leah."

He kissed her then, astonished by the sweetness and the power of her kiss.

"You're *sure* the boys are asleep?" she asked in a whisper-thin voice. "I know Kelsey is…"

"Yes," Paul said, urging her toward the bedroom.

She didn't hesitate.

When they lay in each other's arms, satisfied and exhausted, Paul returned to the worry she'd confided in him a little earlier.

"Please believe me when I say I've never, ever, confused you with Diane. I need you, Leah. Not because of the way we make love together, and not because of all the help you've given me with the children. I don't know exactly when it happened or even why, but I need you in my life. To laugh with me. To share the joy of raising my children, to share the grief of losing someone we both deeply loved."

Paul's hands abandoned hers and moved to softly caress her face. "I call myself a writer, work with words every day, yet I can't find the words I need now. I wish I could say everything I feel for you. I wish I could explain what's in my heart…."

His mouth took her, and, sighing, she lifted her arms and slid them around his neck.

The phone on the bedside table rang just then, and Paul groaned and broke away. He let it ring a second time and a third as he tried to compose himself before answering.

"Hello." Despite his effort he knew he sounded gruff and impatient.

"Paul, it's Rich. Got a minute?"

Paul's eyes met Leah's and he grinned. That was about as long as he was willing to spare. "Yeah, a minute."

"Jamie and I were talking. Actually, Jason was in on the discussion, too."

"What discussion?"

"I'm getting around to that, so quit being so impatient. We all want to take you and Leah out to dinner Saturday night. Sort of a welcome-to-the-family thing for Leah. We should've done it sooner, but with Mom and Dad out of town… Anyway, better late than never."

It took an instant for his brother's words to sink in. He turned his face away from his wife because looking at Leah was too distracting.

"What did you say?" he muttered. "Dinner?"

"Yeah, dinner. Saturday night for you and Leah. Uh, do you want me to call back later?"

"No, that's okay. We'll need to find a sitter, but that shouldn't be too difficult."

"Mom and Dad will want to hold a reception for the two of you when they're back from Montana, but that's not going to be for a month."

"Or more."

"Exactly," Rich said. "It's too long to wait. We all like Leah and want to make sure she feels welcome."

"That's very nice."

A silence ensued while Paul tried to think of an excuse to get off the phone.

"Why don't you check with Leah," Rich suggested. "In case she made other plans."

"Oh…right." Paul realized he probably sounded like an idiot. "Hold on a minute." He cupped his hand over the receiver. "It's Rich. He's inviting us out to dinner Saturday evening. Is that a problem?"

"Ah…not that I can think of."

"It's fine," he said. "See you Saturday, then." He was hanging up the receiver when Rich stopped him.

"You might be interested in knowing where and what time."

"Oh, right." He opened his bedstand drawer and got a pen, then wrote down the necessary information using the title page of the paperback he was currently reading.

There was a slight hesitation from Rich once he'd finished. "You okay, Paul? You don't sound like yourself."

"I'm fine," he answered as evenly as possible. He hung up with a cursory goodbye and reached for Leah. "Now, where were we?"

Leah liked Jamie, Rich's wife. But until Paul had joined the softball team, she'd only talked to her sister-in-law occasionally. Whenever she did, though, Leah was impressed with Jamie's charm and graciousness. She didn't know her well enough to confide in her, but she hoped someday she would.

Leah needed a friend. Now more than ever. Diane was gone, and she'd drifted away from Linda, whose life had become so different from her own.

It wouldn't surprise Leah to learn that the Saturday dinner had been Jamie's idea. The two women had seen each other earlier in the week. Jamie had a doctor's appointment and her usual babysitter hadn't been available, so she'd called Leah. Naturally Leah had been happy to watch Bethany.

Bethany had been no trouble, and Jamie had been so grateful. She'd returned from her doctor's appointment beaming with the news of a second pregnancy. Leah hadn't told Paul, not wanting to ruin Rich's surprise.

Perhaps it was Jamie's happy news that brought Diane to mind. Leah missed her sister in so many ways. Yet she couldn't help feeling that Diane still stood between her and Paul. Between her and the children.

Although Paul had been quick to offer her reassurances that Diane's presence hadn't followed them into the bedroom, Leah's fears weren't completely laid to rest. She hoped Paul had told her the truth—that Diane wasn't part of their lovemaking. But if that was the case, why did Leah struggle with so much guilt?

Leah was afraid she knew exactly why. Without ever intending it, she truly had taken her sister's place.

Although the children called her Leah, they thought of her as their mother. As Elizabeth Manning had pointed out, Leah was the only mother Kelsey had ever known.

She was a wife to Paul, too. A wife in every sense. But Leah wasn't fooling herself. She knew her sister was the children's mother. Although he'd married her, Paul didn't love her. Maybe he wanted her, something he confessed to often. Maybe he needed her, something he demonstrated frequently. But he didn't love her. Not the way he had Diane.

Leah had thought she'd be content marrying Paul so she could raise the twins and Kelsey as her own children. A husband and family were more than she'd ever dreamed of having. But, to her dismay, she found herself becoming greedy.

The realization lay heavy on her heart. She'd always be a substitute. A poor second. A stand-in wife and mother.

Perhaps she was just feeling sorry for herself. It wasn't like her to feel so melancholy or morose, but she was carrying an additional burden now....

It didn't make sense that taking her sister's place should suddenly bother Leah so much. Not when she'd been living with Paul for nearly three months, married to him a month of that time.

Admit it, her heart cried. *You're in love with him.*

So what if I am?

He loves Diane.

That's all right, you loved Diane, too. She asked you to take her place, remember?

Leah did remember, but she hadn't expected to fall in love with Paul. Hadn't expected so many things.

She dressed carefully for the Saturday dinner, wanting Paul to be proud of her, but knowing that no matter what she wore or how she did her hair, she'd never be as beautiful as Diane.

Paul was in and out of the bedroom while she dressed. She'd been looking forward to this evening all week. Now she wasn't sure.

She'd been feeling listless all day, tired, a bit despondent. At noon she'd lain down with the kids and napped. Leah couldn't remember the last time she'd taken a nap. Not since she'd moved in with Paul, at any rate.

"You ready?" he asked, walking into the bedroom.

"I will be in a few minutes."

Paul frowned. "Are you feeling all right?"

She nodded, holding back her news. All her life she'd been far too prone to keeping secrets.

"You're not feeling well, are you?"

She sat at the edge of the bed and picked up her shoe, slipping on the patent leather pump. She hadn't meant to say anything, at least not yet.

"Did I tell you I looked after Bethany the other day while Jamie went to the doctor?" she asked, her voice low.

"I remember you said something about it. Why?"

"No reason." She backed off, not wanting to ruin the evening for them both.

"Leah, what's wrong?"

"Nothing." She pressed her fingers under her eyes, afraid she might start weeping. "I've been feeling...different all day."

"Any reason?" He sat on the bed beside her and reached for her hand.

Leah shrugged.

"Rich tells me Jamie's expecting again."

Leah nodded. "I'm really happy for them."

"Better them than us," Paul said with a small laugh.

Leah withdrew her hand from his. "What makes you say that?" she asked.

"For obvious reasons."

"I...see," she said stiffly.

"What do you see?" He sounded so puzzled.

There was no hiding the truth now. "Did it ever occur to you that…that I might be pregnant, too?"

Ten

"Are you pregnant?" Paul demanded. He couldn't seem to stand still. His heart was in his throat, and the *fear*...the all-consuming fear overwhelmed him. He shoved his hands in his pants pockets and formed tight fists.

"*Are* you?" he demanded a second time when Leah didn't respond.

"I don't know. Not for sure. But..."

He jerked one hand free and raked it through his hair. "How could something like this have happened?"

Leah looked so small, sitting there on the edge of the bed. His question appeared to revive her. Slowly, her hazel eyes burning with indignation, she stared at him. "What do you mean, how could something like this have happened? Think about it, Paul. Just think about it."

"We've been careful." In fact, he'd taken responsibility for birth control himself.

"What…what about the first time?"

He uttered a curse, short and to the point. Then, when he saw Leah flinch, his regret was instantaneous. He would've given his right arm to yank back the ugly word. That first night they'd made love had been one of the most beautiful experiences of his life. But the thought that their first time together might have resulted in pregnancy terrified him to the marrow of his bones.

"There was one other time, too…remember?" she informed him quietly.

Paul did remember. He'd been so eager for her they hadn't taken the necessary precautions. "How late are you?" he asked after a moment.

"Six days."

"Oh, no." Diane had never been late, except when she was carrying the twins and Kelsey. She'd always known by the end of the first week of her missed period whether or not she was pregnant.

"I…I'm not usually late, but…I could be for one reason or another."

Paul nodded, but he wasn't listening as he remembered the past few days. Leah had seemed tired and listless. Diane had been the same way during the first trimester of her pregnancies.

His heart froze in his chest, the dread nearly devouring him. He *couldn't* lose Leah. Not his wife. Not again. He couldn't bear it; he couldn't survive without Leah. Not now, when he was just beginning to live again.

"I…I made an appointment with the doctor for Monday morning," she said haltingly. "I wasn't going to say anything until I'd been to see him…but—"

"You should've said something before this," he broke in.

"Why?" she flared. "So you could be angry with me sooner?"

"I'm not angry."

"You're not exactly overjoyed, either."

"You're right," he answered crossly, "I'm not. Can you blame me?"

"No." The word was a strangled whisper. Her chin came up and tears brimmed in her eyes, ready to spill down her ashen cheeks. Her lower lip started to tremble, and Paul felt a knife twist in his heart.

She was so vulnerable, sitting there, pale and beautiful, bleeding from the wounds his fear had inflicted. He knelt in front of her and clasped her hands in his own. Taking a deep breath, he closed his eyes. "I'm sorry, Leah. I didn't mean to upset you. Whatever happens, we'll deal with it together. All right?"

She nodded.

The doorbell chimed in the distance, and Paul knew it was the babysitter. "Are you ready?"

Once more Leah nodded. "I think so… I'm sorry, my timing's incredibly bad—I shouldn't have mentioned it tonight. It just sort of…slipped out."

Paul kissed her temple and placed his hand on her shoulder. "We'll talk about it later. For now, let's put it aside and enjoy our dinner. Agreed?"

She gave him a watery smile and nodded.

Leah didn't know how she was going to survive dinner with Paul's family.

She desperately wished she hadn't told Paul she might be pregnant. She'd been conscious of the possibility for the past few days, so she'd already gone through the full spectrum of emotions. It hadn't been fair to hit Paul with the news so unexpectedly—just before a dinner party, of all things.

The moment the thought of pregnancy occurred to her, Leah's immediate reaction had been sheer joy. She'd been standing in front of the kitchen calendar when the realization suddenly struck her. It didn't seem possible. So soon? They hadn't made love all that often yet, but it seemed the most logical explanation for why she was late.

Her timing wasn't exactly spectacular—they'd only been married a few weeks—but Leah was thrilled. She loved Paul and the thought of having his baby, *their* baby, had filled her with excitement.

She'd been fearful, too. But not because of her sister. Diane's death had come about through a rare series of events. The likelihood that it might happen again was so slim it didn't warrant consideration. What did concern her were the demands of another child. She loved Kelsey and the twins, but by the end of the day she was exhausted. She was worried, too, about how the children would feel about another sibling.

But her biggest fear of all had been Paul's reaction. For that reason alone, she hadn't intended to mention anything to him until she was certain. She certainly hadn't intended to blurt it out the way she had. Perhaps she was hoping, praying, that he'd share some of her happiness.

Only Paul hadn't been happy. He'd been upset. Then regretful. She could understand and forgive his reaction; nevertheless it hurt. In fact, the pain went so deep, Leah didn't know how she was going to sit through dinner and smile.

"How often have you been late before?" Paul asked when they were in the car.

"Not often, and never more than a few days...that I can remember."

His hands tightened on the steering wheel until his knuckles went white. "I was afraid of that."

"I...thought you said we shouldn't worry about it now."

He sighed. "You're right, but I don't know if I *can* stop thinking about it."

Leah waited a moment, her heart aching. "Would it be so terrible?"

"Yes." His response was immediate. Harsh.

Leah's throat constricted. She turned her head and looked out the side window, wondering how she was going to keep from crying. It wouldn't hurt nearly as much if she didn't know how Paul had reacted when Diane told him she was pregnant with the twins, or when they'd learned she was going to have Kelsey. Paul had been delighted. Exuberant. He'd been so excited they'd celebrated for weeks. Diane had claimed Paul loved her the most when she was pregnant. He was gentle and romantic.

With Diane.

With Leah he was angry and disappointed.

Unexpectedly Paul reached for her hand, gripping it tightly. "Don't worry, we'll get through this."

"I'm not the one who's worried."

From the corner of her eye, Leah watched as Paul frowned darkly. "Maybe you should be."

"Why?"

"Why?" he exploded. "You just don't get it, do you? Look what happened to Diane when she had Kelsey. Do you honestly think I want to lose you?"

"A pregnancy isn't going to kill me."

"I don't want to chance it," he said firmly, leaving no room for discussion.

"Unfortunately, we may not have the option."

His lips tightened. "Do you mind if we deal with this some other time? We're nearly at the restaurant."

"All right," she whispered, managing by some miracle to hold the tears at bay.

When they arrived, Jason was sitting in the restaurant foyer waiting for them. Leah could've sworn it was the first time she'd seen Paul's brother without a baseball cap on his head. He was tall and good-looking, his eyes the same intense shade of blue as Paul's. He stood, smiling, when they entered the restaurant.

"Glad you two made it," Jason said. "Rich and Jamie will be here any minute."

Paul's smile lacked friendliness. He didn't respond to Jason's remark; instead, he buried his hands in his pockets and stared across the linen-covered tables at the view of Lake Union.

"So, Leah," Jason said, apparently willing to try again, "how's married life treating you?"

"Fine." There was no need to exaggerate.

Jason hesitated. "I'm pleased to hear it."

Leah, too, focused her gaze on the distance. The ability to make small talk had deserted her completely.

"Jamie made reservations," Jason announced. "Why don't we wait for them at our table? We might as well relax and enjoy the view."

"Sounds like a good idea to me." Paul said. He placed his hand at the small of Leah's back as they followed the hostess to a table for six by the window.

"Will someone else be joining us?" Leah asked conversationally, hoping to make up for her unsociable behavior earlier. "A date, Jason?"

"Not for me," he said, reaching toward the middle of the table for a bread stick. "I'm leaving all the marrying in this family to everyone else."

"Don't you want to get married?"

"Yes and no…I'm not opposed to it if that's how things go, but it isn't in my game plan right now."

"I know what you mean," Leah said, helping herself to an olive, ignoring Paul, who sat silent and morose beside her. "It would be nice if it happened, but if you don't find someone it won't be the end of the world."

"Exactly."

Paul remained ominously silent.

A few minutes later, Rich and Jamie arrived. Jamie's eyes were bright with happiness. Rich pulled out the chair for his wife, his gaze holding hers as they exchanged a lover's look.

They all greeted one another and then they studied the menu. "Tonight's a dual celebration," Rich announced proudly, smiling at his wife. "As you probably know, Jamie and I are going to be parents again."

"All right!" Jason said, pumping his fist in the air.

"Congratulations," Leah said, continuing to study her menu.

"Congratulations," Paul echoed with a decided lack of enthusiasm.

If anyone noticed, and Leah prayed they hadn't, they didn't comment. Watching Rich and Jamie and seeing the love they shared so openly, so generously, with each other, Leah felt her heart ache anew.

She hadn't thought she could have been any more miserable than she already was, but sitting through dinner with Paul's brother and his wife was agony. The love between Rich and Jamie was like a mirror that reflected all the weaknesses in Leah's relationship with Paul. His reaction to the news that she might be pregnant confirmed everything she'd ever feared about her marriage.

They ordered their meals and a bottle of champagne to honor Leah and Paul's wedding. But Leah didn't feel much like celebrating and apparently Paul didn't, either. For the second time that evening, Leah prayed no one noticed. She wasn't worried about Rich and Jamie feeling slighted; their attention was completely on each other. But Jason was another story. More than once she felt her brother-in-law's gaze. She tried to smile, tried to reassure him, but Leah discovered she had very little reassurance to give.

Not once did Paul speak directly to her during dinner. Leah didn't know if the snub was intentional or not. Nor had he spoken to anyone else unless he was addressed, and then he responded with as few words as possible.

The entire evening was a disaster. Leah fully accepted the blame. She should never have told Paul about the baby…if there even was a baby.

"You barely touched your dinner," he commented on the drive home.

"I…wasn't hungry." And she hadn't taken more than a sip or two of champagne, just in case she *was* pregnant.

After that remark he didn't say anything. He gazed straight ahead, concentrating on the road.

"You didn't seem interested in eating yourself," she said tentatively sometime later.

Still not looking at her, Paul expelled his breath. "I guess I wasn't hungry, either."

That night Paul couldn't sleep. Guilt and fear made for hellish companions in bed. He'd never thought of himself as a particularly heroic man, but he wasn't a coward, either. From the minute Leah announced she might be pregnant, he'd revised that opinion of himself.

He was the biggest coward who ever lived. He'd trembled with fear as soon as the word *pregnant* left her lips.

Knowing it was useless to lie there and toss and turn, Paul climbed out of bed and made his way into the kitchen. He didn't turn on any lights, but pulled out a chair and sat down in the dark. Propping his elbows on the table, he hid his face in his hands as he tried to reason with himself.

He should've been more careful, he told himself. He was an adult. He knew how to prevent a pregnancy. Considering what had happened to Diane, his carelessness, his casual neglect of precautions, horrified him.

He loved Leah, honestly loved her. He didn't understand how he'd been so fortunate as to have married two of the most generous, loving women he'd ever known.

He *couldn't* lose Leah. He didn't have what it took to live through losing her. He couldn't bury another wife.

The memory of the night Diane died came back to him. He recalled Dr. Charman's words as he told Paul how sorry he was, how he'd done everything possible to save her. He'd explained exactly what had gone wrong, but by then Paul hadn't been listening. All he'd heard was that his wife was dead.

A fresh wave of grief washed over him.

He couldn't lose Leah, too. He couldn't!

Not for the first time, Paul realized how selfish and self-centered he'd been when it came to Leah. Without intending to, he'd slighted her in so many ways.

He was just beginning to deal with her news—her possible pregnancy—just beginning to accept it, face his fears and prepare to speak openly with her, when he'd heard her talking to Jason about marriage. Leah had never expected to marry, she'd told his brother, and hadn't really cared whether it happened or not. She seemed so blasé, so flippant. Her attitude had stunned him.

And yet here he was, crazy in love with her. He'd assumed he was well past the point of having his feelings hurt. Nevertheless, her words *had* hurt him.

Perhaps he was overreacting; Paul didn't know anymore. He loved her, and she'd made their marriage sound like…like an accident. Inconsequential. As if she'd only agreed to his proposal because she wasn't likely to get another.

Maybe if he hadn't been so worried about her being pregnant, he might not have taken the comment so personally. Paul wasn't sure about that, either.

His thoughts churned for hours, until dawn crept over the horizon. Somewhere near morning, he returned to bed and crawled between the covers, gathering Leah in his arms, needing her warmth to chase away the chill that had taken hold of his heart.

Monday morning Paul came out of their bedroom dressed for work while Leah was making breakfast for Kelsey and the boys. Ryan and Ronnie were setting the table, and Kelsey was in her high chair, batting her cup against the tray and singing cheerfully.

Not once since they'd left the restaurant on Saturday night had Paul mentioned the possibility of Leah's being pregnant. He didn't need to; it was there between them like a living, breathing thing. He hadn't made love to her, either. Leah didn't know if he intended to ever touch her again.

"What time is your doctor's appointment?" he asked as he poured a cup of coffee.

"Nine."

"I want you to call me."

"At the office?" She'd never called him at the newspaper before.

"Yes. I'll be in all morning."

Waiting for your call. He didn't say it, but he might as well have.

"All right," she said, keeping her back to him.

"I'll talk to you later."

Leah nodded. "Later."

It wasn't until the door closed that she realized he'd left for work. Without kissing her, without even telling the kids goodbye, without saying another word, he'd walked out.

Tears rained down her cheeks; there was no controlling her emotions any longer. She turned off the burner and brought the plate of French toast to the table, where the boys were waiting.

She was grateful that the twins didn't seem to notice she was weeping. She let them dish up their own plates, spread the butter and pour the syrup—half of which ended up on the table.

Rubbing her eyes, she sat down with the boys, but, like Paul, she didn't have much of an appetite. Holding her cup in her hands, she leaned her elbows on the table.

"Leah?"

Ronnie stood beside her chair, his big blue eyes gazing up at her.

"What is it, sweetheart?"

"Here," he said, shoving his tattered yellow blanket into her lap.

Touched by his generosity, Leah hugged him close. It was then that the sobs overtook her.

Paul had gone forty-eight hours on less than five hours' sleep. He'd woken feeling as though the two hours he'd slept had made him feel worse than if he hadn't slept at all.

Furthermore he was dangerous in this condition—to himself and to others. He was halfway to work before he realized he'd even left the house. It wouldn't have concerned him so much if he hadn't been driving. He couldn't remember leaving home or saying goodbye to Leah and the children. If he had, the memory had escaped him.

The phone on his desk rang, and Paul grabbed the receiver, dropping it in his anxiety.

"Paul Manning."

"All right, what's going on?" It was Jason.

"What do you mean?"

"Between you and Leah. Dinner Saturday night was supposed to be a celebration."

"It was…"

"Not from where I sat," Jason countered.

"Leave it alone," Paul said crisply. He wasn't one to share his problems and never had been. If Leah was pregnant, the news would come out soon enough. There was no reason to discuss it with Jason.

"Not this time, big brother."

"I can't talk," Paul said crossly. "I'm expecting an important call."

"From whom?"

"Leah," Paul said without thinking.

"Do you expect her to phone and apologize?"

Paul laughed. "You aren't going to trick me into discussing my problems, so don't even try."

"I wasn't," Jason denied. "But you admit there *are*

problems?" He sighed loudly. "Listen, Paul, would you stop being so almighty proud for once? We're family. You seem to think that just because you're the oldest you should be able to deal with everything all by yourself. Well, I've got news for you, big brother. You aren't any better than the rest of us."

"I never thought I was."

"Then tell me what's wrong with you and Leah. I've hardly ever seen two people look so unhappy."

Paul hesitated and rubbed his face. He was weary in body and spirit. Worried sick. Frightened out of his wits, and he didn't know what to do. Make a counseling appointment, he supposed; spill his guts to a professional.

He pinched the bridge of his nose. "Leah thinks she might be pregnant," he admitted hoarsely.

"No way!" His voice was shocked. Incredulous. Dismayed.

"My sentiments exactly," Paul said, grateful that his brother understood his fear. Grateful, too, that Jason hadn't made some stupid comment about Paul keeping his pants zipped. They were zipped now. He hadn't touched Leah in two nights. It hadn't helped, either. If anything, it had increased the tension between them.

"When's she going to the doctor?"

"This morning. She said she'd phone me."

"How does she feel about it?"

Paul had to stop and think. Darned if he knew. He'd never stopped to ask her. "I...don't know," he said reluctantly.

"What about you?"

"I've never been so frightened in my life! I haven't slept in two nights…. The thought of losing Leah…"

"You won't."

"How can you be so sure?" he demanded. "Diane gave birth to the twins without much of a problem. Who would've believed a second pregnancy would kill her?"

"Yes, but aren't you forgetting something?"

"What?" Paul asked impatiently.

"Leah."

Paul stopped cold. Jason was right. He'd been so wrapped up in his own fears, he hadn't taken Leah's feelings into consideration. Not even once. If she showed any fear of being pregnant, he hadn't sensed it. But he didn't understand how she could *not* be afraid. He was terrified, and they weren't even certain yet.

"But what?" Jason prompted.

"She doesn't actually seem frightened of being pregnant." If anything, Paul had detected a hint of exhilaration, a joyful expectation. With his own fears running rampant, with his guilt and anxiety, he'd ignored *her* feelings.

"In other words, all Leah knows is that you're scared."

"No." It wasn't until now, talking to his brother, that Paul realized how badly he'd bungled things once again. "All she knows is that I'm angry."

"Angry?"

"Yes, angry."

"With her?"

"No," he said forcefully. "That wouldn't make any sense. I'm furious with myself."

"And she *knows* this?"

"Of course she knows it." Or at least he assumed she did. Assumed that she understood his concern was for her, because he loved her so much.

"You're sure of this?"

Paul rubbed the back of his neck. "You know, Jason, maybe you've missed your calling in life. You should be the reporter, not me."

Jason chuckled and Paul smiled, too. "I can see there's some fence-mending I need to do with my wife. I guess I should thank you for being so kind as to point that out to me."

"Anytime. If I ever get married, which is unlikely, you'll be the one I turn to when I'm in trouble."

"Frankly," Paul said, "I don't think that's such a good idea."

"Why not?"

"Because I've got to be about the worst example of a husband you could find."

"Don't be so hard on yourself. You're only human."

"Would you care to explain that to Leah for me?"

"Not on your life. That, big brother, is something you'll have to do."

"That's what I thought you'd say."

It wasn't easy, but with a little begging and a lot of bargaining, Paul managed to get the rest of the day off. What he had to say to Leah couldn't be said over the phone, nor could it wait. He'd been so wrapped up in himself and his own fears that he'd hurt the one person in the world—besides his children—whose happiness meant everything to him.

He drove home, parked in the driveway and leapt out

of the car. He raced into the kitchen to find Leah folding laundry. He stopped abruptly.

"I…I tried to phone the office twice," she told him quietly. "They said you weren't there. Your cell was off. I left messages."

Now that he was home, with his wife, Paul found himself at a loss for words. He held out his arms to her.

"I did try to phone," she said again. "There was no reason for you to rush home."

"Don't say anything else."

She looked at him as though she wasn't sure what to expect. He enclosed her in his arms, cherishing her warmth, her softness.

Holding her face between his hands, he gazed down on her. Her puffy eyes told him she'd been crying. It broke his heart to acknowledge that he was the source of her grief.

"Leah," he said, then paused, not knowing how to proceed. Showing her how he felt seemed easier. He loved her, and it was time she knew it. He kissed her hungrily, deeply, his mouth moving over hers with a desperation that verged on wild. "I love you, Leah," he chanted. "I love you. I love you."

"Paul…I'm not…" She tried to break away from him, and he felt the resistance in her. He knew he'd won whatever battle she was waging when she parted her lips to him.

Leah broke away and hid her face in his chest, her shoulders heaving. "Why tell me that now?" she asked.

"Because it's true…because I should've told you

before. I've been so worried you might be pregnant and—"

"I'm not."

"You're not?"

"The doctor said he doesn't know why my period's so late. It probably has something to do with anxiety, but I can't recall being upset about anything."

The relief that flowed through Paul felt like water on a parched garden. He tried not to show it, not to reveal how grateful he was that he didn't have to face this fear head-on so soon after their marriage. So soon after he'd found happiness again.

"You'll be happy to hear something else."

"What's that?"

"I'm not going to get pregnant, either… I'm going on the pill, so you won't need to worry about me getting pregnant with a baby you don't want."

Eleven

"It isn't that I don't want another child," Paul started to explain, but Leah turned away, not wanting to hear. She picked up a towel and held it protectively against her stomach.

"Paul, I know what your feelings were. Please don't try to sugarcoat them now. You could barely look at me…. You haven't touched me since…Friday night. This morning you left for work without bothering to say goodbye—as though you couldn't wait to get away from me."

"Leah, it's not what you think." His hands settled on her shoulders, but when she stiffened he released her. He walked around the table so she wouldn't have any choice but to look at him, although she still avoided eye contact.

"What else was there for me to think?" she asked. "That you'd be overjoyed if I got pregnant? That you'd arrange for someone to take the children so we could celebrate alone? Did you arrive home with my favorite ice cream and a jar of pickles?"

Her words had the desired effect. He went pale. It was how Diane and Paul had celebrated when they'd learned Diane was pregnant with Kelsey. Alone, their happiness bubbling over, their love and excitement centered on each other.

"I got the message, Paul. Loud and clear."

"It's just that I was so afraid of losing you…."

"Exactly. Who'd be here to wash and clean for you? Who'd be here to raise your children and…and warm your bed?" she added scornfully. "You'd miss me, all right, but for all the wrong reasons."

"Leah…no! It isn't like that. I love you."

"I saw how much you love me." She threw the towel she was folding down on the table and walked into the backyard. Her garden was in full bloom, the tomato plants heavy with reddening fruit. Now that summer was ending, her small harvest was almost ready to reap. Colorful sheets from the twins' beds were on the line she'd asked him to put up, flapping in the wind. On days like this, she hung laundry outside to dry, both to cut down on the electricity she used, and for the clean, breezy smell. The evidence of her life here was all around her.

Leah stood with her back to the house and brushed the tears from her eyes. She heard the door close, alerting her that Paul had followed her outside.

"I may have cheated you in a lot of ways," he admitted, his words deceptively soft. "You didn't have the courtship you deserved or even the wedding you should've had. There are probably countless other ways in which you've lost out in this marriage. But I never intended it to be like this—I never meant to be so thoughtless and self-centered."

A long moment passed. "I love you, Leah. I know you don't believe me. I can't blame you for that, but it's the truth." The words echoed with pain and regret. "What can I do?"

"Do?"

"To right the wrongs…to prove to you I mean what I say. To make up for the way I acted when I thought you might be pregnant."

Leah didn't know. Even if she could have, there was nothing she'd change. She'd moved into his home voluntarily. Married him of her own free will. She loved the children, loved being their mother, and, God help her, she loved Paul, too. With all her heart and soul, she loved Paul.

"Tell me, and whatever you want me to, I'll do."

"It's not that simple."

"I know."

She turned to face him then, her heart hammering. But when she tried to speak, the words refused to come out. "Just…"

"Yes?" He moved one step closer to her. One small step.

"Just…love me…"

"I do. Oh, Leah, I do." He reached for her, burying his face in the curve of her shoulder, his body shuddering against hers.

"…the same way you loved Diane."

* * *

"How does it feel to have the boys in kindergarten half days?" Jamie Manning asked Leah. It was the second week of September, and they were shopping at the mall, pushing their strollers side by side down the concourse, checking out the fall sales.

"They love it."

"What about you?"

"The truth?" Leah said, smiling at her sister-in-law. "I love it, too."

"Free at last," Jamie cried dramatically, then, glancing down at Kelsey, amended the statement. "Well, almost free."

"I can't believe how much more time I have with the boys gone in the mornings. Wait until Bethany starts preschool and you'll know what I mean."

Jamie paused as they neared the food court. "Dare we stay for an early lunch?"

Leah checked her watch. "Depends on how brave you feel."

"Oh, I've always been pretty brave."

"Be warned—Kelsey likes to throw food."

"No problem. We'll sit as far away from other people as we can."

Leah agreed. It felt good to get out of the house for a while, although shopping had never excited her much before. But now that she had Paul and the children to buy for, she enjoyed it.

Taking a morning off to spend with Jamie had lifted her spirits. During the past couple of weeks, things had been strained between her and Paul. He was trying hard to please her, but instead of helping, it had only made matters worse. The harder he tried to prove his love for her, the more forced it seemed. Paul was in a no-win situation, and Leah had put him there.

Leah needed a confidante. A friend. Jamie was fast becoming both.

Leah bought a chicken salad and for Kelsey, an order of french fries. She'd prepare a proper lunch when they got home. Jamie got a slice of pizza for herself and bread sticks for Bethany. In a few minutes they had the toddlers in high chairs the mall provided and were sitting at a small table as far from the other diners as they could get.

"By the way," Jamie said, looking at Leah's watch, "is that new?"

She nodded, swallowing a bite of her salad. "Paul got it for me. I casually mentioned how much I like Mickey Mouse and the very next day he brought me this."

"Your birthday?"

"No." Leah set aside her plastic fork and lowered her head. "He…he feels guilty."

"Guilty? Why?"

She shrugged. "We…thought I was pregnant not long ago. Paul doesn't want another baby. I know a big part of what he was feeling had to do with what happened to my sister, but at the same time I was terribly hurt by how he acted."

Jamie put down her pizza and nodded. "We have a lot in common, Leah, more than you realize. Rich and I didn't come into our marriage in the typical way, either. In fact, we made arrangements for a divorce when we planned the wedding."

Leah knew the gist of Jamie and Rich's marriage story, but not the details. "You married Rich because you wanted a baby, isn't that right?"

Jamie smiled and smoothed the soft blond curls from her daughter's forehead. "Something like that. I wanted a baby, and because I didn't intend to marry, I asked Rich to be the father. It made sense to me, since I wasn't in love with him. Oh, I mean, I *was* in love with him, only I didn't realize it at the time. I told myself he should be Bethany's father because he had the right genetic makeup." She paused and laughed. "We'd been friends since high school and I approached him on that basis. Friend to friend. I wanted him to be my sperm donor."

"And he agreed to this?" It didn't sound like the Rich Leah had come to know.

"He insisted, for a variety of reasons, that we get married. I wasn't keen on the idea, but I went along with it because otherwise Rich wouldn't agree to my plan."

"Then Bethany was conceived artificially?"

Jamie laughed once more. "No, she was conceived the good old-fashioned way. The same way this baby was." She flattened her hand against her abdomen. "So you see, I wasn't exactly a traditional bride, either."

"I imagine you and Rich thought Paul was crazy to marry me."

"No," Jamie said emphatically. "The situation's unusual, but no more than ours. You've been so good for Paul, good for the children, too." She hesitated. "Do you love him?"

"Yes." Leah's whole heart went into that word.

"I knew you did. He loves you, too."

Leah dropped her gaze. She wasn't nearly as confident of Paul's feelings as her own. He needed her, but she'd always wonder if he truly loved her. For herself. For Leah, the shy, plain Baker sister. The plodding math teacher with her logical mind.

When he'd told her he loved her that morning two weeks earlier, it had seemed like a miracle. She realized now it was the only thing he could say under the circumstances, knowing how badly he'd hurt her. He was seeking a way to atone for the pain he'd unwittingly inflicted. Leah wanted to believe him so badly. He had touched a chord in her she hadn't known existed, satisfied a craving that reached far back into her childhood. In all her life, no man had ever really loved her. Not her father, who'd abandoned her when she was barely old enough to remember him. Not Rob. Not the few other men she'd dated. It seemed obvious to her that whatever a woman needed to make a man happy, Leah Baker lacked.

Until Paul. He made her vulnerable in ways she'd never experienced. Vulnerable to love. Vulnerable to a happiness she'd never expected to find. Vulnerable to a tenderness that touched her heart.

"He's trying so hard," Leah whispered. Trying to give her all the things she'd missed before their marriage. In the past two weeks, he'd resumed his courting, with gifts and compliments. He'd wooed her back into his bed and loved her with an urgency that melted any resistance.

He was trying so hard...to love her, for herself.

"Rich and I experienced our own problems," Jamie went on to say. "We never intended there to be anything physical between us. It was supposed to have been a marriage of convenience—but it turned out to be one of *in*convenience."

"What happened?"

Jamie took a sip of her soft drink before answering. "We were secretly married, and I had dinner with a former boyfriend. It wasn't a date, wasn't even close to one. He was married and having problems and needed someone to listen to him."

"Rich was jealous?"

"Terribly. But to be fair to Rich, his feelings were understandable. The woman he'd recently broken up with had been cheating on him, and it seemed to Rich that I was doing the same thing. Everything blew up in our faces."

"But it all worked out, didn't it?"

"Eventually, but things got worse before they got better." Jamie's hand tightened around her soft drink. "I guess what I'm trying to say is, I don't want you to be discouraged. I've known Paul for quite a few years. He's an honorable man. I can't believe he'd ever have married you if he didn't truly love you. If you're having problems now, don't worry about it. All couples do. There's a period of adjustment." Jamie grimaced comically. "I sound like I really know what I'm talking about, don't I?"

Leah smiled. "I appreciate hearing it, but even more than that, I appreciate having someone to talk to.... I miss Diane so much. I not only lost my sister—I lost my best friend."

"Paul understands that," Jamie said quietly. "Diane was his best friend, too."

* * *

It was Friday night. Late Friday night. Leah sat up in bed reading, and Paul was working feverishly on his novel, writing the last chapter. A marathon session. Leah decided she'd wait for him, which wasn't difficult since she was involved in a whodunit by one of her favorite authors.

After an exciting chase scene, the book reached its satisfying conclusion. Closing it with a sigh, Leah climbed out of bed and walked into the kitchen, looking for a snack. Something other than graham crackers and peanut butter. She was bending over the lower shelf of the refrigerator when Paul spoke from behind her.

"Now that's an inviting pose."

"Paul," she chided, straightening quickly, a chicken leg clutched in one hand. She shut the refrigerator door and turned around. "So, are you finished?"

He nodded.

"Are you going to let me read it?"

He crossed his arms and leaned against the door frame. "That depends."

"On what?" she asked suspiciously, narrowing her eyes.

"On how much you appreciate literary genius."

"Oh, I appreciate genius, all right." Paul seemed more relaxed than she'd seen him in weeks. She enjoyed bantering with him, enjoyed his lighthearted mood.

"Might I suggest you lose that chicken leg and come over here?" He held out his arms to her.

Leah gave up her snack to move willingly into his embrace.

His arms slipped around her waist as he lifted her from the floor. "It's taken me nearly two years to get this book on paper."

"But you did it, Paul! You did it."

"I believe a reward would be fitting, don't you?" His gaze focused on her lips.

"What kind of reward?" she asked, batting her lashes in exaggerated enticement.

His eyes darkened in unspoken invitation. "I have a feeling you'll think of something."

"I'm thinking, all right." And she was.

Paul stared into the night, his arms around his wife, feeling utterly content, utterly satisfied. They'd made love for hours....

The urgency he felt to be with Leah hadn't changed in the weeks since their marriage. He didn't understand it, but he'd given up questioning his need for her. It was just there. Powerful and intense.

He'd worked harder these past two weeks at controlling it, for fear she'd accuse him of using her. Maybe on some deep, psychological level he feared it himself. So he was rationing himself. They'd make love once a week—that was all.

Maybe twice, he amended; no need to be stingy. No need to raise Leah's concern should she notice. Yes, twice a week made more sense. Wednesdays and Saturdays. Maybe Monday and Thursdays and either Saturday or Sunday. No, that was three.

Oh, what the heck, three times a week wouldn't be too much. Would it?

He smiled to himself as she nestled her head against his chest. He hadn't slept yet, and it would soon be morning. Close to the time the twins and Kelsey would be waking up.

He didn't care how little sleep he got; tonight had been worth every second of lost sleep. When he'd last looked at the clock, it had been past four. Leah had retrieved her chicken leg and brought it to bed, claiming she was hungry. Who wouldn't be after what they'd just done?

She couldn't let her hunger go unattended, she'd said, attacking the leg. A college professor—even one on sabbatical—couldn't live on love alone. He smiled at the memory.

His book was finished. After two long years, he finally had the story completely worked out. There'd been a sense of fulfillment, an overwhelming sense of accomplishment and pride as he printed out the last chapter. He'd read it over during the next week, do what editing he could at this stage and then mail it off to New York. He'd queried a reputable agent, who'd expressed interest in seeing it. Then the waiting would begin.

Paul was beginning to feel a cautious optimism about life. He was happy. Not *almost* happy. Just plain happy. Once he realized that, he wondered if he should be feeling that way. No, he decided, stopping that train of thought before it could gather speed. He wasn't going to censure himself. He wasn't going to examine his joy under a microscope and punish himself for feeling alive.

He had loved Diane. Loved her now. She'd been his first real love, his first wife, the mother of his children.

But she was in the past. She'd always be a part of him. But she was gone.

Then he'd found Leah. She was his heart now. His soul. His joy.

After the mistakes he'd made during the first few weeks of their marriage, he'd done everything he could to make it up to her, to show her how much he cared. In his own way, on a limited budget, with limited time, he'd been courting her.

Leah was the one who'd brought happiness back to his life. He could laugh again. The grief that had weighed him down for so many months had receded into the background. It no longer dominated his very existence. He still loved Diane and mourned her, but there were other emotions in his life now. Other diversions. He'd been freed from the stranglehold of his grief. His senses were fine-tuned. More poignant. More intense than before.

It was as if he'd woken up one morning and found himself alive after crawling into a grave.

When had it happened? Paul didn't know, but he was sure it had started when Leah decided to move in with him and the children. His whole world had taken a one-hundred-and-eighty-degree turn for the better that day.

They'd had their problems, but then all couples did. Leah was trying to make their marriage work, too. Slowly, as he gained her trust, she was lowering the walls she'd raised. He was winning her confidence bit by bit.

Leah wasn't Diane. She was more sensitive. Less open. A little more guarded, but he was learning. He was learning.

His eyes drifted shut. He was ready to sleep.

* * *

He dreamed of her that night.

Diane.

He'd fallen into a deep, contented sleep, and woke with a sick feeling in the pit of his stomach. A feeling of deep loss and sorrow, of regret.

Try as he might, Paul couldn't remember the details of the dream, only that it had been about Diane. He sat up in bed and held his head between his hands, feeling as though he had a terrible hangover.

Why did he have this dream *now?* It made no sense. He'd set everything in order, made his resolutions, chosen life. Chosen love.

Leah was awake. He could hear her in the kitchen with the children. He staggered out of bed and threw on yesterday's clothes.

Kelsey was sitting in her high chair waving a spoon, while the boys were stationed in front of the television set, watching Saturday-morning cartoons. Leah stood by the kitchen sink, sipping from a cup of coffee. All around him were the signs of ordinary life. Everyday, ordinary, *wonderful* life.

"Morning," he said. "You should've woken me."

Leah didn't answer.

"Leah?" He reached for a mug and poured himself a cup of coffee.

She kept her back to him.

"Is something wrong?"

She shook her head and set her cup aside before walking down the hallway to the bedroom.

He took a minute to drink some coffee, unclog his

mind, before he followed her. She was sitting on the end of the bed, looking lost and small and vulnerable.

He sat next to her, his stomach twisted in tight knots, dread filling his mouth. "What happened?"

"Nothing."

"Leah, don't play games with me," he said sharply. "Obviously something's upset you. Tell me what it is."

She was holding a tissue in her hand and had wound it around her index finger several times. "You…were asleep."

"The dream." It came to him with sudden clarity. "Did I call you Diane?"

Leah nodded.

"I…I had a dream. I don't know why, I just did. That's the thing about dreams—you don't control them. She was in it, which is about all I remember." He paused. "I'm sorry, Leah, but I swear to you that I didn't intentionally call you by her name."

"I know that."

"All I can do is ask you to forgive me."

"It isn't you who needs to be forgiven."

Paul closed his eyes, weary to the bone. "What do you want me to do? Tell me."

"I can't kid myself any longer, Paul."

"Kid yourself?"

"Diane was my sister, I loved her…she was my best friend from the time we were children. Even though she was younger, she was better than me in every area except grades. She was bright and pretty and fun. I was dull and plain and boring."

"Leah!"

"No, let me finish. Please, let me finish while I have the courage. I never competed with her, never allowed myself to be put in that position, because I knew, I always *knew,* I'd be the loser. The problem isn't you, Paul, it's me."

"I don't understand."

"I've discovered I'm greedy and jealous and I hate myself for it. I hate thinking the things I do. I hate feeling sick with envy because you love Diane. I feel guilty and miserable and I can't go on like this."

"Leah, Diane's gone. I've let her go—released her. She's my past. You're my present, my future."

"I wish it was that simple," she said with a sob.

"You don't need to compete with her."

Leah turned to look at him, her gaze unflinching. "Do you love her?"

He didn't hesitate. "Yes, but I love you, too."

"I need some time…to think, sort out my feelings. I'm sorry…."

"Time?" He went cold with fear. She was going to leave him. His heart was in turmoil, his head spinning. Could he have found happiness only to lose it again?

"I…can't sleep with you anymore, Paul. You want me, you desire me, but it's Diane you love. It's Diane you call for in the middle of night. Not me. For the first time in my life, I'm not willing to take second place to my sister. For once, just this once, I want something just for me. I want to be loved for *me.*"

She started to cry then, and Paul knew that nothing he could say would comfort her.

Twelve

Paul drove around for several hours, trying to clear his head. A light rain had begun and the skies were gray, which only depressed him more. He parked his car when he passed the small apartment complex his brother Jason owned. He sat there, wondering if he should talk to his younger brother.

He never discussed his problems with anyone, not even family. Generally he preferred to work things out by himself, without the counsel of relatives or friends.

But Jason had said something recently that had struck a chord with Paul. His brother had said it was time Paul realized he wasn't any better than the rest of them—that he should quit being so arrogant.

His brother's assessment had taken Paul by surprise. Jason and Rich viewed him as pompous! He'd thought he was just being strong.

Not dragging out his troubles for others to analyze wasn't a matter of pride, Paul had reasoned. More a question of habit. He was the oldest in a family of five. The others looked up to him. He was their role model. He could almost hear his parents' words, often repeated, reminding him how important it was to be a good example to the others.

He'd gotten so accustomed to keeping his worries to himself that he wasn't sure he knew *how* to ask for help. Or even if he should.

After several minutes, Paul climbed out of the car and ran toward Jason's apartment. He'd assumed Jason had made a mistake when he'd recently bought the eight-unit complex. As far as he was concerned, renters were nothing but trouble. But his brother didn't seem to be having much of a problem. He managed the building himself, made sure he got the right tenants, then sat back and collected the rent money every month.

Jason answered the door, wearing a football jersey and a baseball cap. He'd been a sports fanatic since they were kids. He'd been on the varsity cross-country, track and swim teams in high school, and he'd continued with cross-country in college.

These days all Jason played was softball, and the season had ended a couple of weeks earlier. But he still loved to watch any kind of sport.

"Paul!" He sounded surprised to see him.

"Morning."

"It's afternoon."

Paul checked his watch, shocked to see that his brother was right. "So it is."

"Come on in out of the rain. Notre Dame's about to kick off." He motioned toward his sofa, where a bag of potato chips had spilled across the coffee table and a can of soda was sitting on the morning paper.

Paul had only been to Jason's home once before, shortly after his brother had bought the building. A look around told him Jason wasn't much of a housekeeper. Newspapers, at least a week's worth, were carelessly scattered across the beige carpet. A partial load of laundry, towels it looked like, was heaped on the recliner. Several glasses, plates and eating utensils littered the living room.

Jason plopped himself down in front of the television. "Make yourself at home."

Paul sat on the sofa beside him and for a while pretended to pay attention to the game.

"You want something to eat?"

"No, thanks," Paul said. He reached for a potato chip and munched on it before he realized what he was doing.

"So things aren't working out between you and Leah?" Jason asked in that easygoing manner of his.

"How'd you know?" He hated the fact that his younger brother could read him so well. Paul had always thought of himself as aloof, adept at hiding his emotions. Apparently he wasn't as good at it as he'd assumed.

"You got the look, big brother," Jason said, grinning.

"The look?" Paul frowned.

"Yeah, the look of guilt. What'd you do this time?"

"Why are you so sure it was me?" Paul muttered.

"'Cause it usually is the guy," Jason said without taking his eyes off the television screen.

"For not being married, you certainly seem to be an

expert on this." Paul almost wished he'd gone to Rich, instead. He knew Leah had gone shopping with Jamie earlier in the week and he was delighted the two of them had become friends. If he was going to spill his guts, Rich was, for a number of reasons, the more logical choice, yet it was Jason he'd turned to.

"You're right, you know. I *am* guilty."

"You want to talk about it?"

Paul nodded and rubbed his palms together as he gathered his thoughts.

Jason reached for the remote and turned off the TV. "You want a drink? Soda? Beer? Coffee?"

With so many other things on his mind, Paul found making even a simple decision almost impossible. "Coffee, I guess." He followed his brother into the kitchen and marveled that there were any clean dishes left in the house. Dirty pots and pans lined the sink and counter. Ah, the joys of the bachelor life.

Jason opened the dishwasher and pulled out a mug. He examined it before filling it with tap water. Then he opened the microwave, removed a pair of socks and set the mug inside.

While the water was heating, Paul paced the small kitchen. "I had a dream last night…about Diane." He paused, half expecting Jason to comment. When his brother didn't, he continued. "I don't remember anything about the dream—only that she was in it."

"Has this happened before?"

"Not that I recall." Paul hardly ever remembered his dreams. "I don't understand it. If Diane was going to haunt my sleep, why now? Why would she come back just when I've made my peace with her death? It doesn't make any sense."

Jason apparently didn't have any answers for him, either.

"I've remarried and after almost a year, I can finally say I'm happy. Leah and I are…were," he amended sadly, "working everything out. I've been doing my best to be a good husband, to make up for the things I didn't do earlier. Now *this*."

"Don't go hitting yourself over the head because of a dream."

"It was more than that," Paul admitted sheepishly. "Last night, Leah and I—" he hesitated "—I don't know how to explain it. It was as though for the first time all the barriers were down. I'd finished my novel and—"

"Congratulations!" Jason said.

Paul smiled weakly. "Thanks." He wasn't as excited as he had been. The book, or at least the first draft, was finished, but the exhilaration was gone. Nothing was more important to him than his relationship with his wife.

"Leah and I made love and…I don't know how to describe it, Jase, it was so…beautiful. I held her in my arms and I realized how much my life had changed since I married her.

"I feel so whole again. I loved Diane and I always will, but she's gone and I'm alive, and for the first time since I buried her, I'm not sorry to be."

"You've come a long way, Paul."

Paul shook his head. "When I went to sleep I was at peace with myself and my world, and then I had that dream…."

"Did it occur to you that maybe Diane was saying goodbye to you?" Jason asked softly.

"Saying goodbye to me? I don't understand."

"You just finished telling me you'd accepted her death."

"Yes."

"Perhaps your subconscious allowed her the opportunity to release you, too. After Kelsey was born—before Diane died—there wasn't much of a chance for the two of you to talk, was there?"

"No. It happened so fast. Within days she was gone."

"I know." Jason's eyes were somber.

"I wish I remembered more of the dream," Paul said after a moment's silence. "There's a glimmer, but... Maybe it'll come back to me."

"Does it really matter?"

Paul pulled out a kitchen chair and sat down. The burden of his guilt had never felt heavier. "There's more. I don't know how it happened, but apparently at some point during the night I called Leah *Diane.*"

"You didn't do it on purpose," Jason said. "Surely Leah understands that."

"I don't know what she understands. She was crying and, to be truthful, she wasn't making a whole lot of sense. She kept saying she wouldn't compete with Diane anymore, and that she's moving out of our bedroom because I loved Diane. I'm not supposed to have loved her?" he demanded. "She was my wife!"

"Give Leah time. She's obviously upset, and when you think about it, you can't really blame her."

"As a matter of fact, I'm upset, too," Paul said heatedly. "Where does this leave me? I'm supposed to tell Leah I don't love Diane anymore?"

"She wouldn't believe you even if you did."

"I know," Paul admitted, slumping forward in his chair. "I remember the day I married Diane. It's clear as anything, but it seems like a hundred years ago now. I recall thinking I was going to love this woman all my life. And the amazing part is, I *will* always love her. I can't stop loving her. But I don't understand how it's possible to love two women so intensely."

"You love Leah, too, then?"

Paul nodded. "I didn't go into this marriage with the same rosy vision I did when I married Diane. It made sense to marry Leah. It was a practical decision. I have to admit I was attracted to her, though. I admired and respected her, and she didn't object. But I didn't truly love her when we got married, not the way I loved Diane."

"But now you do. That means something, doesn't it?"

"Apparently not a lot," he answered vehemently. Then he sighed. "I didn't know I could love both of them so much. I struggled with that, thinking I was cheating one or the other." It was a moment of self-realization for Paul; talking to his brother like this was helping him clarify his feelings.

Jason didn't say much, but he sat down across from him.

"Leah and I didn't start our physical relationship right away," Paul continued, a bit chagrined to be discussing his sex life with his unmarried brother. "Neither of us was ready for it."

"At least you were wise enough to recognize that. Not everyone would have."

"For a while I felt like I was being unfaithful to Diane, to Diane's memory, by loving Leah. But try as I might, I couldn't make myself *not* love her."

"She's your wife," he said simply. "You should love her."

In his heart Paul knew Leah was as miserable as he was. He'd tried to talk to her that morning, tried to reason with her, but she was beyond listening. Not knowing what else to say or do, Paul had slipped out of the house.

He'd felt numb as he drove around. Numbness frightened him. For the first few days after Diane's death he'd experienced the same lack of emotion. Gradually, a red-hot pain had overtaken him, and the grief had dominated his every waking moment. The agony had been so consuming that his mind had blotted out whole weeks. He'd functioned, gone to work, taken care of his children, lived day to day, but he didn't remember much of what had happened.

It had all started with a numbness, the same numbness he'd felt that morning when Leah told him he'd called her by her sister's name.

"What are you going to do?" Jason asked him.

Paul had to pull his thoughts together, mull over his dilemma. "I don't know yet," he said honestly. "Try to rebuild her trust. I'll love her without making any demands on her, give her the space and time she needs."

"Sounds like a good place to start."

Paul smiled. He never did get the cup of coffee his brother had promised him—not that it seemed very palatable. It didn't matter, though. He was finished—or rather he'd found a place to start.

"How'd you get to be so smart?" he asked Jason.

His brother grinned. "Guess it just runs in the family."

Eager now to go home to Leah, Paul left his brother's apartment. He was ready to talk to her, to explain everything he'd realized when he was talking to Jason.

More than anything, he longed to take her in his arms and tell her how much he loved her, how much he needed her, how much he wanted her.

He parked in the driveway and nearly leapt out of the car. He dashed to the front door, throwing it open.

"Leah." Her name was on his lips even before he entered the house.

No response. He hurried into the kitchen to find Kelsey standing up, holding on to the seat of a chair. She gave him a four-toothed smile and thrashed her free arm about with excitement.

A neighbor girl, Angie somebody, was slicing a banana at the counter.

"Oh, hi," she said, smiling broadly.

"Where's Leah?"

"She left about an hour ago."

"Did she say where she was going?"

"No. I'm sorry, I didn't ask. She gave me the phone number to…" She reached for a slip of paper. "Here it is, Jamie and Rich's."

"Yes?" Paul prompted.

"She wasn't sure when you'd be back, so she said I should call Jamie if you weren't here by dinnertime. Apparently Jamie was going to come over and pick up the kids."

Paul's heart was pounding. "Did she tell you when she's coming back?"

Angie shook her head. "I don't think it's anytime soon. She must've been going on a trip or something because she took a suitcase with her."

Leah had no business being behind the wheel of a car and she knew it. Tears streamed down her face, blurring her vision, making her a hazard on the road.

She stopped when she came to a red light and blew her nose, then ran the back of her hand across her eyes. The rain that spattered her windshield was the perfect accompaniment to her mood.

She didn't know where she was going, only that she had to get away. The logical thing to do was to check into a hotel. She had to sort through her emotions, try to make sense of why she'd said what she had to Paul. She needed to understand what was going on between her and Paul. Between her and Diane.

Finding somewhere to spend the night might have been rational, but Leah was in no frame of mind for rational behavior. If she had been, she would never have done anything as stupid as packing her bag and walking out on Paul and the children.

But he'd left *her.* He'd left the house, and she'd been

all alone with her pain. Everything was crowding in on her, and she'd felt the overwhelming urge to escape.

Leah hated what was happening to her. What was happening to Paul. She'd reacted in anger, lashing back at him for the pain he'd caused her. The same pain she'd carried most of her life, standing on the sidelines while her mother fawned over Diane. She'd smiled and swallowed back the hurt when it was Diane who received new clothes at the beginning of the school year while Leah got hand-me-downs from neighbors and friends.

She'd carried the hurt with her all those years, and yet she loved her sister. Diane couldn't be blamed for being pretty and sweet, any more than Leah could for being plain and serious.

Then Diane had died and, ironic as it seemed, *wrong* as it seemed, that had given Leah a chance at happiness. She'd jealously guarded her heart for so many years. If she was going to fall in love, why did it have to be with her dead sister's husband?

Paul had adored Diane. He still adored her. It didn't seem fair that the only man Leah had ever loved had to be a man who loved her sister so completely.

They were very different, Leah and Diane. Leah could never hope to gain Paul's devotion. He loved her, Leah realized that, but what he felt for her paled in comparison to the depth of his love for Diane.

Once again, she stood in her sister's shadow.

She was jealous of Diane, but why now, when she'd never been jealous before? Early in life she'd accepted her lot, understood her place. So why now? Why, after

Diane was gone, did Leah feel this way? It was crazy. *Unfair.*

Leah continued driving in the rain, taking side streets and staying off the busy thoroughfares. Her aimless route led her past a golf course. Golfers carrying umbrellas ambled from one green to another.

With a jolt, it came to her then. She needed to talk to Diane, and even if it was a one-sided conversation, Leah had things that had to be said.

Because she didn't know what street she was on, it took her some time to locate the cemetery. She parked, then walked slowly across the damp lawn, ignoring the drizzle that still hadn't let up.

Nearly a year had passed since Diane's death. In all that time Leah hadn't once visited her sister's grave. She'd stood there as the coffin was lowered—her heart breaking, her breath coming in tortured gasps—and had no desire to ever return.

Paul came often, or he had in the beginning. For months he'd brought fresh flowers each and every week. Leah knew because she'd often looked after the children while he was gone. Sometimes he'd be away for hours; other days it would only be a short while.

Leah couldn't recall the last time he'd come here. If he still came as often, he hadn't mentioned it to her.

Leah wandered around, ignoring the drizzle, searching for her sister's marker.

Diane Sandra Manning, Wife, Mother. The dates of her birth and death were listed along with a Scripture verse from Proverbs 31.

So few words.

Yet they said so much.

She stood looking down at the headstone. An overwhelming sense of sadness came at her and fresh tears filled her eyes, mingling with the rain.

After several minutes, she composed herself enough to speak. "Hi, Sis," she said when she could, her voice tight. "I bet you're surprised I came to see you."

It was probably foolish talking to a patch of lawn. In her heart Leah knew Diane wasn't there; she knew her sister would never hear the words she spoke. But none of that mattered to Leah.

"The boys started kindergarten. Oh, Diane, you'd be so proud of them! They're growing up so fast. Ryan came home from class last week and announced that anyone who could read five whole words didn't need a blankie. He gave it to me and hasn't asked for it even once. Ronnie's given up his thumb, too." She smiled as she smeared the tears across her cheeks.

She began again. "Kelsey's such a precious baby. She's walking now. Three and four steps at a time—she's so eager to get into everything. She's drinking out of a cup, too, but she still has two bottles a day." Leah folded her arms around her waist. "She has your coloring. Her hair's so blond it's white. She's a beautiful little girl."

Leah opened her purse and took out a fresh tissue, which she wadded up in her hand. "Paul finished his novel the other night," she said haltingly.

Then, squaring her shoulders, she closed her eyes. "I love him, too," she cried. "Is that what you wanted—for me to love Paul? I didn't mean for it to happen....

I'm not even sure when it did. One morning I woke up and I realized it was too late—I realized I love him.

"What do you want me to do, Diane? I can't fight you for him. We can't sit down and talk this out the way we did when we were teenagers. You can't hug me and tell me everything's okay." She took a deep, shuddering breath. "Paul is your husband. But now he's my husband, too. Is that what you intended? Is it what you wanted? For me to raise your children and…and to love Paul?" She was sobbing so hard now, she could barely speak. "Because…that's what happened and I feel so wretched."

Suddenly, unexpectedly, it stopped raining. The dark heavy clouds that had blanketed the sky most of the day parted, and a dazzling display of sunlight broke through, shining on the grass, making it glisten.

Leah looked up at the sky, feeling the sun's warmth seep into her bones.

Paul tried to keep the panic at bay as he called Rich's number.

"Hello."

His sister-in-law picked up the phone—for which Paul was grateful. "Jamie, it's Paul," he said, managing to keep his voice smooth. "I just got home. I don't suppose you've heard from Leah?"

"Oh, hi, Paul. No, I haven't. At least not since she phoned this morning."

"Did she say where she was going?"

Jamie didn't hesitate. Paul was listening carefully, waiting for the slightest pause, hoping he wouldn't detect one so he'd know she was telling the truth.

"No, she didn't. Is everything all right? You seem worried."

"Everything's fine," he said abruptly, far more interested in getting the information he needed than in providing polite reassurances. "How did she sound when she talked to you?"

"About the same way you're sounding now. You're *sure* everything's all right?"

"Yes. What did she say?" he asked again.

"Not much. She phoned to ask if I could take the twins and Kelsey for her if you didn't get back before dinnertime. I told her it wasn't a problem."

"That's it?" Paul was beyond the point of concealing his distress. Despite his insistence a minute ago that everything was fine, he knew Jamie wasn't fooled. She didn't need him to spell out that he and Leah were having problems.

This time Jamie did hesitate. "It wasn't anything she said, exactly…"

"Yes?" he prompted.

"She sounded upset, Paul, as though she'd been crying. When I asked her about it, she laughed. But her laugh sounded more like a sob."

Paul felt wretched. He should never have left her. If he needed time alone, he could've mowed the lawn, or cleaned out the garage, organized his thoughts that way. "You're positive she didn't give you any indication of where she was going?"

"I'm sorry, Paul, she didn't. I don't think she knew herself."

That made sense to Paul. Then again it didn't. Leah

was methodical about everything she did. She didn't often act—or react—impulsively. The realization that he'd driven her to this was like a nail through his heart.

"Thanks, Jamie, I appreciate the help."

"I'm sorry I couldn't tell you more."

"You've helped." She'd given him something to hold on to, and Paul needed that.

"If there's anything I can do, call me back, okay?"

"Yes," he said.

"Anything," she reminded him.

They spoke for a few more minutes. Jamie asked if he wanted to talk to Rich, but Paul said no. He was in a rush now, wanting to check the closet. If he could figure out what Leah had taken with her, he might be able to guess where she'd gone.

He practically raced into their bedroom, going through the closet and drawers. Whatever she'd packed, it hadn't been much. The murder mystery that had been on the nightstand was missing. She planned to go someplace and read? That seemed odd.

As far as he could tell, there weren't any clothes missing. Maybe a pair of jeans and a shirt, if that. She hadn't taken her pajamas or her housecoat. Or her toothbrush.

The phone rang just then, and Paul's heart shot into his throat. He hurried into the kitchen and grabbed the receiver, hoping to get it before the ringing woke Kelsey and the twins. They were napping, and Angie had gone home, although she'd promised to come back if he needed her.

"Hello," he said as calmly as he could, although he doubted he was very convincing.

"Paul, it's your father. I'm calling from Montana."

"Dad, hello." Why was his father contacting him? Had he heard from Leah?

"Christy had her baby. A little girl. Six pounds, seven ounces. Cute as can be. She's got lots of dark hair." He paused. "Your mother said she would. Christy had heartburn real bad, and according to Elizabeth, that's a sure sign the baby would have a lot of hair and by heaven, she does."

"That's wonderful, Dad. Another granddaughter."

"They've decided to name her Erin Elizabeth. That has a nice sound, doesn't it? Naturally your mother's pleased—and that's putting it mildly."

"Erin Elizabeth Franklin," Paul repeated.

"Cody's proud as a peacock, as well. He's been handing out cigars to everyone in town. 'Course hardly anyone smokes anymore. Even in a cowboy town like this."

"Congratulate him and Christy for us, won't you?"

"You bet I will," Eric said enthusiastically. "Taylor says to tell you hello. She and Russ are going to be adding to their family again. About time if you ask me, but then no one ever does. Including your mother." He chuckled at his own joke.

"Okay, Dad," Paul said casually, not wanting to alert him to his troubles. "I'll let Jason and Rich know. Do you have any idea when you and Mom will be back in Seattle?"

"Oh, I imagine we'll be back in the next couple of weeks."

"Drive carefully."

"You know I will. Take care, son."

"Thanks, Dad." Paul replaced the receiver.

So Christy and Cody were parents now. Despite his current problems, Paul was elated for his sister and brother-in-law. He recalled his own excitement, not so long ago, when Kelsey was born. His joy had soon been dwarfed by concern for Diane, but those precious moments when he'd heard his daughter's first cries would stay in his heart forever.

He sagged into a kitchen chair, knowing there was nothing he could do until he heard from Leah. He could fret and worry, but it wouldn't help. He could list everything he'd done wrong, but that would only depress him further.

Paul was reviewing his conversation with Jamie when the front door opened. Feeling a surge of new hope, he moved out of the kitchen and into the living room. He stopped suddenly as Leah walked inside, suitcase in hand.

She froze when she saw him. Her eyes were red and puffy, her face so pale he wondered if she might be ill.

"Hello, Paul," she said softly.

Thirteen

"Leah." Paul stepped toward her, then hesitated, as though he was afraid of saying or doing something to intimidate her. "Are you all right?"

She nodded. Tears filled her eyes and her throat, and she hated herself for being so weak. "What about you?"

"I'm fine...now that you're home."

His gaze fell to the small suitcase in her hand, and her eyes followed his. She'd forgotten about the bag and was embarrassed now that he'd seen her with it.

Packing her things had been an empty gesture. She'd been distraught, barely aware of what she was doing. All she'd taken was a murder mystery and Ryan's yellow blankie. Maybe the five-year-old didn't need his security blanket, but she sure did.

A book and a blanket! What did she intend to do, curl up under a tree? Spend the rest of her life in hiding?

Even more foolish had been her belief that she could leave Paul and the children, for even one night. They were her breath, her substance, everything that mattered to her.

"I went for a drive," she said, her voice husky with emotion.

"So did I," Paul said, his own voice so deep and rich she could listen to it forever.

"I...I thought I should get away for a while...clear my head."

"Me, too. I did the same thing."

Courage rose inside her and she took heart, smiling through her tears. "Did you come up with any solutions?"

Paul's eyes held hers steadily. "The same ones that've been staring me in the face for months. What about you?"

"A few."

"Do you want to talk about them?"

Leah nodded. Paul came forward and took the suitcase. "I hope you won't be needing this."

"No...I won't be," she whispered as he set it aside.

Then, taking Leah by the hand, he led her to the couch and they both sat down. A small space separated them, but the force of their attraction—no, more than that, their love—seemed to draw them together. Leah shifted closer; so did Paul.

They were silent at first, perhaps afraid of saying the wrong thing, of misunderstanding each other again. It was all Leah could do not to blurt out everything she'd learned, how much she loved Paul and the children. How peace had come to her in a cemetery, standing before her sister's grave.

Paul spoke first. "I went to my brother's," he said.

"Rich?" Leah had talked to Jamie earlier. She'd tried to disguise her unhappiness and done a poor job of it.

"No, Jason. For some unknown reason, I...I found myself outside his apartment," he said, staring down at his hands. "I'm glad I went. Jason didn't say much, which meant I did all the talking. Whatever he was thinking, other than to defend you, he kept to himself."

Leah smiled. She didn't know him well, but she'd always liked Jason. He seemed like an overgrown kid, but under the baseball cap was a man with a warm, generous heart.

"So talking helped?" she prodded.

Paul's hands reached for hers. "Yes...I realized what a fool I've been."

"We've both been fools."

"When Diane died, I never expected to fall in love again," Paul said. "I didn't think it was possible." He hesitated and looked at her uncertainly. "I don't mean to hurt you by telling you this...."

"You aren't hurting me." She encouraged him with another smile, although emotion was clogging her throat—tears of release and relief.

"I figured a man only finds that kind of love once in his life. Then you came to live with me and the children. In the beginning I was so grateful that I assumed everything I felt for you had to do with appreciation. I owed you so much."

"You never understood that I was the one who had reason to be grateful. It was me—"

"I still have trouble believing that," he said, cutting her off. "You gave up your life for us."

"No, I found it instead. If it hadn't been for you and the children, I would've spent my whole life teaching the quadratic formula and attending faculty meetings. I would've grown old without ever knowing what it means to be in love."

His gaze dropped, as if he had to look away in order to continue. "I don't know if marrying you when I did was the right thing. I was attracted to you. I suspect I was afraid of losing you to Rob Mullins."

"Rob." Leah gave a short laugh. Paul had no idea how much she'd come to dislike her colleague and friend. Former friend. Their last evening together had been a disaster. Rob had tried to pressure her into confessing a sexual relationship with Paul. It seemed beyond his comprehension that the two of them could be living together without sex.

Leah had been insulted and infuriated. She was attracted to Paul and had been for weeks. They'd experienced that one explosive kiss and both had worked hard to avoid repeating it. They'd been constantly aware of each other's proximity. They'd fought their sexual attraction every moment they were together. Some days the tension had seemed intolerable.

So Rob's innuendos had struck a raw nerve. Leah had barely made it through the evening. The poetry reading was nearly two hours north of Seattle, and she'd hardly spoken a word on the long drive back. Rob had tried to fill the silence with questions and snatches of conversation, but she'd met his attempts with one-word replies.

He'd grown impatient with her, and by the time

they'd reached Paul's house, he was angry and demanding. Leah had jumped out of his car, said she didn't plan to see him ever again and escaped inside before he could argue or delay her. She hadn't heard from him since, for which she was grateful.

"I was jealous of Rob," Paul was saying. "And I hated myself for it—because it made me aware of several things I wasn't ready to face. First and foremost, I was *feeling* again.

"For months my emotions had been numb. I was desensitized. There were times I laughed, but I was never happy. There were times I looked forward to another day, but I wasn't whole. I wasn't at peace with myself. Six months after Diane's death I was still clinging to her, deathly afraid of what would happen if I ever let her go."

"When your parents suggested we get married, I was stunned." Leah had her own confession to make. "I didn't think you'd want to marry anyone like me…."

"Why not?"

All the old doubts and fears had come back to plague her. All the insecurities of her youth. "I'm not…Diane."

"No, you're Leah. Warm, beautiful, gentle Leah."

Leah didn't feel she'd possessed any of those qualities until she'd fallen in love with Paul. "I was afraid."

"But why?" Paul wanted to know, looking bewildered.

"I was convinced that sometime down the road, a year from now, or maybe sooner, you'd wake up and realize you were saddled with me and—"

"*Saddled* with you? Leah—"

"Please, listen." She couldn't allow him to distract

her, to keep her from addressing her fears. "I'm not beautiful. I've known it all my life, and I've accepted it." She paused when it looked as though Paul was going to protest again. Pressing her fingers to his lips, she continued, "I don't have a gregarious personality. Or Diane's charm and sense of humor. But I couldn't change who I am, not even to please you. When I agreed to marry you, I did so for purely selfish reasons."

"Leah—"

Once more she stopped him. "I did so because I couldn't bear to leave the children and because... because I was falling in love with you, and it scared me to death. I finally had a chance of finding what had always escaped me. A husband, a family, people who loved me, and I grabbed it with both hands."

"Our marriage was unfair to you."

"Don't you understand?" she cried. "*I* was taking advantage of *you*. I knew the time would come when you'd regret marrying me, yet I went ahead with it anyway."

"Leah, I'm never going to regret marrying you."

"Maybe you should."

"No." He got to his feet and walked to the window, gazing out. "Because, you see, Leah, I discovered I loved you as deeply and profoundly as I've ever loved anyone in my life."

"And I...I discovered love through you and the children." Leah's voice was tranquil. Thoughtful. "I discovered what it is and what it means."

Paul turned toward her. "I expected to feel guilty for loving you and I fulfilled that prophecy. Only, to my surprise, I had to force myself to feel the guilt. Anytime I examined my feelings for you, I realized loving you was what Diane would've wanted. But I couldn't admit it, because that would mean letting Diane go, and I wasn't ready to do that.

"I was caught between the two of you. Trapped between the past and the present. The more time I spent with you, the dimmer my vision of Diane became, and that frightened me. Yet I couldn't make myself stop loving you." He looked away from her again.

"Until you thought I might be pregnant... Then you couldn't bear to touch me." Leah lowered her eyes because the pain was still there.

"No!" Paul covered the distance between them in three strides. He sat next to her and took her hands in his. "It wasn't that, Leah. It wasn't *anything* like that. I've never known a greater fear than when you told me you might be pregnant. The thought of losing you terrified me. I think I went a little crazy."

He leaned his forehead against hers, and his voice grew rougher. "It was when you thought you might be pregnant that I understood how much I loved you."

Paul's arms came around her then. "I was confronted with my greatest fear. Losing the woman I loved. Now, looking back, I realize how badly I behaved, how much my attitude hurt you. I'm sorry for that, sorrier than you'll ever know."

"You were so angry."

"But never with you. If I blamed anyone, it was myself. At the same time, I recognized how much I loved you—and how much I loved Diane. I didn't know it was possible to love two women so deeply—and then it came to me—I didn't."

Was this what he'd realized when he talked to his brother? Leah wondered. Her heart started to pound louder and louder.

"Friday night..."

She pulled her hands free from his and lowered her eyes. Their lovemaking the night before had moved her in a way that went beyond sensual excitement or gratification. Paul had held her in his arms afterward, teased her, laughed with her. He'd made her feel more wanted and loved in one evening than she'd felt in her entire life. She'd gone to sleep content, basking in the joy she'd experienced. A joy that exceeded anything she'd ever hoped to feel.

Then she'd woken to the sound of another woman's name on her husband's lips.

"That night," Paul continued, "was indescribable. Yes, the lovemaking was great, but it always is. You went to sleep in my arms, and as I lay there I realized what was different, what had changed." He tucked his finger under her chin and raised her face until her eyes locked with his. "On Friday night I released Diane. I let go of her and stepped out of yesterday and into today, tomorrow—my life with you."

"But...you called me Diane."

"I had a dream," Paul said, his words heavy with regret. "I can't explain it, but...in my dream Diane was there. I can't remember exactly what happened, just bits and pieces of it."

Breathless, Leah stared at him.

"Jason thinks my subconscious had something to do with it," he went on. "He thinks Diane was releasing me, too. I don't know if any of this makes sense to you. But I'm at peace with her death, at peace with myself. It didn't come easy, but…" He seemed to be waiting for a reaction from her.

"Diane came to me in a dream once, too," Leah said in a whisper. It was the first time she'd ever told anyone about that experience. "It was the night she died. I was exhausted and I was sure my mind was playing tricks on me. She looked so happy. I couldn't understand it. She was standing under a tree with wildflowers all around her."

"What kind of flowers?"

His question seemed odd to Leah. "I'm not sure, except she was holding a—"

"A daisy."

"Yes." Her eyes widened with surprise. "How'd you know?"

"In my dream she stood under a tree. I remember that much now. She seemed so happy, plucking the petals from a yellow daisy."

"Yes!" Leah flattened her hand over her heart. "Yes," she repeated. "There was a light, too."

"A brilliant light."

Leah nodded again.

"What did she say?" Paul asked her.

"She told me she was going away. I tried to argue with her, tried to make her stay, but she didn't have time to listen to me. She said she'd had to get us away from the hospital because we were holding her back. And then...then she explained that she hadn't wanted to go away in the beginning, but had come to understand it would be all right to leave. She...she asked me if I'd take her place."

"Take her place?"

Leah nodded. "I didn't understand what she meant, but I didn't question her, either. She looked right at me. I'd never been able to refuse Diane anything, so I promised her I would."

Paul was silent for a moment. "I don't remember what she said to me, but I think Jason might be right. I think she came to say goodbye."

They grew silent, each lost in the memory of the one they'd loved so much.

"It was because of the dream that I eventually decided to live here, in your house, but I never intended to fall in love with you," Leah confessed. "You talked about feeling guilty and being trapped between the past and the present—that's how I felt, too. I was afraid to love you, fighting it, but at the same time I'd never been happier, or more fulfilled."

She didn't know how to put into words everything that was in her heart. How could she explain that she belonged to him in ways she didn't even belong to herself?

"You felt guilty?"

Leah grinned sheepishly. "When I left today, I...I went for a drive and ended up at the cemetery. I hadn't been there since the funeral. I wasn't sure where her grave was, and it took me a long time to find it. When I did I just stood there, not knowing what to say, but knowing I had to say something."

"I haven't been there in weeks." Paul's voice was low, incredulous, as if he'd just realized it. "I guess the need to talk to her left me after we got married."

Leah went on. "I told her how well the twins and Kelsey were doing, and then I got angry. I so seldom raise my voice that I think I frightened myself. I hated what was happening to me. Hated competing with her when I'd never wanted to compete before. For the first time in my life, I wanted something she had, and I didn't know how to handle it."

"Oh, Leah…" His thumb caressed her cheek. Leah closed her eyes, loving the glorious feel of his skin touching hers.

"I asked her if this was what she wanted—for me to love you. Because it was killing me—loving you, when you loved *her.* I was jealous, and I'd never been before, not once in all the years we grew up together."

Paul pulled her toward him, adjusting their positions so she was cradled in his arms, her head on his chest.

"Did you receive any answers?"

"Yes." She smiled, a smile that radiated out from her heart. "I was standing there, weeping, knowing I was asking the impossible, demanding an answer when there was none to be had. Only…there was."

"But how…what answer?"

"It'd been raining most of the morning. The sky was dark and overcast."

"Yes," Paul concurred.

"As I was standing there, the sun broke through the clouds. I watched as the sky parted and this brilliant stream of light shot down." Leah wasn't sure whether she should continue, whether Paul would believe her or not. The sun parting the sky wasn't a spectacular miracle; it was an everyday phenomenon. An everyday kind of miracle.

"I had my answer," Leah whispered, close to tears. "You and the children are Diane's gift to me. She gave me what she loved most—you four. She knows me so well. All along she realized I was going to fall in love with you. It's what she wanted."

"She knew I'd love you, too," Paul added. "That we'd both fight it because of our loyalty to her, and yet, if she'd been able, she would've told us our love was by design. Her design."

"She loved us both so much."

"Loves," Paul corrected softly, tightening his embrace. "I don't think that'll ever change." He was still holding her when Leah sensed they were no longer alone.

Slowly she opened her eyes and glanced at the hallway. Ryan stood there, rubbing his eyes. As she watched the child—her child—her heart seemed to expand with all the love she felt.

"Did you sleep well, sweetheart?" she asked.

Ryan nodded. "Kindergartners are too old for naps."

It was a point he argued loudly and often, and yet he fell asleep of his own accord every afternoon.

"I'm too old for naps, too," Ronnie announced, appearing by his brother's side and yawning widely. "Only babies go to bed in the daytime."

"I'd like to be in bed right now," Paul whispered in Leah's ear. "You wouldn't hear me complaining about taking a nap. If you were taking one with me, that is."

"Paul," she chastised.

"Come here, boys," Paul called his sons. They climbed onto their father's lap as Leah got up to check on Kelsey. If the boys were awake, then their sister probably was, too.

Sure enough, she was standing in her crib, bouncing excitedly. She broke into a grin when she saw Leah.

"How's my darling?" Leah asked. "How's my darling baby girl?"

Kelsey raised her arms to Leah and delivered a sentence or two of happy gibberish.

Leah and Kelsey joined Paul and the boys, and the five of them sat together on the sofa—Paul holding the twins and Leah holding Kelsey. The five of them were truly a family, Leah realized. One formed in love. A gift she'd received from her sister.

Paul's eyes met hers and he smiled.

Leah smiled, too. She felt his love—in his smile, his touch, the warm look in his eyes.

Love… It was more than she'd ever dared to dream. More than she'd ever thought to have.

Love had found a place for her.

* * * * *

You've met Taylor and Christy in
THE MANNING SISTERS,
watched as Rich and Paul met the women of their dreams in
THE MANNING BRIDES,

now look out for two more Manning family weddings in
THE MANNING GROOMS
by Debbie Macomber

It was one of those days. Jason Manning scrubbed his hands in the stainless-steel sink, then applied ointment to several scratches. He'd just finished examining and prescribing antibiotics for a feisty Persian cat with a bladder infection. The usually ill-mannered feline had never been his most cooperative patient, but today she'd taken a particular dislike to Jason.

He left the examining room and was greeted by Stella, his receptionist, who steered him toward his office. She wore a suspiciously silly grin, as if to say "this should be interesting."

"There's a young lady who'd like a few minutes with you," was all the information she'd give him. Her cryptic message didn't please him any more than the Persian's blatant distaste for him had.

Curious, Jason moved into his book-lined office. "Hello," he said in the friendliest voice he could muster.

"Hi." A teenage girl who seemed vaguely familiar

stood as he entered the room. She glanced nervously in his direction as if he should recognize her. When it was obvious he didn't, she introduced herself. "I'm Carrie Weston." She paused, waiting expectantly.

"Hello, Carrie," Jason said. He'd seen her around, but for the life of him, couldn't recall where. "How can I help you?"

"You don't remember me, do you?"

"Ah…no." He couldn't see any point in pretending. If a cat could outsmart him, he was fair game for a teenager.

"We're neighbors. My mom and I live in the same apartment complex as you."

He did his best to smile and nod as though he'd immediately placed her, but he hadn't. He racked his brain trying to recall which apartment was hers. Although he owned and managed the building, Jason didn't interact much with his tenants. He was careful to choose renters who cared about their privacy as much as he cared about his. He rarely saw any of them other than to collect the rent, and even then most just slipped their checks under his door around the first of the month.

Carrie sat back down, her hands clenched tightly in her lap. "I—I'm sorry to bother you, but I've been trying to talk to you for some time, and…and this seemed to be the only way I could do it without my mother finding out."

"Your mother?"

"Charlotte Weston. We live in 1-A."

Jason nodded. The Westons had been in the apart-

HMIRA_WEB2

Printed by RR Donnelley at Glasgow, UK

ment for more than a year. Other than when they'd signed the rental agreement, Jason couldn't recall speaking to either the mother or her daughter.

"Is there a problem?"

"Not a problem…exactly." Carrie stood once again and opened her purse, taking out a thin wad of bills, which she leafed through and counted slowly. When she'd finished, she looked up at him. "It's my mother," she announced.

"Yes?" Jason prompted. He didn't have a clue where this conversation was leading or how long it would take the girl to get there. Stella knew he had a terrier waiting, yet she'd purposely routed him into his office.

"She needs a man,"

© Debbie Macomber 1992